HINTERLAND

Arno Geiger was born in 1968. His novels include *Der alte König in seinem Exil* (2011; translated as *The Old King in His Exile*) and *Selbstporträt mit Flusspferd* (2015). He has been the recipient of numerous prizes; in 2005 he was the first ever recipient of the German Book Prize (Deutscher Buchpreis) for his novel *Es geht uns gut*. A huge bestseller in Geiger's native German, *Hinterland* (*Unter der Drachenwand*) was first published in 2018. In French translation, it was shortlisted for three major prizes – the Prix Femina, the Prix Médicis and the Prix du Meilleur Livre Étranger. He divides his time between Vienna and the small town of Wolfurt in the west of Austria.

Hinterland

ARNO GEIGER

Translated from the German
by Jamie Bulloch

PICADOR

First published 2022 by Picador

This paperback edition published 2023 by Picador
an imprint of Pan Macmillan
The Smithson, 6 Briset Street, London EC1M 5NR
EU representative: Macmillan Publishers Ireland Ltd, 1st Floor,
The Liffey Trust Centre, 117–126 Sheriff Street Upper, Dublin 1, D01 YC43
Associated companies throughout the world
www.panmacmillan.com

ISBN 978-1-5290-0319-2

Originally published in German 2019 as *Unter
der Drachenwand* by Carl Hanser Verlag

1 3 5 7 9 8 6 4 2

A CIP catalogue record for this book is available from the British Library.

Typeset in Stempel Garamond by Jouve (UK), Milton Keynes
Printed and bound by CPI Group (UK) Ltd, Croydon, CR0 4YY

Visit **www.picador.com** to read more about all our books
and to buy them. You will also find features, author interviews and
news of any author events, and you can sign up for e-newsletters
so that you're always first to hear about our new releases.

High up in the sky

High up in the sky I could make out a few clouds drifting past and it was then that I knew I had survived. / Later I realized that I was seeing double. Every bone in my body was aching. The following day I contracted pleurisy, which fortunately I recovered from. But I still had double vision in my right eye and my sense of smell had disappeared.

Once again the war had only managed to throw me sideways. My first thought was that I'd been devoured by the blast, not to mention the steppe and the waters at this rugged knee of the Dnieper, which devoured everything in their path. I saw blood flowing in bright streams from beneath my right collarbone. The heart is an effective pump, and my blood was no longer circulating inside my body, but pumping out of me, boom, boom. Fearing for my life, I ran to the medical officer, who plugged the wound and gave me a temporary bandage. I watched, marvelling at my luck that I was still breathing. / Some shrapnel had injured my right cheek, another piece was lodged in my right thigh and a third had penetrated a major vessel beneath the collarbone. My shirt, coat and trousers were soaked in blood.

That indescribable, incomparable feeling of having survived. As a child you think: when I'm older. Today you think: if I survive. What can be better than staying alive?

It happened in exactly the same area where we had been at the same time of year two years earlier. I remembered everything in detail, I recognized the area at once, the roads, nothing had changed. Nor had the roads improved in the meantime. We were grouped beside a destroyed village, for most of the time under fire. During the night it was so cold that the water in our bucket froze. The tents had iced over too. / Our retreat was one long band of fire, horrific to watch and sobering to contemplate. Every last haystack was alight, every kolkhoz, only the houses remained standing for the most part. The local population was supposed to be evacuated westwards, although this was only partially successful as most of them refused to leave. They didn't care about being shot, but they were not in any circumstances going to leave.

And the war went on, forwards for some, backwards for others, but always in the bloodiest, most incomprehensible frenzy.

On the day I was wounded I was taken away by ambulance. If a large lorry hadn't been assigned to escort us we would have got stuck in the mud right outside the village. We made our way to the collecting station, where my wounds received a few rough stitches. I watched the process, again in great astonishment. / The clothes I had first put on at the end of October had been on my body for almost a month; the shirt was literally black when it was removed.

I saw a doctor who broke five matches trying to light a cigarette. He stood there, his head bowed, until a Red Cross nurse came and took the matches from him. The doctor closed his eyes as he took two drags on his cigarette, holding the smoke in his lungs for a long while. Then he uttered a few words before staggering off between the bloodied stretchers.

Two days later we moved on. On one occasion our car almost turned over after we slid into a ditch that had been invisible up to that point. By the time the others had salvaged the vehicle, the road was blocked both in front and behind, as it had started to snow heavily. It took us the entire morning to travel nine kilometres because the path had to be cleared with shovels. Behind us the road was then better, but I felt pain in every one of my ribs. / It was terrible on the main road too. Six times we had to seek cover from aircraft strafing us. Once when I moved too quickly the wound in my thigh opened up. / At Dolynska railway station we were attacked three times over the course of an hour by bombers. I was relieved to get away from there.

In Dolynska they threw boxes of boiled sweets and chocolate into our carriage. It's always the same: when we're retreating they empty the supply depots before they fall into Soviet hands. Boiled sweets and chocolate are the only good things in a soldier's life. Everything else is just terrible.

I lay freshly bandaged in a hospital train. Most of the time we were at a standstill because the lines were so busy. It took us five days to get to Prague, and from Prague two more to the Saar Basin. / You wouldn't think it possible to be transferred from the east to the far west, but that's further proof of how small so-called Greater Germany is. / We had a small stove in the carriage to prevent frost from getting into our wounds. My sense of smell had returned. In the warmth, the stench of pus and iodoform worked like a narcotic; I fluctuated between total clarity and a fuzzy head. Sleep, sleep, sleep. Pain? The medical officer said I should grit my teeth; the morphine was only for the most serious cases. And I'm not a serious case. Besides, we were heading westwards, and pain is easier to bear when you're going in that direction. / Some of the wounded in my carriage would doubtlessly be back at the front soon. The sheer joy of travelling west made them better. Which was a mistake of course. / Again I had the feeling that everything inside my head was droning and humming. And again I slowly slipped into a state of unconsciousness.

The whining, the groaning, the smell of inadequately treated wounds, the smell of filthy bodies. All of these combined to produce something that for me is the essence of war. I tried to sleep as much as possible. Almost everyone in the carriage was smoking. Those who couldn't hold their own cigarettes got their neighbour to help them. I developed a severe headache and thought it must be down to the stench of pus and all the smoking. Like the doctor at the collecting station, I held the smoke in my lungs for a long while.

And practically everyone tried to get their story off their chest. Perhaps by telling your story you ensured it would have a future.

The Saar Basin. That pretty much says it all; it's not particularly beautiful. In itself, the countryside is all right, but then you have to ignore the soot from the collieries. The military hospital I'm in used to be a children's home, founded by a mine owner apparently. The drive is covered in white gravel, not really appropriate in an area so full of soot, and the hospital stands in a park laid out with exotic trees, clipped shrubs, Roman statues and other extravagances. Inside, the building is furnished simply as a hospital, white beds with box-spring mattresses. / After such a long time at the front, this hospital is like heaven. How strange that I should be lying here, my body in one piece, with women in shining white aprons bringing real coffee, two fellow soldiers playing cards next to me, and outside the sound of church bells. The first white sheets in over a year. How strange!

I like it when the nurse takes a needle wrapped in white cotton wool from the box. 'Relax,' she says. 'Try to imagine that the pain isn't yours.' / Earlier a doctor, who showed little interest in me, came and said he was being replaced tomorrow. I don't care. / How lovely it is to be touched by clean hands again. / Once in southern Russia I left the front line for a few hours in the field mess. It was just like here at the hospital. I couldn't believe my eyes when I saw flowers arranged in glasses.

I arrived at nine o'clock in the morning and then spent the whole day lying in a recess in the corridor, behind a white curtain, where it was frightfully cold. Later a doctor came to examine me. That evening I was transferred when a bed became free in a ward. Various blood samples had already been taken, and the next day there were X-rays and more blood samples. Over subsequent nights I slept well for the first time in ages. It was neither cold nor damp, nor did I get straw in my mouth or flies up my nose.

On 2 December they operated on my thigh and collarbone. I felt queasy after the injection, everything was spinning and the beds on the ward floated like little sailing boats on a lake. All that was missing was the palm trees. I began to hear voices and became aware that I was receding away from myself. I said my name, over and over again; as long as I knew my name, I thought, I still had my wits about me. *Veit Kolbe . . . Veit Kolbe . . . Veit Kolbe . . .* The last thing I saw was a nurse in a white bonnet bending over me. Then I was gone.

These nurses had worked here when it was still a children's home. They are older and wear long dresses. Sadly I'm no longer a child. The first time I borrowed a small mirror from the man in the neighbouring bed so I could have a shave, I was shocked by the cuts and exhaustion on my face. / I hadn't shaved for around a month, not since Kharkov – Taganrog – Voronezh – Zhytomyr – I had no idea. I looked like a submariner returned from a tour of duty: ghastly. And I had to borrow a razor too. I had left my belongings behind and felt like one of those bombed-out people.

It's worrying how time passes. I can clearly see myself growing older, I can see it in my face. Only the war remains the same. There are no seasons any more, no summer offensive, no winter break, just war, incessant, without any variation, unless you consider it a variation that the war is no longer seeking new battlefields, but returning to the old ones. The war always returns.

Dear Mother and Father, I will write to the brigade again and tell them to send my things and the three months' wages that are still outstanding to my home address. But I fear that our baggage has fallen into enemy hands, and thus there is little prospect of seeing my belongings again. And so I beg you to send me some money, writing paper, my spare razor, a toothbrush and some toothpaste straightaway. I've been given new clothes by the hospital. / I'm sure to be granted some sick leave, I'll tell you everything then.

There are a few very young girls running around here: sixteen, seventeen. It's impossible to believe that they have had any training; they can't even take a pulse.

I like the clean smell; it reminds me of when Hilde was in the sanatorium. But the sanatorium wasn't as warm as it is here. For some reason the doctors hoped that the cold would help the patients with lung diseases recover. / I thought about this when the afternoons refused to pass. I don't know whether it was a result of the medication, but for several days I saw everything more vividly. Unfortunately, each time I moved, my head hurt and my pulse throbbed in my ear.

First they said that my eardrum was damaged, so I should simply leave my ear alone. Then it turned out that my upper jaw was broken. My cheek was numb. The sound my teeth made when tapped had changed, now it was hollow. I had to take off all my clothes for the examination; that must be terribly important for fractures of the jaw. I often get the feeling that I'm amongst madmen here. Luckily, the teeth hadn't got any darker, so there was still a hope of preserving the nerve. The cheek had swollen badly and it hurt when pressed. / Every day my cheek was given short-wave treatment, which was meant to reduce the swelling and possibly stimulate the affected cheek nerve too. They also put me under a sun lamp every day. Unfortunately my headaches didn't get any better. / The wound on my thigh also took a long time to heal, copiously oozing pus; every morning the bandage was greenish-yellow and it stank. I couldn't bend my knee properly, but they said this would soon get better once the wound had healed. But first it had to be scraped out a few times, because granulation tissue was growing where the shrapnel had torn my flesh, forming a skinless bump on my thigh. If they just left it, the doctor explained, a crust would form that would look like a large, dark wart. They had to remove the granulation tissue to allow the excess growth to die off and skin to grow. / Every few days the doctor examined it and scraped out the wound, after which everything wept and oozed again.

The wound beneath my collarbone gave me the least concern. To begin with I'd thought it would kill me; now it was the first thing to heal.

All good fortune is relative. My passenger was killed by the shell that injured me. I was sorry that he died, but I also felt relief. The misfortune of others makes your own lucky escape all the more appreciable.

One Sunday all the wounded soldiers in the hospital were given four cigarettes: one from the F, one from Keitel and so on. I gave mine away because I didn't particularly want cigarettes from the F or Keitel. I also got the Wound Badge in recognition of my bad luck. / Four years of war, hardship and worry. I'd driven my lorry, a Citroën, from Vienna to the Volga, and from the Volga back to the Dnieper. Countless broken springs, several broken axles, shorn drive shafts and steering arms, defective alternators, frozen brake drums, fuel pipes, fuel pumps, oil filters, starters, hours spent beneath the vehicle in winter, permanently rough hands from the beastly cold and petrol. Whenever I knocked against anything, shreds of skin would tear off. In truth, the Citroën's resilience had been my own resilience, and I'd never received the slightest acknowledgement for this. And now I was getting a badge for having stopped at the wrong place at the wrong time, a badge for three seconds of bad luck and for not having snuffed it. I accepted the award with as much composure as I could muster, then took it off the moment I was alone again.

A baker boy from the city, whose job it is to bring us fresh bread daily, said that the hospital used to be a nursing home. He had the easygoing manner of a local, but only outlined the bare details: the nursing home had been emptied a few years before, freeing up space for a military hospital, beds to help the war effort. Those sound sleepers who'd preceded us were probably asleep in heaven now. The baker boy said he'd heard from another baker boy delivering to another sanatorium that patients arrived there by the busload, but the daily bread requirement always remained the same.

There's nothing quite like a stay at a military hospital, you meet people from all branches of the armed services, including the rear echelon staff. The captain next to me spoke about his time in Warsaw, describing scenes one would have thought unbelievable in the past, executions of civilians in the middle of the street.

This captain's entire right arm had been thrown in the bin, his face was yellow and he was only allowed to eat semolina. After telling me about the executions he said, 'I made a promise. If my stump of an arm gets better I'll make a pilgrimage to Altötting. Will you come with me? Right then, we can go together, can't we?' / I raised my eyebrows, I got on well with him, as I did with all of them. We didn't talk much, that was the best way. But a joint pilgrimage to Altötting? / 'Right then, we can go together,' he repeated. / Certainly not, I thought.

Then an ulcer burst inside his stomach. Shortly before supper he felt sharp pains, that night he suddenly started screaming and from midnight onwards he lost a lot of blood, from the front, from behind and from out of his mouth. The nurses didn't move from his bed. In the morning his face was the grey colour of death, they operated and apparently he was given fourteen bottles of blood. Over the following days they examined him in the mornings, always checking his left eye to see how much longer he would live. Although they continued to clean his body, otherwise they'd given up on him. / One man whose head was thickly bandaged said, 'Rather than being terribly sad when someone dies, I'm happy. I mean, he's come through his examination, achieved his goal and is now entering the kingdom of everlasting pleasures. If he is on his way to hell then it's also right that he dies, because he won't be able to commit any more atrocities. He would only add to his eternal misery.' / He kept blathering away beneath his head bandage, but I'd stopped listening and was thinking of those five lost years, including basic military service in the last year of peace, years that grew ever darker, ever more compact, rounding themselves into balls, and then just kept rolling on. I'd been a soldier for long enough now, I thought, and wanted to go home before I flew into a rage. I wanted to leave here as soon as possible because I found myself suddenly becoming scared of the patients.

Several positive things then came together on the same day. I was allowed to get up and go to the lavatory on my own for the first time, albeit with crutches. I even managed to make it to the orderly room, where I submitted an application to be transferred to a hospital back home. They said they would discharge me and I could receive care at home, if I had a doctor in Vienna who would regularly cauterize the wound in my thigh. / While I was in the orderly room they changed my bedclothes. I got into my bed and wrote to my parents saying that I'd be coming home soon. I told them I was still weak and tired, but happy to be away from Russia for a while; almost everyone came back from there with something or other.

The captain in the bed beside me was on the mend; he could drink unassisted and sit up in bed for hours at a time. All the same I'd had enough of this ward, enough of hanging around and the doctors' jokes about helping us gymnasts to get back onto the horizontal bars. It is a peculiar quirk of mine that I mistrust anything dressed up as a joke. / I was issued with a uniform and boots, excellent quality, although completely stiff. Everything was new – and it would have taken two further years for the uniform to become threadbare again, barely covering the body of a mental cripple, alive, or a corpse in a mass grave in Russia. / Once again they refused to discharge me.

On the day before my departure I went to the local soldiers' hostel where I ate my fill of bread and cheese, and drank a beer. I hobbled around the small town on my creaking crutches because I wanted to buy a few apples. But you could only get them with a ration card. By chance I came across a shop where I again asked in vain for some fruit. Afterwards I readjusted the bandage on my thigh because it had slipped. Then the woman said she'd bought a kilo for herself and she'd give them to me. I stood in a side street eating apples with another wounded soldier, and a boy came up to us and brought us two more beautiful apples. His father had seen us enjoying the fruit from a window and sent his boy down. / And so I have fond memories of the town of Leubach – Neunkirchen – Homburg – Merzig. / On this first venture out of the hospital I was virtually pain-free; there was a slight tugging around the wound in my thigh, but nothing worse than that. The way my bandage kept slipping was irritating, but I was fit and ready to travel home.

As it turned out my departure was delayed by two days. A few bigwigs had been in contact and overnight the hospital was prepared for inspection, meaning that the wounded received less care because all the nurses were busy tidying, washing and cleaning. They were busy with other tasks in the orderly room too, and so fell behind with processing the discharge papers. Everywhere they fussed to make the whole place clean and beautiful. On the day of the inspection a particularly fine lunch was served, after which they had to economize again for several days with boiled turnips and potatoes. Fortunately this didn't affect me any more; I was angry enough as it was.

And so I left the sooty town in the Saar Basin. They'd given me some medication just before, which saturated my entire body, and I was still quite sluggish when the train was caught up in an air-raid alert in Kaiserslauten. The train left again immediately, which I think was sheer luck because from a distance I could see the British bombers releasing a fair amount of ordnance. There were forest fires in the area too; from the train I heard detachments busy trying to put them out.

The train rolled slowly, unbelievably slowly, towards Frankfurt. Central Station . . . nothing. In the frenzy I gave my rucksack to a boy and was happy when he showed me the way to the dormitory in return for some bread from my marching rations. It was full, but in a nearby hotel I secured a room with two beds. Burning soles and chafed feet from the stiff boots. After a brief snack of salami, bread and black coffee, I lay on a sofa, weary and plagued by a nagging unease. For the first time in more than a year, I heard trams outside and sounds of the street, with laughing and intelligible voices. I slept until six o'clock, when the cold insisted I got up. Then I returned to the station and waited, trying to imagine what it would be like to arrive home. In Russia I'd found it easy to imagine my homecoming . . . haring down Possingergasse at top speed and running through the creaking front door to the stairs. Now I thought this would never happen.

For a day and a dark winter evening I trundled through Germany. The stations the train passed through were not illuminated, with only a solitary blue lamp lit at some of them. Soldiers and lots of refugees were camped almost everywhere. Only the train crew knew their way around the night-time jumble of tracks, and I was astonished when we pulled into Munich: change. I hauled my rucksack onto a carriage of the packed train and dozed, dozed . . . not a word passed my lips, only smoke into the lungs, an antidote. / My despondency, now increasing, was joined by an extraordinary physical tiredness and aching limbs, my chafed feet had got worse, I tossed and turned, and sometimes my eyelids closed as I ruminated. Finally, at half past twelve, we arrived in Salzburg. Shivering, I waited in the dark of night and dozed until five in the morning. Outside it was cold and grey. The tiredness dulled my nerves. What, over the past days and weeks, had been my most fervent desire was now on the verge of being fulfilled. But I wasn't awake enough to take in what was going on.

It was mid-morning when the train pulled into Vienna. Another station, the Westbahnhof, which seemed like an opera house after such a long absence. Memories popped up and then disappeared, like everything. I continued on foot and with crutches along Felberstrasse to home. Nothing mattered apart from the fact I was alive.

Fifteen months had passed

Fifteen months had passed since I was last in Vienna. On the slow journey back my wishes for home had taken shape, stemming from the hardships of the war. I wanted to sleep on my own in a bedroom, without a pair of boots beside the bed, and didn't want to have to lie in the snow with frozen hands beneath a defective lorry. I wanted to drink coffee from the cup I'd been given by Hilde for my fifteenth birthday. And I wanted a new toothbrush every four weeks. But despite the fact that all my wishes had been granted, I didn't feel at ease there, because for someone returning from war, home is a different place from the one they left.

Mama was not in a good way, she felt the cold as well as all the snow, rain, wind and fog. Although she had to cope with the household on her own, it seemed to me that in some respects this burden was no bad thing because the work left her with no time to think. On several occasions when I would have been grateful for her support she said, 'It's not my place to judge.' / Papa gave me wonderful advice, nothing but inanities which made me lose my temper. He said he'd been born at a bad time, whereas I had the fortune to be young on the threshold of a great era. A man couldn't ask for any more, it was just up to me to make something of it.

I served my time at the kitchen table as if it were punishment for having survived. I also found it a punishment having to talk after such a long time. But naturally it was only my parents' right to find out what had happened to me. I would have been disappointed if they had come back wounded from the war and been reluctant to talk. And yet I wasn't in the mood. Moreover, my injuries were not what preoccupied me the most. But my parents showed no understanding of these things, especially not Papa, whose nonsense got on my nerves.

On the way home from school he had popped into the Party offices to donate clothes to the German People's Collection. The uplifting feeling of having made a contribution prompted him, at the first bitter comment on my part, to gibber on about the necessity of the war and its long-term benefits. I felt crushed by such absurd logic. When I'd read about his optimism at the front, in letter form, it had been bearable. But to have to listen to it in person was another thing altogether.

Whenever I could, I retired to my room, the room I'd lived in as a schoolboy. Since I'd been conscripted for military service in late summer more than five years earlier, the room had barely changed. My schoolbooks were still on the desk, a reminder of the years that nobody would give back to me. I could have tried to catch up on my studies, but instead I lay on the bed without any impetus, my heart hollowed from the inside. And I kept thinking: I've lost so much time that I'll never be able to catch up.

I would have breezed through a course at the College of Technology, needing only the minimum time prescribed to complete it. I'd now be independent, standing on my own two feet, and my father's tutelage would leave me cold. / Often in Russia, when the clouds of dust drifted across the landscape, I would tell myself: *Look, my days . . .*

Another indication that something was wrong with me were the pictures of me hanging on the walls in almost every room of our apartment – memories, I was everywhere. These photographs had participated in family life while I'd participated in the war. They'd given me the prime spot in the living room, beside the portrait of Hilde. Mama said she wanted to be able to see her lad wherever she was. Papa said we had to indulge her. / But now I also made an appearance on the bookshelf as a wounded soldier in the Saar Basin. Papa again showed his generosity, saying how nice this photograph was; he couldn't fault it at all.

It came as a surprise to me that Hilde's asparagus fern was still there. Hilde had been dead for seven years and her asparagus fern was thriving. And Hilde's guitar was still leaning against the wall; for seven years it had been as silent and useless as I was. Can there be a sadder sight than an instrument that nobody plays any more? / What was going through Hilde's mind when she played the guitar in her room? Was she despondent? Was she frightened? I will never know. Why did I never ask? And why wasn't I able to help her? If I had asked I'd feel better now. / Every tiny object breaks my heart, everything that belonged to Hilde and which now stands around sad and forlorn. There is so much Hilde could have done with her life, she took such pleasure in things, whether it be music or a glass of beer outside on a warm evening. Almost until the bitter end she always found something positive in life. Whereas I stare at my empty hands, lie in my lumpy child's bed, feeling sorry for myself, filled with regret, sorrow and shame. Hilde knew how to live, but had to die. I, who have been allowed to live, have no idea what to do with my life. How dissatisfied Hilde would have been with me. But how can I change things? How can I change myself?

I wandered around the city as if I belonged nowhere after so many years of being away. The tram stop near our house had been taken out of service to save the electricity used when coming to a halt and pulling away again. Some drivers reduced their speed near the stop so passengers could jump off and on. I hobbled along the pavement. The streets were so crowded it was enough to drive you crazy. I was still imbued with the sluggishness of the military hospital; I felt like an annoying foreigner.

Another problem with going out was that the bandage wouldn't stay in place, no matter how carefully I walked. I kept having to tug at it to prevent it from slipping down to my ankle. Eventually Mama gave me a garter belt and showed me how to put it on. She laughed so much, more than I'd seen in years, with such a lack of inhibition. Later she said she hoped I hadn't become homosexual during the war and it would be good if I found a wife soon. But this garter belt was something we shared, in more than one respect, and I treasured her laughter.

When we visited relatives I was treated to cakes and wise words. Aunt Rosa said, 'Keep your head up and mouth wide open, and everything will work out.' She was still the most civil of the relatives on my mother's side. I also sat through an hour of politeness at Uncle Rudolf's.

I was particularly irritated by his surprise that Thaler Heli, a neighbour's son, should be voicing complaint in his letters. But instead of slamming my fist into Uncle Rudolf's face, all I said was, 'It won't be completely unjustified.' / I was mistrustful of anyone in Vienna who talked the big talk or felt sorry for themselves, which was virtually everybody. If you could earn money collecting phrases, Vienna would be the City of Gold: 'Everything comes to an end sooner or later, even the war.' / 'Yes, the war, it niggles away at you.' / 'The F is master of the situation, as ever.'

My most important visit was to the army district command, as per my instructions. The doctor's certificate was validated and I was granted several months' convalescent leave, but once again they refused to discharge me and let me return to my studies. My employer was intent on waiting. Once he has a hold on you, he doesn't let go easily / At least as far as Mama was concerned, I came home with some good news. Because of my injuries I'd been promised a Führerpaket: food stamps and money, as well as a bottle of Sekt. This was a real help to Mama, because the package contained stamps for five kilograms of flour, legumes and fat.

Shortly before Christmas it started to snow, and in abundance. By chance I managed to obtain nine yellow roses for seven Reichsmarks through a friend of Waltraud, my eldest sister. I visited Hilde's grave in Meidling Cemetery. The cemetery was covered with a thick layer of snow, only the main paths had been cleared. At the spot where, in March 1938, Papa had added another flag to the sea of flags and cried real tears, tears of joy, I placed the nine yellow roses, lit the graveside lantern and said my prayers. Apart from that there was nothing more I could give Hilde. The snow kept falling. I'd always imagined her to be an angel watching over us.

Frau Holle is said to be one of the ringleaders of the wild horde of spirits who haunt the earth between Christmas and New Year. During this time the gates to the underworld are open and the dead come back to their past abodes and pass judgement on the living. / Snow, snow, snow. And beneath the snow my sister sleeps.

Two days later shoes and vehicles had trampled the snow into a light-brown crumbly mass. The wind occasionally swept a few white flakes from the roofs and they fell onto the elderly, women, children, cripples and soldiers. The streets were full of soldiers, which didn't exactly enhance my love for Vienna. Although the crutches were no longer strictly necessary, I always kept them with me as it meant I didn't have to keep thrusting my arm up in the air. / Even the shop mannequins now had the poise of soldiers and were thinner; clearly this type must boost business. So long as there were goods to sell.

I wore my cap at home too, albeit far back on my head, which I claimed offered relief from my headaches. / The coat is the garment of transition; the cap connects worlds.

In conversation with Papa I suppressed many a comment I would have loved to get off my chest. I'd developed a high degree of self-control in an environment where a bold tongue brought you nothing but trouble. If there had ever been any free spirit within me, this had been smothered; I regarded a free spirit as belonging to the private sphere and no private sphere existed any more, it hadn't for years. My conversations with Papa? They weren't private, the clock couldn't be put back. / Papa said, 'We're living in a time of greatness. Our descendants will envy us the privilege of being able to live in such a time.' / Suddenly I had an inkling of how often things like this must have been talked about over lunch. It was one of the few bitter moments when I felt relief at having been away for five years. And although I'd decided not to talk politics as I had in the past, I said I'd had my fill of the privilege of this momentous time, which Papa had been going on about to his children for years, and I refused to hear any more. I wanted nothing to do with a future that resulted from such nonsense, and anyway, this future had already written me off.

Papa was upset that I'd rained on his parade. The following morning his face was devoid of expression. It wasn't until he'd finished the last sip of his coffee that he said anyone who'd lived through the last war and its consequences had to be resolute in their insistence that it must not go wrong again this time. / Then he talked about 'our soldiers', always with the intention of making the horrors I'd experienced appear tamer. Mama pointed to the window. A bullfinch sat perfectly still on a flowerpot, its breast towards us. Papa ignored it, he ignored Mama's pointing too. She had a spoon in her hand, and Papa kept talking.

These conversations got us nowhere, they merely wore us out. Even without this discord with my parents, the personal relationships in my life were appalling. That was why I didn't want to let matters descend into open confrontation. But I grasped that in my parents' apartment I was incapable of being the person I had been during my absence. I'd swapped the lunacy of the front line for the lunacy of family life.

Christmas was approaching. This year you could only get Christmas trees with a coupon issued to households with young children. My parents and I celebrated quietly with a bowl of apple rice, which was now the most appropriate way of marking Christmas. There was an air-raid alert too.

Over the festive days a Christmas card arrived from Uncle Johann, Papa's eldest brother. I'd sent him tobacco from the front a few times; now he was sorry that he hadn't heard from me in quite a while. Uncle Johann was the local police commander in Mondsee. Back at the hospital the captain in the next bed had told me, 'If you ever get the chance, pack everything up and move to the country.' And as I read my uncle's card I decided that this was exactly what I'd do: escape to a more peaceful world.

It took me three attempts to get through to Uncle Johann on the telephone. I told him that I didn't know what had happened to my bed, it was too soft and too lumpy. And I could feel the springs in Hilde's bed, it felt like lying on cabbages. Could he find me a room in Mondsee? / 'Consider it done,' my uncle said. A telephone conversation of robust brevity.

I was authorized to travel thanks to another doctor's note. The authorization was written on my clothing ration card. Mama was upset. 'Do you want to go away? I think you ought to be here with me.' / When I saw her sitting at the kitchen table, worn out, haggard, tired, her hair completely grey, her fingers bony and crooked, I felt like embracing her. But I stood by the sink, just staring, until she caught my eye and burst into tears. / 'What should I say if somebody asks after you?' Papa said. 'Nothing. Because it's really nobody's business. When Mama went to visit her relatives in Markersdorf it was nobody's business either.' / Mama had taken some excess linen and a few pieces of porcelain to relatives in Moravia. Codes of conduct for the Viennese were continually being published in the newspapers; people were suggesting that major attacks on the Danube cities were imminent. In the end, the reason my parents weren't more critical of me leaving was that secretly they no longer felt safe in Vienna either. / Mama wiped the tears from her eyes, and she said again, 'I think you should be with me now.' / And Papa, eloquent once more, said, 'But don't let the pious riff-raff in that part of the world get you down.' A few hours later he thought of something else. No doubt to justify himself, he said, 'I recall that you were in favour of this war from the start.' / I was not going to let myself get embroiled in another lengthy discussion, and so all I said in reply was, 'There's actually nothing here to make me feel proud.' / Papa said nothing for two whole days after that. Fine by me.

With a garter belt beneath a lance corporal's uniform and a crutch under my arm, I hobbled around Vienna and used up my ration card. I bought a cardigan, a woolly hat, mittens, shoes, provisions, and a sun lamp to treat the damaged nerves in my face. I had the wound in my thigh cauterized again with silver nitrate. Then came New Year's Eve. I was especially disturbed by the blackout that night. We hoped for a better year ahead for all of us, sure in the knowledge that a lot would happen before it was out.

The first thing the new year brought was my departure on the morning of 1 January. I bolted out of that apartment as fast as I could, to avoid any pangs of conscience over the kitchen table making me waver. On the way to the station I reluctantly bungled a few military salutes, but luckily I was one of the first on the train that was ready and waiting. I'd bought myself an early-boarding ticket, to which my wounds entitled me. / With a sigh of relief I leaned my head in a corner of the carriage so I could pretend to be asleep. Then I fell asleep.

Half an hour's train ride from Salzburg

Half an hour's train ride from Salzburg, but part of the Upper Danube district, on the shore of the Mondsee, which some say gets its name from its crescent moon shape, lies the town that shares its name with the lake. To the south the Drachenwand puffs out its broad chest above the towns of St Lorenz and Plomberg, which also sit on the lake. To the south-east the Schafberg raises its striking nose, now covered in snow. Due to its proximity to the main crest of the Alps, the climate around the lake is harsh, even though it's not that far north. When the landlady met me at the station and saw how cold I was, she said, 'Here you need your winter coat from November through to April.' / Although I was disheartened by the icy, cutting wind that penetrated even my coat, I replied, 'Four years of war have given me sufficient opportunity to wean myself off any sensitivity.' / She looked at me from head to toe like a cow up for sale.

On the coach box was a heavy blanket, which I wrapped twice around my waist. In spite of this I was so dreadfully cold during the drive that I could barely climb down when we reached the house. Aching bones from the journey and a twinge of uncertainty in my stomach. Overall, however, I was too exhausted to feel anything particularly acutely. At first I didn't even register much about the house we'd come to. It was a compact farmhouse of the sort you regularly find in this area, in a slightly remote location on a hill, with an adjoining barn. Projecting from the wall beneath the gable was the frame for a pulley; a rope with a hook dangled in front of the dark square of the attic window. The frame pointed towards a small brick house opposite, to which a garden and greenhouse were attached. I took a few steps towards the greenhouse to stretch my legs. A dog lying there leapt up and barked at me.

The landlady told me gruffly to carry my own case. She hadn't said much up to this point; she was the epitome of a rugged, uncommunicative charm that very much appealed to me and which I hoped would be widespread around here. I followed the woman to a side entrance and she pointed to the privy, which I used at once. It was right next to the pig shed, which meant you could have a good chat with the animals while going about your business. Then we went up some dark stairs that led up into even blacker darkness. The stairs were so steep and so narrow that as a child I would have tackled them only with the greatest trepidation. At the top stood a tin bucket, which in spite of the darkness the landlady managed to avoid. I, on the other hand, knocked straight into it and was startled by the sudden clattering. I just managed to avoid falling over. / 'Do watch out!' the landlady said. 'The lighting,' I muttered apologetically. / But at once she set about badmouthing 'the Viennese'. I was really far too tired to be as surprised as I might have been. / Outside the door of what was now my room, the woman handed me a ten-centimetre Chubb key and welcomed me to the house.

The worst thing about that evening were the sleeping arrangements. To call it a bed was stretching it, what with the rickety frame that lurched this way and that. The smell was also unpleasant. A stale, sour odour of dead animal rose from the depths of the mattress. / There was a stove in the room, which had been lit and which sighed as I entered. Running water was only available in the cramped bathroom down the corridor. No wardrobe, but an upholstered chair on wheels. And a breakfast table with a retractable writing surface. At least there were enough beams I could hit nails into to hang up my things.

That first night I thought I was going to die of cold. I kept permanent watch over the fire and added more wood several times, but the heat raced straight up the poorly fitted stovepipe into the chimney. The dog barked repeatedly, a furious barking that set my teeth on edge. At moments like this, my body could still, at a stroke, switch to a critical state of alert. Then it would be half an hour before my heart started beating normally again. I lay awake, my eyes wide open, listening to the mice scurry across the room, and thought of the thing I hoped had forgotten me: the war, which was presumably absorbed with its earthly pleasures.

Plagued by coughing and breathlessness, Hilde often had difficulty sleeping. I remember her saying, 'If I can't get to sleep I will sew another button on. When I sew buttons I forget everything else.' / What a shame that I didn't have any buttons to sew. / I got up to fetch my military coat as an additional blanket. Then I continued to lie there awake, still overpowered by the heady stench of dead animal that I couldn't identify.

By now I was well used to waking up in strange places, and so when I opened my eyes I didn't know where I was, but had every faith that it would come to me very soon. From the dog's barking I remembered that I was in Mondsee. Grey light seeped through the dirty windows.

On this first day I contented myself with an exploratory walk accompanied by a visit to my uncle. I limped into the town centre. There was no snow on the plain, a desolate winter palette. Welcome, grey man! Mondsee was pretty, I thought, with dark farmhouses on the outskirts and candy-coloured town houses, especially around the market square. The oversized palace beside the oversized parish church with its two chunky towers and a clock on each tower. The clocks had stopped at different times, which cast a dissonant atmosphere over the town. To the right a war memorial in the customary crude style, externally a dead structure. What saved the memorial were the names engraved inside it. / I had to give the yapping yard dogs a wide berth. / Nonetheless, Mondsee appeared to be a promising enough place. Not isolated and yet secluded, not some peasant backwater, yet small enough and away from the military roads. As throughout the entire Salzkammergut region, it was slightly antiquated, many things appeared hermetically sealed, so the place was ideal for my current requirements.

Just down from the market square stood the town hall, an old, ochre stone building with several windows that looked out onto the rear of the Sparkasse. Not far from there, on the other side of the cemetery, was the forestry administration. The gendarmerie was housed on the ground floor to the rear of the building. I entered through the door facing the street and found myself in a hallway covered in bottle-green linoleum. I got the impression that it hadn't been mopped in quite some time.

I gave my uncle a good bottle of wine and two packets of cigarettes. He ventured a polite protest, of course, but he was thrilled with my offerings. I hadn't seen him in years; he'd turned grey and put on weight. One could see from his skin that he'd been smoking relentlessly for forty years. His cough was dry and croaky, and sometimes he choked.

He showed me a pretty calendar from Denmark with pornographic photographs and a nude photograph of a girlfriend. This was in the staffroom. Then we went back into his office where we spoke for about an hour. He smoked some of the cigarettes I'd brought, then put the wine on the table with bread and a jar of schmalz. I should have eaten some bread and schmalz first, because after the cold the wine burned my throat like battery acid. Uncle was surprised to see my eyes fill with tears and he enquired about my emotional state. He was reassured when I said it was just that I couldn't take the wine. 'A different time will come again,' he said. 'I found it used to taste better in the past too.'

In the gloomy ground-floor room it smelled of files tarred with cigarette smoke. There was dark-green linoleum here too, which was more worn and lighter by the door and under the desk. On the wall there was a fold-down bed for emergencies, and above it a colourful sign: *The Seven Golden Ws / Who killed / whom / when / where / why / with / what?* To the right of the seven Ws was a pool of blood with jagged edges that frayed.

My eyes kept drifting to the pool of blood as I talked to Uncle in great detail about my parents and two sisters. I said that it didn't look as if Waltraud's lung problem would come back, she had got her PhD and was now teaching in the Protectorate. Inge was married and living in Graz. My uncle asked about my time in Russia, and I said I wasn't particularly sad to have left; the place wasn't to my liking. Nor did I find our manner of waging war to my liking: people had no idea of the brutality . . . But Uncle interrupted me and said that the key thing was that we stuck it out until the victorious end. / To avoid getting me deeper into the subject he asked about the military hospital. I told him that the nurses had been deaconesses; the pious nurses were the most popular even amongst those who believed in the devil, if anything at all. He coughed and laughed and said the priests would return via the back door. / 'Papa could have said that.' / But strictly speaking it was true. The hospital was a back door of the war and I was happy to have made use of it. I reminded my uncle of the saying that the road back home leads via the military hospital. He said, 'There you go, there's a kernel of truth in everything.'

Was I getting my bearings in the town? Yes. Had I already seen the community doctor's house? Yes. Was I happy with my room? No. / I told him that the stove was too feeble for the room. Maybe it could be fired by coal rather than wood, but for that I'd need an allowance. / He said that could be sorted out. And I should take comfort in the fact that the previous two winters had been harsher. I pointed out that I'd spent them in Russia. He nodded thoughtfully. / It brought to mind the snow-storms that had hurt my eyes as if someone were throwing gravel, and then the fear that the gun oil might freeze, leaving us helpless in that wasteland with frozen toes, unable to defend ourselves. / Two stretcher-bearers trudging through the snow with an empty stretcher. / In Russia it was so cold that one might believe the winters were a direct product of the war years, an emanation of the period. / My uncle reached for another cigarette, in the process clearing his throat with a cough. The cold season was pretty severe here too, he said. He'd seen things . . . metre-long icicles hanging from the roofs in April, being unable to go out in short sleeves until June. / As I was leaving he advised me not to sit around indoors; that just made you soft and gloomy. You have to get out, fresh air boosts the morale. 'Promise me you won't just sit around in your room,' he said. I gave him my word and hobbled off.

In the house where I now lived I climbed the rickety stairs and went into the cold room I'd been allocated. Out of instinct from my time at the front I was about to take off my rifle and got a shock when I found the strap wasn't on my shoulder. I was weak at the knees and shivering, and for a moment everything vanished, time, space, there was no in-between, nothing to protect me. Fragments of the past fell down and buried me, I felt as if I were about to suffocate. / When I came to, I gasped for breath. My heart pounding wildly, I sat on the bed. Was this a fit? I'd never experienced anything like it before. I was quite unsettled. And shocked too, for I couldn't recall ever having found the war so terrible when I was actually there. It was bad enough, but not that bad. / I felt a little better when I remembered where the face I'd seen was from. It was the face of the Russian woman we'd been billeted with when the stove exploded that night. The thatched roof caught alight instantly, and at the very last moment I was able to leap to safety through the window. Burning to death must be horrific, I imagine. / Afterwards we stood outside, some without field tunics and overcoats, six men without boots. And the woman sobbed; yes, her cottage burning down wasn't nice, but none of us was to blame. A single giant red flame blazed into the icy air, with a cloudy tinge to its edges as if it were evaporating moisture. / I didn't know the woman's name, but I did recall the name of the place: Yavkino.

To take my mind off things I lit the stove. I was bathed in sweat and panting with exhaustion. Later I tried to get to the bottom of the dead animal smell. The mattress was in a such a revolting state that I was seized by anxiety again and knew that I didn't want to spend a second night in this grave-like bed. Gasping for air, I went outside. After a while the landlady came out too and played dumb: she hadn't found anything wrong with the mattress when getting the room ready for me. I explained that the stove was too feeble and I couldn't air the room all day long either. Eventually she saw my point and admitted that the bed had been in a shed full of junk before my arrival and that she hadn't been inside the shed for years. She said she could offer me straw sacks instead of the mattress. Better than nothing. / I lugged the mattress outside and burned it with the help of a little petrol. The Polish housemaid watched, we exchanged a few words in Russian, she offered to clean my boots in return for a few Reichsmarks each week and I took her up on this. Then I washed the bed frame with an old sponge and some vinegar. It riled me that I should be the one who had to carry out this task. But despite the anger I also felt relief at having something to do that I was in charge of.

In the dark storeroom next to the bathroom I found a second chair which I could use as a bedside table. I drove a dozen nails into the beams, then sat beside the oven so the ink wouldn't freeze, and wrote.

In the room next to mine is a German woman with child of a few weeks that's not yet able to lift its head. The woman is

from Darmstadt, she's slim with long, brown hair, she stands
very straight and she's married to a soldier from Vöcklabruck.

On the day after my arrival the Darmstadt woman was summoned to Linz because they said her husband was leaving the barracks for the front. She dropped everything, took her child, left for Linz, visited her husband and returned on Wednesday night. I was already in bed. On Thursday morning she'd only just finished cooking when an express card arrived calling her back to Linz because her husband's transfer had been delayed. I heard her crying in the room next door. Shortly afterwards I bumped into her in the corridor. The corridor felt oppressive on account of the low ceiling and because the only daylight came from up the stairs or through an open door. / The Darmstadt woman said she was getting a boil on her hand and now she had to leave again. I helped her wrap up the child as she found it so difficult with one hand. She asked me to open her door occasionally. During her absence over Christmas it had turned so cold in the room that everything froze: water, milk, even the potatoes she'd kept well covered. / She'd laid sacks and a blanket over her crate of potatoes. / When she came back on the Sunday she was ill, a cold, which she treated with hot-water bottles and putting her head in a mist of steam. The landlady told me that the Darmstadt woman had also contracted a more chronic condition, something 'with a discharge'; once a week she had to go to see Professor Bernhardt in Salzburg. She couldn't say what caused the discharge, it could be from her cold. Perhaps the visits to Linz had come too early and the encounters were too tempestuous. The landlady laughed spitefully and, after a moment's thought, continued, 'Her perineal tear is causing a bigger headache.' / Embarrassed muttering on my part. / 'Professor Bernhardt says he can't operate *there*, so he cauterizes it once a week. Indescribable pain. And in any case it has to get better on its own.'

The landlady's talk was disconcerting. After all, war was the only thing I knew. I had no idea about anything else any more. It's only when you mix with normal people again that you notice how twisted your own mind has become.

The days passed with a lot of time-consuming toing and froing. The first thing I got was my coal allocation certificate, for which I required a heap of documentation. At the same time I registered with the police, obtained my ration card, bought a wireless (second-hand), and registered the wireless, which required the presentation of another certificate. In the fifth year of the war the Reich could afford a bureaucracy unparalleled anywhere in the world, and which was as unrestrained as it was obstructive. Total mobilization was perfect fodder for the authorities, but not good for anything else. Wherever I went I was asked for my police certificate of good conduct, my Party membership and my doctor's certificate. I was lucky the baker would sell me bread without demanding to see my papers. / I purchased food supplies. Shopping with a degree of normality – I hadn't done that in ages. For years I'd been used to being provided for. And when the supplies ran out, we requisitioned. To go to a shop and buy something with money was for me the epitome of normality.

My thigh, now that really was a strange tale. In hospital they'd taught me how to treat the wound: rubbing ointment, regular dressing, a weekly visit to the doctor to cauterize the swelling that was still there. From time to time it looked as if the wound would dry out, but then it started oozing again and would seep through the bandage and my trousers. And for every boil that healed beside the wound, a new one would form because of the ointment. / The landlady said I should pay a visit to a medicinal herb salesman in Bad Aussee. My uncle advised me to get injections of ram's blood. / If I wasn't careful with my movements the pain was hellish; everything went spinning before my eyes. I often suffered from headaches for which I had to take powder and lie down. Hours that felt like being under water. Some warmth would have helped my head and leg, but that would have required a warm room, and I had precisely the opposite. I sat regularly in front of the sun lamp, but it was totally inadequate. / The community doctor said my ongoing difficulties chewing were down to my fractured jaw and I shouldn't overexert it. / At any rate I didn't feel in a good state. And when you're not in good health, everything bothers you.

I pushed the bed closer to the stove. When reading in bed I wore gloves. And every night I also covered myself with my army coat, as I had in the driver's cab of the lorry, as I had in the bunker and as I had in the tent. The straw sack rustled all night long. / Whenever an icicle fell from the edge of the roof and shattered with a crash, I awoke with a start.

I was flush with money. Since the invasion of Czechoslovakia I had been on four campaigns and had saved a large proportion of my pay and all the bonuses for front-line service. Money can buy you a better life, and so I reported to the local group commander and, mindful of the needs of the hour, prattled on about the link between the Volk's health and its achievements. He took a look, and as a result he allowed me to have a slow-burning iron stove. / The landlady bristled, grumbled and asked me what on earth I was thinking of – I'd be turning the entire house upside down. I found her blatant rudeness almost interesting. / She finally gave in, but only after a long argument and her claiming she was only permitting it out of the goodness of her heart. In truth she realized that the new stove would increase the value of the room, and at my cost too. And because I didn't believe that the currency was going to keep its value I ordered a bed as well. The carpenter was already working on it. I also bought a seagrass mattress at some point, but for the time being I slept on straw sacks; it was all very difficult. But as Uncle Johann kept putting in a good word for me, I could count on the benevolence of the local people.

I listened carefully when they gave the temperature out on the wireless. Thank goodness it wasn't cold enough for ice skating; only the troughs and puddles were frozen over.

I'd managed to sort out the bureaucratic aspects of my relocation. Now, sentenced to a life of indolence, I took to going on walks. My body had become stiff during my time in the military hospital and while using crutches, and I felt like the frozen leaves that had crunched beneath my boots the previous year. There was still no snow, and the ice in the ruts of the swampy fields made the landscape appear as if it had been patched together. / In mid-morning my strolls were accompanied by air-raid sirens and the drone of bomber formations in the sky. The American squadrons would take off from Sicily at sunrise and head for the southern cities in Germany. Usually around ten o'clock they would fly over the main crest of the Alps. / Exhausted, I stood on a swimming jetty, eating the sandwich I'd brought along with me and listening to the polyphonic droning. And the squadrons passed overhead. Then I continued on my way, blinded by the low sun, surprised to be walking here, all my bones intact, almost twenty-four years old, with my own thoughts and my own feelings. By the Mondsee, the moon lake. Beneath the Drachenwand. A few patches of mist lay above the dark-grey water.

One day in the middle of January, I took my uncle's advice to boost my spirits with fresh air a little too far. In St Lorenz, on the western bank of the lake, my leg started to ache and gradually the cold crept through my gloves. I ought to have turned back earlier. It was so cold that I didn't fancy resting on a tree stump, and so I went to Gasthof Drachenwand to recover my strength.

There were several men standing by the bar, while the innkeeper sat at a table writing a letter. I'd already sat down when I remembered that my uncle had mentioned this pub. The previous owner, a Herr Lanner, had been beheaded eighteen months earlier for illegally slaughtering animals, together with his son of the same name: Anton and Anton. Although the recent history of the place made me feel uneasy, I asked the landlord whether he had any ration stamps and fortunately he said yes. It was the same routine everywhere: people always said yes. Then you'd beg the person to give you some stamps, in return for remuneration of course. And so you got something to eat. You never actually set eyes on the stamps, as you had to give them straight back to the innkeeper anyway. Ultimately what it meant was that you could eat even if you didn't have stamps, albeit at an inflated price. But what did it matter? Money was not what I was most in need of.

An old farmer who'd been standing at the bar came up to me and said they'd had a handsome dump of snow in the Waldviertel, and in some parts of the Innviertel too, and people there were able to make their deliveries. It was a strange winter, he also had all manner of deliveries to make and no sledge. Hopefully February would show a bit more mettle. / A shiver went down my spine when he said that. Papa had often used these words to describe what was expected from me: I had to show some mettle. I'd tried to meet expectations, show myself to be worthy – to my country, my forefathers, to history. But who was history? Where did it come from, where did it go? Why wasn't it the other way around: history having to prove itself worthy of me? Why didn't others do their bit, or not, as the case may be? And why were we permanently having to *prove* ourselves?

Sullenly, I stuffed myself with the roasted dumplings and washed them down with a beer. After I'd paid, I went back outside. The sun had come out so I kept hold of the scarf for a while longer and enjoyed feeling its warmth on the back of my neck.

As I was finishing my lunch I'd heard the whistle of a locomotive, so it was unlikely there would be another train to Mondsee any time soon. All the same I hobbled, my leg still painful, to St Lorenz station, where I ran into a crowd of people: a group of twelve- or thirteen-year-old girls and two chaperones. The girls were wearing immaculately clean clothes, pretty hairdos, and you could tell that they'd still been at home that morning. When they told me that they were pupils from the secondary school in Zinckgasse, behind the Westbahnhof, my heart missed a beat as they came from the same district in Vienna as I did, although I recognized none of the girls' faces. I looked around again: nothing but unfamiliar faces, with an air of expectation about them, but they also looked hungry. These girls would have been about eight when I'd had to leave Vienna. And suddenly I was struck by the sheer sadness of my life with an intensity that I hadn't felt before. I had to turn away and act as if I'd been distracted by something.

Local boys loaded the suitcases and rucksacks onto handcarts. The girls watched wearily and occasionally rubbed their eyes at the sight of the Drachenwand that towered steeply above the village. Then the teacher called out, 'Hats on!' The boys pulled the carts and two girls had to push behind each one. The other girls followed in twos, at more of a trudge than a march, a small, shy herd. They headed down to Schwarzindien on the lake, the village with the strange name: 'Black India'. As they crossed the tracks a rucksack fell from a cart. The wheels broke the frozen puddles. I heard a girl say, 'It wouldn't be quite so dreary if there was some snow.'

While the new stove

While the new stove was being fitted I attended to my correspondence. In the afternoon I painted the stovepipe, also new, with a metal lacquer. The pipe gave off an unpleasant smell afterwards, but that would go away within a few days. The first time I lit the stove I lay on my bed and laughed in triumph. I felt as if I'd achieved something for the first time in five years.

Now I paced around my room all day without shoes on. I could take the liberty of doing this because I never had any visitors, which was fine by me. When it got light in the mornings I no longer saw clouds of condensation above my bed, which was also fine by me. The space still wouldn't match everyone's idea of a bedroom. But it was bearable. And in spite of all the difficulties it did me good to have a place that I didn't have to share with anyone apart from the mice. Every morning I found crumbs from bread that had been gnawed. / Every day I made toast by putting slices of bread on the stovetop and toasting, or burning, them on both sides, then spreading them with butter and jam. It tasted very good. If the bread was still warm I could polish off large quantities of it.

At last, I was able to heat up as much water as I liked. My preference would have been to wash from top to toe every day. The words 'Come back!' were embroidered on my flannel, which I'd been given for free by a linen shop in Thaliastrasse. I'd had the flannel since I was a child, and whenever I was on leave I told myself that as long as I had this flannel I would always come back.

The new stove also produced a turnaround in my physical state. I gradually started to put on weight and my muscles, which during my time at the front had ached from tension, sometimes for weeks on end, now relaxed. Only seldom did I wake at night from cramp in my leg. My ability to concentrate, however, was still at rock bottom; I felt burned out and needed more sleep than before. Whenever I read a few pages of the electronics textbook I'd brought from Vienna, it all breezed through my head like a draught.

And yet I was over the worst, I could feel myself coming to life again. With a bottle of wine in my coat pocket, I ventured out into the frost and went to see the local group commander to thank him for having authorized the stove. It might sound strange, I told him, but for me the stove represented an element of freedom. The commander gave a hearty laugh. He was a tall, thickset man, around forty-five, obliging, and a dentist by profession. But he turned down my offer of wine; his secretary was Mondsee's gossip-in-chief and he did not want to give the impression that he bestowed favours on individuals. / We chatted briefly about how I was; I told him that regular nights spent sleeping outside in roadside ditches had ruined my health and that I didn't think I'd ever feel completely well again. Then he gave me a paternal clap on the shoulder, told me not to be so miserable and urged me always to strive for greater things. Immediately afterwards he excused himself, saying he was a very busy man. / I'd already seen in the pub that the commander wasn't one to hang around. When he'd sat at the neighbouring table he was already wiping the plate of his main course clean with a piece of bread while I was still on my soup.

Apparently the commander had denounced his own brother for having two bicycles in his cellar, complete with tyres, which ought to have been surrendered long before. I was told this by my uncle, to whom I brought the bottle of wine. I took advantage of the opportunity to dispel any remaining suspicion he might harbour that I was going to try to live off him.

Uncle and I had grown closer over the past few weeks, so I asked him why he and my aunt had separated. He said she didn't like his attitude to work. He himself had always lived by the rule that it was one's highest duty to avoid working one's fingers to the bone. My aunt believed the contrary. She held the view that a man needed to accomplish something for his money, otherwise how could he have any respect for himself? More to the point, how could any woman? My uncle had sunk so low, she said, that he wasn't even ashamed of his behaviour. As far as she was concerned, my uncle said, he ought to have found himself a gruelling job earning five hundred Reichsmarks per month, but he'd tried to explain to her how important it was for a marriage for the husband to come home relaxed and in a good mood. If he slumped down exhausted and annoyed into a chair, barely able to speak, it would be detrimental to the relationship. His wife had countered this by insisting that a man mustn't let his feelings get the better of him, he must control his temper. In other words, she'd shown herself not only to be egotistical, but stupid too, and he told her this in no uncertain terms.

Such folly on her part made the separation easier in the end, although he could have forgiven her the egotism.

We went out into the street together and bumped into the girls' teacher I'd seen at St Lorenz station. She was around my age, slim, with shining brown hair down to her shoulders. She wore a rucksack and was breathing on her spectacles, which she then wiped with the end of a scarf that was wrapped several times around her neck. / Was it the presence of my uncle that gave me courage, or the fact that we came from the same district in Vienna? In any event I asked whether she and the girls had settled in. / She greeted me, but with some reticence; clearly she couldn't remember who I was. / After I'd explained, she proceeded to talk to my uncle. In a decidedly businesslike tone she said that they hadn't been given enough fuel so she'd sent the girls into the forest, where there was plenty of wood lying around to bolster their supply. She didn't want to get into trouble on account of this, however. / My uncle pandered to the woman slightly, but she seemed intent on keeping her distance from his smoker's cough. And ultimately all she was interested in was whether she'd get into trouble, a question she asked him again and again. My uncle sighed and told her she definitely wouldn't get into trouble.

After my uncle took his leave because the priest hurrying towards us from the cemetery had beckoned him over, the teacher sighed gently too. 'I'm curious to know what's going to come of all these assurances.' / 'Front fatigue?' I asked. / She frowned and I realized I hadn't made a particularly good impression by using this military term. Unsure of myself, I said, 'The war has worked its way into every bone of my body, I need to get it out of my system.' / Now the teacher braced herself to give me an answer: 'I know the theatre in Schachen, where I was in an evacuee camp last year. Here it's all right for now, but you should see the coal cellar in Schwarzindien, where there's half a metre of coal dust which you can't burn. You have to dig around with a pitchfork to find the occasional lump of coal, and filling a bucket takes an age. You can imagine how much the girls dread being on heating duty, especially as on more than one occasion they've discovered that the coal cellar has also been used as a lavatory.' / 'Not nice,' I said. / 'Not nice at all!' the teacher said in disgust, then wrapped herself in her three-metre-long scarf and took her leave with an outstretched arm.

As I saw her taking the path down to the lake I limped after her and asked if she minded my walking with her for a bit. I'd become as stiff as a frozen fish during my time in hospital, I explained, and so I had to keep moving. She smiled dutifully, but nodded, and so I joined her. / We had already reached the path that runs around the edge of the lake when I found an opportunity to introduce myself. The teacher told me her name too: Grete Bildstein. She knew Possingergasse, where I had grown up; she herself lived in the Heimhof. When she said 'Heimhof' something must have happened to my face, some expression of surprise. She frowned again and asked whether there was something wrong with people who lived in the Heimhof. This completely threw me and it took me a while to reply that I didn't judge people by where they lived. But I must have hesitated slightly too long, for she fixed her grey eyes on me and sneered, 'Oh yes, it's what people are like on the inside that counts, isn't it?' Then she changed the subject to something trivial, but in such a way as if she was done with me. It shocked me how life concentrates itself into moments. / Later she said she was overwrought and on edge because they'd announced the evacuee camp was going to be inspected. That morning she'd shuddered whenever she'd heard a car.

The path took a sweeping curve and then headed south-east for a good kilometre towards Schwarzindien. To our left the lake lay calmly, the water's edge marked by a narrow strip of frozen rushes. Whenever you looked in the direction of the lake, you saw a bright landscape with the snow-covered ridge of hills above the eastern shore. On the other side, harshly defined trees along depressingly poor paths and squawking crows beneath grey clouds. / Three young nuns came our way. Having passed us, one turned around, a beaming smile on her face, and made the victory sign to me with two splayed fingers.

The teacher had quickened her pace and I was having difficulty keeping up. I got the impression she'd forgotten me again. / 'Not so fast,' I said. But she merely kept going. For a while I let her stride ahead, and when I caught up again after she'd had to let an ox-cart pass, she said, 'Your boots squeak awfully.' It was true. I apologized and explained that the boot grease I'd bought in town was poor quality, it didn't work its way into the leather, and when I put my boots beside the stove to dry the leather became stiff. / Although we didn't talk about anything important, it did me good to escape myself for a while.

After about half an hour we reached Gasthaus Schwarzindien. The sun was above the Drachenwand and moving over towards the Schober, behind which it would presumably sink. From the other side of the building I could hear low numbers being shouted out as if instructions were being given. In the shadow of the steep, jagged cliffs, and set between parcels of cattle pasture at the edge of the ever-cold, unfathomed lake, were three garden terraces leading down to the shore and a large boathouse. / You could tell which were the girls' rooms by the food piled between the windows, which they had been sent from home.

To my surprise the teacher invited me to accompany her to the rear of the building. The girls were doing gymnastics to the orders barked by the camp leader, all of them in black sportswear. The teacher said the girls were getting fed up with the isolation here, whereas her nerves were being frayed by the never-ending commotion. She was barely able to formulate a clear thought in her head, but she needed to because the children were approaching her with all manner of questions. Then I realized that by walking with the teacher I'd robbed her of half an hour to herself. / She put her rucksack down by the wall facing the lake, against which leaned a portable blackboard with an unsolved sum written in chalk. I could see that it was a rule of three, but as we sauntered past I was unable to solve it in my head.

As we approached the girls the camp leader stopped issuing her commands, which was also a signal to the girls, and they came running up to us with that excess of movement so typical of children. The teacher said, 'Don't let the little beasts mow you down, there's really not much for the girls to do here.'

The teacher had fetched a rather large package from the post office in Mondsee. She pointed at her rucksack. One of the girls near me was so delighted she kept hopping on the spot like a goat. There was no mention of what exactly was in the package that had been sent from the school back in Vienna, but I assumed it was some handicraft materials. The girl hopping up and down like a goat was given the job of taking the rucksack inside. She seemed pleased that she could be of assistance to the teacher. Then the girls in room 3 were told to rearrange the tables for dinner; six girls wandered off morosely. A girl who asked whom it was the teacher had brought along was given the answer, 'Blow your nose.' / We then chatted for ten minutes about my injuries and where I'd sustained them. Amongst these girls I felt as much of an outsider as a pupil who's sent to another classroom to ask for some chalk. What a shame there hadn't been more happy moments in my life until now, I thought, when, quite unselfconsciously, the girls burst out laughing at the mention of my garter belt, despite the unsettling nature of their lives at the present time.

The children were fidgeting with excitement. The presence of a soldier was of great interest. I was pleased that they seemed to like me. It must be down to the fact that the official news only said the best possible things about German soldiers. They pestered me for more details, and when I replied that I could only talk of horrible things about the front line, one girl with hanging plaits said, 'My father says you don't die that quickly.' / I refrained from contradicting her, even though my experience was different. Instead I said, 'An attitude like that would impress even a general.' / I asked the girls if they were frightened when enemy planes flew over. Many said 'Yes'. One of the girls said, 'You just have to keep calm, always. It's when you're most calm that something's least likely to happen to you.' She said she bet I wasn't afraid. I waved a hand dismissively and told her I was always the first in the cellar. Laughter all around. Having survived hazards in the past, I added, didn't protect you from those in the future; at some point all of your luck was used up.

Because some of the girls had started to stamp their feet in soldierly fashion to keep warm, the teacher brought our gathering to an end. She rubbed her red, frozen hands together, upon which some of the girls did the same. / 'Everyone indoors!' the teacher called. / In accordance with the rules that had been forced down the children's throats, they obeyed immediately. As she got to the door one of the girls called out, 'Do come and visit us again!' She consciously caught my interested gaze and smiled. I returned the smile. Then all of them turned around and ran off, giggling.

The teacher stayed there a moment longer, inwardly torn. Then she said goodbye too, without the slightest visible emotion, grabbing the blackboard with the unsolved sum under her arm. Meanwhile I lit a cigarette, anxious to stifle the trembling in my hands. I pondered what might be wrong with me. My head was aching from the activity, the noise, the talking. / As I left I turned around. Gathered at every window on the upper floor I saw girls' faces, wide-eyed and joyful. / What a strange life the children were leading here, in this secluded bolthole, where the attempt was being made, via drill and training, to acquaint them with the seriousness of life. At night the animals emerged from the forest, the owl fluttered around the house and the foxes barked. During the day the birds visited the feeder and the lake lapped at the frozen swimming jetties. And inside the building, instructions were already being barked again.

When I got home I met the Darmstadt woman outside the house. She was standing in the street beside the water fountain, waiting for the postman who was doing his evening round. He came at the usual time and gave the woman two letters. One she put in her coat pocket, the other she tore open with a smile and mumbled, 'Risen from the dead . . .' As she read she wandered back to the pram which was parked beneath the porch of our house.

Thus our conversation ended. Now I knew that the little girl had turned eight weeks old that Saturday, which meant she'd been born two weeks after I was injured. And I knew that the girl was just a couple of hundred grams shy of five kilos, and that she slept from ten o'clock at night through to six in the morning, or woke up only once at most. I would have known this anyway as the walls between our rooms were so thin that we were practically cohabiting. When I made a remark to this effect the Darmstadt woman replied that I talked to myself in my room, my favourite phrase being: 'We'll see!' / I said that sometimes the floor shook so badly that it was impossible to pen a letter or write in my diary. That must be her exercises, she admitted, ten minutes, three times a day, and she thought her stomach was already slightly smaller. But overall she wasn't happy with it yet. / What I neglected to mention was that she sometimes cried in a soft but throaty voice. If the crying went on too long I would crash my boot to the floor, giving her a fright. That stopped her crying.

When I entered the house via the barn door the Darmstadt woman silently put two outstretched fingers to her forehead and moved them away again. It was her way of saying goodbye.

We were fooled by a very brief spell

We were fooled by a very brief spell of warm weather, followed by crystal-clear days with sharp frosts. Half of the village had colds, children's noses were running and women pressed their hands to the sides of their heads. The landlady said that the Anglo-American dogs might have dropped bacteria on us, she wasn't ruling anything out. / I asked her what she meant by bacteria. / 'Germs, what do you think?' she replied. / I told her I thought that was humbug. / Then she snapped, 'That cutlery and crockery I lent you, I need it back. You've got to bring it down for me. Now. Yes, now!' / I had half the food I'd cooked the previous day in it and had to go begging for cutlery and crockery to the Darmstadt woman because I didn't want to eat with my fingers. / She told me that the landlady was notorious throughout the town; everybody pitied us for having to stay with this crook. She reeled off a few examples of her meanness, and it reminded me of the milkmaid back in Vienna at number 4. The landlady hadn't even wanted to hand over the bucket of coal that the Darmstadt woman had already paid for and had been obliged to ask for several times. Apparently the butcher said that the landlady had been at the Frankenmarkt on Monday, but they hadn't allowed her on the bus on the way home. Why not? Because she was a bloody cow, the butcher had said. So she was even popular at the Frankenmarkt. The Darmstadt woman rolled her eyes and said there were times when she preferred all the air raids back in Darmstadt to living with a woman like this. She pointed across the street to the gardener, who everybody just called the Brazilian. Dressed in a dark-grey poncho, he was washing a mattock in front of the greenhouse. Only a few days ago the Darmstadt woman had found out that he was the landlady's brother, and that neither of them ever said a word to each other.

I spoke as little as I could to the landlady now. That evening she called up to me from the bottom of the stairs. I didn't respond. She called again, then it went quiet; she was too lazy or polite to come up and see whether I was in.

I continued to feel regularly tired, often subdued. Lots of enemy aircraft in the sky, sometimes three hundred or more. My employer had nothing to offer against this. / I watched the enemy aircraft twinkling in the gorgeous sunshine high in the blue sky. It was an eerily beautiful sight.

Yesterday evening three mice were caught by my simple wooden trap. I had to take them out in the night apart from the last one, which I didn't discover until morning because I didn't hear it get caught.

On the third day my impatience got the better of me and I went back down to Schwarzindien. My boots were freshly greased and weren't as squeaky. Now and then I stopped, blew my nose, listened out for noises, then went on my way again. The merciless wind stung my skin right through my clothes. In the soft January light of a sun that hung aloof in the sky, the path crept its way there. When I reached Schwarzindien I buried my hands in the pockets of my low-slung uniform trousers, and at that moment the teacher stuck her head out of the window. When she spotted me she immediately shut the window. I walked past the building without looking up again.

The following day took me back to Schwarzindien, the entire village festooned with flags, as it was the Day of the National Uprising. Some girls were outside and I heard singing coming from inside. Down by the lake girls were trying to get the cat that belonged to the innkeeper and his wife to do tricks. They were using a piece of salami to encourage the cat to jump through a hairband. It kept sneaking beneath the hairband and trying to grab the salami with its paw. After several fruitless attempts the cat ran away and one of the girls chased after it to bring it back. / Another of the evacuees from Vienna said she hoped it would snow soon; someone would have to buy St Peter a schnapps. Then she said that the Viennese school in Zinckgasse had been relocated to Märzstrasse and now female foreign workers were living in Zinckgasse. One of her fellow pupils, Lisl Svirig, had gone back to Vienna to say goodbye to her father who was about to enlist.

The teacher came outside, a peculiar person: nice, spirited, and yet I didn't know what she thought of me. But from whom did I know that? Nobody, to tell the truth. So it didn't matter. / The teacher said that the camp leader had gone with three pupils to Vorchdorf to fetch plates and pots from an abandoned camp. They would be away for a day and a half, which meant that she was tied to thirty-five girls without any help or chance of a rest. The compositions the girls had written about their arrival in Schwarzindien were still unmarked. / I told her that my father had once dictated a composition to me because I didn't have time for homework, and I'd got a poor mark for it. / She shrugged. 'You ought to have written the essay yourself.' / She swept her hair behind her right ear and called after one of the girls, 'Sascha, you're losing your scarf!'

I wasn't for a second able to bridge the gap between us. My attempts to get close to her probably made her uncomfortable and she tried her level best to discourage me. Why was she like that? Why didn't she like me? I don't know. Perhaps she didn't like me because I was a soldier. Whenever I mentioned the war she frowned in that now familiar way and looked at me as if it were all my fault. / Then she mentioned the local supervisor of the children's evacuation programme, who lived in Mondsee and was forever creeping around the camp, without it being clear why, for she got no help from him and had to do everything herself. Finally she said she'd seen enough men over the past few years and was fed up with their seal-like smell. / I don't think she noticed how hurt I was by those words. If she did, she didn't let it show. But now I realized that there was no point in trying to force the issue; I might as well save myself the embarrassment.

One of the evacuees, who was very hoarse, told me that she'd tried to print her name at a machine at Mondsee station, but what came out was *Annemarie Schall*. Her name was two letters too long, the machine only printed sixteen characters, and if she'd known she would have tried *Nanni Schaller*. She blew into her hands and peered at me with curiosity over her knuckles. There was something appealing about her that I couldn't put my finger on, something extraordinarily self-assured. Her inquisitive, challenging eyes were still fixed on me; perhaps it was because I didn't know how to reply. She said at Easter she wanted to climb the Drachenwand with her cousin, then shielded her eyes with her hand and gazed dreamily at the cliffs to the south-west, cascading terrifyingly. / 'There'll still be snow up there,' I said. / Nonetheless, the girl beamed, as if she'd already set off in her mind, and she said, 'Kurt will go in front.' A second later she awoke from her reverie, looked at me uncertainly, mumbled something and turned away.

How odd this all is, I thought on my way back. I stopped, tossed a few stones into the lake, and I realized what the emotion was that I felt when I saw the camp teacher: shame. I felt condemned and was sure that in the presence of this woman I'd never be able to fully regain my self-respect.

Back home I wanted to make potato pancakes. Because the landlady had demanded her kitchen things back, I cut a tin in half with an axe, bashed the metal flat, made holes in it with an old bayonet, and my grater was ready. Wretched army life teaches you crude habits. The bayonet clanked when I threw it back onto the rubbish pile. From nowhere I had another attack of the nerves, a sense that something was happening to me over which I had no control. I dashed outside like a hunted animal and supported myself with both hands on the frozen fountain. Familiar images and fears shot through me, accompanied by a trembling. Familiar isn't the right word, perhaps, because everything I'd experienced in the war remained alien to me. And yet it felt as if everything were stored inside my body, as if there were things you never fully recover from, even if you appear to have returned to normal life. The fire in Yavkino was one of these things, as were the partisans sweating profusely while they dug their own graves, as were all those mutilated bodies.

After an attack like that I was jumpy and nervous for the rest of the day. Sometimes I was still subdued the following day too. Uncle said I literally dragged myself through the streets, worse than an old man. The images remained like a bitter aftertaste in my mouth. Often there were multiple attacks that came in waves, but they decreased in intensity.

As I peeled the potatoes I had to rest my head on the table and almost fell asleep with exhaustion.

That evening I went to bed early, heating the room thoroughly beforehand, because it was forecast to drop below minus ten overnight. I lay awake for a while, having abandoned plans to read because my head was throbbing badly again. Through the wall I could hear the Darmstadt woman talking to her child while she must be changing her nappy. 'I need to repack you, I bet it's not nice lying in that wet. But it's easier for you, I have to go down to the barn and sit in the damn cold like a pearl amongst swine. It's so cold there that my bottom sticks to the board.' / She also told the child that she needed an electric bulb for the bedside table lamp; the old one had gone. Things like that. Then I heard crying, comforting, and I caught myself listening more attentively to the comforting than the crying. The woman's voice made me again aware of my loneliness, and I fell asleep more quickly than her baby.

In the bottom-most pit of sleep where it's always cold and damp, I stumbled upon the war again, its one thousand five hundred terrible days, the stench of blood and at the same time the corn swaying peacefully in the wind while the partisans line up alongside the ditch as sweat pours down their faces. And towns where nothing is left save for the chimney breasts when we finally move in and, as if guided by a ghostly hand, one of the chimney breasts topples straight towards me. The last thing I remember before the fright was someone calling out to me in a menacing voice, 'Life? It's a kopek!' And once again I couldn't recall ever having found the war so terrible when I actually lived through it as I did now in bed.

Panting, I rubbed my brow on the sweat-drenched pillow and lifted my head. It was dark, everything lost, the only thing I could make out was my watch with its luminous face on the chair I'd put beside the bed. Now I realized where the smell of blood was coming from: in all the tension I'd bitten my lower lip. Scared, embarrassed, wary, I got up as if I were crawling out from a hole in the ground after the front had overrun me. I found a handkerchief in the pair of trousers hanging by a belt loop from a nail hammered into a beam, and pressed it to my mouth. Then I went and opened the window, a feeling of trepidation still hovering over me. Fresh air streamed in, but it was cold, very cold, and as I breathed it in, it was as if the air contained some of the blackness from outside. The town was in strict blackout, not a shimmer of light anywhere, and the houses sat in their gardens like boulders. There is a Russian saying that goes: The night carves robbers from posts.

Then I heard music coming from somewhere outside, a strange, almost lethargic guitar spinning into the depths and conveying the sense of a slow fall. At the same time it was very warm, weirdly buoyant, occasionally reminiscent of the music they play in Viennese wine taverns. Looking outside I strained my eyes until I felt dizzy. But there was nothing to see in the blackness. / As I didn't think I'd be able to sleep any more I got dressed. Maybe a stroll through the neighbourhood would allow me to tear myself from the war-filled air.

It was a clear, starry night and outlines gradually came into view. I could still hear the music, hypnotic jazz, no, not jazz, but something I'd never heard before, sleek with elements of upheaval, suddenly boiling over, then slowly returning to a gentle simmer again with a solitary instrument. I stood there listening for a while; the music was coming from the greenhouse. Clearly the gardener didn't care if it was day or night.

'Close the door!' the gardener called out gruffly because of the cold draught that swept into the greenhouse as I entered. I shut the door quickly and it clicked. I couldn't see anything, but the music had been switched off and I heard the dog growling. Only when I took my lighter from my coat pocket and sparked a flame was I able to orient myself. I lit up the central aisle between the seedlings and reached the orchid bed. From my uncle I knew that the gardener was a returnee from Brazil, the only remaining grower of equatorial orchids in Austria. Wrapped in a woollen blanket up to his chest, his legs fully stretched out, he sat in an armchair beside the stove, a lean man with a hooked nose. He'd quietened the dog, which lay rolled up into a shaggy ball on a blanket that had been folded several times and stared at me with its lively brown eyes. / 'Why are you here?' the Brazilian said. / 'I heard the music,' I replied. / He looked at me with calm interest. And after having pointed to a wooden crate I could sit on, also beside the stove, I extinguished the flame of my lighter. Right away it was as if bitumen had been poured over everything again.

The music the gardener had been listening to was by a man called Villa-Lobos. Did I like the music, the gardener asked me. Yes, I said. 'Rich is he,' he said, 'who is lucky enough to be able to live in Brazil.'

He explained into the gloom of the greenhouse that the plants would freeze if he didn't heat the stove half the night. In Brazil he couldn't sleep because of the sheer zest for life, here because of the cold. In Roman times, he said, this area had been a terrible place for the legionaries, comparable to exile: cold, inhospitable, a severe climate and severe people. In Brazil, on the other hand . . . there was no way you could understand it if you hadn't experienced the country for yourself in all its warmth, tranquillity and opulence.

I listened to the gardener fiddling around with something, he was grinding his teeth and sounds came from the back of his throat that suggested he was concentrating. I thought about what my uncle had said: the Brazilian had desperately submitted requests to get approval for an assistant. But there was no prospect of this as two years ago he'd been stripped of his German civil rights after making a careless remark about the F, which meant that now he was rather isolated. / I heard a hissing and crackling, then individual sounds and the same music started to play again, not as loud, but emphatic, agonizing, then without warning switching to cheerfulness, before it plummeted and sank right down with the solitary guitar. / For a while I just listened to the music, nothing else, my eyes closed. When I opened them again I could vaguely see because the Brazilian had opened the stove, where a wood fire was blazing away. He threw a few large logs in, red light illuminated his wrinkled face, his fox's eyes shone and the dark pores on his nose looked burnt. He briefly jabbed at the embers with the poker, then closed the stove door. / 'In an hour's time the last load will go in: four hunks of burr. It's harder and lasts longer. That'll be it for today then.'

I asked him what he was growing. / 'Tomatoes at the front, orchids and some cucumbers at the back,' he said. 'I started eating tomatoes in Russia,' I said. / 'A good thing too, tomatoes are very healthy, better than anything else.'

The music, the greenhouse and the night were all around us, and the stars shone in the sky, and the squadrons didn't arrive from the south that night, but from the north, and didn't reach us. He told me, more-over, that a Brazilian, the aviation pioneer Santos-Dumont, had asked the League of Nations to outlaw internationally the use of something so beautiful as an aeroplane for the dropping of bombs. At first this demand seemed naive. Then again . . . why not? / After that we discussed the Brazilian's vegetarianism. People said he gave his dog vegetarian food, was that true? He said it was, laughed and told me that this was the reason they let him have the dog, even though she was still young, she ought to have been seized for the war effort. It was too time-consuming for the F and his cronies to cook vegetables for a dog, he said; she couldn't eat them raw. / I automatically looked to where the dog was lying. All I could make out was darkness and silence. Lost in thought I sucked my bitten, swollen lip. / 'Once upon a time,' the Brazilian said, 'there was a country called Austria, you'll be familiar with that.' / 'Yes.' / 'It's such a long time ago that it's no longer true.' / There was something uncanny about his voice now.

The next thing I remember was the Brazilian putting more wood in the stove. 'You nodded off,' he said, 'and I thought about the Serra do Roncador, the Desert of Snorers. I crossed it.' He laughed. The dog lifted her head and looked towards the aperture in the stove, from which waves of heat were streaming.

It was time to go back to bed. The Brazilian said he'd have to heat up the greenhouse by six o'clock in the morning at the latest, otherwise everything would be ruined and all his efforts wasted. He offered me his rough, chapped gardener's hand, which I shook, and as I left I couldn't help thinking that in the hospital I'd lost the hard skin on my hands and feet, my war skin.

In the morning

In the morning I tolerated fifteen minutes of the local newswire from the landlady, whom I'd had the misfortune to run into outside the house. What's new in Mondsee? Pipi Reuss has come home, but he's in a very bad way, just skin and bones. At the textile recycling plant in Lenzing a Polish girl got her hair caught in the machine and the skin on her head was torn right off. And Klara Hufnagel's pregnant by a French prisoner of war, she's in prison in Linz. The Frenchman was working for her father as a farmhand and they marched him straight back to the camp. Also, Josef Strobl died. His wife wanted to fetch the doctor, but Josef Strobl said, leave it, I'm going to die, there's money for you in the drawer of the table, I don't owe anyone anything, I'm owed two hundred Reichsmarks by Ramsauer, just so you know. And the very next second he was dead. / I had to get away quickly or the landlady would have gone on talking at me forever.

The pregnant farmer's daughter cropped up again that afternoon. My uncle had sent for me because he needed a clerk; the prisoners of war were doing lots of work, he said. Farmers' daughters thought it was their only chance in life to . . . with a Frenchman. My uncle laughed bitterly. 'With a Frenchman!' / Perhaps I was tired from the previous night, when I'd undertaken the last two refuellings of the stove for the Brazilian so he could get some sleep. At any rate I put some of the carbon copy sheets between the five sheets of typing paper the wrong way around. When this happened a second time, my uncle dismissed me with a few less than friendly comments. I felt terribly embarrassed. But the episode showed how distracted I was; my mental deterioration after five years with the army was clearly visible. Others might be less affected, but I had been particularly hard hit.

I went back home. The weather was cold, damp, misty, and light snow was falling, as was typical for November. Smoke rose from every chimney, crawling beneath the roofs and into the streets, where it prickled the throat. When I crossed the Zeller Ache, I gave a start again. *Where is my rifle? Where is my kitbag?* Both were leading a life of their own somewhere in the east and only the routines and habits had followed me here to Mondsee, to unsettle me.

Waiting for me at home was a letter from Mama, telling me that the few belongings of mine which had stayed on the baggage train had arrived in Vienna. She got the impression, she wrote, that quite a few things were missing, such as my fountain pen. I was particularly sad about the fountain pen, because the one I was using at the moment wrote very poorly.

Even hens scratch more beautifully on the dung heap than that. And recently I'd been writing more than I ever had. It didn't matter what I did with my time, it was all a change from the war.

Now it's already starting to get dark again and I can barely make out what's on the paper. The lines and letters are all higgledy-piggledy, sentences in strange formations, strung together, meandering from one day to the next.

When I got up in the morning I was always slightly woozy. I wasn't right. Almost every day I had a headache. Now and again I took pills to relieve it, and they helped to some extent. My leg gradually improved. But no matter how often I dabbed my open wound, a few seconds later the shimmering red liquid would be there again. Although I was in no particular hurry to get my leg back in adequate working order for my employer, it was unpleasant all the same.

On one of these days I took the bus and train to Vöcklabruck to visit the infirmary there. I told myself it was wise to go regularly so that my complaints were recorded in the medical file. Unfortunately the doctor didn't examine me; he just asked a few questions, then decided he'd done enough asking and sent me away again.

Wild horses wouldn't get me back into a butcher's shop. I couldn't look at the meat hanging from the S-hooks, while the smell of blood made me feel queasy; I was worried that I'd have another attack of the nerves. / From time to time the Darmstadt woman would ask whether she could get me anything. I handed her my ration card and gave her the choice of whatever was available. Usually she would cook it too and we ate together. When I protested that she had enough to do without worrying about me, she said she had to cook anyway and I should feel free to knock on her door regularly. It would stop her going completely round the bend. / On my trip to Vöcklabruck I'd managed to get hold of some electric light bulbs, one of which I gave to the Darmstadt woman, at which she almost threw her arms around me. / She even offered to do my laundry, not out of sheer enthusiasm, but a lack of soap, something which I had. There may have been a touch of mistrust too: she simply couldn't believe I possessed sufficient housewifely qualities to look after myself properly. I said that washing and cleaning were amongst the very few sensible things I learned in the army.

I now drank tea regularly, heating the water on my stove. I made it as I had in the war, using a scrap of an old handkerchief as an infuser, which worked perfectly. / Sad, grey light came through the window.

The Darmstadt woman's child was thriving. She could whoop already, sometimes so loudly that she gave herself a fright. She wouldn't lie quietly for a minute, but thrashed about with her hands and feet, kicking the blanket away and saying, 'He . . . ho . . . mu . . .' / I liked watching the little girl. When the woman asked me about this, I said, 'It's better than any opera.' / Where, in my room, a uniform jacket hung from a beam, here hung an infant scale. The baby had finally hit the five-kilo mark. / Whenever the child cried, the Darmstadt woman tried to calm her down by producing a sound at the very back of her throat, which sounded as if her own mother back in Darmstadt might have hummed in exactly the same way.

On Saturdays the evacuee girls were usually free to do as they wished in the village. The streets would be teeming with uniformed girls between the ages of ten and fourteen, their hearts seemingly brimming with sunshine. The girls were delighted for the rare opportunity to escape the vigilant eyes of their guardians. Some were holding packages with shoes that needed repairing, others were minding a bag of wool that they'd bought after conferring with their parents by letter, so as to knit a flute pouch for a friend's birthday. The girls never tired of gazing at the animals in the gardens or the food on sale in the shops. Two girls who were playing with the Brazilian's dog told me where the boys from their school had gone. I'd said, 'Surely there aren't just girls in this world, there must be boys too.' Scarcely looking up from the dog, they replied that the boys had been evacuated to the Bačka and had even been to a local fair there already.

The Brazilian emptied the ashes from his oven and scattered them over the tomato plants. He said that bone ash would be better, but he wouldn't have anything to do with that. I asked him how he'd made it through the much harsher winters of the past few years, the most severe winters in decades. He said his mother, who'd died last autumn, would heat the greenhouse until midnight, while he would get up at five o'clock in the morning. The room where the Darmstadt woman now lived used to be his mother's room.

At night I sat in the greenhouse with the Brazilian and we gradually sounded each other out. The Brazilian gave me some of the apple slices and onion rings which he was drying on his stove, convinced that the really difficult and desperate times still lay ahead. In a tone of amazement he told me his life story, but he became so confused that only occasionally did I manage to grab a thread hanging loose from the tangle, for example that the Brazilian had lectured as an alternative biologist before being cheated out of all his money. / He kept punctuating his sentences with long pauses and I often thought he'd stopped talking for good. Then he would resume at some random point, his eyes probably closed, uttering phrases into the darkness with only a very loose connection between them. It felt to me as if he were indulging in fantasy when he talked of corpses laid out in the undertaker's shop window and of minstrels singing their ballads out in the open wearing full-length black coats. / We were disoriented by the late hour, and an aimlessness in both of us was no doubt a reason why we kept losing the thread. I found myself listening with one ear only and dreaming of crooked trees with yellow fruits and a woman in nothing but an apron playing guitar between head-high blue and pale-pink orchids.

I asked him why he'd come back home. / 'Yes, it was a mistake, and because of my parents.' Later he added, 'If I'd had an inkling of how ruined life was here, I'd have rather died in Brazil three times over. It's not worth me working my fingers to the bone for this. All the work in the greenhouse has given me rheumatism in my arms. When I finally get to lie in bed I can't sleep because of the pain.' / Now and then he whispered 'Adeus!' in his thoughts. And the dog whimpered.

The Brazilian missed the cheerfulness of the people in Rio de Janeiro, the way they were so relaxed and unbothered by things. He missed the vibrancy of the colours; there were birds in Brazil that looked as if they were illuminated from inside. The moment they let him he'd go straight back to Rocinha, back to the southern hills above Rio, into the sun-kissed hills with their sea view, where in Europe the rich would live, but in Brazil it was the poor. At night he used to watch pilots fire flares from the windows of their seaplanes before landing in a bay. From where he lived he got a good view of this.

The full moon passed. As the moon began to wane, it grew warmer, and just as the first cowslips had come into bloom the landscape was transformed. In the morning snow lay all about and the snowfall continued. Everything was white, covered, packed, every branch thickly laden. Only the steep cliffs of the Drachenwand were as grey and black as before, towering above the lake. It was peaceful, with the occasional flyover. The temperature was mild. Not even small streams had frozen over. I heard on the wireless that there was a thaw in the Carpathians too. The poor devils there.

I had dry nostrils from the snowy air, but my feet were permanently damp. Although I'd given my boots a good greasing to prevent the snow from sticking to them, the wet crept its way in. So I resorted to another tried and tested method: stuffing newspaper under my socks, which made my feet slightly warmer. / Once when I was out for a walk I met Grete Bildstein, the teacher from the camp at Schwarzindien. As we approached each other I felt myself getting nervous. But then we had a normal conversation, normal in the sense that, as ever, the teacher emphasized just how much she had to do. She said her sphere of work was expanding all the time, children and parents were beating a path to her door, which was a good thing in some respects, but it left her little time to think. / A pallid sun swam behind the snow clouds. When the teacher raised her head I was surprised to see her face lose all of its severity. 'The girls,' she said, 'well, *good* would be an overstatement, but they're all right. It turns out that one of the girls is involved in a rather distasteful correspondence with her cousin.' The teacher told me the girl's name, Nanni, and the name of the cousin, Kurt. While their mothers were busy defending the homeland in oil-smeared metalworkers' clothes in a factory, Nanni was letting Kurt feel her up. / I gained the impression that the teacher was telling me all this to make up for some of the humiliation she'd subjected me to. And all of a sudden I felt as sorry for this tall, diligent, anaemic young lady as she probably did for me.

In mathematics two minuses multiplied together make a plus, but not in psychology. In psychology two zeros make a double minus. And there we stood silently for a few seconds, the spurner and the spurned. / When I continued on my way I recalled my life as a soldier, straightening my back as if I had to make a show of marching upright. Hopefully the teacher wasn't looking back, because I was trying to strike a pose that wasn't me and which meant nothing to me either. But this only dawned on me after I'd gone a hundred metres or so.

If I need to debate something with myself I do it in bed if possible. That's why I didn't get up the following day until just before noon. / What had happened was this: I'd made advances to the teacher and she'd rebuffed me. Indeed she'd rebuffed me on several occasions, and she no longer meant anything to me. I mean, I'm not so stupid as to set my heart on a woman who doesn't like me. A waste of time and effort. And I wasn't going to let this matter get me down. After all, it wasn't the first disappointment in my life and it wouldn't be the last either.

I got up when I heard the pre-raid warning. During a red alert the shops would shut, a sort of siesta, not a Spanish one under the walnut tree, but a German one in the cellar. That's why I wanted to dash to the bakery. Outside the house I ran into the landlady, who said how outrageous it was that I lay in bed for so long. She contrasted me to the F, who got up at five o'clock every day, sacrificing his health for layabouts such as myself. / I was still on my way to the town centre when the red alert was sounded, and in the distance I could hear a muffled rumbling and a persistent rattling and banging; it sounded like a dogfight. I didn't feel at all safe between the houses, so I hobbled to the avenue lined with huge lime trees, which led down to the harbour.

Other people, young and old, were already gathered there. A squadron approached from the south-west, around fifty Flying Fortresses, without escort and without becoming embroiled in combat. They flew very calmly, leaving two hundred streaks of condensation trailing from their engines, four to each aircraft. I could hear a regular drone, as if the aeroplanes were dragging their bellies along the smooth, hard runway of the sky. The aircraft had almost passed overhead when a second squadron appeared above the Drachenwand, this second wave, much closer to Mondsee, also neatly ordered, but considerably smaller than the first squadron. I reckoned it must have already lost one-quarter of its number. It was attacked by German fighters, which was clearly visible because they came from above, out of the sun. The noise rapidly gained in volume and I saw what there was to see. / A slender boy with a sailor's gait worked himself up into such a state of excitement that he had to run away and pee up against one of the lime trees.

The war didn't shift one millimetre. The noise was overbearing, the shooting and whining, the harsh, pointed outlines, my heart was pumping from just watching. The bomber closest to the town, at the tail end of the squadron, was under permanent fire. All of a sudden it was unable to keep up with the others' speed and it veered off to the side. I could see from the streaks of condensation that only one engine was still working. In the end the aircraft plummeted in a spiral. A Messerschmidt circled the crew dangling from parachutes, but then rejoined the pack which was strafing the next bomber, always the last one, on the very outside. / Beside me an elderly woman with a face chiselled to perfection like a Punch-and-Judy puppet had her hands over her ears. A small child had its eyes closed. War's good reputation is based on a fallacy.

Two women standing behind me started talking about men. 'It's perfectly clear that all the decent men are away. If that Hirsch ever gets a woman, it'll be quite something.' / 'Just imagine having to go to bed with him!' Both laughed gleefully. / 'Wendt has been conscripted now. He left with his head down. But he's too stupid to keep his head down at the front.'

The next Flying Fortress broke away from the formation and fell to earth. All ten crew saved themselves, the last being the captain if custom was being observed, dropping into the wild blueness, or into the metre-deep snow for those who had the bad luck to land in the mountains. The bomber burned and broke in two in mid-air. The men hovered in the ice-cold atmosphere, as tiny as dandelion seeds, to the north of Attersee. See you on the ground. / The squadron rapidly vanished, heading north-eastwards. Then the noise lost its ferocity, mingling with the squawking of gulls, and finally dissipating altogether like a bad dream.

The sirens had sounded the end of the alert. The episode was discussed on street corners. People were saying that the boot was on the other foot again now, for a long while the Americans had been flying around here as if they owned the skies. / But less than twelve hours later the Reichsgau of Upper Danube was paid another visit, this time from the north, around two hundred aircraft reaching unchallenged the target they'd been heading for at midday from the south: the ball-bearing works in Steyr. The bombers encountered no resistance worth mentioning; during the day my employer had resorted to *total* overspend.

One day later, 26 February, it was my twenty-fourth birthday. As in previous years I celebrated quietly and peacefully, there was no plate of fruit or cake to greet me, I ate hotpot and nobody was any the wiser. Afterwards I lay on my bed, staring at the ceiling, my confidence eroded by multiple setbacks. For today was the day I'd decided would be the start of my university studies. It passed uneventfully. I was now an old fool, older than my sister Hilde had been when she died.

Hilde died when I was sixteen. I'd found it baffling that a person can be alive and although they're alive they can never get well again. It was likewise incomprehensible that Hilde could walk but would never run. When we were both younger Hilde had often caught me in the garden or when we were out on a walk. She would have been the same age as the girls in the Schwarzindien camp, the same age as Nanni Schaller.

When Hilde had a relapse I was in the fourth year of primary school, and the year afterwards I started secondary school too. Hilde spent a lot of time at Hochzierl sanatorium and Papa would read out her letters at the kitchen table. When Hilde was in Vienna I carried her bag to school, while she walked unsteadily beside me, smiling sheepishly whenever we had to stop for a rest. / Once we couldn't stop laughing and afterwards Hilde said, 'My chest hurts. But it's worth it for the laughter.' / In Russia when I sat alone in my driver's cab and tried to pass the time by thinking of Hilde, I ran through my memories, the day of my return from holiday camp, the day Hilde finished her school-leaver's exams and how the two of us went ice skating together and how she'd embraced me. And then I would smile, rubbing my face, or lean back with the thought that at least I was still alive.

Uncle was able to tell me that an American who'd bailed out in the area hadn't tied the laces on his boots. When his parachute opened, the force of the jolt tore the boots from his feet and he landed knee-deep in snow in his socks. One has to bear these things in mind too, my uncle said, there's an unbelievable number of things one has to bear in mind.

On Friday in Darmstadt

On Friday in Darmstadt eight hundred rabbits were shared out, taken from the sheds of other people who were deemed to have too many. The feed situation isn't good, and it's bad for me too because both bicycles are broken. Bettine's packed up straightaway, while the inner tubes and tyres on mine burst two days after you returned to Mondsee. It's at the Walters' shop on Elisabethenstrasse. It's not good, but if I had it I could go into town and pick up scraps of waste. The bus is always too full.

Are you coping with the nappies, Margot? Do you have enough warm things? What are the beds like for you and the child? They *won't* be as good as at home. And I hope you've got enough to eat in Mondsee. You're always so hungry and now you've got a baby to breastfeed. I remember what it was like when I breastfed you, always a lot of biting. I hope you have a better time of it. / Tonight I'm sleeping back in my bed. I've been in yours since the last air raid. Bettine will use it from now. Ernst and Helen are sleeping in the little room until they can move into their new apartment in Saalbaustrasse.

Papa's still in Metz, he's far too gloomy and the thoughts going round his head are wearing him down. Men of his age certainly won't get sent to Russia, but he lives in permanent fear, and besides, it offends him that he and others his age are still being dragged away. On the other hand it might not be such a bad thing, as your father will learn to appreciate his home and realize that a good word is worth more than all that shouting and screaming. I'm just hoping he comes back to us safe and sound, that's what goes through my head day and night.

Bettine writes from labour service in Berlin that she's got new shoes and a new hat, and she's not going to get rid of her artist's mop of hair, even though the kepi doesn't fit properly. That sister of yours is behaving like she's straight out of a twenty-pfennig novel. I'm really worried about her. Berlin's a dangerous place and at sixteen years of age your sister can't see past the end of her nose. I've written to her several times to say she should try to get them to release her from those damned trams, but she won't listen.

My legs are better now. I went to the doctor's yesterday. He says I can take the bandages off at night. / I've just thrown Peterle out after she made a right mess of my kitchen which I'd just cleaned. Otherwise everything is pretty much the same as usual.

I stopped writing for a few days because I don't have a grain of happy news to pass on and I don't fancy writing about sad things. Everything's so hard to get hold of, no manure, no fencing, no cardboard, there's a shortage of everything. You run around all you like, but for nothing. The worst thing is that I don't have enough tobacco. If I had a husband with a tobacco ration it would be all right, but my card doesn't stretch far enough, and when I've got nothing to smoke I have no desire to get on with any sort of work. Unlike lots of other people, I won't smoke anything else, I've tried and I feel sick just thinking about it. What's more, the beer here is just water, no trace of beer, Papa would say it's all crap. / So I find myself running around the whole time and whenever I want to write, something gets in the way, while all those air raids do the rest. I've become really quite nervous of late, and am fearful whenever evening comes. Last Saturday evening the sirens wailed, they bombed Frankfurt and did serious damage, but Darmstadt copped a few too, including a heavy 3.5-tonne bomb that tore a fifteen-metre-deep crater in a field, as well as phosphorus canisters and firebombs. There were several fires, including a factory and the labourers' barracks beside it. The blazes made it as light as day outside and the foreign women screaming could be heard as far away as ours.

As you can imagine, we've had some really worrying times here again. We've now got cracks in the walls too from the blasts. In the kitchen so much paint has come off the ceiling that it looks as if we've had the decorators in. But according to the flyers they dropped the worst is yet to come, we're going to get what others have already had. Yes, dear Margot, if only you could see beautiful Frankfurt. I was there after the last raids and I don't wish to see it a second time. The city has been reduced to ruins, and there's no way of removing those enormous piles of rubble. The bodies of tenants still buried beneath, it's terrible. And yet, amidst the ruins and the rubble, life goes on. We've already got everything in the cellar, the cupboards are empty.

About the suit, Margot, I told you in my letter to have a good tailor make it, but once again my words fell on deaf ears. Now look where we are! It's not right, it's too short and whatever else is wrong with it. When all is said and done, it's never going to give you any joy. There's nothing to do apart from put it on when you're doing the laundry and that's that. I'm not going to let myself get worked up any more over it.

But I'm pleased that some sign of life from you has made its way home again. As for me, so far I'm all right, I mean, we are in the middle of a war. And no, I don't go out in the evenings, the blackouts keep you busy, you have to watch out you don't trip over a bicycle that hasn't been put away properly. Hans Bader broke his leg on the way back home because he didn't see a step.

The Feuerbachs' son was home on sick leave, with malaria apparently, while their son-in-law is in Poland, tasty things are always coming from there. Some people are bragging that they barely notice the war. / Old four-eyes in the house opposite makes me livid. Believe it or not, he stands at the window or on the balcony all day long. And he's constantly smoking: a pipe, cigars and cigarettes in turn. Then I see him stretch or cross his hand behind his head. Papa's wearing his fingers to the bone for people like that, and others are working like Trojans. He must have connections. Herr Becker too: the doctor's diagnosed him with cardiac neurosis. Now he's complaining of having to work ten hours a day on fire duty at least twice a week, and so he says he'd rather join up. Only a really stupid fool could say something like that. I'd rather work round the clock with cardiac neurosis than freeze my backside off. Papa says the infantry are lying in holes in the ground, many in tents, and all the time it's minus five or minus ten – who'd want to swap for that? And a shell can explode right beside you at any moment, bang. Nobody knows when they're going to get it. They should be pleased they're at home. It's all very gloomy here, men being called up left, right and centre. How's your husband? Is he still in Roumania?

Käta gave her first children's cookery lesson yesterday: cold dishes for children up to the age of ten, including boys whose mothers are in the labour service. The children were really good, but Käta's awfully hoarse after all that talking and can't talk at any volume. I've had the most dreadful Saturday myself, and if I didn't have to stay up waiting for something in the oven I'd be in bed already, rather than writing letters. I haven't sat down at the window in a fortnight now.

One night I had such a vivid dream about you. You were walking down a country lane fully armed, you were a soldier in uniform with your child on your back. / Let's hope the war comes to an end soon.

I can't stop thinking of Bettine on the trams in Berlin. Write and tell her not to get mixed up with any men. She could ruin her entire life, there are all those diseases and most of them don't know. The men are only in town for a few days and after that she'd look like a right charlie. It wasn't a good decision you took, either, to marry a stranger in the middle of the war and then have a child straightaway, or the other way around. So write to Bettine and tell her not to make the same stupid mistake. She won't listen to me. She's already acting the Berlin know-it-all towards me, maybe her sister will have more influence. Tell her even a kiss can ruin your entire life. I've only got her best interests at heart. Hopefully she'll listen to the warning from you and remember her whole life long. Guess what? Fräulein Gramüller gave me fifteen Reichsmarks' travel money for Bettine. Bettine gets this every month and she's kept it a secret from me, even though I give her the fare too. That's not nice of her, I'm most disappointed and wouldn't have believed she'd do something like that. You tell her this too and say we hope nothing of the sort ever happens again. / I've spoken to the caretaker of the AOK, who was pleased to meet me. She kept saying: What's Margot up to? She sends her regards. I showed her the photograph of you and the baby you had taken in Linz. She went running with the picture to her husband, leaving me standing there, and she just kept calling out, 'Look at our little minx!' The people there really like you, they had tears of joy in their eyes.

In the letters you send home you write lots about the child and little about yourself. I'd rather it were the other way around. I'm thrilled that the baby can already say 'ho' and 'mu', but how are you? Was I really out of order to say you ought to be ashamed of yourself? Did you expect me to say it was fine for you not to reply to me, that's how I like my daughter to be? I think not! So, please don't let me wait another four weeks for an answer. And of course I'm sorry to hear you're freezing like that. You'd be better off at home. I often lie down at night, embarrassed to be the only one in the family with a warm bed. Papa's also complaining that he's cold. The handwriting in his last letter was so poor I could hardly read it. Maybe his hands are completely frozen. There's no prospect of any leave at all at the moment. I'd be so happy to see him again, and you and the child. I'd love to have the child close to me for a bit. Forgive me if I grumble at you from time to time. You know me, I don't mean to be unkind. Whenever I go into the back bedroom and see your bed, I really miss my little Nuschi. We can only hope that you'll soon be here with us again for a while. / Yes, dear Margot, I'm going to sign off now and have something to eat so I can go straight to the animals when the all-clear sounds. I'll give you a few of these bread stamps this time, because you don't get enough bread in Mondsee. And when you say that the woman you're living with is a witch, let me tell you that you'll return to your parental home richer in experiences and disappointments, and I hope you'll have learned to appreciate how lovely it is here and won't want to go away again. Lots and lots of kisses, dear Margot, from your mother! And best of luck, always!

I almost forgot, Gretchen died on Friday. Seventy-nine, she was. It's not nice for Otto, he slept one night *in* bed next to his dead mother. Send a card of condolence, would you? Offenbach, Taunusring 109. / Fritz Stömer had a fatal accident on Thursday on the Siegfried Line. He slipped while laying mines, fell on one and died instantly. Kammerer has become a father again, they keep going on their merry way. It won't be long before she gets a German Mother's Cross, silver class, let me tell you. His wife is still in hospital because the ligaments in her uterus are too weak. She's got to stay in bed and they're giving her calcium injections. I see nothing but prams out and about. / I'd be keen to know what you're standing up for. I didn't understand what you were saying in your last letter.

A dark-grey rabbit's died, I'm sorry to say. I feed them so carefully and I'd have been so proud if I could have kept them all alive while

Papa's away. It hadn't eaten anything since Sunday. If only I'd got Erb to slaughter it, but I was worried that Papa would say, 'Everything goes to seed when I'm not at home, now she's killing my rabbits on purpose.' But it won't happen to me again. Even if a surgeon major had come from the field hospital, he wouldn't have been able to help the rabbit either, that's what I reckon.

Only eight days until Easter now, yes, dear Margot, all of us apart, but in our thoughts we're all together. I might be frightened of the enemy aircraft, but I get the feeling they're sparing me. But the rest of you in distant parts, some not getting enough to eat, others freezing, Bettine's exhausting work on the trams, and all of your lives in danger. I'm ashamed to crawl into a warm bed every evening. I'd really love you to come back home with your child. But I know you've got your misgivings.

It's now half past one in the morning, there's an air raid and I can hear the droning in the distance. We're on red alert, so ta-ta for now. Back later. Hopefully. You've always got to give thanks to God if you come back up from the cellar in one piece. / It's morning again now, just before eight, and I'm going to keep on writing this letter. We were in the cellar half the night, not sheltering from bombs, thank God, just aircraft passing overhead. But let me tell you, just the prospect of a bomb crashing into your roof is enough. There's an alert every day, sometimes twice a day, all that's missing is them coming at breakfast time too. It really gets on your nerves though I try to remain calm, outwardly at least. I hear a siren in every creak of the garden door, every cry of an infant. Every time there's a sound I have to check it's not the pre-alert signal. But enough of that, I'm sure you'll have everyone telling you the same thing, so it's not worth me blathering on about it.

Lulu is asking whether you got her letter. I told you about Kresser und Luft's, and how we stayed in Eichbaumeck during the alert while everyone else fled to the bunker in the forest. Nothing happened at Kresser und Luft's. But those strafers can't distinguish a barracks from a goat shed. Guess what? They opened fire on our shed.

When I went to hospital for my examination I was two hours in the air-raid shelter there. I don't know if I've already told you this because I write my letters to you in my head when I'm working, when I'm cutting up the rabbit food. Well, there I was sitting in that underground shelter, then they, a strafer, shelled Eichbaumeck with an on-board cannon. They fired at Herr Kreng, who was digging over his garden. He was right in the thick of it, but they missed him. They shelled the Sulzbachs' cellar, and at the Winters' place they shot holes in their cot and a fist-sized hole in the wardrobe. Some of the Gusers' rabbits were killed, but nobody was injured, thank God. That caused quite a commotion in Eichbaumeck, it did, but I was in the cellar and completely unaware. It's just lucky that they didn't strafe our hayloft. / Lies and Lotte are still jolly. They haven't had any babies yet, only the piebald and Vienna Blue. The garden's all fine, tomatoes doing well. The oats haven't grown much, there hasn't been enough rain. The clover's very sparse, everything's too dry. Grandpa was here yesterday getting some plants. He didn't even go to see the rabbits. If I hadn't said he ought to take a look inside the shed he wouldn't have bothered.

Grandpa said that thirty rabbits of some friends of his had burst lungs after a bomb exploded nearby. Grandpa slaughtered three for them so they could preserve them and he's going back to slaughter the others too. Things look bad everywhere.

Hopefully we'll all have a bit of peace and quiet tonight. I ought to be darning stockings, but the light in the cellar isn't good enough. I wish you could sit around the table with us like you used to. I hope you'll be back soon and we'll all see eye to eye and won't argue. We could have spared ourselves some of those spats, don't you think, Margot? If you weren't afraid of an air attack during the train journey you could spend the odd couple of days here with the baby. It would make me so happy. And do write as often as you can to dear Papa, you know what it means to him. He mixed up our letters, so I'll send you yours. Do follow his advice.

How are you, dear Margot? Are there a lot of explosions in your neck of the woods too? I still haven't had a reply to my letter. Now it's Saturday again and it's been raining the whole day. Bettine has arrived from Berlin with a cold. She's lying on the sofa with a scarf wrapped three times around her neck. I reminded her that when Auntie Resel worked as a conductress on the trams she developed her condition because she went in to work at Christmas with a fever. / And how are the two of you in Mondsee? Is your neck better? Is the child's bottom better? Can you sit normally again? I do hope so. Always wrap up warm. And if you're feeling a bit poorly, see to it that you stay in bed. / That's it for now, I know that I've forgotten half of what I wanted to write, I haven't quite got my head together at the moment, my thoughts drift back and forth.

Two days ago Lulu came home from Landkronstrasse in the pouring cold rain in her stockings. Her shoes got so soaked that they went out of shape and she threw them away.

She's not going to the bank today because she doesn't have any other shoes yet. She's asked a few times whether you've got her letters. She doesn't like spending her time at home any more, she wants to be with other people, but I'm sure a little time away from Darmstadt would make her see sense. I've only ever wanted the best for you. You understand that too, don't you? I don't want you to see me just as your mother, but as a loyal friend you can pour your heart out to at any time. Write and tell us more about Mondsee and what you're up to. I always read out your letters in the cellar so the others can enjoy them too. They're amazed that you can now eat potato salad with onions. But why can't you do that with your mother, who's only ever wanted the best for you? Instead I find myself getting worked up into such a state. If you're able to eat anything now, you can come home soon too. You've been away far too long and I hope you've learned to appreciate home. / I'm sending a few stamps, mind you don't let these ones expire too.

Susi was waiting for me

Susi was waiting for me at the tram stop to give me something, a letter from you. She said she wanted to *notify* me about something. I think that nosey parker suspects something's afoot, she just doesn't know what. Do you know what I mean, dear Nanni? By then it was already too dark to read in the street, so I hurried home and could have jumped for joy. I couldn't read your letter often enough and by now I know it off by heart. / My one regret is that we parted company so coolly. In front of my parents I lacked the courage to say goodbye in the way I'd have liked to. All the same I was very happy to see you again. It's not something you can really say in the moment, it only comes afterwards. When you were in the street with your rucksack on, I was standing up at the window and in my mind I can still clearly see you trotting off towards the Westbahnhof. My heart felt so heavy, but I didn't know you felt the same.

You say that Schwarzindien is a very forlorn place, and there are only a few boys coming and going outside the camp. Where are the boys from? And anyway, how do you know they're all stupid if you're under constant supervision and have nothing to do with these boys? Don't you ever go into the village? Don't you meet any boys there? Don't get up to any mischief, I don't want to be disappointed. Please don't forget your Kurt. And hopefully what you wished for when you found Burski's eyelash will soon come true. I'd be happy enough just standing under the railway arches with you again. Do you remember? I don't mean like outside the front door, more like that Saturday when we were in the Prater and I was standing behind you, you know. Whenever I think of it my heart begins to pound and won't stop. What I'd give to wander down Mariahilferstrasse with you again too. When we walked together in autumn you kept giggling and how I liked that! My dear Nanni with the strange dwarves beyond the seven mountains. Do you already know the mountains there by name?

I'm sure you'll get used to the drill soon enough. I hate it when somebody's watching every crumb that falls to the floor. And your morning roll call outside whatever the weather doesn't sound nice either. I can imagine it must be quite sinister sometimes when all you can hear in the morning mist are the cries of the herons. But why do you stand in a square when hoisting the flag? Is there a particular reason? Do you like squares? I hate the way the world is so square.

Do you know the mountains by name yet? I've asked you that already. You ought to have answered my questions instead of drawing on the last sheet of paper the hunk of smoked meat you got on Sunday. I really want to know about the boys that come and go outside the camp. What about them? Do you talk to them? Please write and tell me. / And I can well believe that your belly swells after eating. I'd love to drum on it. I miss you, Nanni, especially on Sundays when I feel very alone. But you mustn't put on too much weight or I might as well marry my mother right now. They seem to be fattening you up there like hippos.

Something quite different now. Yesterday I went with Mama to see your mother, who was in floods of tears. Whenever you write to her you've got to say that you're well and everything's fine. You can pour out your heart when you write to me, I can cope with it. But your mother's frightfully worried and very unhappy. There's a new foreman in the factory where she rivets infantry spade carriers, and your mother says he's hell-bent on working all the women there to the bone. She doesn't want to stoop that low, not for a boss who just lounges around. They're all crooks, she says, who've been deferred from military service because they don't fancy risking their criminal necks. That's what the foolish masses are for. The factory overseer isn't to be trusted, she says. Either he's being intimidated by the management, or he's spineless and a coward, or both. It's piecework and your mother is supposed to produce twenty-five spade carriers per hour, but that's only possible if you hammer continually without speaking, and she can't keep up this rate for any longer than two hours with the fifty grams of fat she gets a month and all the worries she has. In the evenings, she says, her hands are incapable of touching anything, and in any case all that graft is a waste of time because the war's going to go on forever. I write this to give you an idea of what's going on and so that you can adjust your letters accordingly.

What you absolutely mustn't tell her again is that you don't want to live in that boring dump any more. I'd do anything to get you out of the camp, but I'm afraid I can't. You just need to stick it out and it will all be fine. And if it gets really bad then write to me, which will make things easier for both of us.

There's tension all the time here at home, that's to say nothing but harmony between Mama and Papa, but Susi's getting on my nerves and vice versa. As a result my parents think that Susi's the poor sister and me the wicked brother. I shut myself away and practise the trumpet so loudly that Papa hammers on the door with his fist. Then I'm forced to talk to him about common decency until I can't take it any longer and escape into the street. You know the rest. My shoes will soon start rotting. They won't dry any more because I'm so seldom at home.

Now Mama won't stop nagging me because I'm writing you such a long letter, which is why I've started another sheet of paper, even though I don't know what else to say. Your friends' eyes will be on stalks when they see this essay. It might be the longest letter ever written, apart from the time when they used to correspond on clay tablets. If someone finds it in a few centuries it'll end up in a museum and they'll have to build a special cabinet so it has enough room. It's funny, but I find it really easy to write on stolen paper, so much more springs to mind. But my fingers have gone stiff already.

Susi's cat has just jumped on the cupboard and is now balancing its way along the front edge. And you can see from the greasy marks on the paper that I've been eating a sandwich while writing to save time.

Attention! Attention! Breaking news! The high command of the Grassingerhof estate has an important announcement: Kurt Ritler's request to take a trip to Mondsee at Easter has been approved by his father on the condition that his end of term report contains no grades below *Satisfactory*. / Ferdl and I are planning to visit you during Holy Week. We hope the snow will have all gone by then and we'll be able to climb the Drachenwand. Hopefully I'll have enough money. Papa has a book of proverbs, ordered by country. One Indian proverb says: Money can even buy you tiger's milk. / I'm sending all the very best to my Nanni in Schwarzindien! A kiss on the hand for your teacher Frau Bildstein, the deputy queen of Schwarzindien, and lots of kisses on both cheeks for you! Not to mention many more pecks on the lips. And please pack up some of your countryside and send it to me. After all that snow the mountains must look particularly beautiful now.

By the way, you no longer have to be so cautious when writing because I've stopped Mama from reading the letters I receive. / What you write about post being handed out after lunch is like the soldiers you see on the newsreel. I can well imagine that those who don't get anything make themselves scarce and think, I can't watch. So I'm going to send this letter *right now*.

Erhard arrived home two days ago and he's going to be here for a fortnight. As the leader, he's taken charge again in the bedroom. I've tried asking him about his deployment but he's not especially talkative. All he says is that he wants to come out of the war unscathed. I don't mind having to share the box room for a few days, because in the evenings I can put on Erhard's uniform and have a better chance of getting into films that are for adults only. I'd love to finally watch *Much Ado about Nixi*, but I have to see whether I can get tickets. I should spend the night before in the cinema, Papa complains, so I don't miss the first performance in the morning and can save myself the journey. He's annoyed that I have so little idea of all the things that need to be done to keep a household running. I'm not rushing to experience what Papa calls the seriousness of life. After all, he says I'll soon get to know what it means. 'Soon enough. Soon enough,' I reply.

Did you know that there is a uniform hair length for women between the ages of fourteen and twenty? A directive from the Reich youth leadership to the professional association of hairdressers. While the ingenious Reich government continues to come up with ideas like this, Germany is not doomed. Don't laugh, in six months' time you'll be subject to this directive too. But I beg you once again, don't demean yourself – you know what I'm talking about. And I'm not interested in what other people say, I don't listen to them. Also, what you say about your mother and the spade carriers isn't nonsense and it doesn't bore me either. Do you know what I mean? I love it too when you say funny things such as *opinions are divided on that* or *the two of us*. Coming from your mouth it always sounds wonderful. I really, really like you. When I first told you to kiss me you burst into uncontrollable laughter. But then you liked it, didn't you? / Right now they're playing 'Springtime in Vienna' on the wireless. Perhaps you're listening to it as well and thinking of me.

Do you know that now we have a strict blackout here too, just like in the west? There are new fire regulations as well. Mama had to take her cushions off the windowsills so that there's nothing flammable by the windows. She says it's not so comfortable to sit there any more. But overall it's boring in Vienna. The most exciting event of the whole day is when the postman comes. But he's not coming again today. I'm sitting in the kitchen, writing to you. 'Springtime in Vienna' is on the wireless again. Are you listening to it too?

I'd love to have been there on your bath day instead of Burski. And afterwards I would have also scrubbed off the dirt for you according to time-honoured custom. Do you remember?

Last night we were visited by an aircraft that did a few laps of honour and dropped flyers rather than bombs. I was happy with that. Having said that, it's only very recently that enemy planes have started flying so far, which is less good news. I fear we're going to have many more visits in the future, at least that's what people are saying.

The mood is pretty gloomy here at the moment. Papa and I are tired because last night we attended an air defence course and after that went to play tarock at Uncle Hans's. Then, at four in the morning, the doorbell rang and Frau Michelreiter told us that Erhard was lying on the stairs, drunk. He looked terrible. I got quite upset. I hope it doesn't happen again. And Mama's angry because earlier I got some ink on the tablecloth, while Susi is sitting at Papa's desk sorting out her schoolbooks. She's quietly talking to herself and I get the feeling it's about me. Occasionally she stares at me as I write this letter, I can't help but laugh with embarrassment the whole time. I'm such an idiot, oh, I don't know.

And please don't be angry with me if now and then I write something I don't even understand myself. I'm pining for you so much, I miss the knocking in the morning, sometimes I imagine I hear you knocking and in moments like those I just want to pack up my belongings and come to see you in India.

PS: *squeak* is written just with *qu*, not *quw*. I only write this because you added the extra *w*. And thanks for the little card with your name. How stupid it is that the machine discriminates against people with long names. I expect a Chinaman invented it. / Do the people in India have short or long names? / Here is another proverb from Papa's book: Animals die while they eat, humans die while they think. Don't worry about me, I've been faithful to you for four months, how could you have any doubts? And if Sascha's saying I'll find someone else quickly enough, tell her to mind her own business.

Tell me, Nanni, do you think life is beautiful? I'd love to know. I think it's strange. Take, for example, all the time that I waste, fritter away or sleep. I'll *never* have that time back. It's impossible to stop it or even, sometimes, to make it pass more quickly. Nobody can re-live an hour they've already lived. Isn't that strange? And often I just need an hour, a quarter of an hour, or even just a few minutes and I haven't got them. But then, what about all those hours that pass you by?

Has it sunk in yet that Ferdl and I will be coming to Mondsee at Easter? Or are you still gasping for air? I can well believe that you leaped over the beds with joy. I'll scrape together the money for the train ticket. But I can't say it's definitely going to work until I get my Greek exam back. I've been revising like a madman to push myself up to a *Satisfactory*. I think I'll get there, worry not, you know that one spring day happiness will come knocking at your door. And hopefully your teacher is right when she says that we'll all be together again in summer. I almost believe it myself. Then, early on Sunday, I'll knock on the wall and wake you up, and we, the two of us, will go for a morning stroll alone in Penzing, and then the two of us will come back somewhere for breakfast and buy goulash with raspberry water, as well as some sausages with a glass of juice. And when we're nice and full we'll lie down in a flowery meadow and look up at the sky, relieved and happy that there are no more sirens wailing and no more enemy bombers flying over our heads.

I'm writing nonsense again, I know. I'll continue this evening, when it flows better, so long as Mama and Susi leave me in peace. And please excuse me for not having rustled up any red writing paper. I can't get hold of it anywhere. So don't be angry, the blue letters express just as much as the red ones would.

I'm bringing Ferdl with me at Easter so my parents agree to the trip, that's why. Without my parents' approval I couldn't come. They don't think I'm independent enough to travel on my own. I can already hear Papa's words in my head. And forgive Ferdl for having called you a stupid cow at Christmas. I'm sure he's got a better heart than you would think when he opens his mouth. / Here's another Indian proverb for you: The world is divided into five parts and the sixth is Schwarzindien. Long live India! Long live the roof of the world!

Today, the day of dullness, I have to write quickly because tomorrow is the thirteenth and I don't write letters on the thirteenth. Yesterday we had a geography and history exam all in one. Right in the middle of it the sirens wailed and we had to go into the basement and continue our exams there. We heard large bombers fly overhead and explosions in the distance. In the afternoon dark smoke still hung over Simmering, so thick that the sun barely shone through it. Please write home straightaway if something happens near you. / One thing's certain, it's no fun writing an exam paper on your knees in the basement, it's exhausting. On top of it all, Ferdl and I went to the hospital in Liniengasse after school to give blood. They took 470cc from me and said my pimples might disappear as a result. I also got a special allocation of 200 grams of chocolate, 125 grams of butter, 250 grams of salami and 8 eggs. Now Mama can't say that I eat more than my ration. It's not my fault anyway.

I have to sign off now, even though there's still so much more to tell you. For example, Erhard has gone back to the front. Mama told him not to gaze deeply into the eyes of the young ladies as she absolutely doesn't want a Russian for a daughter-in-law. I said that this was such an important topic that we ought to have a family meeting, because I don't want a Bolshevik for a sister-in-law either. But Erhard, who's lost all sense of fun, got angry and said it was none of our business and so there was no need for a family meeting. Nor did we have to worry, he said, he wouldn't be bringing anything back home except for sheer fury. I said he was a Bolshevik himself and got worked up about everything. Papa slapped me on the head and said that wherever Erhard went his complaints would soon stop, as would mine if I kept talking like that. I needed to help out more actively around the house, he continued, or I'd get an even greater shock when I started with the labour service soon, where you were screamed at for the most trivial matter and called all manner of names.

Do you now know every mountain by name, Nanni? I can well imagine that you were tired from the long walk in the snow, I mean, you're not used to the heavy shoes. On the wireless they keep talking about how light-footed young people are, and then you have to go around with such clogs on your feet. If you want to climb the Drachenwand with Ferdl and me at Easter you'll need more stamina, so get exercising, I've heard it's a three-hour climb. / What do you do all day long? Did you go tobogganing on Saturday or Sunday? Did you use your b—m to brake again? How's the weather? Is Sascha still writing to the boy from Sturzgasse? Or are you, perhaps? I hope you got my card. Have you seen the soldier again? Has he got something going with Frau Bildstein? Have you been to the cinema yet? And please send me a photograph of you. Keep your chin up, don't have black thoughts in your India. Lots of kisses, lots and lots of kisses from Kurti!

Dear Nanni, my Schorsche, are you poorly? Or has the ink frozen where you are? Have the air raids frightened you so much that you can't hold a pen any more? I haven't had a letter from you in a week, I've lost my appetite, I'm getting more and more worried by the minute.

Did you know young Frühwirt who lived at Tellgasse 18? Twenty-five years old and always used to drive a motorbike? He died in Russia a fortnight ago. His mother gave me some of his trousers a couple of years back. The parents have lots of children, his mother is short and hunched, you must have known him. And do you remember Frau Binder on the upper ground floor of block 2? Small blonde woman with a little daughter? She's been in prison for two months. / They're playing 'Springtime in Vienna' on the radio again.

I'm sure Sascha's told you that from now on I'm going to write to poste restante in Mondsee. You can imagine how furious I am! It's outrageous that your teacher is reading my letters and that my parents are forbidding all contact with you. 'The party's over!' Papa says. And I've told them that if there's no letter from you again today I'll go berserk. / Papa grumbles that his efforts to educate me have failed. For my own part, I try to educate myself in such a way that all the magic leaves me cold. Which isn't so easy, unfortunately. Papa was just in here and I had to quickly stuff this sheet of paper under my pillow. That explains why it's creased. Papa said, from now on Nanni is going to be your little cousin again. I replied that I wasn't going to put up with it all any more. He laughed scornfully and said there was plenty more I'd have to put up with as I'd be going to war. They'd be fitting my boots soon. He gave me a warning about harsh reality, and when I said, 'as harsh as our cat's tongue', he gave me such a hard slap that I fell over. 'Is that clear enough?' he said. How I hate that question! / Dear Nanni, I'm getting totally worked up. Do they still burn widows in India? Do you know anything about that? Burning, that must be so awful. I could howl with rage!

I'm coming to Mondsee at Easter and if I have to do it by bicycle I'll get there in two and a half days. Keep a regular eye out around the camp. I'll probably arrive on Wednesday.

It's such a cheek that your teacher reads my letters. I wouldn't put up with it! When Mama told me I thought I was going mad. And Papa hit me so hard that he deserves to spend a year in prison. Mama says there won't be any more letters from you, so I should stop hanging around like a starving beggar. Is that true? Write to me at Ferdl's address: Walkürengasse 4. And please, Nanni, I want you to tell me if you still like me and if what your mother and my mother are saying is nothing but lies. Feel free to tell me the truth, it's better I know straightaway as I'll find out sooner or later.

How am I?

How am I? That's not a question to ask, I'm miserable in every respect. On 1 January 1939 we were both given another name. Wally's second name is now Sarah and mine is Israel. The same is true for Georgili and all our relatives. It feels as if a bell has been hung around our necks. / The worst thing is that they want to take away our apartment too. They came and asked us to move out voluntarily. You can imagine what it's like trying to negotiate with that lot. Because I resisted, the matter is now being dealt with by the Party. So, the question is: where to go? It's very hard for us Jews to get a sublet in Vienna, especially as with Wally and the child there are three of us. I really don't know what to do, but I hope God will not forsake me. / Wally is very despondent too. Sadly, someone stole her bag on Thaliastrasse today, including her money. What bad luck. She's devastated. It was her mother's bag, it was so precious. Such is life.

On Tuesday I redeemed the things from the Dorotheum that went with the crate, to have them valued on the fourteenth with the rest of the furniture in the apartment. I'd imagined the whole process would be simpler. Two men I got cheaply loaded the furniture and we drove to the Dorotheum. As I was registering the objects for auction, the gentleman taking delivery asked whether I was right in the head: why hadn't I let them know I was coming beforehand? After that he wouldn't look at me any more, but went on working with his furniture and left me to speak. It got to the stage where he'd clearly had enough of my rambling or my despair must have appeared so genuine that over my shoulder he said I could go to see the director of the Dorotheum, and if the director gave authorization for me to leave the objects here – which he very much doubted would be the case – he would accept the

furniture. / We went to see the director, I went inside while my assistants waited outside. I'm not going to go on about it at length, but the
director spoke in the most disdainful terms about us Jews. But then he
went personally to take a look at the cart and said they would take the
lot. / In my excitement, idiot that I am, I forgot to put the film pro-
jector and screen on the list. And I also slipped up during the valuations.
I didn't know that you could put pictures, microscope and rugs on the
same form, because different valuation experts were involved and three
copies were made for each valuation, which meant I had to pay for nine
forms rather than three. Nobody pointed out my error to me. Some of
the things have already been auctioned off, but at prices considerably
below their value.

On Thursday I handed over the apartment, and the witch who
moved in started clearing it out at once. I still have to replace the two
windowpanes that were smashed and which she complains about at
every opportunity. She's a most disagreeable individual, not because of
that, but in general. I have to go back again tomorrow and put the
books in the cellar. As I always feared, I haven't been able to sell them
even though I put the word out to everyone I knew. The witch is forever sneering at me, asking what I'm going to do with my books. I
reply in a similar tone.

Unfortunately I haven't had confirmation yet of my birthday greetings to Mayflower (1) nor have the greetings to Winternitz (2) been
passed on. Please write and tell me when these were received.

Our neighbours in Possingergasse are not especially sympathetic to
our difficulties, which is sobering. Frau Hofreiter openly expressed
her satisfaction at the new regulations and said she would now take
what was her due. I took one final look around the apartment.
Surely there can be no sadder sight than one's own apartment one has
just been booted out of. I left the house like a stranger, without a
goodbye.

I'll write more about our private affairs later. Today it's more
important to me to sort out that issue relating to your move, particularly as I don't have a good feeling about it. More and more we're
hearing that war is on its way. Unfortunately the tax matter hasn't been
resolved yet and, as I heard today, you'll have to pay a further 362

Reichsmarks. I need to go back on Monday. / Seeing how strapped for cash you are, you don't need to send us anything at the moment. If we don't have anything, we'll just have to make do with nothing. Wally could go to England as a domestic help, but with two children she doesn't want to work all day. Mizzi says she feels sorry for us because we don't know what we want. Coming from her it may sound harsh, but unfortunately that's how it is.

In the meantime we've sold most of the apartment and hopefully we'll be able to get away soon. There's more good news from Bernili in England. Georgili on the other hand is still sick, though he's feeling better. We've heard next to nothing from cousin Robert Klein-Lörk, only what he wrote to Bernili and Bernili passed on to us. So all we know is that he's in good health.

It's an ordeal living in this house we're sharing with illegals. We're also being tortured by the tenant in the Possingergasse apartment. Wally has been driven mad, in fact she's still quite unwell after contracting botulism and spending a fortnight at the Rothschild Hospital. Then there's the terrible hunger, which you couldn't begin to imagine. Jeannette, dearest cousin, you would be shocked by how ghastly I look. As we're living here in Vienna practically without any support, I can forget the idea of emigrating unless you're able to send us some money. We need at least one hundred Reichsmarks per month to live, with the cheapest dump costing around forty Reichsmarks. You can imagine how it breaks my heart.

There's been no progress with our affidavit, you know the ruses of the American consulate. As it's a friendship affidavit, there is questionnaire after questionnaire, and it takes weeks for a reply to arrive from overseas with the current shipping situation. After all that, the regulations have changed. / It's unfortunate you haven't been able to get us an entry into South Africa but, God willing, perhaps a permit of affidavit will come our way soon.

Lots of people are going to Italy, but for this you also need money, which we don't have. So I'm stuck here. Maybe we'll go to my brother in Budapest. / We meet up regularly with Uncle Monath. The poor fellow is weighed down too. His daughter Irma wanted to go to Cuba and ended up in Brussels, that's quite something. But they're doing fine in Brussels, because they're being supported from America. Irma writes that she was badly cheated by the Cubans. On the *St Louis* they formed a guard of male passengers to ensure nobody leaped into the ocean in despair. There were deaths all the same. / Adieu! A thousand kisses from Wally, Georgili and Oskar.

My scant resources are running dry. It's hard to get anything at all here, and even then only briefly. We've sold almost everything from the apartment and eaten it all up, so to speak. Uncle Monath says it seems as if all the shenanigans and hatred are just an excuse to get hold of our things cheaply, a vile acquisitiveness. At the same time they keep pointing a finger at us. 'They're so wicked!' Wally says. / It's really very difficult now. And of course some deals go pear-shaped, and sometimes I come away empty-handed. Without a sound knowledge of how to strike deals, in a legal vacuum you're anybody's fool. You can imagine I feel thoroughly miserable a lot of the time. / We get meals from the Jewish Community and fifteen Reichsmarks allowance per month for rent. As Mizzi and the aunts pay ten Reichsmarks each, our rent is covered.

Irma Wasservogel is still in Brussels, waiting for her American visa. We are supposed to be getting our affidavit in September, but how to get tickets is a thorny question. Besides, my acquaintances are warning me about the US. But if things keep going in the same direction, we won't hesitate to grasp the nettle.

We've unexpectedly received a new export licence for your lift. I'm doing my best to see that it works again soon. I remember that sweet time when Hermann was still alive and I would go up in the lift to your apartment. But to finally bring this matter to a conclusion you would have to pay the export duty, which has been increased again as it's wartime.

Just imagine, Jeannette, dear cousin, all men with both legs still intact are being shipped off to Poland to build roads, and they're showing an interest in the women too. And whenever a rumour does the rounds it soon becomes the truth.

Yesterday I was spat at in the street. I was so shocked that I stopped in my tracks. The man was in uniform and, keen to give his patriotic act some style, he spat at me a second time. The second time was much more spiteful. / Such things herald the end of life as it used to be. We have to endure severe trials. They mean to make life wretched for us, and it's really miserable already. Our freedom of movement in the city is very restricted, and in my own street I have to press myself along the walls of the houses. And still the women lean on cushions, watching out of windows with indifference. They used to look at each other, now they watch the men in their brown uniforms who act as if they're trying to teach some bespectacled Jews how to march. You know, you've seen it yourself, and in truth the only point of this charade is so they can kick the men from time to time. After years of practice, the women on their window cushions don't change expression.

Life has become very arduous, day after day. I don't have the faintest idea of what to do, everything has come to a standstill. I'm not even allowed to go to the sports ground any more, and so my interest in football has waned. These days I rarely bother reading the reports in the newspaper. / Regulations are issued which leave me utterly speechless. Sometimes I stand facing a notice and think someone must have taken the wrong piece of paper from the wrong drawer, surely tomorrow they'll paste over the right piece of paper. But soon afterwards a new, even harsher measure is introduced. We have to put up with so much here. We're not even allowed to cycle any longer, we had to hand over Bernili's bicycle as per the regulations, which lends everything the veneer of legality, even stealing from children. This is a sort of public-spirited robbery. / Bernili wrote asking after his bicycle, now his letters are coming via Switzerland. I wrote back saying that the bicycle was safely stored away.

We're still working on our emigration plans, but with increasing reluctance. First you have to pay a flight tax, then you go to another country where you're a foreigner and don't understand the language. Wally says we should live where we feel at home. / Whenever some new fast-track legislation comes into force, we promptly comply with it, as a patriotic act, so to speak. We think it's a real achievement that we're able to go on living here. If many leave, it will placate those who are against us. The fact that they're going to such efforts to make our lives intolerable is a sign that there must be some good reason for staying here. At some point they'll leave us alone again. You can see we're comforting ourselves with rational arguments. And I know that rational arguments might be no match for people's malice.

That double-enveloped letter which came via Hungary was the first communication I'd received from you in ages. You say I should take the family to safety. Yes, I'm doing my best, dear Jeannette. And I know you'll do everything in your power to ease our hardship. Wally is not in a good way, unfortunately, sometimes she appears muddled, her mind seriously confused. She's so angry that she claims to have forgotten which river flows through Vienna and which district St Stephen's Cathedral is in. She says she's forgotten all of it.

Wally often sinks into lethargy, saying practically nothing, lying on her pallet and staring at the ceiling. When there's a knock at the door she refuses to answer. 'I won't be bullied,' she says languidly. Sometimes in the mornings I can still see the effusive Wally I married, and at such times she makes plans for the future and jokes about Hlatikulu. But it's all a bit crazy. In the afternoons it's impossible to rouse her from her passivity. And when she wants to listen to the wireless in the evenings then realizes that she's no longer allowed to, she exudes such unremitting despair. Even Georgili can't cheer her up. Occasionally she'll laugh, but we can hear that it's a fake laugh and not particularly convincing at that. Sometimes a sign of this strange laughter will remain on her face as if forgotten.

We had another ugly argument today. 'Maybe Italy after all,' I said. / 'I wouldn't dream of it.' / 'What have you got against Italy?' I asked. / Then Wally said icily, 'Why don't you go, then! What do I lose if I'm alone with a child or together with a pessimist?' Then she started up again with the line that there was no way they could drive us out, she was a free woman and a born citizen of this city and it would be foolish to run away from such ridiculous regulations.

Wally says, 'The Torah too teaches us that things are never quite as they appear at first glance. So let's not mope around, Oskar.'

Our accommodation is becoming increasingly cramped. We're sharing one room with Georgili and four other people, the healthy and the sick, the young and old all together. It's an ugly room, not at all homely and quite eerie. There's always something unfamiliar in the room we can't get used to. And when you're all sitting in such close proximity, arguments spring up by themselves. Sometimes one person can't bear to see, smell or hear another any more. There are moments when I feel like killing the others. / Wally can't sleep for more than two hours at a stretch any longer, she keeps sitting up, then often goes to the window and I worry that she'll fall out. Sometimes she won't even look at her food. And sometimes she says weakly, 'I can't go on any more.' / Sadly she also says this when I suggest we make another approach to the American consulate. She says, 'I can't go on any more.'

Because we're so miserable we also stick out in a bad way, as people who create a bad mood. Yesterday on my way to Prinz-Eugen-Strasse, where the Central Agency for Jewish Emigration is housed in the Palais Rothschild, I met a former work colleague and unburdened my sorrows on him. He seemed surprised that I was still alive, clapped me comfortingly on the shoulder and said it was always the good ones who got hurt. I asked whether he might not know anyone who could help us get an affidavit. He looked embarrassed and said he didn't get mixed up in such matters.

These things gnaw away at one's self-confidence and they gnaw away at one's natural ability to make the right decisions. You know that I'm not by nature a risk-taker anyway, or someone with initiative, so all this is quite a challenge for me.

There are days when you have to be wary of the rabble, then others when it feels as if you're invisible. Recently in Rotenturmstrasse one man said he was offended by my wearing glasses, he felt provoked by them. But without my glasses I can't see ten paces ahead of me. He hurled the usual insults at me, and a tailor's apprentice standing in the doorway of the shop laughed. One ought not to laugh at the misfortune of one's fellow citizens. / Naturally, the apprentice was very young, and so I decided to make a mental note of his face.

Just imagine, lately I came across a job advertisement in a specialist journal for a dentist or dental technician in Accra, the capital of the Gold Coast in West Africa. They're looking for someone to run a practice independently. More out of curiosity than interest I replied and, to my surprise, after a fortnight – I'd almost forgotten the whole thing – I received a letter from a lawyer in Vienna requesting that I visit him. It turned out that the owner of the practice was his brother-in-law, who recently lost his right hand following an infection. Now he was looking for someone to run the practice. The lawyer offered me a five-year contract, free board and lodgings, and a salary of thirty-five pounds sterling per month. There would also be free second-class travel for the whole family. I would have to depart from Marseille in the middle of June. The whole thing is quite genuine, the British consulate would assume liability for the contract, but there is a snag: the weather. I was told that apart from two rainy months a year the Gold Coast has a tropical climate with average temperatures of 35 degrees. When we considered 35 degrees the matter was settled for Wally and me, because we cannot cope with heat like that. But I've got until 17 May to consider the offer.

As far as duties for the lift are concerned there are endless new complications. And there are endless new complications too regarding the affidavits. Despite all my efforts I cannot manage to assemble the thousands of papers, each time something gets in the way at the last moment. Only the exit permit seems to be possible. But the consulates change their regulations more rapidly than they process the applications, which means that with a stroke of the pen they can easily keep a tight rein on the procedure. I'm forever trying to keep up and wasting my energy. The end result is nothing.

We finally received an affidavit yesterday from Wally's relatives in America, but we can't do anything with it because all of a sudden the quotas are full, that's what the American consulate is saying, with unjustifiable brutality. I can't describe to you what it feels like . . .

Joszi has disappeared without any announcement or a goodbye. Another one gone. Mina has left too, in a sealed emigrant train from the Westbahnhof. I waved from Rustensteg footbridge until I couldn't see the train any more. The web of family and acquaintances has been torn apart, only a few connecting threads remain. And we know too few people in the city who still have influence – none, in fact – which makes our situation so bleak. Uncle Monath is also broke because he was forced to buy into the Jewish old people's home in Seegasse.

Time is passing, dear Jeannette, and I know that we ought to have moved abroad long ago. I hurry through the city in search of any remaining bolthole. The Gold Coast came to nothing and the regulations for leaving the country are now so convoluted that nobody understands them any more. I've drawn up another list, and when I look at this with its thousands of items and sub-items my heart starts to pound. The list stands before me like a ten-metre-high wall: official authorization to leave the country, quota number, visa application, birth certificate, tax assessment, bank statement, certificate of good conduct, in duplicate, triplicate, quintuplicate, guarantee, affidavit, flight tax and back to square one, duplicate, triplicate, quintuplicate. Dear God! And tomorrow another regulation will be issued and the quotas will be reduced.

Time and again someone comes up to me and says, 'Listen, comrade, we're in great danger, go away from here, this city will be your downfall.' And it's true, I no longer recognize my beautiful Vienna. Though the houses are still standing, it is destroyed on the inside. We still feel intact on the inside ourselves, but externally we are marked.

Now that America is at war with Germany too, everyone of the wrong blood must visibly wear a yellow star. All Jews in the German Reich have been forbidden from leaving as well. And two days ago I received in the mail an order to go to the transit camp in Castellezgasse, wearing work clothes. But I have no desire to be a slave of this state. Moreover, the particularly suspicious individuals amongst us, who notoriously keep their ears to the ground, say the impression suddenly being given is as if they wanted to keep us now. This is highly suspicious, they insist, seeing as Rosenberg emphasized that *the question* could only be considered solved once the last Jew had left the country. So the question is: leave, yes, but by which route? Some people laugh grimly and this new development worries me too.

Today the Weiss family departed from the neighbouring apartment. A man from the Jewish Community came in the morning and asked the family to go with him: husband, wife and three adolescent daughters. The man from the Jewish Community stood by the door to the apartment and prevented me from being able to talk to Herr Weiss. For a year we cultivated a neighbourly relationship, and now we were parting company with the most fleeting of goodbyes. / The man from the Jewish Community marked the luggage and took the keys to the apartment. Then he took the Weiss family down into the street, where others with yellow stars on their chests were already waiting. They all headed towards Taborstrasse. Whole lives are being shovelled away, because somebody thinks they're in the way. / The Weiss family looked baffled and forlorn as they stood outside our building with their sparse luggage. I looked down, it was a great shock. And most of all, this episode has set me thinking. A threat is hanging over our heads too. I discussed it with Wally, who said, 'They'll kill us in the end.' / I was nonplussed. / She said, 'I don't give a damn about this horrid life, I don't give a damn about this horrid city.'

I realized that our days in Vienna are numbered. At the Jewish Community I heard talk of people in Burgenland assisting Jews to escape by keeping routes to Hungary open. I went to Seitenstettengasse and tried to make the necessary contacts. That same afternoon I had a meeting in a wine tavern in Margaretenstrasse, negotiated a price and received concrete instructions. In four days' time we are to be at the Gasthaus zur Linde in Bruck an der Leitha, either late afternoon or early evening.

For years all our efforts had been in vain. We contemplated the few options that remained to us. We weighed up the chances of success and the consequences of failure. But now there was no longer much scope for objections. Did we want to go to my brother who lives in a Budapest slum? It would be better than living a life in permanent fear. Wally agreed with me. I breathed a sigh of relief.

Our thoughts were now focused squarely on our forthcoming escape. It became evident that fleeing the country illegally was what Wally had been waiting for all these years, without ever coming up with the idea herself. She was pleased that we were about to do something without first seeking authorization, slightly irrational, but good. / Wally said she'd always been a proud Viennese woman. But what was that worth if you wished your vile neighbours didn't exist?

The most difficult thing for us was financing our flight. We no longer had anything we could sell, apart from Jeannette's lift from the house in Lagergasse. We redeemed it with everything we had left and I sold it at a fraction of its value to a building contractor. I was given small amounts of money by the Jewish Community and an aid committee acting behind the Red Cross. But this still didn't cover the fee I'd been quoted for our flight. If Uncle Monath hadn't dug deep in his pockets, all our struggles would once more have been in vain. What a lovely, lovely man! Blessed will be the day when I can repay to Irma and Olga what Uncle Monath has done for us.

We swiftly decided what of the things we still possessed we should pack and take with us. We weren't sorry to have to leave behind the few items of furniture remaining from the Possingergasse apartment, as they'd been hollowed out from the inside too. / 'Is there anything we absolutely must take with us?' I asked Wally. / 'No, but there are a few things that don't deserve to be abandoned here.' / We packed these things and at that moment the idea of leaving Vienna no longer felt so alien. I didn't feel an attachment to Vienna any more. One final glance at the fragments of our life adrift on the floor. I wondered where these things would wash up. No doubt they'd be scattered across the city – so what? I couldn't care less about anything. Even had it been possible, I wouldn't have wanted to put the Possingergasse apartment in my pocket and take it with us. How much things had changed.

We didn't say a word to anyone apart from those people who needed to know. We paid visits to the cemetery again, and again I walked past the house we'd moved into after we got married. In my head I took my leave of the city, but without feeling sad. I just wanted to get away. / We drank a liqueur at Uncle Monath's. He said we should grasp this opportunity. He wished us the best of luck and hoped we'd see each other again soon. But I doubted we would. Uncle Monath stayed behind, alone and without any protection. With tears in our eyes we looked at each other and said again that we'd see each other soon.

Our first problem was that we had to get to Bruck an der Leitha. We split up and made it to Schwechat, Wally with Georgili and no yellow star on her chest, me in my work clothes. It was meant to look as if I was a member of one of those labour brigades working on the airfield or at the refinery. I took off my star at Schwechat. / Then we had to wait more than two hours for the bus, it was pouring and we were cold, although luckily each of us had a woollen jumper. At least the bus driver was so preoccupied by the condition of the roads that he showed no interest in his few passengers. / Finally we arrived at Bruck an der Leitha. It was still bucketing down, but it wasn't the worst weather for a border crossing. We weren't even checked when we arrived. And at Gasthaus zur Linde we met the individuals who would get us out of the country. They were wearing firemen's uniforms and took us in a fire engine to Halbturn. / As the roads in the Seewinkel area were strictly policed, special authorization was necessary. Everything went well. / At the end of the drive, as the rain was letting up, we passed Halbturn Palace, and for a moment I thought how lovely it would be simply to walk in and live there. Then I realized just what an idiot I was, me, Oskar Meyer, the palace resident!

When we left at midnight Wally was in a good mood. She wasn't anxious and felt so strongly we were doing the right thing that she strode across the fields, as if she were at home there. By contrast, my heart was racing wildly. My suitcase was twice as heavy on this soft, muddy ground, and I could feel my armpits getting damp beneath my coat. I led Georgili along with my left hand. He shook at it several times, saying, 'Not so tight!' / 'We have to stay together . . .' I whispered. / Soon we were wandering amongst vines, and once our leader was assured that the guards were not in their usual places he gave us a sign. 'Keep going straight, you can't miss it.' As far as he was concerned his job was done. / Georgili wrenched his hand free of mine and hurried along ahead. It was winter and the ice wine grapes were still hanging on the vines. As we walked past I pulled off a few grapes and put them in my coat pocket. I told myself that I wouldn't eat these Austrian grapes until I was in Hungary. And that's exactly what happened.

A snowstorm all day long

A snowstorm all day long with the temperature hovering around zero. The roads barely passable, but many farmers made use of what hopefully will be the last snow to spread manure. The house in utter chaos, unpleasant, the Darmstadt woman's child kept crying for long periods. Only at night was there peace and quiet. Ever since I've had the new seagrass mattress I haven't wanted to get out of bed because it's so comfortable. I lay in bed until mid-morning and wrote. I fried wrinkled apples on the stove.

I'd received a letter from a former co-driver, who was in the thick of heavy fighting in Tarnopol, munitions from the air, provisioning from local people, he said he was now writing to everybody he could think of. I could well imagine what was happening in that cauldron – dreadful. / I wrote a few lines in answer, but with a queasy feeling. Then I braced myself for a letter to my parents, whom I hadn't written to in weeks. From a letter Waltraud had sent I knew at least how things were at home: the same as ever. After the usual pleasantries about the weather and my health I asked my parents not to stint on money when it came to visiting the cemetery. Hilde's birthday was approaching and I wanted her grave to look beautiful. I didn't write much more than that, just trivial stuff, such as how I had to mix my ink before writing because I could only get it in tablet form in Mondsee. I said I hoped I wouldn't need another litre before the war finished, for I had enough tablets to make that much ink.

At lunchtime the sun came out, I stuck a stamp on the letter to my parents and underlined the field post number on the envelope for Helmut's letter. Then I left the house, looking forward to a walk by the lake, for now the wind had dropped and the temperature had risen.

At the postbox I bumped into the Darmstadt woman, who was posting letters too. I asked why the child had been crying so much of late and she told me that it had a sore bottom. She said what she could really do with was a sun lamp. I was able to relieve her of this worry as I had that selfsame device to treat the pinched nerve in my cheek. My cheek still felt numb, but the nerve was significantly improved. I told the woman from Darmstadt that she should have the sun lamp until the child's bottom was better. She was delighted.

The following day the landlady took me to task about the sun lamp, saying I ought to have told her I had one. A wireless didn't use much electricity, she said, but a sun lamp was altogether different. She'd recalculated the electricity costs and now wanted an additional one Reichsmark per month. / I was about to protest when she interrupted, saying she didn't want to hear my opinion, she was familiar with that already. Well, well.

That sort of thing can really ruin one's day. I found the matter so awkward that I didn't say anything to the Darmstadt woman. The landlady took care of that personally. A few days later there was a knock at the door, early in the evening. The Darmstadt woman put her head round to see whether it was an inopportune moment. I invited her in. She raved about the sun lamp, saying that her child's bottom was much better already. She also thought that it was crying less, which I confirmed. Then she wanted to give me two Reichsmarks, which I firmly refused, it was a point of honour. The woman insisted, but then relented, oh well, she didn't want to offend my honour. Then she grumbled about the landlady, saying it was a mistake to have told her about the sun lamp. There were some people who felt the need to snuff out any hint of happiness, she said, and the landlady was a shadowy individual. As it said in *Faust*: 'Let the sun remain at my back!' / Surprised, I asked whether she'd read *Faust*. / No, she hadn't. But she knew a few nuggets from it, this was a point of honour on her part. Had I forgotten that she came from Hesse?

She marvelled at the cleanliness of my room. It looked, she said, as if I were awaiting an inspection from the sergeant major. Cleanliness is next to godliness, I mumbled. She allowed her gaze to roam until it alighted on the garter belt that was hanging on a nail with my things.

'Oh!' she said. / I turned red and tried to explain the circumstances: the wound on my thigh hadn't quite closed completely yet, it was still weeping a little, but the opening was now just a finger's width and I wore a plaster rather than a bandage which kept slipping down. / Did she believe me? I had no idea, but I hoped I'd managed to sound sufficiently plausible. / The woman had blushed faintly too, she looked with embarrassment at the sausage casing in my wastepaper basket. After a moment's silence she said, 'Dinner's almost ready. There's enough for two.' / It was hard work trying to turn down the invitation. Eventually the Darmstadt woman relented and gave me her usual greeting of putting two outstretched fingers to her forehead then moving them away again.

At noon the following day the Brazilian used a board affixed to a pole to clear the snow that had fallen that morning from his greenhouse. The air was sparkling and glistening from the sun which had just broken through, and in the distance I could hear the drone of dozens of aircraft, already on their way back. The flyovers were slightly sinister. On a nice day it seemed as if they were going to fetch milk, flying to their destinations, dropping their load then returning to their bases as if this were the most normal thing in the world. With a bitter laugh the Brazilian said, 'The magic of technology! If I were to try to explain to an Indian what was going on here he'd be offended because he'd have to assume that I thought he was an idiot. Perhaps he'd respond to my not particularly edifying jokes with a weary smile.'

His initial abruptness and aloofness towards me had virtually disappeared. Now I sought his company more often during the daytime too. I no longer found him as strange as I had at first, all in all he was an affable man. Besides, I had spent enough time amongst people willing to submit to every demand and who accepted the war like they would rheumatoid arthritis in the shoulder, so I enjoyed spending time with someone who didn't automatically conform.

The girls from the Stern camp marched past in double file, singing, thirty well-dressed girls, eyes fixed on the back of the neck of the girl in front, beautiful clear voices. When they passed they saluted us in unison, as if their arms were being tugged on strings, with the eagerness of children. The Brazilian muttered scornfully that it would never occur to any animal to proceed in double file, it was absurd. And as for frail bones, well, you just had to list all those times Herr H had broken his promise, then you'd see frailty in all its glory. Only the threats should be believed, he said, and the threats were testament to extremely base convictions. / A slab of snow fell onto his shoulder, snow crept inside the collar of his shirt and he shook himself, cursing. / Enjoying marching in step, the girls disappeared into a hollow, and soon all one could hear of their singing was a high tone in the air. The drone of the bombers had faded into the distance.

Later I followed the Brazilian to the greenhouse, where he set about his work. The sunlight, filtered and tinted yellow through the grubby panes of glass – partly icy on the outside and partly fogged up on the inside – fell softly onto the beds. Not just the warmth, but silence too seemed to be trapped beneath the glass. But although I felt a sense of the unreal in this stuffy atmosphere, I liked spending time here and enjoyed the pleasant smell of damp humus and the fragrances of the various plants. / The Brazilian weeded the orchids. His face was filthy, furrowed, his red nose was dripping and he blinked a lot. In the day-light his face looked older than at night. He wouldn't have been able to deny that he'd crossed the threshold of fifty some time ago, and I could also see that he was overworked, his eyes sat deep in their sockets. And because he didn't get enough sleep he was always freezing. / Now he bent over and snapped off some dead shoots. The first orchids were in flower and the tomato plants were growing well too, taller than knee-high and showing the first signs of fruiting. At my urging he put on a record of Brazilian music. As if in response to a signal he began to talk about the Southern Cross and of his wish to emigrate once more to a distant, warm part of the world, as unspoiled as possible, where the people were full of warmth too. He would rather live poor and dirty abroad, he said, but amongst good people, than in a palace here amongst madmen.

It was obsessive, the way he always returned to the same topics. I'd found it interesting to begin with, but now that I realized he was merely repeating everything over and over again, I became bored. I tried to change the subject at the first opportunity. The southern climes the Brazilian evoked reminded me of the conversation I'd had with the

Darmstadt woman the evening before. Unlike him, I said, his sister didn't give the impression of being cut out for a life in the tropics. I quoted the line from *Faust* that the Darmstadt woman had come out with: 'Let the sun remain at my back!'

The Brazilian pulled a face as if he were being forced to swallow a wire brush. The winter light that penetrated the glass made the air shimmer. Whenever there was a break in the music I could hear the struts of the greenhouse creak. Straightening his back, the Brazilian said that with a heavy heart he'd parted company with his sister. She'd been a lovely little girl, and young woman too. He would have taken her to Brazil if she'd been prepared to come. Sadly, during the years that he was away, she'd opted for a bad lifestyle and dragged that knave of the devil Dohm into the family, the varnisher who was currently playing at being a New Man in the General Government, he said. But a pasty face in boots with dark thoughts who drank beer and smoked would never become a New Man. The Darmstadt woman was probably right, he said. Trude and her husband, and all of H's fellow sewer rats, with H leading the way – H, who always looked like regurgitated milk and grabbed at everybody with his corpse's hands – all of these vermin were underground dwellers and the lack of light made it easier for them to keep going with their messed-up lives.

Once again I thought the derogatory way in which the Brazilian talked about the F was very daring. The Party was what had given my life meaning as a boy and even now I couldn't completely disabuse myself of the idea that the F was a great man. I urged the Brazilian to be more careful in his choice of words, for there were laws that forbade such talk. He laughed sadly and said, 'But you can't act dumb for years on end, nobody can put up with that. I'll go mad eventually, not that I'm far off now.' / As I stood hesitantly amongst the orchids, my worried face looking down at my boots, he added, 'You don't have to believe the truth, Menino, but don't claim you never came into contact with it. This loathsome European civilization, which regards hatred as a cultural achievement, has had its day.' / And I heard a tone of regret in his voice, as if he felt sorry for my stupidity.

With a mournful look on his face, he returned to his gardening work, dolefully muttering odd words that he may have picked up from the

Brazilian jungle. After a couple of minutes he seemed to have regained his composure and he expressed his relief that winter was mostly behind us. In Holy Week he would sell the orchids in Salzburg. He knew that anyone cultivating orchids in the fifth year of the war was the unwitting enemy of all those who pondered what apart from blood belonged in the soil here. He hoped to do good business all the same. And as soon as the firm for blood and soil had gone bankrupt, he, Robert Raimund Perttes, would make another journey of liberation to the southern of the two Americas. His prospects weren't so bad.

A few days later I asked him whether he'd calmed down yet. / 'Who was the one who needed to calm down?' he said, firing the question back at me. And with his finger raised, almost severely, he rebuked me: 'I advise you, Menino, remain calm on the inside and use your head. And try your best to keep your mind, body and soul healthy. I think you're perfectly capable of that, you're a sensible lad. And also be aware that it's easier to incite hatred in people than to make them love and respect. A hint of this lies dormant in all of us.' / He gazed at me with serene interest as I scratched my head in embarrassment, while trying not to look too witless.

Then Hilde's birthday came around, 11 March. Unable to go to the cemetery, I lit a candle in Mondsee church. A new candle was also flickering in front of the war memorial, where the stonemason was engraving a few more names just in time for heroes' commemoration day.

The landlady ordered the flagpole to be erected and the flag hoisted so that the moon colony could pay homage to the motherland. / It was the same a week later on Wehrmacht day, the whole town bedecked with flags, and endless processions by the army and Party members. To mark the occasion the landlady spoke kindly to me, saying that the entire house ought to be one big family and everyone should stick together. Yes? / I said I was in favour in theory, but ultimately everyone was an egotist and community only existed on paper. / Was I doubting the existence of the Volk Community, the landlady asked crossly? Unfortunately, I replied, I'd never encountered the Volk Community, only people who spoke in its name, principally in their own interest. To avoid getting the landlady even more worked up I assured her that I was looking forward to coming across the Volk Community soon. / 'It can go fuck itself,' I muttered as I walked away.

I went for a stroll by the lake, which took me as far as Plomberg, directly beneath the Drachenwand. Because of the snow, the paths were in very poor condition, especially the farm tracks, and all that trudging brought me out in a sweat. But I enjoyed my solitude, it was a splendid walk. When you're outside, enjoying the fresh air, you wonder why it's taken so long to decide to put on your shoes. Snatches of brass band music carried across the lake. I saw a few deer and a fox. The latter had a patchy coat of fur and trotted across a snowy meadow, stopping from time to time, but never listening out or raising its nose in the air. Then it went off to the side and disappeared amongst the firs.

In Plomberg I had a coffee which was so revolting that the ghastly aftertaste still lingered in my mouth half an hour later. To get rid of it I stopped on the way back in St Lorenz and drank a lemonade in the pub that used to belong to Lanner before he was executed. Having done this, I headed for the camp in Schwarzindien, where I heard a babble of excited voices, although I couldn't see the teacher or any of the girls. The only person I saw was the innkeeper, decapitating five young cockerels and leaving the bloody heads in the snow for the cats. We greeted each other and that was it.

Two hundred metres from the camp I could still hear laughing and screaming behind me, and the further away I got I became more downcast at my loneliness. For a while I was irked again by the idea that my youth had been stripped away from me. I don't know, perhaps this was because of Wehrmacht day, which made me realize once more how the years in uniform had raced past. I remembered vividly that after finishing school I was convinced I was about to enter a time of passionate emotion. I was sure that I'd find love for the world in a mature way. My inherent ability to almost burst with love . . . I could have sworn that it *had* been inherent, but was never able to break out. Now it felt as if this ability had been taken from me.

I stood by the shore of the lake, my hands thrust deep into my pockets. The thought of those years which had been ground to dust stuck in my mind with an annoying obstinacy. All at once – I don't know whether it was down to a noise in the air or my mood – I had another attack. The images came like a roaring wave and sluiced me into the cold shaft of war.

My body clenched, I felt all the humiliation of death, convinced this time that my number was up, luck had finally abandoned me, the light was about to go out. The chimney breast towering forlornly in Zhytomyr again toppled forwards slowly and fell right on top of me, grenades whistled. I was wired into the deadliness of the moment, I struggled to breathe and I could clearly see the bodies shot dead in the ditch. These were tremendously powerful images, as for minutes I crawled through the snow on my knees. The surge was extreme, worse than ever, I gasped for breath, first bent over, then sat upright.

When finally I'd managed to haul myself out of the cold shaft, a girl was standing beside me in H Youth uniform, a blue brushstroke against the grey of the water. She looked down at me with large eyes, concerned and not at all fazed, it seemed, by my peculiar behaviour – I was still breathing fitfully and both hands were pressed against my chest. / 'Can I help you?' she asked, and when I took my right hand from my chest to show that I was now feeling a little better, she seized it and said, 'Mama gets short of breath sometimes too. It helps if I hold her hand.'

The girl's voice and her simple words comforted me. I stroked my chest several times with my free hand, happy to be unscathed. A few heart-stopping moments continued to rise like bubbles, only to suddenly burst again, then the knot in my throat loosened and, relieved, I took in air and let it out again. Why did I get these nervous fits while out walking? After all, till now I'd survived everything, been equal to every task, as a son, schoolboy and soldier. So why now? Was this the rude awakening? The feeling that I couldn't go on any longer, did not want to, the final straw, the collapse? And in the end, perhaps, admission into an institution? Was this what awaited me?

'Everything's all right,' the girl said. She continued to stare at me curiously with her big eyes. She had frizzy, dark-blonde hair, cut short above the shoulders. Only now did I realize she was the evacuee I'd chatted to briefly in the camp and about whom the teacher spoke to me later: Annemarie Schaller. I looked at her in surprise. / 'Are you feeling better?' she asked. / 'I think so, yes, I'm able to breathe again now,' I said, looking at the hand that was circumspectly holding mine. 'I get breathing problems sometimes,' I gasped. / 'Is it your lungs?' she said. / 'Fear,' I said. / 'You need to take glucose.' / The girl knew how to smile too. A hint of pride flashed in her eyes, pride that she'd been able to give me some advice. She helped me to my feet, I knocked the snow off my trousers and shook myself, partly due to the cold and partly to banish the shock of the fit. / 'Glucose calms you down,' she said.

'Thanks, many thanks,' I replied, collecting myself. A few smoke-like clouds drifted above the lake, somewhere a cock crowed in commemoration of his decapitated brothers. / 'Where did you appear from?' I asked the girl. / 'I've got a stabbing pain inside my head,' she said. 'We were making Easter presents, the lacquer dried quickly but it gives off such a terrible smell that we almost passed out, the lot of us. So we've been given an hour off to get some fresh air.' / 'And you're on your own?' / 'I don't have any friends any more. But I'm a good comrade to everyone.' / The expression that accompanied these words gave me cause to say, 'Life isn't easy for you at the moment, is it?' / She looked horrified for a moment, then stared at me again in her open way. / 'Because of your cousin, I mean.' / She sucked her lower lip and nodded. Brass music resonated fleetingly across the lake again, and when it was no longer audible the girl said, 'I'm in love.' Another smile darted over her round face, not quite as free as before, but full of clan-destine happiness. / 'Well,' I said, 'it's wonderful to be in love.'

Red blotches appeared on the girl's cheeks and, as if she had to choose between bursting into tears or doing something completely dif-ferent, she felt in the side pocket of her jacket and pulled out a letter. 'From my mother,' she said hastily. 'As a soldier, would you write to her and tell her what you've just told me, that being in love is wonderful?' She looked at me as if mesmerized and sucked in her lower lip once more. The images and voices that tormented me were still close by.

The letter was written in curved school handwriting, legible, simple in places, but full of criticism for, and threats against, the girl. I'd barely read more than half a page before I found it hard to look at this humil-iated child, while for her part Nanni stared at me expectantly, saying how unfair it was that Kurt wasn't allowed to write to her any more or come to visit at Easter. She kept her eyes on me the whole time, pushed her cap up and wiped her brow. Like me, she seemed bewildered by a world hard to understand and by unfamiliar feelings. I sensed she had an inkling of the forlorn fate of her love affair. A bird with wings in the form of a scythe soared over us and away, while the ghosts of my breath hovered in the cold air. It felt as if the temperature had dropped by at least ten degrees in the past few minutes. The coldness came from the water and I was blinded by the crystalline glare of the snow.

'Will you?'

After summoning all my strength, I said, 'What your mother writes isn't nice. She's worried about you, I'm sure she doesn't mean it like that. And when you're back in Vienna . . .' / 'Will you write to Mama?' she interrupted, shooting me such an expectant glance that I felt uneasy. What unnerved me the most was that a child intimidated so cruelly still had the strength to stand up for herself. / 'Please!' she said. / My heart pounded. I ought to have made the girl realize just how exhausted the attack had left me, but in such moments one's faculties are very much reduced. Even before I opened my mouth I knew how awkwardly I would express myself, and I said, 'Listen, when someone on the outside gets involved something always goes wrong. And this would be the case even if I tried to do it as well as I can. Your mother doesn't mean it like that, I'm sure she doesn't, and she doesn't know me either. I'm a complete stranger. She'd take my letter the wrong way. Chin up, young lady!'

She stood there, listening to me, and accepted what I said. All of a sudden I understood her cousin, I could see the fascination of this girl, of her reactions which were sometimes sluggish, sometimes abrupt. She appeared to be a completely free spirit, not a calculating individual, she didn't seem to understand what her parents' arguments had to do with the matter, unswerving in her conviction that Kurt and she were meant for one another.

'If I can help you in any other way, do come to see me,' I said, exhausted. / She looked at me as if she were slowly waking up. And, as if this were connected to her own problems, she said with a sudden bleakness, 'We're going to lose the war.' Then, in a flash, she grabbed her mother's letter, scrunched it up firmly and tossed it towards the water. After that she turned her back on me rather abruptly and hurried away with poorly coordinated movements, as if her arms and legs were working against each other. As I watched I immediately became anxious again. With her heavy shoes she stumbled several times in the snow, but without falling over. It looked as if she were wading through a trench full of sludge.

The way home was a struggle as I wrestled with my anxiety. Back in my room I cleaned my boots as a distraction, and as I did this I was revisited by a feeling of the unreal. Even now, as I write, I'm starting to sweat at just the thought of it.

Nanni! / The grief you've caused me! I can't contain myself. You've blocked off the path to your own future! How could you become a teacher now with your bad reputation? Your conduct will be noted down in the schoolbook, you see, and will haunt you all your life! You can do an apprenticeship with Uncle Mark, he's straightened out plenty of others in the past. What did I tell you time and time again? Preserve your decency, don't waste glances on such stupid boys, they're not worth losing your reputation for! Was it nice when the bad girls of your age went noisily past our window with a pack of adolescent louts? You'll have time for such distasteful things when you're twenty, when it will all look very different! You're ruining your lovely childhood, and you'll never get it back again! What goes on in your head to make you say such things to the children in your room there? Have you no sense of shame? Surely you must realize that the children will report it immediately! If your head is full of such disgusting ideas then keep them to yourself and don't say a word, keep your lips sealed! You're smart enough to get up to such antics, aren't you now? So be smart enough to keep silent! I think I failed to let you feel the back of my hand for too many years. I kept telling myself, no, I don't need to hit my child, she'll obey me anyway! All those things you told me about other children getting sharp clips around the ear from their mothers! You were always so happy to have such a good mother! How poorly you've paid me back! What were you actually thinking, having that thing with Kurti? Did you not blush with shame, corresponding with a soon-to-be seventeen-year-old boy in such a way? I mean, you're only just thirteen yourself! I've already given Kurti a piece of my mind, and Auntie Elsa and Uncle Albert too! Well, you can imagine what Auntie Elsa thinks of you now. She says you're to blame too, and I must say I agree with her. Lizzi on the third floor is treated like a right stepchild, she gets slapped and hit every day. But what do they say at the Krimml camp where Lizzi is? The director there is full of praise for Lizzi and impatient to meet the mother who has raised such a model child! Yet I, who've always treated you with nothing but kindness, and done everything I possibly could for you, I'm going to be known as the mother of the vulgar girl! Can you imagine if I paid a parental visit to Schwarzindien? I'm not going to come, I'm too ashamed! The children will tell their parents everything and I'm a marked woman wherever I go! All that's left for me to say is this: obey Frau Bildstein's every word and be happy to have a teacher like her, understand that your head is spinning, keep everything neat and tidy and maybe your good teacher will forgive you! What an imposition it must be for her to have to educate a child like you! Behave modestly, be unassuming and hardworking, then you will make up for some of your guilt! If you don't change, you'll never go to the Grassingerhof again and you'll find yourself in an institution straightaway. / So, the choice is yours! / Greetings from your mother!

March had been unusually

March had been unusually cold. It snowed again in the first few days of April, but then it promptly turned warm in Holy Week, the snow quickly thawed and small streams burst their banks. On a sunny waste tip beside the railway track to St Gilgen I discovered the first coltsfoot of the season. The Russians called these yellow, scrubby plants 'German seed'. In Kharkov last spring, where we'd ensured that everything had been bombed, ploughed up, shot to pieces and clubbed to death, large swathes of coltsfoot had appeared amongst heaps of rubble and where buildings had burned. I couldn't help recalling this when spring finally came.

The community doctor cauterized the wound on my thigh with silver nitrate one last time. I told him about the nervous fits I regularly suffered, describing the feelings of suffocation, the sweating and the fact that I had difficulty walking. Something wasn't right with me, I said. I wasn't mad, but that might be the impression I gave whenever I struggled my way to the next seat with small, stiff steps. / The doctor stuck a large plaster over the wound on my thigh, which was virtually closed now, and frowned. He was no expert on the attacks I was describing, but he was reluctant to admit it. After a few comments such as 'interesting', 'difficult' and 'that happens', he prescribed me Pervitin, but said I should only take it as a last resort. He gave me the pills from his medicine chest.

The Brazilian was now extremely busy with work and moreover he was bothered by the fluctuating weather. On a few occasions it had looked as if his now permanent cold might deteriorate, but his medicinal herbs had worked wonders, he claimed. Only at the start of Holy Week did the work almost get the better of him, he said, refusing to leave him in peace even during the few hours of sleep he was able to snatch, for he kept waking with a start, anxious that he might have forgotten something. / He had to get up at five o'clock, then by six in the morning he had to cut and pack one hundred large orchids and prepare them for rail transport. This meant wrapping each individual flower in tissue paper, then bundling them into fives in packing paper, the stems in damp moss, then putting fifty into a cardboard box, covered by a protective frame to prevent damage to the flowers. Finally the Brazilian placed packing paper over the frame. He mustn't waste a single minute, or his consignment wouldn't leave with the early train, and then the flowers wouldn't arrive at the Salzburg shop on time and more than half of them would be ruined because the orchids couldn't survive in packaging any longer. In addition, for Easter he had to send twenty orchid plants to Salzburg and Linz three times that week. And in between times there was work to do in the vegetable garden, which meant more hurrying, for even before he stepped out of the greenhouse he needed to be back in there with his orchids. How he'd love to keel over in the middle of his work, he said, and not get up again. Without his plans for an escape to freedom in South America he'd never be able to summon the strength to keep going.

The quiet winter period came to an end for my uncle too. The patrols to check and enforce the blackout regulations couldn't be undertaken in late afternoon any more, for the days were rapidly lengthening. An order came from Vöcklabruck to check the stability of all landing stages on the Mondsee. Then word got around that a young man with both hands thickly wrapped in bandages had claimed to be a wounded fighter pilot and had asked one of the evacuee girls to take out his penis so he could pass water. He told the girl she needed to rub it a bit too, to make something come out. They had a description of the person. / The endless proscriptions relating to daily life also created lots of work. A farmer in the Gaisberg district had been reported by neighbours for feeding his chickens with wheat, which was forbidden. My uncle abandoned the investigation before he'd even launched it. He said he had no desire to analyse chicken dung under a microscope.

And so the weeks passed. Everyone slipped further into the year. The war proceeded at the cost of a better life. I was horrified by the thought that the day when I would be examined for re-employability was gradually approaching. / They talked on the wireless of the destruction of Frankfurt city centre, while the first major air raids had occurred over Vienna too. German troops marched into Hungary, and sometimes it was disquieting how long the trains were, heading east via Salzburg and carrying war equipment. / In Mondsee, however, daily life continued as normal. They played back-to-back springtime melodies on the wireless. The farmers sawed wood, the puttering, whistling and screeching of the circular saws resounding through the town for hours on end. The Darmstadt woman occasionally popped into my room and poured out her heart to me. The child had recently started turning onto its back from its stomach, it had discovered its thumbs and a new humming noise, which it was practising hard. On the Friday before the Easter holidays the second term of the school year finished, and even the girls in the evacuee camps were given reports. The day after that saw the official heating period come to an end.

I saw the girl, Annemarie Schaller, once more after that. She was wiggling absent-mindedly on the rickety camp bicycle in my direction when she noticed me, moved to the side of the road and sat up stiffly on the saddle, as if her torso were detached from the process of cycling. She scowled at me and rode past, her face blurred by an unspeakable sadness. I said hello, and perhaps she returned the greeting, perhaps not; I couldn't say with any certainty, maybe it was something in-between. A hundred metres further on I saw her disappear into the woods, now snaking from side to side again.

Two days later, on Maundy Thursday, news made its way around Mondsee that Annemarie Schaller had gone missing from the camp at Schwarzindien. The rumour spread so quickly that it had already gone full circle by the evening. 'I know, I've already heard, the girl did a runner with a sixteen-year-old boy from Vienna.' / As it later turned out, this was not true, for her cousin, Kurt Ritler, had spent the whole of Holy Week training at a marshalling yard in Kledering, where he'd slept in a heated couchette wagon. After the holidays he and his fellow schoolboys wouldn't be returning to school for lessons, but going to an anti-aircraft installation at Schwechat, next to the refinery. / Officials in Vienna interrogated 'the little rascal', as Uncle called him, but without success. Kurt had apparently been most upset and was very worried about her.

It was assumed that the girl would find her way to Vienna. Unfortunately she didn't turn up there, nor at her paternal grandmother's in Engelhardtskirchen. Her father had died five years ago: tuberculosis. Uncle disclosed details of the incident to me early on; he needed the services of a clerk more often now. Young girls created a large amount of work, he said, it was far worse than the murder of a policeman.

What could be established beyond doubt was that Nanni had feigned toothache and the camp teacher had given her a written exeat. She didn't turn up at the dentist's, but spoke to a woman in St Lorenz and asked whether she could buy her a box of biscuits on her ration card. Nanni counted out the money for the biscuits into her hand. Then she made for the station, at least that's where the camp bicycle was found. Nanni's luggage was left behind in the camp at Schwarzindien; Uncle refused to rule out the possibility that this was a deliberate ploy to deceive the authorities. Besides the usual girls' things, they had found some letters from Kurt and a piece of paper on which she'd scribbled: *It's how I am to the core, hooray! It's how I am and how I'll stay, yes, Sir! /* This was roughly all that could be gleaned. The railway guards couldn't provide any information. There were too many girls around and they all wore the same dark-blue uniform of the youth organization. Nor could anyone else help; nobody knew where the girl had gone. On the day she disappeared, moreover, the wind had scattered the clouds and the sun soon melted the remaining patches of snow. It all turned to water, obliterating any useful traces. The beautiful season was now beginning in earnest, and I took in the warm air with a sense of relief, having spent the past few springs fighting in Russia. The bees were active again too, finally. The Brazilian said they'd overwintered well.

When Annemarie Schaller still hadn't turned up by Easter Monday, I wasn't the only one to feel increasingly worried. The authorities began to consider the possibility of some sort of accident, and after a telephone conversation with Linz the decision was taken to send the local H Youth to the lake, to search beneath all the overturned boats that were out of the water, as well as every accessible boathouse, always in groups of at least three to prevent anyone else from going missing. They wouldn't rule out the possibility that the girl had drowned; almost annually every lake in the vicinity had its own dead child. But nothing pointed directly to this eventuality, and they had to leave it open, especially as it was well known that large bodies of water allowed for restricted visibility. Experience showed that the lake would return the body, assuming there was one, over the course of the year. / Unfortunately, the alleged fighter pilot with the thick bandages on his hands couldn't help resolve the matter either. He had tried to pull his stunt a second time in Bad Ischl and was soon afterwards taken into custody. As he had an alibi for those days in the middle of Holy Week, he was unable to offer a glimmer of light in the murkiness of the investigation.

Uncle said that such things simply happened from time to time. For example, the thirteen-year-old son of a policeman from Wels had run away from home and taken the train to Italy because, he said, he wanted to see the theatre of war. He himself would be very happy to stop having to make educated guesses, but that was all he had to go on for the time being and so he was just writing what reason and logic dictated to him: *Annemarie Schaller has run away.*

After several attempts at straightening a pile of registers on the desk, he leaned back and crossed his hands behind his neck. He said he wasn't going to tell me in detail what he thought about women, but the younger a woman was, the crazier the places you found their dirty laundry. The older ones, on the other hand, had basketfuls of the stuff! In the past Nanni had come home late on several occasions. Her fondness for the opposite sex was well documented. And on top of this, now she had wanderlust. He was going to draw up a missing person's announcement, indicating that a name tag was sewn onto every item of her clothing. And that was it. There were so many people disappeared, in hiding, roaming around, escaped prisoners of war, foreign workers, deserters, idlers, conspiratorial communists and conspiratorial ministrants: welcome to the Greater German shadow Reich!

Uncle emphasized how valuable his time was. The more valuable your time, the more relentless the era you were living in. He said he was going to go out on a patrol now to stop him from contracting lung disease from the stale archival air of his office. / We both stood up at the same time and went outside. When Uncle fetched his dog from the kennel, I said, 'It's all so . . .' / 'So depressing?' he said. / 'Yes.' / 'I think the same. It's dreadful, young man! What godawful times we live in! My digestion's giving me gyp. It's always the same. I can't think and digest at the same time.' He rubbed his stomach wistfully. 'And then I went to get some tobacco from the tobacconist's this morning, but couldn't buy any. What use is a smoking ration card if there's no tobacco to be had? Life used to be very different, not everything was weighed out by the gram.' / He tied up his dog again, an Alsatian, which gave me an indolent look. Right next to the kennel, in a room at the end of the shed with a window, were the rabbit hutches. Uncle fed the rabbits, coughing as he did so. / 'I'm really worried about the girl,' I said. / 'Well, well!' / 'She ought to have been in Vienna by now, she could have easily made it in this time. And seeing how much in love the girl is, Vienna is the only logical destination. There's something not right about the case.' / 'There are a number of possibilities, of course,' Uncle said. 'But over time one develops a nose for this sort of thing, you know? To my mind it's perfectly understandable that she hasn't gone home. If my teacher and mother tried telling me in unison that I was mature enough to recognize my immaturity, I'd run away too. I have great sensitivity, believe you me.'

When we went into the street the sun was shining. The Schafberg stood there in the blazing light, gleaming at us so white and pure that I immediately felt the need to eliminate my own blemishes. I think I have plenty of them. A group of girls in uniform was marching in double file from the station. They saluted by stretching out their arms and they continued on their way with brisk movements. I felt a sudden tension in my muscles and had to force myself to walk normally. All those years away were making themselves felt here too. / In his blood-spattered apron, the fat butcher's apprentice hurried towards the market square to fetch beer. The red postal van turned into the street, forcing the girls to stop. I turned away.

Almost another week passed like this. All manner of important and trivial things happened, while my own life was lacklustre and dismal. My uncle relayed all the developments in the Annemarie Schaller case.

And so I knew that her mother had been requested to stay in Vienna in case the girl turned up at home. Eight days after Annemarie's disappearance, however, Frau Schaller arrived unannounced in the Upper Danube district. The many evacuees rehoused in St Lorenz meant there were no available rooms, so she stayed in Mondsee. I recognized her at once. The day when they broadcast the fall of Tarnopol I saw her in front of the church, the same round and open face, albeit severe too. She sucked her lower lip in the same way. And she also had this unbelievable expression of astonishment that was so pronounced it was as if it stood proud of her face. Miserable and forlorn, her head bowed, the woman wandered off. It seemed to take her an age to cross the square in front of the church.

For the former occupiers of Tarnopol I laid a bunch of coltsfoot by the memorial to the fallen. I'd heard in Kharkov that coltsfoot grew directly on lignite, which seemed fitting to me. Then I went to the post office and sent a package with the garter belt back to Vienna. / A few members of the H Youth were roaming the village, given the job of picking up flyers from the ground. These had been dropped the previous day and cast doubt on the wisdom and integrity of the Reich leadership. When a scrawny little chap in a cap that was too big for him tried to have a pee against a garden fence, one of the H Youth tore strips off him.

After a lie-down in the afternoon I broke out into a sweat. I got up immediately, splashed myself with cold water and put on a fresh shirt. I had a throbbing in my temples and my forehead ached, while my pulse rose to one hundred. / I stood at the window for a while, looking over at the garden. There was not much activity; the dog was trotting around the house while the Brazilian, in his rubber boots but without a coat, came out of the greenhouse and looked up at the sky. I moved back from the window to warm myself by the stove. / A little later there was a knock at the door. Uncle had sent for me because he needed the services of a clerk again. I felt such an outsider and so redundant that it gave me a lift when I was needed. And as I've already mentioned, it didn't really matter what I did with my time, so long as it proved a distraction from the war.

Nanni's mother sat in the office, my uncle opposite her. She'd tied her hair up in an old-maidish bun. She wore a grey skirt, white blouse and a very wide, dark-blue necktie. The round face, still pale from winter, was full of shame. She blinked a lot, not because the wind had blown dust into her eyes or because she was blinded by the sun, but as if she still had to wake up, as if she were unable to believe what was being asked of her.

I fed the copy paper into the typewriter and took care not to make any mistakes. Frau Schaller stated that Nanni had started menstruating when she was eleven, far too young. And from then on she'd developed so rapidly that soon she could have been mistaken for a fifteen-year-old. Regrettably, she said, Nanni had always had the sorts of friends who saw to it that she learned all about the opposite sex. She'd realized this and forbidden her daughter from having such friendships, but unfortunately Frau Schaller had been called up for wartime labour – she did piece work, riveting spade carriers – and so Nanni was generally left to her own devices during the daytime. At half past six in the evening, when Frau Schaller came home from work, Nanni would tell her what she'd been up to that day and Frau Schaller had no choice but to believe the girl. Nanni must have lied occasionally, she said, all hell was let loose in those years when children developed. Nanni had a fertile imagination, moreover, she could immerse her mind so deeply in something that she really believed she'd experienced it. But, contrary to what she'd told the other girls, Nanni had definitely not spent the evenings away from home and in the park, something Kurt confirmed too. Otherwise, Frau Schaller said, she was a good girl, smart, she did everything you asked her to without question. She just needed reining in on account of her overactive imagination. But as a mother, she insisted that Nanni would simply never gad about the place indiscriminately. She knew her daughter, she was desperately worried about her child.

The mother talked, my uncle didn't ask many questions and there was little change in expression on her face. From time to time her flow dried up, at which she would raise her head anxiously and look at Uncle with red eyes. Uncle looked back with every semblance of kindheartedness he could simulate. When the mother resumed talking, she always began quietly, her eyes downcast, then her voice slowly gathered strength, but her gaze remained fixed on her lap. I saw the severe line that cut down the mother's forehead between the eyebrows. She said she'd lost three and a half kilos in the past week, which was quite a lot given how little she weighed in the first place, and there had been a noticeable effect on her health. She was taking glucose for her bad nerves. / As I typed *glucose* I thought of my meeting with Nanni by the lake. I hadn't told anyone about our encounter. Frau Schaller said she had terrible nerves and she hoped she'd get her child back safe and sound, nothing else mattered.

Uncle had been sitting there distantly, daydreaming in front of a mountain of paper. When he realized that Frau Schaller needed a break, he took out one of the now rare cigarettes, looked at it long and hard, as if it possessed some superior knowledge, then offered it to Frau Schaller. Frau Schaller declined. In the end, Uncle put the cigarette between his own lips and lit it, on a habitually grey day in life.

When the assistant walked across the room, Uncle scolded him. 'How many times have I told you to wash your face in the morning? You've always got that dirt around your eyes and so you never see what you ought to! You're not being paid to have dirt in your eyes.' / Uncle rubbed his permanently dry smoker's hands and coughed three or four times as usual. Afterwards he calmly pointed out that of course it was well known what young girls like that were like. / 'Really?' Frau Schaller asked uncertainly. / He rolled his eyes dismissively. Then with his customary impassive voice, as if he were talking about turning left or drinking water, he said, 'Who buys a large box of biscuits? Someone who needs provisions. Nanni has money, a pair of sturdy shoes and a uniform in which she doesn't stand out. Circumstantial evidence proves nothing, but it does support the probability that your daughter *is* gadding about.' / He referred to the skittish frame of mind brought on by sexual maturity and quoted from a letter to Kurt in which Nanni made the suggestion that they emigrate to India. The girl was surely capable of such an attempt. / 'But for heaven's sake, Inspector, no, no, never! She's still a silly little child!' the mother said, bursting into tears. / 'Yes, that's precisely why,' my uncle said with a mollifying gesture of the hand. 'Clearly she needs to bang her head hard against a wall to come to reason.' Then, in a cloud of smoke, as if his words were part of the smoke too, he added, 'She'll turn up again soon.'

He waited until Nanni's mother had stopped crying, then blew a thin trail of smoke up to the ceiling and asked a few questions about Kurt Ritler, but in a way that made it sound as if he were just passing time rather than particularly interested. Frau Schaller blew her nose and answered willingly. I was touched by the fact that, until Nanni's evacuation, she and Kurt had lived in neighbouring apartments in the Grassingerhof, and slept separated only by a wall. When they got up, Frau Schaller said, they used to wish each other good morning by knocking on the wall. / For a few seconds I stared at the wall facing me, on which hung the sign with the Seven Golden Ws: *Who killed / whom / when / where / why / with / what?* Then I had to hurry so as not to lose the thread of the conversation. Frau Schaller said that deep down Kurt was a good boy too.

Uncle brought the interview to an abrupt end, saying he had to go to his air-raid warden course in Vöcklabruck, for which he'd already had to miss choir practice three times. So the interview was over and Uncle hastily fastened the coat of his uniform. Frau Schaller watched him helplessly. She wanted to see a glimmer of hope in Uncle's eyes, but there was no glimmer, only impotence and indifference, although my uncle did say, 'We will do everything in our power . . . everything will turn out all right . . . everything will sort itself out . . . your daughter just wants to give us one hell of a fright.' / Frau Schaller shook her head in disbelief; my uncle offered her his hand. Baffled, Frau Schaller smoothed down her skirt with both hands before giving Uncle's hand a curt shake. Then she left the room, sobbing. / Uncle looked at me and said, 'A most stupid business indeed!'

Frau Schaller stayed in Mondsee for another couple of days. I saw her once by the lake, sitting desolately on some steps that led down to the murky water shrouded in mist. And once I bumped into her at the bakery, where we exchanged a few words. She told me she was waiting for the nightmare to go away at any moment and she was so terrified. Without the camp teacher, she said, she'd die of loneliness, she was so desperate to see her girl again. / But Nanni remained missing, without trace, as they say. Finally Frau Schaller left on the day before the regular parents' visiting day. She didn't want to meet the other mothers, she said. She left a number of addresses and telephone numbers at my uncle's office. / Uncle narrowed his eyes like a cat and told me, in all confidence, that he wouldn't rule out the possibility of Frau Schaller's being mixed up in the affair. As far as I was concerned, the woman's pale green face made that unlikely. I pointed this out to my uncle. He said the woman probably drank, and he shook his head as if bewildered by the irrationality of the world.

On the evening before Frau Schaller left I had another nervous fit. I took my first Pervitin pill, lay trembling on the bed and waited for the medicine to kick in. I heard the Darmstadt woman in the neighbouring room talking to her baby: 'Your grandmother has written to say she's looking after the goats and rabbits. She'd love to give us some goat milk, our goats are called Lies and Lotte and they're both healthy, but the British shelled our goat shed, just imagine that. And Papa has sent us twenty-five moleskins from Estonia that he found in an abandoned house, already tanned. He says they might be enough for a pram blanket. Your papa is fighting up there in the cruel war.'

She spoke in her thick Hesse accent, and the way she said *cruel* lent it a realistic edge, it sounded like *crawl, crawl into holes in the ground*, it sounded like those dark, damp shafts I tumbled into when I had my attacks. I was happy that the Pervitin was gradually taking effect. Or maybe it was the woman from Darmstadt's talking that calmed me down.

'Did you know, Lilo, that all those victory torches were nothing but common pitch torches. Now your papa is sending us moleskins from Estonia. The soldiers up there are living like the first human beings. Sad, isn't it?'

Parents' visiting day

Parents' visiting day actually stretched out over two days. Even before Easter, H Youth boys had gone through the town with lists, enquiring as to who could provide how many beds for which day. Two mothers and a newborn slept in the landlady's parlour. One of the only two men in the entire group stayed at the Brazilian's with his wife and another woman. I recognized this other woman, for she'd been a sales assistant at a shoe shop on Thaliastrasse when I was at school. / When the train bringing the parents arrived, the girls' howls of delight echoed across the lake. The camp teacher, Frau Bildstein, whom I saw for the first time in a long while after the parents had left, said that when the cloud of smoke from the train came into view the girls had knocked each other over in their excitement.

All the same, there was a nervousness hanging over the parents' visit, just as when the lamp flickered in my room and I waited spellbound to see if it went out, as it habitually did. The rumours had done the rounds in Vienna. A letter dictated by the camp teacher ought to have reassured the parents in advance. But the fact that nobody would or could provide adequate information about Nanni's disappearance only fuelled the parents' anxiety even further. / The two mothers who slept in the landlady's parlour sat in the garden chatting until late in the evening. My window was open and I listened to them. At such a critical time the two of them were keen to know their children were in safe hands. And now they asked themselves what was more dangerous: the anticipated bombings of Vienna, or the jungle of Schwarzindien with its secrets. The war was going to cause a lot more headaches, one of the women said. But there was nothing to fear in Mondsee at the moment apart from a possible emergency jettisoning of bombs.

One woman was breastfeeding her newborn child, which the other woman remarked on several times. 'The way he sucks, I take my hat off to you! He'll be a professional wrestler one day.' After a while the breastfeeding woman said, 'Just look at his big head, it's no wonder I still ache all over. I need to go for a bit of a walk.' / Then the two women went away.

The mothers concealed their concerns from the girls as best they could. But all of them were anxious to spend as much time with them away from the camp as possible, not just to have time alone with their girls, but also in the hope that, separated from the group, the girls they knew from back home would reappear. The slightest change in any of the children was viewed against the backdrop of Nanni's disappearance. Even I, an outsider, had noticed how the girls had grown in confidence over the past few months; they were told often enough that they were the F's most precious possessions. / The anxious mothers went on walks with their daughters, seeking out quiet corners. And whenever I saw one of these mothers with her daughter, she almost always made use of the difference in height to lean on the girl. The mothers were tense, their emotions suppressed, they kept looking around while the girls gave free vent to their feelings. As she took a look at the Brazilian's greenhouse with her daughter, the former sales assistant at Bata on Thaliastrasse was told, 'Stop pulling me around!'

The Brazilian withdrew for a nap in the hammock. Frau Nowak sat on the stub wall out on the street. In spite of all the difficulties she seemed happy to be in this peaceful place, and yet deep in thought, a frown on her face, mistrustful of both the present and the future. She watched her daughter play with the Brazilian's dog. It'll be all right, I wanted to say, but I kept quiet. / All around, the mountains towered silent and sombre, covered in a canopy of snow and impassable woods. The mighty stone skull of the Drachenwand stood grey in the haze of the beautiful weather.

The women staying with the landlady returned from the lake. The one with the infant was wearing a flowery yellow dress, the other was in mourning clothes. The girls behind them were chatting merrily. The taller of the two said, 'Apparently my brother's become really fat. He must be missing that sister of his who annoys all his excess fat away.' The girls laughed spitefully.

When Frau Nowak left for the station, her daughter was carrying the small suitcase. 'Stay healthy and look after yourself!' Frau Nowak said. / 'I will,' the girl said. The following day I met Frau Bildstein, the camp teacher. I hadn't seen her for several weeks, and still she didn't appear to show any real interest in me, but now I was more relaxed about this and didn't find it upsetting, for this wasn't the time to make a fuss. But I was plagued by dissatisfaction with myself because I wasn't able to make the transition from the theory of life to life in practice. I realized that I shouldn't expect any help from the teacher in this regard, as her prejudice against soldiers was irreversible. I still found her appealing to look at, but otherwise things had gone cold on my side too.

We talked about nothing in particular. She said she'd needed some nails to repair her clogs. They cost four pfennigs, but that morning the shoemaker had received three letters from his son, who was fighting in Russia, and out of sheer joy he'd given her the nails for nothing. She, Margarete Charlotte Bildstein, had been given something as a present. Normally she had to chase everything.

She complained that she'd had to deal with one problem after another of late. Fortunately two of the mothers had been to the school in Vienna and brought books with them when they came for the parents' visit. The post was making no exceptions to the restriction on packages. She didn't expect any help from Linz, from where they just bossed her around, and since Nanni's disappearance the campaign against her obviously hadn't abated. / 'Sympathy is not provided for in the system,' I said. / She fixed her harsh, grey eyes on me, which looked so alien and detached that I felt embarrassed. I tried to light a cigarette, but the heads broke off two matches. The teacher didn't even react to this. She said she'd finally got an old lid and egg whisk for their PE lessons, which were now her pride and joy. Even this she said with great earnestness; she didn't like to laugh, or at least not in my presence.

So I was most surprised when, just as we were about to go our separate ways, she remarked on my poor appearance. If I didn't put on some weight soon and get a little colour I would get a spanking. She said *spanking* in all seriousness. The word went round in my head for hours afterwards and I couldn't help smiling. Fundamentally all people are strange.

I couldn't, in truth, feel satisfied with my appearance. I'd never looked like I was brimming with health, but now my face was more drawn than it had ever been. It couldn't be down to what I was eating, as I was being provided for adequately. The Darmstadt woman and I helped each other out with various rationing difficulties, I ate with her two evenings a week and I turned down her invitations on at least two other occasions per week. Quite simply the past few years had left a visible mark on me. Whenever I wrote my diary, I needed nothing but a cup of black coffee, and never felt the urge to get up from the small table and eat a snack. I wrote and wrote, and from time to time took a sip of coffee.

I often lacked the energy to visit the Darmstadt woman, for in the evenings I was dog-tired. I regularly slept twelve hours at a stretch, without which I wouldn't have been able to get through the day. I found it astonishing how little food can keep a man going without him starving. I always had something to do. I saw to it that my things were in order, washed my own handkerchiefs, underwear and socks, and I even sewed up a loop on my trousers, which at some point a skilled woman's hand would have put right. The Polish woman just polished my boots for the one Reichsmark per week I gave her. She urgently needed this one mark for minor outgoings.

The Polish woman, Joanna, was another sad case. Twenty-three years old, she worked very hard from early in the morning till late in the evening. On the Sunday of the parents' visit she had a sudden emotional outburst; she cried and told Frau Nowak she just wanted to die, there was nothing for her in this life. For four years she'd been away from home, doing forced labour, and every day was the same. Not even Sunday brought any relief: she wasn't allowed to go to the cinema, wasn't allowed to go swimming, nor even to church, even though she was very religious. She didn't have any children, nor any clothes, and what she did have got torn through the hard labour. As a Pole she didn't even get thirty points on her card per year. What was she supposed to do with thirty points? She'd soon be turning twenty-four and her youth, none of which she'd been able to enjoy, was almost over. A terrible life. And the most awful thing was that Joanna was onto a relatively good thing with the landlady because she was able to cultivate a patch of the garden. Many foreign workers were poorer, and looked in bad physical shape too. When they were unable to work any more they were simply sent back.

They've just said on the wireless that the struggle for Simferopol is over. My sense of humour is gradually being eroded. It makes me dizzy thinking about what will have happened there, all the people who will have died.

Uncle said the front will reliably come to a standstill at the gates of Germany. This will happen without fail, for the Bolsheviks aren't that mighty. At the beginning of March they were sending sixteen-year-old boys to the southern section of the front, which suggested they weren't in such great shape, so now we had to . . . / I calmly listened to everything he had to say and came to my own conclusions. I didn't believe anything, for nobody knew anything for certain. Finally I did give my opinion, saying that after all we'd done on the Eastern Front, the Red Army had a colossal score to settle. And those who now claimed to know how we could worm our way out of this yet again, I added, were by nature the right ones to send to the front, sparing the rest of us the most terrible things. If there was one thing you could be sure of about the armchair strategists, it was that they allegedly had everything under control and that they'd be able to last another ten years of war so long as they never had to trade places with those at the front. / Uncle plucked a thread of tobacco from his lower lip and rubbed it between his fingers. The staffroom slowly filled with smoke.

He said he'd seen me with the teacher from Schwarzindien. 'Are you interested in that filly? Is she to your taste?' / 'She gave me the brush-off weeks ago.' / 'Sorry to hear that,' he replied, clapping me on the shoulder.

Later I heard him on the telephone to one of his superiors, which I could tell by the way he kept barking 'Yes, sir!' into the receiver. Meanwhile I read one of the occasional letters that Kurt Ritler had sent poste restante to Mondsee, and which the postman had given to my uncle.

Uncle read the letters just to be sure that nothing in them merited his attention; I read them out of personal interest, for I liked the boy. Now he was stationed at a flak position in Schwechat, opposite the road that ran to the south of the refinery.

We're doing a lot of training, but right at the moment I'm sitting all on my own in my acoustic locator, listening to an aeroplane far away. If you didn't know what it was you could let the distant, deep and regular sound lull you to sleep. There's nothing menacing about the sound. / It's a shame that I ended up with the listening personnel, Ferdl is on the floodlights so at least he can see something. I'd love to look for you with one of those floodlights. I'm so worried about you, Nanni, I'm afraid something's happened.

I asked Uncle about the girl, and he said he didn't have any news of her. But he was convinced that all the important details would soon suppurate from the case of their own accord. That's how he put it. / I left, claiming to have a severe headache. The weather had turned, and individual raindrops signalled uncertain conditions. Time to move quickly.

Back home I was intercepted by the landlady, who again demanded I erect the flagpole, this was a man's job. / The celebrations to honour my highest master were fast approaching: the so-called F's birthday. For this occasion too it was necessary for the moon colony to pay its respects to the motherland. / With an eye to the weather I asked if the flagpole couldn't wait until tomorrow. But the landlady humourlessly said that surely I'd be wanting to sleep in late. It was hard to find an adequate response to that. / With an unerring sense of how the conversation would proceed from here I did as instructed. This was routine now. While the landlady, arms crossed and a spiteful smile on her lips, stood beside me waiting for the operation to go wrong, I manoeuvred the pole into the hole. The landlady hoisted the flag and a few minutes later it hung heavy and limp above the house. It had started to rain. And how!

The water gushed out of the gutter in an arc, overshooting the drain tiles in the garden. The village cowered miserably beneath the downpour. Toads crept out of their holes, and in the field beside the greenhouse a fox waited for a mouse to be washed out of its hole. Twice I watched it run away with a mouse in its mouth.

That evening I ate with the Darmstadt woman. The child's bottom was all right now and she gave me back the sun lamp. What a wonderful life this would be, I said, if there weren't damp squibs all over the place, here in the form of our landlady. The Darmstadt woman asked me why exactly I was in Mondsee. Because I didn't like living with my parents at home, I said. She gave a sudden laugh and told me she was in the same situation. She planned to stay here until the end of the war, then she'd see. I said I'd also be very happy to stay here, but it wouldn't be long before my employer came looking for me again; I feared his long arm. At the moment I was not fit for duty and had another eight weeks until my examination.

After dinner I poured us some wine while the Darmstadt woman ironed at the table. When I casually asked her if she missed her husband, she said she had her child and she had her cream to rub in at night, which was something at least. I thought she meant at least some sort of physical contact.

I didn't trust myself to pick up the baby. But before dinner I held out my finger and the child grabbed it and played with it. The child's encrusted nostrils looked bad. But the woman reassured me that it was nothing serious. When I bent down to take a closer look, the girl squealed and kicked with her legs.

The following day the bad weather had blown over. The market square was subjected to further colonization as the Party sought to extend its Lebensraum inside the children's heads. This took the form of a speech in front of the assembled evacuees, delivered by the regional officer of the children's evacuation organization, Oberstammführer Pleininger. I saw him chugging on his motorcycle behind a shuffling herd of cattle, in the finest-looking boots I'd set eyes on in months, chrome leather, French. It struck me that if those at the front knew how good life was for those who'd stayed behind, they'd desert at once.

Because the evacuees were also celebrating their three-month anniversary – that's to say they'd been evacuees for three months – there was dancing in all the camps until ten o'clock at night to F's birthday music on the radio.

The Brazilian's existential brooding had lately been interrupted by bouts of good spirits. He groaned under the burden of his work, saying it felt as if it were made of rubber, all of life was made of rubber, sponsored by Buna, Made in Poland, General Government. But he predicted that the invasion in the West was close at hand, and then it wouldn't be long before he cleared off from the obsolete civilization of Europe. His hour would come, he said, and then nobody on earth would be as happy as he. He would shake the hand of the God's Finger peak, listen to the polyphonic humming of the Serra dos Órgãos and lie down in the Desert of Snorers. He just had to get away from this continent burdened by villains and war. / When he wrenched an old nail from an old plank, the noise this made was not unlike the scraping of chalk on a blackboard and my bladder contracted. / As he worked, the Brazilian's elbows stuck out through the holes in his pullover. He said he wouldn't be buying a new one now. In Brazil, yes. 'Viva Brazil!' He gave a grunt of satisfaction and went with the rusty nail down the flagstone path to the greenhouse.

Word had also got around the evacuee children that there was a Brazilian in Mondsee. When the girls had free time to go into town they would seek out his company and question him about parrots, hummingbirds and coffee plantations while lending a hand. Sometimes the Brazilian tossed away careless remarks: 'In Brazil the races mix as a matter of course. There are lots of half-breeds, it's normal over there. Anyone who elevates race to the most important category by which to judge people, more important than any other human characteristic such as intelligence, wit, discretion, talent – they give no proof of their superiority.' / There was a frisson as the children listened inquisitively, exchanged surprised glances or made fun of him slightly. One of the girls came out with a loud 'Yuk!' / The Brazilian just shrugged and the girls took note of this.

His fate was sealed, not by his love for the more southern of the two Americas, but by a remark he made three days after the F's birthday during a speech by the minister for public relations. The Brazilian arrived at the bar of the Schwarzer Adler with his first delivery of radishes and cucumbers that year during the middle of the broadcast being played over the wireless. The minister was trotting out a few phrases to mitigate the impact of the reality of the war. And the Brazilian said he hoped they'd soon find a stern, well-built nurse for old Goatfoot, who'd strap him into one of those jackets made for lunatics. / A few people looked open-mouthed at this comment, and apparently one customer, who was trying to be helpful, warned him not to talk such nonsense, he was clearly drunk. The Brazilian refuted the accusation that he was in his cups, however, and said that the country had no need of an F, who for tactical reasons and sheer egotism refrained from indulging in alcohol, tobacco and large quantities of meat, but provided his underlings with such things in pathological abundance. But amongst the freaks who had brought this country under their sway, the minister for public relations was one of the least extreme.

The Brazilian wasn't arrested overnight

The Brazilian wasn't arrested overnight or at daybreak, as people always said when talking about such things, but at lunchtime. I got the impression that the authorities, who weren't making any progress in the Annemarie Schaller case, that is to say they were stuck, used the opportunity to give the appearance that they were still on their toes. / As I ate my late breakfast I had a rather bad headache. Noises from the garden sounded muffled to me. I looked at the two tomatoes waiting to ripen on my windowsill facing the street and thought about how Hilde too had enjoyed looking at the tomatoes ripening on her windowsill in the sanatorium. Mama and Papa had sent them wrapped in paper or wood wool to her in the sanatorium, which was possible back then. It's part of the story that shaped me. And next door I heard the rapid, busy footsteps of the Darmstadt woman, as well as the clattering of crockery and the occasional knock on the wall.

Then a vehicle drove quietly down the road. Only the butcher usually came this way, making a completely different sound on account of his trailer. Coffee cup in hand, I wandered to the window. Squeezing its way between the handcart and the front compost heap, a dark Peugeot pressed two tracks in the grass all the way up to the greenhouse entrance, where the Brazilian was washing his socks in the fountain trough.

Two men got out. One was so stout that the back of his neck concertinaed if he lifted his head even slightly. And they approached the Brazilian. And the dog came running out of the greenhouse, barking all the way. And the slimmer of the two men immediately struck the dog twice with his stick. And the Brazilian put his wet socks over the edge of the trough. And the fat one grabbed the Brazilian's arm to make him realize that they needed him more urgently than the dog did. And the dog crept, whimpering, beneath the handcart. And soon afterwards the men went into the house with the Brazilian. And I thought, what sort of men are these who don't remove their hats when they enter a house? Answer: it's probably not the most important thing on their minds.

When the men came out again, the briefcase under the arm of the slimmer man was now fatter, and half the neighbourhood had gathered in the street, for the appearance of a car with tinted windows hadn't attracted just my attention. / Being in uniform, I took the gamble of approaching the men. Without letting me say a word, the fat one said I was just the man: I should get rid of all these onlookers. I turned around and saw that the landlady had ventured forwards too. I asked what was going on. / 'A flawless arrest,' the man replied with a slight sneer, fixing his gaze on me in the way he would have been taught on his fast-track secret policeman's course, or as he'd made his habit. It looked rehearsed, but it didn't fail to have the desired effect. I stopped in my tracks.

All too often during those winter nights in the greenhouse I'd listened to the Brazilian with one ear only. I now felt as if he'd once said that our ideas of what constituted civilization could not be sustained. And I recalled another remark he'd made: he said that sometimes I was like a plant which needed repotting. He got the impression I'd stopped growing years ago.

Now under his arm he had what must have been a hastily gathered bundle of underwear. And as the fat policeman went back to him, the Brazilian sought my gaze and said, 'Look after my tomatoes, Menino. I'm sure I can trust you to do that.' He threw me a bunch of keys that sailed straight into my hands in front of my belly.

Then the fat one said to the Brazilian to keep his mouth shut and clean his wretched galoshes so they didn't soil the car. In spite of everything, the Brazilian, in his chunky, stubby work shoes, still kept his sense of humour, saying that good shoes were worth a lot all around the world, but even in the Brazilian jungle it was true that those wearing the finest and most expensive boots brought the greatest misfortune. / The policeman gave the Brazilian a derisory look, slightly contemptuous. Then, as if all of a sudden remembering the regulations in force for the fifth year of the war, he gave the Brazilian such a furious punch in the face that the latter fell backwards into the grass. The other police-man kicked the Brazilian, and so the whisperings about such procedures were confirmed after all. They grabbed the unconscious man by the collar, dragged him through of the essence of life, the dirt of the earth and the grass of the days, shoved and kicked him onto the back seat and then chucked in the bundle of underwear and one lost work shoe that a local child had handed to them. And everyone else just gawped, including me. And the Peugeot shunted its way back between compost heap and handcart, and bounced back onto the road, forcing some neighbours to step aside. And it sped away, lurching to avoid the pot-holes. And now it was so quiet that I could hear the pitiful whimpering of the dog from beneath the handcart. And I had a brief peek and the dog looked fearful, but my heart was beating so wildly that I didn't care, not about anything.

In the wake of that episode I felt so unsettled again that I strolled aimlessly around Mondsee until, exhausted, I went to the police sta-tion late that afternoon, only to be told by my uncle that he knew less than I did. The complaint had gone via Linz, as did everything else. But whereas he hadn't been particularly interested in Annemarie Schaller's disappearance, the Brazilian's carelessness seemed to pre-occupy my uncle. It was no trifling matter, how could one be so stupid as to suggest putting the minister for public relations in a straitjacket? Everyone involved must realize that there would be no avoiding a punishment in this case. The Brazilian ought to have kept his mouth shut, he said, as others did, then he would have spared himself many a night on a hard bed. I asked what he meant by *many a night*, what sort of figure were we talking about? Without thinking long about this, Uncle said, 'Six months if he sees sense. Otherwise, like Anton and Anton Lanner, he'll find out that it can be much worse.' / Then he nodded as if he knew it all.

I felt the sudden urge for a drink; the Neue Post was just around the corner. Because I was so despondent the alcohol went straight to my head; after a quarter of a litre of wine I already felt giddy, I wasn't used to it any more. But the air in the Neue Post was so thick with tobacco smoke, kitchen fumes, alcohol and sweat that I could practic-ally lean against it. And those who were drunk may have been staggering about the place, but in that thick air they never fell over. Even lost souls found some support here. / There was a lively discussion about the Brazilian's arrest. One man said the Brazilian had ended up in the wrong place because he belonged in a madhouse rather than prison. All in all, however, there was a basic consensus that what the Brazilian said hadn't been particularly clever. If you wanted to talk, it was best to save this for the cows, and even then you should only whisper. Better to slap your hand over your mouth, otherwise you were responsible and nobody else. 'That's my opinion,' an old man said. And for no apparent reason a hat fell from the hook on the rack and rolled in a puddle of beer.

When I got home I was startled, as I had been several times that day, by the clinking of the keys in my trouser pockets. / The Darmstadt woman was insistent I should have a schnapps seeing as how my nerves were shot. She already had the bottle in her hand. But if I took even a sip of her medicine, I'd be totally gaga. It felt as if nobody could ever remedy the disorder in my life.

Sniffing circumspectly, a mouse slips out from behind the doorframe, where there's a hole. It scuttles across the floor until it finds something it can eat, then vanishes back into its hole. / It's already starting to get dark. I can barely make out the lines on the paper any more.

I kept getting up and going to the window. The Schafberg and Drachenwand stood unperturbed in their places. The Brazilian's garden lay there, abandoned, the greenhouse shimmering peacefully in the light. Somebody had to look after the business, that much was true. And yet I couldn't make up my mind, for deep down what business was it of mine? I didn't want to be drawn into it. The war had taught me to weigh up risks, and if I were careless here I ran the risk of my employer coming to fetch me earlier than anticipated. So it would be better if I ducked out of it; a good soldier never forgets a lesson like that.

Soldier? I felt slightly uneasy having uttered that word in my mind. And another word popped up beside it: *friend*. The Brazilian and I, were we friends? If so, who had actually chosen whom in this friendship? More me than him.

The Darmstadt woman took the rest of the dinner to the dog, which hadn't budged from its position beneath the handcart all day. The woman stroked its back, the dog whined, at which the woman quickly withdrew her hand and gave the dog a reassuring stroke on one of its front paws. She put some water down for the animal. On her way back she looked up and greeted me with the two outstretched fingers that she brought up to her forehead and flicked away again. I saluted in the manner I'd been taught.

Long after darkness had fallen and the child was already asleep, I heard the dog barking feebly. I didn't think anything of the barking at first, but then I heard a tinkle, followed by another and then another. I threw open the window and heard several more tinkling sounds. Figures were scurrying around the greenhouse, and I shouted into the night as loudly as I had done only once before: when screaming for the orderlies after I'd been injured. I was so agitated and my heart was thumping so wildly that I no longer know whether I really did shout. What I do remember is that I fetched my rifle. I was incensed. The shadows scurried away towards the field and meadow, and I fancied I could hear suppressed laughter. Then it was quiet and once more I could hear the dog whimpering.

Not long afterwards I was standing outside the house with the Darmstadt woman. She was rocking the child in her arms and said that if things went on like this it would turn her milk sour. / The landlady briefly poked her head out of the window to ask why I was making such a row, I'd torn her from her sleep. I wanted to hurl the crudest insults at her, but asked myself what the point would be, and so just said, 'There was good reason.' / When the landlady closed her window again we heard from inside her wild, eerie laugh. The Darmstadt woman said, 'I hope the dear Lord grants me the patience to put up with this till the war is over.'

The dog's eyes gleamed beneath the handcart. I held my hand to her muzzle and she licked it. The Darmstadt woman said she suspected they'd broken the dog's spine. She wondered whether the vet should be called and whether now it was a good idea to keep feeding the dog a vegetarian diet, which she felt uneasy about anyway. Still completely agitated, furious and unhappy, I put everything off, saying I would deal with it all in the morning. / I filled the dog's bowl with fresh water.

Overhead the stars were a dense tangle. But I'd had ample opportunity in Russia to get closer to the constellations and they no longer interested me. A few bats fluttered through the darkness with a paper-like sound, those restless souls.

I lay awake by the open window for a long while, listening for every sound outside. In the room next door the Darmstadt woman twisted and turned in her bed. And then I dreamed that Uncle was rising to the ceiling of his office, feet first. Waking around five in the morning with stomach ache, I staggered downstairs to the latrine and exploded, diarrhoea, pure liquid. The pigs slept on undisturbed, ignoring my moans. I lay down again, awake, until the sun came up, then I finally got dressed and went over to the Brazilian's property to inspect the damage.

Eight panes of glass in the greenhouse had been broken and the larger sections of the broken panes were still in their frames. Inside, the orchid beds had been harvested; a few days earlier the Brazilian had planted up some more cucumbers. Large and small shards and slivers lay on the dark earth. Larger pieces of glass had shorn off some of the tomato stems and two plants had been decapitated. Amongst the glass I found stones the size of fists. I left them there until my uncle came to inspect the crime scene with the panting of a heavy smoker. He made no effort to feign any interest in the case, nor did he sacrifice any of his record sheets, arguing that it would be a waste of paper in view of the serious shortage at present. / 'Young and boisterous, that's understandable. Although I'd agree it's a touch excessive,' he said.

Uncle gave off a sour, sweaty tang, he looked sleepy and moved sluggishly like someone who squanders his time waiting and standing around. I stared at him with a mixture of bitterness and anger, and then he referred to himself as an old nag, lamenting that a few years back he'd virtually had his retirement in his pocket, but now it was being postponed year after year, and he was forced to play with fire at every turn, always at the limits of what was respectable. He turned so many blind eyes in every direction that he'd be able to start a second career with the circus after the war. Yet sometimes he thought he'd get nothing in the end but a sound thrashing. What a shame, for in better circumstances he'd have long ago taken to his boat to fish in the lake.

He then asked me to clarify my relationship to the Brazilian. In the town people were already grumbling that I'd do more good at the front than here. They could well believe that Mondsee was a nicer place than the Carpathians for the soldier from Vienna. But it was no good, we were at war, the needs of the moment and all that. / I began by gathering up the shards, saying that the day of my follow-up examination was fast approaching and that my uncle shouldn't rob me of my remaining weeks here. I told him not to worry, I wouldn't become a vegetarian, and after all it had been he who'd arranged the room for me, I hadn't chosen the neighbourhood, I got on well with everybody. / 'Well, well,' he said, twitching his bushy eyebrows in a gesture that I interpreted thus: 'A likely story!' / He watched me pick up the pieces of glass for a while longer, then he let out a 'Bugger it!' and pushed off, coughing, because he'd left his cigarettes on his desk.

Convinced that something had to be done, I set a number of things in motion. I asked Herr Tecini for advice and spoke to the local Party leader. It took a huge amount of effort and several kilograms of cucumbers to get everything on track and secure the glass allocation. Uncle had provided me with the key phrase: *In view of the serious shortage at present.* I reminded the local Party leader of the two hundred evacuee children in his care and that we were talking about seven hundred kilos of tomatoes, a not insignificant sum these days when goods were more valuable than money. The exhausted-looking Party leader confirmed this; there was indeed money, he said, but a shortage of pretty much everything else. I negotiated a price, we agreed a deal verbally, and I thought to myself, what a greedy old hag the Volk Community is!

I was in despair at the amount of work over the following few days. Most of my time was taken up running around to acquire the necessary materials. Again, I was only able to get hold of putty in exchange for a variety of yellow, green and round items. To keep him on my side, I gave my uncle a packet of cigarettes too. As far as he knew, Uncle told me, the Brazilian had been hoarding a few crates of cigars in case things turned really bad. For years these cigars had been sent to him at Christmas by a certain Frau Beatriz de Miranda Texeira, and I should take care that the cigars didn't fall into the wrong hands.

The putty was tough and difficult to shape. The rungs of the ladder were loose, which unnerved me. And from up there, my head above the greenhouse, the flyovers seemed endless. As the squadrons from Italy crossed the lake in glistening formation, it felt as if I were not in the real world. Luckily the feeling passed after I drank some water from the fountain. And I kept struggling with the tough putty. When I came back down the ladder I saw that the leaves of the plants were drooping; they hadn't been watered in three days. And the cucumbers still hadn't been harvested.

It was Friday afternoon and my back was aching. As I wasn't able to attach the hose to the fountain tap, I worked with the watering cans, irrigating with one while the other filled. I had blisters on my hands, which filled up too. And although the door to the greenhouse was open, the sun heated it up inside and sweat poured down my back. / I was about to finish for the day when I heard a squeal. The Darmstadt woman had entered, and in her arms the baby was exploring the range of its vocal possibilities in this very different light and temperature. At least there was somebody who was still able to be happy. / The woman went over to the rear of the greenhouse, laid a blanket on the ground, put her child down, started up the gramophone and took from the pile a record by Rosita Serrano. As the first bar of 'Red Poppy' played she asked me to look after the baby. Then she went outside and attached the hose. I asked her how she'd managed it. She showed me and then beamed with delight at having known exactly what to do. Back home in Darmstadt she had the same system. Then she harvested the cucumbers. 'Better than washing nappies,' she said. She handed me a tomato and told me to take a break. 'You need to relax a little, you're completely worn out.' / I sat on the toolbox, where I'd always sat in winter. At my feet the child lay on her back, her legs in the air, bent at the knees. She watched me eat the tomato. After a while she rubbed her cheeks with her plump little fists as if she were thinking. / I turned the record over and Rosita Serrano sang 'The Stars Were Shining'.

Overnight the weather changed again, bringing more snow, which took everyone by surprise. In any case I needed a rest. I took the diary from my field tunic, which was hanging on a nail to one side, and crossed off the days that had passed. On balance I concluded that April 1944 had been a most unsatisfactory month.

In the jungles of Schwarzindien

In the jungles of Schwarzindien everything went on as normal. There was no further commotion in the camp, the cheeky girls were as cheeky as ever, and Emmi howled at least once a day, so I was told. All the rooms smelled of meadow flowers, and yet the mood was much darker than it had been in winter. This was chiefly down to Nanni and the fact that nobody can be more present than someone who vanishes without trace. The entire camp was fed up with Nanni because she received more attention than all of them put together. The impudent girls grumbled and the more obedient ones shook their heads disapprovingly.

The girls who came with the trolley to fetch the first tomatoes, showing the exeats their teacher had written them, said that they were getting fed up with the stricter supervision they now had and the fewer opportunities to leave the camp. In their free time they were now having to gather plantain and other herbal remedies for the school in Vienna until they were ready to collapse. Nettle salad was appearing more frequently on the menu. And the weather was more changeable now too. They'd only once had all their lessons outside, with the bench by the lake serving as the teacher's desk. There had been talk of swimming when the weather was warmer, but then it had changed again.

The Brazilian was awaiting his trial in police custody in Mozartstrasse, Linz. The legal profession had been raking it in for a number of years now. I received a letter from a lawyer in Vöcklabruck, in which he informed me that the Brazilian was well, albeit black and blue all over from the wooden bed he had to sleep on. There was no reason to assume that the incident in the Adler would have serious consequences. The lawyer then enquired about the greenhouse and my intentions in relation to it. His client, by his own admission, ran the business on his own and begged me to keep it going. / I sat down to compose my reply, mentioned the dog and that the vet had said he couldn't help her, nor would he, because he considered it abnormal for a dog to be fed a vegetarian diet. Finally I set down my proposals. / A few days later I received the letter I'd requested authorizing me to run the market garden, in the name of the Darmstadt woman. At first she said she found the idea surprising and had to think about it. But in the end she agreed after I'd explained to her that my future was uncertain too. From one day to the next I couldn't be sure whether I'd have to return to the front soon.

In the evenings, absolutely shattered, I would fall onto the bed, unmade from the previous day. Often I didn't even bother to wash. Occasionally I still had the strength to plump the pillow, but not always. I frequently worked without pausing for breath, all the while thinking of the Brazilian, picturing him at that moment staring at the walls of his cell. As I listened to the ticking of my watch, the words *doing time* came to mind. And when I looked down at the lake I thought of the phrase *going down*. There are so many words related to imprisonment that I couldn't help regarding it as a fundamental human experience on a par with eating and sleeping.

My life was now one of blistered hands, broken fingernails, bruises and aching muscles. The blisters made me grumpy and the broken fingernails despondent, but the bruises and aching muscles gave me a feeling of satisfaction. I would wrap my blanket around me at half past nine in the evening and rarely lie awake for longer than ten minutes.

Whenever a feeling of unreality came on during my monotonous work in the greenhouse, I took a Pervitin. This soon calmed me and occasionally even made me feel happy. Under the influence of the medicine I also had more stamina. And overall I preferred working to thinking. / Occasionally, when I had the time to take a longer break, I would lie in the Brazilian's hammock. Once the child lay on my stomach and fell asleep. And I slept too until the Darmstadt woman woke me.

She looked after the business side of things. She'd done an apprenticeship in insurance broking at the public health insurance company in Darmstadt before being summoned for wartime auxiliary work in signalling at Frankfurt central station. The tomatoes for the camps were fetched by evacuee girls or the housekeepers. The Darmstadt woman did the deliveries to the restaurants in Mondsee with a trolley. When she was away I looked after the child. She couldn't crawl yet, but would shuffle around in circles on her belly. / My least favourite task was getting rid of those weeds that seemingly never go away. After two hours of weeding I was worried that I'd get a permanent stoop. The hands and the back are the main victims of the horticultural profession. / The Darmstadt woman said that if you were too exacting when gardening you'd never get anything done, something I'd already discovered by now.

The first couple of weeks in May were largely dry. The countryside turned green and the fruit trees started to blossom. The storm season began too, and whenever one broke it didn't do it by halves. The rain would roar so loudly that I could barely hear the thunder, but I did feel the bed shudder. And when lightning flashed through the room I felt a shiver run down my spine. I was permanently worried about hail falling. I feared every cloud in the sky. It struck me that ever since I'd assumed responsibility for the market garden, my fears had increased. I kept wondering how this would turn out, how that would go, and what would happen tomorrow.

The mood in the town continued to be marked by the nagging landlady, bomber squadrons flying overhead, deaths, the stench of latrines, and power cuts. If the landlady didn't like the Wehrmacht report, she would kick the empty dustbin across the yard. At times like that it was best not to talk to her. / No matter how one imagined the war would progress from here, a bad Wehrmacht report put so many people in a foul temper that this inevitably rubbed off on everyone else.

In mid-May the Crimean peninsula fell back into Soviet hands. Entire armies which had once paved the way now no longer existed. In the first few years of the war, following reports by army high command about progress on the front, the wireless would fall silent for the so-called *fallen heroes*. These pauses were five minutes to begin with, then three minutes. But no silences had filled my room since Stalingrad, even though my employer had been relieved of entire armies on several occasions. Now all we ever heard was that part of the front had been retaken. And no mention was made of the fact that soon the whole of Ukraine would be lost, a territory with such huge importance, something the newspapers hadn't tired of demonstrating with statistics a few years ago. The Ukraine, for the conquest of which the bloodiest, most ruthless and brutal campaign in the history of humanity was fought, with me part of it, for a full thirty months. The portion of the Ukraine still occupied was basically worthless swamps and forest, which Germany had as little need of today as she'd had three years ago. And there was the vague impression that people now would be satisfied with the Reich in her old borders. Nonetheless, somebody somewhere was trying to develop a miracle weapon. And no doubt those people who today were lauding the progress of the weapon's development would soon claim that the undertaking had succeeded, this was bound to happen one day.

For my uncle's birthday I left a bottle of wine and a packet of tobacco by his door. Later he told me that the tobacco didn't agree with his stomach. Some things could make the adjustment to bad times, but not an old stomach. Tobacco had become such poor quality that he could hardly stand cigarettes any more. He had such a sour taste in his mouth, he said.

Yesterday evening there was a gas mask exercise in the primary school. The Darmstadt woman stayed at home with her child. I almost fainted. The heat under the tight gas mask, the low-ceilinged shelter with all those people and the emergency lighting. I felt claustrophobic and my heart was thumping.

In a pullover, which she'd put on inside out because she liked it better that way, the Darmstadt woman sat outside the greenhouse, unravelling old socks. We didn't have any more string to tie up the tomatoes and there was no new string to be had anywhere, for it was always sold out before it had even been delivered, all of it needed for packages to be sent to the front. / I was carrying two buckets of weeds to the compost heap.

The heat inside the greenhouse drew the fragrance from the earth. During the day the doors were open, wooden wedges preventing them from closing, to allow the bees inside. It always smelled as if it had just stopped raining an hour earlier and now the sun was shining in the sky again. But whenever I stepped outside I was startled by the cool air and relentless wind that came down from the mountains. / Nappies flapped on the Brazilian's washing line which hung between two apple trees.

When it was time to finish work for the day the Darmstadt woman would go on ahead and prepare something to eat. A quarter of an hour later I washed my hands, swollen from their activity, climbed the irregular steps, took off the old man's clothes that belonged to the Brazilian and which I wore while working, and put on my lance corporal's uniform. Sometimes I'd have a quick cup of coffee and watch the child play until dinner was ready. Some of her toys were broken. I was shocked when the Darmstadt woman said, 'Papa will come soon and fix it.'

I asked her to tell me how she'd met her husband. She said that the soldiers on their way to the West used to throw pieces of paper with their field post numbers out of the train windows, and they frequently found them littered beside the railway tracks. A colleague in signalling had given her Ludwig's address and she'd thought, an Austrian, why not? / Her signalling work had been extremely exhausting, strapped to some apparatus for hours on end without a break. At night she often only got one hour's sleep on three chairs put together. Most of the time she was so tired that she used to nod off on the train back to Darmstadt. After three months of writing to each other Ludwig paid her a visit, following which her friends said they could hear the wedding bells ringing, and then she got another slap from her father, that's enough thank you, and then she wasn't careful in bed any more, and then wantonness, or whatever one might call it, made her get carried away. Did I understand, she asked me, that attitude? Not caring about anything, just wanting to live? Did I understand what she meant? They'd got married at the first opportunity.

She explained she'd been going through a strange phase recently, which she attributed to her belief that she hadn't married the right man. Marriage had seemed to her the best opportunity to get away. And it had nothing but advantages for a soldier too. 'War bride!' she added, bursting out laughing. 'These days the cruel war sticks to every beautiful word there is.' / Once again she said the word in that particular way, so it sounded like crawling, like squatting in holes in the ground. / 'Are you shocked?' she asked. / I uncorked the bottle and mumbled sadly that it didn't surprise me; in my company it often seemed as if the married ones were on leave permanently, meaning there was nothing left for the single ones.

The child burned her tongue while she was being fed, she cried for a while and then was ready for bed. The Darmstadt woman wanted to put her infant down, but she protested so vehemently that she took it out of the washing basket again. I did the same thing a little later: laid the baby down then picked it up again. The child was finally in bed at half past eight and soon fell asleep after a little more whining. The Darmstadt woman and I finished the wine and moaned about the state of the world until I said, 'I must go, it's time for bed.' / As she stood she smoothed down her dress.

Spring had properly sprung now and a mild southerly wind blew over from the mountains. The Darmstadt woman and I were already quite tanned. In the afternoons when we worked in the field outside, it was so warm that I wore my shirt open. A wonderful time or, to put it more accurately, wonderful weather. / That evening we ate under the Brazilian's walnut tree for the first time, listening to the frogs' long evening prayer, and I thought of what they called 'combing the forests', ribbit-ribbit-ribbit. And shooting partisans, from our point of view, was like trying to catch the wind, it brought no advantage, it was all totally pointless, horrible, inhuman. Then onwards in stifling heat, kilometre after kilometre through huge jungle-like areas, and all the while the frogs went ribbit-ribbit.

Because I was worried about having an attack I took a Pervitin and soon afterwards I was in a good mood. The Darmstadt woman and I talked and laughed a lot. We had a peculiar relationship or, to be precise, I found it peculiar because we were so natural with each other, we weren't as stilted and stiff as young people are.

The dog barked. I saw a fox coming out of the greenhouse and my mood immediately soured. Even tiny things like that made me nervous. / I washed my hands at the fountain then spoke to the dog. This creature, to whom the gift of understanding had been granted only to a limited degree, looked at me hopefully with her young eyes as if she were begging me to give her back her hind legs. I gave the dog some watered-down milk to drink. Then she hauled herself with difficulty to the compost heap, dragging her hind legs behind her, had a pee and crawled back to her straw sack beneath the handcart, where it was cooler. Nobody disturbed her there and she could be part of our day, because she had a view of the greenhouse and we often walked past the handcart.

When I rose from my knees I felt dizzy, so I waited until it had passed. Then I wiped down my trouser legs. Once again the sun set, heralding the next rotation of the earth, which regulates natural life with its day and night, not totally insignificant for a market garden.

The child was now really chubby and had red cheeks. The Darmstadt woman did gymnastic exercises with her, stretching and kicking the feet, hanging in the air by the arms, hanging in the air by the legs, standing the child on its head etc. She said she hoped Lilo would become a beautiful and clever girl. / The child slept from seven in the evening until five or six in the morning. During the day she played with her hands or feet, telling them things that nobody else could understand. And she loved visitors. When the evacuee girls came to fetch tomatoes and spent ten minutes with the baby she couldn't believe her luck. People asked whether she had toothache. But it was just her fat cheeks. / Her favourite foods were spinach and semolina pudding.

Once I asked the woman from Darmstadt what she liked about me. To begin with she said a few obvious things, then finally said I made her feel that I liked having her around. She never got the impression that she was disturbing me. And that was true. / She said all women liked that. But it probably didn't mean much to men, on the other hand. / 'It means a lot to me,' I countered. Her face lit up. / She said she was surprised to hear that. Because it was always very loud back home, she said, everyone was delighted to get the chance to spend some time alone. In her experience community had always been an absurd idea. I told her that a large Breughel picture hung in the Kunsthistorisches Museum in Vienna called *Peasant Wedding*. The wedding feast was held in a place of work, I said, and I liked that. Everybody ought to get married in a place of work.

We stood in the greenhouse, looking at each other. Then, plop, plop, plop, there was a brief shower, fat drops of rain. For the next few minutes in the greenhouse it sounded as if someone were rattling their piggy bank. / We sat on the toolbox at the back where the child lay on the floor, staring at her hands, and we drank a beer. 'I like being with you,' the Darmstadt woman said. / It took me a few seconds to realize what she'd just said. Then I said, 'I feel the same.' / And without ever having touched each other outside of work before, we'd probably already been a couple for a week or two. If I hadn't been so flustered and nervous I would have really enjoyed the moment when we admitted this to each other.

The following morning we decided to reward ourselves with the day off. Carrying the child on our backs we took a walk to the lake, drank a quarter of a litre of wine in St Lorenz and shared a cake. Thus refreshed, we were in good spirits when we left. The child was jolly because she was being carried around the whole time. And outside the cafe the Darmstadt woman gave me a kiss, it was our first kiss. And we went on our way, arm in arm. And later she kissed me again, very intimately this time.

She asked me to tell her about myself. I told her about Vienna and my parents. Then she said I should tell her about the war. I said that it had been a terribly slack time for me, and yet not much had escaped me at the front. By which I meant that I'd seen all those things that nobody wants to see. If a village was in our way, we just wiped it out, young and old alike. All that remained amongst the piles of rubble and corpses were a few dishevelled chickens running around. The Russian people had dug themselves into holes in the ground, covered themselves with a few planks, bringing with them a little straw and the few belongings they could salvage. Horrific images. / 'The people were so destitute and starving . . . if we threw even a piece of paper away they would pounce on it like lunatics. And the old ones would kiss your hand if you gave them a piece of soap or bread. And if children kissed the soldiers' boots, I could be fairly sure that something terrible was happening.

'What a shame,' I said, 'that none of these things in my past can be changed any more.'

When we approached the house the landlady looked over from the barn door, and although I moved away from the Darmstadt woman, our last few steps were accompanied by a disapproving stare. In the end the landlady threw her cigarette, only half smoked, into the water trough, and there was a brief hiss.

As I'd had no experience of relationships

As I'd had no experience of relationships I assumed that I would have to start by overcoming a mountain of ignorance. But a few days after Margot and I first slept together I'd learned all the essentials. Here was somebody who was interested in me, who liked me and would rather spend her time with me than with others. There were many things I could tell Margot, far more openly than I could friends and relatives. She was happy to listen and didn't immediately put the worst gloss on things, seeing me in a bad light, as most people do. She laughed when I laughed. And she didn't try to school me. I think she was the person closest to me who didn't try to school me. I knew all of this after four or five days, and there couldn't be much more to find out. I was astonished. And I went around with a self-confidence I'd never experienced before, sensing that I wasn't missing out on anything, that everything was as it should be.

I felt more at ease in Margot's room than in my own. I liked Margot's company and the company of the child. Both made me relax; I forgot my inner turmoil and my envy of others. / I lay on the bed, my hands crossed behind my head. As Margot changed the baby's nappy, she explained what she liked in bed, talking about the pluses of my being on top of her, the pluses of her being on top of me, and why she liked feeling herself. I listened with eyes closed. There were moments when my bitter thoughts left me alone and there was nothing I wanted for.

She said how happy she was that we got on so well, she thought a friendship had to work, that's how she put it. When she said *work*, it was plain she was referring to bed. She said it was only possible to sustain a relationship if the requirements in bed were met and it worked. It worked terribly well for us, luckily, for you always had to consider the possibility that it might not work. Margot said this to me with a wink. / I started to get a sense of why sexuality, even without love, has validity, more validity that love without sexuality, which is like a candle without a wick. / 'Is it a problem for you that it's so important to me?' she asked. / 'I'm happy it's that way,' I said.

After Margot had rubbed moisturizing cream into the child's bottom, she rubbed the rest into her hands. There was still some cream left so she put it on my hands too.

I lay beside her, deep in thought, my left arm beneath her neck. I now had some practice at lying in bed during the daytime. It's strange what war can do to you. Before the war I'd never have voluntarily gone to bed during the day, only when I was ill. Hilde had often spent the day in bed, but nobody else would have ever chosen to. At the front I'd lain down out of boredom, in the driver's cab of my lorry, in the bunker, in the tent, in the former experimental plant, in the cleared-out chicken farm. And now in Mondsee, on a sunny afternoon, I was lying in bed beside a married woman. And on the floor a six-month-old child was sitting on a blanket, smiling at a wooden fire engine.

Margot supposed that in some respects I must be delighted that she was already married. Every man, after all, desired to have a relationship with a married woman. I felt terribly insulted. What made her think I was such a bastard? I requested her not to say anything of the sort again, and she gave me her promise. / 'The fact that you're married and have a child prevented me from wondering whether I might be interested in you,' I said. 'There are natural inhibitions, and when it comes to inhibitions I'm grateful to have them.'

Later, the child sat outside the greenhouse in a warm puddle left behind by the rain, gleefully splashing the dirty water with her hands. Margot and I harvested tomatoes and loaded two crates of them into the trolley the girls from Schwarzindien had brought. / The girls said that the lake was nice and warm already, and they hoped Frau Bildstein would soon relent, for they couldn't wait to experience the lake. / The girls hadn't only grown taller in spring, they'd put on weight too. As nobody bothered to let the hems down, they were all going around in unusually short skirts, like Shirley Temple.

Sometimes I fancied I saw Nanni Schaller snaking her way along a farm track on the camp bicycle. But when the girl came closer I realized that she was younger, an evacuee from the Stabau camp.

Margot fed the dog cooked potatoes and carrots, and the child was given carrots too, but mashed. I breathed in the nettle-like aroma of the tomato plants and felt relaxed. If it hadn't been for the flyovers, reminding me every few days of how unpleasant our times were, the world outside of Mondsee would not have concerned me one bit. On occasion, the lightness that had entered my life seemed to be a completely new beginning. It will all be fine, Margot said.

'I think what I needed most was someone to tell me, "Don't be afraid."' / 'How often do you have to tell yourself that to believe it?' Margot replied, referring to something else. / 'Depends on the individual,' I said.

We didn't make any plans for the future, and I think that was one of the reasons why we found these weeks so enjoyable. You just had to look at the faces of my Berlin employers to see how old they'd grown in the past few years, jaded faces, jaded gestures, jaded arguments. Too many plans. / Every person, at various times in his life, has the opportunity to decide whether to go swimming or make plans. In Berlin they'd been making plans for more than ten years non-stop, and this destroys your personality. I'd given up making plans and felt younger than I had in six years. / What of the future? I couldn't believe in a great future any more; I'd learned to distrust the great future. And so I was absolutely fine with a modest future.

When Margot handed me a letter from the lawyer, I was lying in the Brazilian's hammock with the sleeping child on my chest. The Brazilian had been sentenced by the special court in Vienna, which had sat in Linz, to six months' imprisonment for thinking illicit thoughts and for a failure to keep his counsel. As my uncle had predicted. Two witnesses had downplayed the Brazilian's comments, and one had insisted on several occasions that the Brazilian had appeared to be in a world of his own. The long winter, the lack of a mother, the nights in the greenhouse, the work in the cold frame. Anybody who spent weeks sleeping only fitfully, like an animal in the forest, one eye open, must at some point become overwrought.

The lawyer wrote that six months was the same sentence handed down to a farmer in Gaspolthofen who had chased a bailiff from his house with a pitchfork. With good behaviour the Brazilian ought to be back home in September. But he wouldn't get off so lightly next time, the judge had warned him of this in writing. At present the Brazilian was a Class One criminal, which meant that only family members were permitted to visit and he was allowed to write every four weeks, starting in mid-June.

I asked the landlady whether she would visit her brother. She said her nerves were so bad that the mere thought of chains rattling upset her.

The next morning the child, having lain with us for a while, flopped off the bed. We were worried, but she crawled away with a 'Tatu!' and fetched the wooden fire engine that was still under the table from the previous day. Margot and I stayed in bed, chatting and cuddling until one of us got up to make coffee. / I liked being in her room in the mornings. We were almost always in our pyjamas, drinking coffee. We listened to the wireless, its five frequency bands arranged on top of one another and the magic eye shining green. Margot would breastfeed her child. And sometimes, when the child was lying back in the washing basket, we made love.

Two people who for a while had found their peace, a peace which didn't, as so often, have anything to do with solitude, but with security. When we drank coffee in the morning, the child crawled around on the floor and Margot sat at the table keeping the nappies going by endlessly darning them. New nappies weren't to be had, another sign of our golden age. I leaned at the window and we spoke about various things. And that was it. I'm fully aware that more eventful love stories have been told, but I maintain that mine is one of the loveliest. Take it or leave it.

'You always have to consider the possibility,' Margot said, laughing.

Rome had fallen. That raised a few questions. But we didn't hear much from my employer in Berlin. It was silent for so long that clearly they hadn't yet managed to concoct some favourable explanation for the defeat. / I thought it unlikely that victory would commence in this way. The landlady must have been of a similar mind, for she was despondent and irritable.

Two days later the Allies made their attempt to land in Normandy and gained a foothold. This was part of history too. The Wehrmacht reports made the Polish domestic help sing as she worked. I told her I had nothing against her singing voice, but in her own interests she ought to be more restrained in her delight, her time would come. / Much depended on the West. If the British made advances, as it looked as though they would, then the Soviets would turn up the heat in the East too. The optimists interpreted the invasion of France as an act of desperation by the Anglo-Americans, who must be in serious trouble, otherwise they'd continue to bank on time coming to their rescue. But yet again I didn't think it very likely that my employer would be able to salvage any advantage from his defeats. When the poorest-resourced powers came face to face with the richest-resourced ones, and the latter also enjoyed a clear advantage in population numbers, what might the outcome be?

On the Saturday following the invasion, the Reich athletics competition for all evacuees took place at the Stabau camp, comprising running, long jump and ball throwing. The crickets had chirped loudly the previous evening, a sign that the next day would enjoy fine weather. And yet it was so miserably cold on the Saturday that the girls practically froze in their outfits. / At the invitation of some of the girls, Margot and I watched the competition for an hour. There I saw for the first time the landlady's husband, Dohm the varnisher, who'd arrived on leave the previous day. He'd done well for himself in the General Government; it was said he had his finger in several different pies over there.

Dohm was one of those men who wear black to try to give the impression of greater substance. He was a tall, determined man with angular shoulders and a flat face. The cut of his brown hair was as accentuated as that of his tailored uniform. He arrived by motorbike and inspected the rows of evacuees, nodding contentedly, then gave a short speech in which he insisted that the things you missed out on in your youth were extremely difficult to catch up on later. It was in your youth, he said, that emotions were most heartfelt and distinct, for the personality and the heart were still malleable and all impressions of life still new. Nothing, nothing at all was more damaging during this time than undue haste. Young people could not process too much all at once, it was during this stage of life that problems and defects put down their roots, which was why it was so important for children to do plenty of singing and plenty of sport. He closed with the words: 'Always keep nice and clean, girls!'

He smoked two cigarettes, walking amongst the girls as they ran, jumped and threw, and I couldn't tell whether his scrutiny of the evacuees' backsides was to check their physical development, barely concealed by their outfits, or the food situation in the camp. From time to time he exchanged a few light-hearted words with one of the girls and sometimes he frowned. When the girls whispered behind his back he spun around and said, 'Did I just hear something? Why are you all looking as if there's been a lightning strike.'

Afterwards he came over to me. I saluted, but he gestured to me not to bother. I doubt that he knew who I was yet; it was the first time we'd exchanged friendly words. We began with men's talk. Looking at Margot he used the expression *earthy woman*. Then he talked about shooting marmots, and this made me remember something the Brazilian had said about his brother-in-law: the varnisher had swallowed too much varnish in his peacetime profession. And yet I didn't dislike him. There was something endearing about the buoyant self-confidence of a man who felt appointed to renew the world for his own benefit. / We talked about the war situation, which he judged to be critical: for the hundredth time in the past five years the next few weeks were going to be 'decisive for the war'. / When the host of the Stabau camp came and invited Dohm to lunch, Dohm turned down the invitation, muttering as we walked away that he wasn't so keen on children's food. Then a broad smile spread across his face, and for a moment I could understand why women overlooked some of the less appealing things about him. He vaulted nimbly over the fence and went back to his motorcycle.

Another girl leaped and the sand in the pit flew up, and the girl got to her feet and turned around and saw the imprint of her body in the sand. She swept the hair out of her face. The teacher from Schwarzindien declared the jump legitimate, they measured it and the girl brushed the sand from her arms. The sandpit was smoothed with a rake. A young man, recipient of the Reich swimming certificate first class, who'd trained at the Reich sports school to be a Reich sports official, recorded the distance on his list. The next girl, who had plaits and was swelling with pride, got ready to jump. Her white knickers peeped out of her black gym shorts.

Behind Margot and me the girls' cries still rang out across the meadows and the lake, becoming softer and higher in pitch. I thought of Nanni and pictured her rocking from side to side as she prepared to take her run-up, and counting in her head the paces to the line from where she would have to jump.

I enquired about Nanni when I bumped into my uncle in the street, but again he said that he had no new information. Then he explained just how much you had to know if you wanted to be a good policeman. He underlined the importance of perspicacity, which he implied he possessed in above-average measure, while also emphasizing that you found evidence on your knees rather than in the imagination. On the other hand, given the immaturity of a thirteen-year-old girl, you could not merely count on logical behaviour, you had to consider the possibility of illogical behaviour too, that's to say, imagination. In Nanni Schaller's case, however, he said he was relying on the most likely course of events; the coherence of the clues suggested that the mother must have threatened the girl too severely and so she had run away. / Uncle talked and talked, seemingly trying to make my head go around in circles. I found his chatter at least as boring as waiting all day in a hole in the ground for something to happen, your bleak sense of impotence growing stronger by the hour. / Finally, Uncle used one of his favourite phrases: 'A silly business indeed!'

On Monday the child fell off the table. As Margot bent over to put the dirty nappy in the bucket, the child slid down her back and landed on her head. Margot was distraught, but fortunately it was nothing serious. When I tickled the baby's tummy she laughed and kicked with her legs. Margot said she'd been terrified. I was slightly cross with her and said she ought to be more careful. She swore she hadn't done anything wrong, it had all happened so unbelievably quickly. / 'Take better care, then!' I said. / And at that moment the unreal feeling was back, and I felt the fear flood in and wash me away. Panic-stricken, I rushed out of Margot's room and into mine, took a Pervitin and lay on the bed, where the fear sloshed over me in big waves, engulfing me completely.

Margot clearly sensed something; she came over and said, 'Is something wrong?' / I was shaking as I described to her the solitary chimney breast in Zhytomyr falling towards me and the shootings I'd been forced to watch as an onlooker for months. Margot stroked the sweat-bathed hair from my forehead and said, 'Don't worry, Veit, it's all going to be fine.' / The Pervitin began to take effect very slowly.

Another reason why my anxiety attacks were on the increase was my imminent examination to check whether I was fit for service. As Margot slept, I lay awake, listening to check whether she was still breathing. Why wouldn't she be? Why would she be dead? – Everything is possible – Whenever Margot grunted faintly in her sleep, inwardly I sank back into myself, relieved, but my heart still thumping. I am such an inherently gloomy individual that I'm delighted by the slight snoring of the woman lying beside me, like a single, stray aircraft, its tank almost empty. When Margot finally emitted one of these grunting sounds I was even able to listen to her normal, regular breathing for a while, and then somehow I managed to get back to sleep. / But the periods awake were ever more frequent. Margot lay there, breathing peacefully and deeply, and I lay there with open eyes. In the upper left-hand corner of the window Venus was unnaturally large and bright. A lucky star? How lovely that would be.

I awoke in the morning to find Margot bent over me, smiling, as if she'd been awake for hours. I rubbed my eyes and had a stretch beneath the blanket. When I looked back up at Margot, she was still smiling so I smiled back. Margot got up and opened a window. Outside the sun was shining.

So long as you were not desperate for a swim, it was beautiful now, everything green and vibrant. Margot went into the woods with the child and picked a whole soup bowl full of wild berries. She said it was very relaxing. The potatoes flowered, and dead cockchafers lay everywhere, which was how you could tell that we were well into June. It rained from time to time, and in these moments it occurred to me that the swimming season ought to have begun by now. I felt sorry for the evacuee girls, but otherwise I couldn't care less. I had a nice suntan from my work in the field.

Margot often mentioned her husband and no longer pretended that her marriage had been the best possible decision at the best possible moment. I came to her husband's defence; quite possibly he was sitting in a hole in the ground right now. But she silenced me and said that it wasn't my fault; the marriage had been a mistake. I pointed out that maybe their separation was to blame – the war again. She doubted that, saying, 'Ludwig and I aren't right for each other, it doesn't work.' / Margot certainly wasn't wishing her husband would stay in Russia, but she didn't appear particularly sad when there was no letter from him for ten days.

I hope you received my letter in which I told you that we were entrained. Another week has passed since and in this time we've done all manner of things. We've now been deployed between Vilnius and Lida. Wherever the dust flies around, our division is there. We had a day of rest today and so I'm writing you these lines to give you some news of me again. The dreadful heat is very uncomfortable. But overall I'm well and I hope that everything's all right with you. Because of the situation here I haven't had any post from you in a long time and so I'm slightly concerned. Hopefully some will arrive soon. How is Lilo? Please let her sleep beside an open window even at night and don't forget to lie her on her tummy and on the other side to stop her from becoming lopsided. And please don't be angry with me for writing so little. I want to get some sleep because we've barely shut our eyes for the last seven days. / One year on my parents have now finally received the news that my brother Franz is no longer alive. His submarine went missing.

That evening a storm raged. Time and again the wind tore branches from the trees and hurled them against one of my windows. It sounded as if someone was trying to break into the house. Whenever the wind subsided for a few seconds, I heard Margot next door calming the child. And I thought of how in Mondsee people were now saying Margot was one of those women who jumped into bed with anybody. It hurt me that in the eyes of others I was just any old person.

Even my uncle took a dim view of our relationship. He'd brought the matter up when I'd met him in the street and enquired about Nanni. / 'So you're messing around with the Reich German woman, are you?' / 'Who told you that?' / 'It's hardly a secret.' / I didn't respond and listened to the crackle of burning tobacco as Uncle took a drag on his cigarette. / 'Your domestic arrangements are none of my business,' he said. 'But people think you've been idling around here long enough and you might as well try your luck at the front. Seeing as you're my nephew, I can't merely ignore this talk.' / We parted company sullenly.

The following day began with a mist, but it soon cleared and the steep peak of the Schafberg stood out abruptly, growing up out of the distance, partly covered in snow and shifting its gaze southwards. The Drachenwand looked gruffly over at us. / As I harvested tomatoes, Margot did cartwheels in the Brazilian's garden, then she washed her hands and face at the fountain, came over to me and stroked my face tenderly, which made my spine tingle. I felt as if she'd sought me out.

In front of the house the landlady's husband stood in the black uniform of the order, smoking with his head back. After a while he crossed the road and came over to the handcart where the dog was lying on its straw sack. A few days earlier the dog had started squinting and now she spent most of the time with her tongue hanging out. The varnisher spoke to the animal, presumably about the merits and demerits of those aspects of life relevant to him. The dog pricked up her ears as if trying to understand the varnisher. But she didn't understand him. I watched the two of them, shadowy figures through the dirty panes of the greenhouse, and when I realized what was about to happen it was too late. Dohm, still speaking, pulled the pistol from his holster, placed his left hand on the creature's head and set the pistol at her neck. I ran, and was just in the doorway of the greenhouse when the shot was fired. A wild, uncontrollable twitching ran down the dog's spine, with a violence one wouldn't imagine those shattered bones could still possess. A few more mild twitches followed, then the creature lay gently on her side and stretched out her white paws with a soft mutter. Every muscle relaxed. And Dohm, who had stood up again, slipped his pistol back into its holster and looked at me close up with a curiosity that no longer contained any hint of sympathy. / All worked up, I asked him if he'd gone mad. I saw the blood trickle from the dog's large, soft ears, very dark blood, trickling down the fur of her neck and slowly seeping into the straw sack beside her head.

'Stand to attention!' Dohm said in a gruff, cold voice. I froze, and after a brief pause for thought I saluted as befitted my rank. / 'Is there a problem?' he asked. / 'I'm going to report you,' I said. / 'You will kindly refrain from that,' he said, bored. And all of a sudden I felt so intimidated that I reacted with a curt bow.

For several minutes Margot and I sat on the ground beside the dog, gazing at her. I stroked her soft back several times and Margot caressed her white paws. / Later we buried the creature beneath the elder at the rear of the garden, where the meadow began. I felt listless.

Margot dragged a stone over, placed it on top of the grave and said, 'It's about time this war came to an end.'

This was the day before I travelled to Vienna for my follow-up examination. I sat alone in my room until half past one in the morning, crunching coffee beans between my teeth and writing.

In the morning I packed

In the morning I packed my things and left Mondsee with the milk van. As I said goodbye to Margot I hadn't yet realized how happy I'd been over the past few weeks. When the train pulled out of the station I suddenly found myself in the middle of a jam-packed carriage, all alone. I felt so isolated and lonely that I would have happily got out again at St Gilgen. The further I was from Mondsee, the more desolate I felt. I slept as best I could or dozed.

As ever during the war, the train was unfortunately very busy. It was also stiflingly hot. In my compartment was a nun who had a migraine, which meant the window had to stay shut. She wore a long, black tunic and a bonnet. The only parts of her body showing were the face and hands. I enjoyed talking to her. When I hinted at my dread at possibly having to return to front-line duty, she waited for a suitable moment then whispered that I ought to smoke aspirin.

The train made good progress, but in the Lower Danube district we were diverted because of damage to the overhead wire. The conductor said the cargo of a goods train had derailed, tearing down a few pylons and destroying the electrical line. / Soon the countryside became flat. Where they were still cutting hay, some of the work was being carried out by women and prisoners of war.

Margot had made me two sandwiches for the journey. I didn't want to eat them at first, because the bulge in my jacket pocket filled me with affection. Later on it was too hot to eat and so I didn't have the sandwiches until we were almost in Vienna.

And my thoughts kept returning to that strange, mad world I'd been part of for five years and which possessed a door I might have to step through again soon. I was terribly worried about the examination, the chemistry inside my body wasn't right, and when I got off the train my arms and legs felt stiff as if I'd just recovered from a bad case of flu.

At the exit my papers were checked by plain-clothed policemen, who let me pass after about a minute of close scrutiny. Relieved, I stepped out onto the station forecourt and turned towards Neubaugürtel. The number of cars had decreased again, but the pace at which people walked had accelerated. Chins pressed tightly to chests, they hurried on their way as fast as possible. Get away from here, just get away, they seemed to be thinking, no matter where they happened to be. / On the side of a building was written large the slogan: *We will prevail*.

My parents' apartment stank so horribly of moth powder, mothballs and moth cream that I almost passed out. Mama had to give me a glass of wine straightaway. My parents were living a really primitive existence. Half of their furniture was in the cellar, the books were packed in crates, the bed linen rolled and tied up, everything in the cellar, the cupboards and chests of drawers virtually empty, the moth poison stewing inside them. / Papa said they were now living like bears; their real home was the cellar. / In Russia, right at the beginning of the campaign, we'd made passable conversation with the local population. Their eyes were on stalks when some soldiers showed them pictures of home and their apartments. The Russians asked us what we were doing here when it was so lovely back home. That's what I told Papa.

At least Papa's claptrap about inevitable victory had finally been superseded by claptrap insisting that defeat must not be allowed to happen. Allowed – allowed – allowed. But of course nobody was asking Papa for permission. And what also struck me on that first evening was that, when he talked about the war, Papa no longer used the words *definitely* and *without fail*, but *hopefully*. His new favourite phrase was: 'Hopefully we will hold out on every front.'

Because Papa was my father, I refrained from giving him my views on this in all its consequences. But he sensed I was trying to go easy on him, which he found aggravating because it gave him the impression, not without some justification, that he was being patronized. He snapped at me that it made him feel like a village idiot. 'We're all village idiots,' I said.

On New Year's Eve 1938, Papa had raised his glass and said, 'What a year for me and the world!' And I had drunk a toast to him. When the speech to celebrate the surrender of France was broadcast over the wireless, Papa couldn't stop crying, as Mama wrote to me in a letter. And Papa had hovered over the wireless like a vulture ever since. If a few days passed without any reports he became jittery. I suspected that something would be missing from his life when the war was finally over.

A few days after the Anschluss we went up to the cemetery and laid flowers on Hilde's grave. And Papa stuck a swastika pennant in the earth roughly where Hilde's heart would once have been. Papa kissed Mama, which was such an unusual event that I found it embarrassing. Years later, when I was no longer at home, I received letters in which Papa commented on reports of victories with phrases such as: 'If only Hilde could have been around for this!' / A crow flies above the city, pursued by spirits.

I visited Hilde's grave this time too, on the morning following my arrival. My lucky star was rotting beneath the earth. / From the cemetery I went to the barracks. I saw on the way there that a large number of individual houses had been gutted by fire or reduced to rubble. At the gate I showed the soldier on duty the order from the recruiting district headquarters, and he pointed me in the direction of the sickbay where the examination was to take place. A medical orderly said, 'Take a seat, you will be called.'

Sitting in the waiting room were two men, a little older than me. They didn't acknowledge me and I didn't acknowledge them. One was missing three fingers and he was squeezing his hand. The other had a dented cheek, though he could still see out of both eyes. The eye in question was not fully protected by the lid, it clearly protruded, and to begin with I thought it was double the size of the other one, a veritable bull's eye. I was happy when the man immediately lowered his head again. Nobody talked. We were all thinking about how alone we would be when we faced the doctor.

For three-quarters of an hour nobody took any interest in me. My mood . . . I felt so impatient and tense, as if they were going to break my arms and legs. I sat there as if I'd turned to stone. And my thoughts shifted between Margot and the child, and my uncertain future. I was fully aware that my hopes of the call-up being deferred again were over-optimistic, given the changes in the war situation. At present barely anybody was able to keep himself out of harm's way. The conflict carried off everyone who was young and male. / I felt myself being watched by the bull's eye. I was tortured by fear. In my helplessness I wished I could freeze my life until it resumed in a better world.

At last they called my name. I handed the doctor the file with all the findings – I had certificates coming out of my ears. He briefly skimmed them all, examined me and diagnosed severe tension. I'd known that for ages. I listed all my complaints, but he was barely interested in what I had to say and just examined my tonsils. So I described again my headaches and suggested that they might be connected to my jaw fracture. I also told him that my headaches meant I couldn't wear a metal helmet. / 'Right, good,' he said and sent me away. / His report arrived at the office half an hour later. I learned that the doctor had certified me as fit. *Fit for active service.* I immediately went to see the medical officer and demanded to be examined by a specialist. I wasn't going to be sent back to the front that easily.

The doctor came out again, not especially pleased that I didn't think much of his report. He said that the examination I was demanding wouldn't change anything; not even a specialist could do anything to cure my headaches or nerves, they would just prescribe tablets too. / 'But I can't be permanently swallowing pills at the front,' I said. / 'Out there you'll soon wean yourself off them,' he said. / The conversation went back and forth. I demanded to be X-rayed. That wouldn't help, came the reply. But I insisted, because I expected it would offer some insight into the cause of my headaches. The cause had already been established, he said, the headaches were down to the jaw fracture and weren't that severe anyway. / 'Do you know that?' / After lengthy discussion I managed to secure an appointment with a specialist for the following day, having emphasized that this was an injury sustained in combat. Was he seriously going to deny me a consultation with a specialist? / I came within a whisker of being sent back to the front, and there nobody would have cared two hoots about me.

When I came out of the barracks I took a Pervitin. I just couldn't cope with this misery any more; the mere thought of anything military made me shudder, it was all so pointless. And whenever I thought of how life had been before the war I felt miserable. / On my way home the entire city seemed to be in a state of chronic irascibility. If I got in someone's way even slightly or took my time because I was deep in thought, I had a confrontation with that golden Viennese heart which is notorious for the intensity of its emotional outbursts. Otherwise just wax masks and grey faces and men missing arms and legs, this difficult time a burden on all of them, everything bleak, even the shop windows that had nothing on display save a few scrubbing brushes. / Luckily the Pervitin started to take effect. When I arrived in Possingergasse I felt less weighed down.

I bumped into Hupferl Gmoser on the stairs. Hilde and he had been the consumptives in our block. Hupferl still coughed into his hand, he was two years older than me and I asked him how he was feeling. / 'Comme ci, comme ça,' he said. / I took his shoulder and joked, 'One might think you'd just come back from the Western Front.' / 'I should be so lucky!' he replied, coughing into his hand again. Presumably we were thinking the same thing. / 'Don't be so glum, Hupferl, you're not missing much.' / He laughed bitterly. 'Being healthy is a national duty, which makes me a burden on the nation.' / Once he'd said that his head sank forward momentarily, as if he regretted something he didn't dare say out loud. One sad day I would get a letter from Mama with the death notice enclosed, consisting of a pious saying and a portrait of Hupferl in shirt and tie, which he'd never been seen in apart from that occasion at the photographer's and at the memorial for his dead brother. And I would recall one final time how we always used to play football with Hupferl Gmoser as our spectator behind the fence. And that would be it.

On the day before Hilde died, the sun had shone from the morning onwards, and early in the afternoon Hupferl had summoned the football team. Later, Papa Glaser had tried to take the ball away because we were being so noisy, and even the Jew on the first floor had called out of the window that we should be quieter. Hupferl stood by the fence and jeered, sometimes applauding, sometimes coughing. / Then Waltraud came down to fetch me because Hilde wanted to see me. I wiped the sweat from my face and lent my plimsolls to one of the Stanek boys while I was gone.

'I've so been looking forward to this tryst,' Hilde said in her thin, fluttery voice. Her use of the word *tryst* made me falter briefly, as I associated it with lovers. I often thought about this later, after Hilde's death.

The spit-bottle stood amongst various boxes of medicines on her bedside table. I can recall the names of some of these: Coramine, strophanthin, tuberculin. And I remember all those fattening diets Hilde had to undergo. She was always having to eat as much butter as possible, butter by the pound, but it didn't help one bit. In the end she had a yellow face and hollow cheeks; she looked as if a gust of wind would blow her over. A few days before she died another tooth snapped off.

From out of the blanket came her right hand, scrawny and yellow, followed by an angular wrist. I saw this hand lay itself on my knee, stroke my knee tentatively. This made me feel uncomfortable; I couldn't help thinking of the skin on Hilde's fingertips that was always open. I sat there, unable to return her gesture of affection with anything affectionate on my part. My heart was throbbing and I just wanted to be back with the footballers outside. We talked a bit, she asked me about school, and from time to time she said she was feeling slightly better today, but she was afraid of jinxing it, for whenever she said she was feeling better something went wrong again soon afterwards.

I am still touched by the word *tryst* today, and I can see Hilde's hesitant smile, utterly lost in her yellow, hollow face. / I also remember Papa's comment: 'She's not going to get better.'

I shook Hupferl's hand and briefly placed my left hand behind his right ear in a friendly gesture. Then I went up to our apartment and wrote a long letter to Margot, outlining my fears that our life together would be brought to an end for the foreseeable future. It was the first letter I'd ever concluded with a declaration of love. / I just hung around for the rest of the day, which I would have loved to have spent sleeping but couldn't because my mind kept returning to the examination. And all the while I listened to what was going on outside. Fear sharpens the senses.

When, at supper, Papa insisted once again that the nation's very existence was at stake and that we had to fight it out to the last, because we had no other choice, I got up and left the room. What *the last* actually meant was something only soldiers really knew, that's to say people like myself.

Papa always pretended he was being harshest on himself. But if one took a closer look, this harshness was rather fuzzy. He seemed to live the life he considered to be right, and by coincidence it happened to be a comfortable life too. Mama ironed out any difficulties for him. And Volk Community or no Volk Community, Papa sent his private letters to Inge in Graz via Inge's husband's field post address. This didn't just save on postage, it was strictly forbidden.

My appointment with the specialist was at the military hospital in Liniengasse. The doctor was an old man and not particularly considerate. He peppered his talk with swear words; I soon stopped listening. Peering up my nose with the help of some device, he said it was only possible to relieve the headaches and the whole bloody nasal bone might have to be removed, but that could wait until the end of the war. Overall, someone like me could be presented to students as an example of robustness.

I begged him not to mock me. In June 1938 I finished school with distinction, but hadn't yet seen a university from the inside. If the war hadn't got in my way I'd have easily finished my studies by now, I said. My passage to a better future, beyond mediocrity, was being forcefully blocked by people like him. 'I would like to know,' I told him, 'what I did so wrong to warrant this punishment of being stuck in the mire for almost six years now.' / He looked up and said, 'What the hell do you mean?' When he asked me a few questions I sensed he could understand how pained I was by the years I'd lost. / I said that in Berlin they were calculating that an entire age group would be wiped out, which in the overall scheme of things might not be such a calamity because another generation was on its way. For me, however, it was a disaster. / He asked whether my real problem was my studies. I replied that I had lots of problems. He nodded and pointed out that this was true of almost everyone; just having lots of problems wasn't enough.

The doctor skimmed my entire file again. It was a good thing that

I'd twice visited the infirmary in Vöcklabruck because of my complaints, otherwise it would have sounded implausible when I now said, 'I'm a bone that's been sucked dry.' / 'Hopefully you'll be up to working in the garrison.' And although the doctor had overruled every one of my objections to begin with, this comment was partially uttered as a question, and so I felt prompted to say, 'As far as I'm concerned, life in the garrison is like a stealthy suicide.'

He gave me a disapproving look, but behind this professional scowl I could make out an old man's smile. And for a fleeting moment I felt totally clear-headed and said exactly what I felt. 'The Krauts are so long-winded and boring.' / At this the doctor burst out laughing, wiped tears from his eyes, laughed again, grabbed my arm firmly, convulsed with laughter once more, going bright red in the face, turned away, calmed himself a little, then burst out laughing yet again. He tried to repeat what I'd said, but failed. He tried a second time, but failed again. Finally he gave up.

It was a while before he was able to talk again, then he said, 'So, you have headaches on a daily basis, which are so bad that they can impair your vision from one moment to the next?' / I nodded. / 'And you're also a suicide risk?' / I nodded. / The doctor scribbled a few notes. I asked whether it might be worth applying for a permit to study. He pulled a face and said that such a move was risky because some of the worst shirkers hung around the universities. Would there be any problem with my remaining an invalid for the time being? I shook my head. Then he dismissed me.

With a new certificate of deferment in my hand I felt giddy. I don't know why, but I expect it was due to happiness. Back home, however, I was totally exhausted, which must have been the nervous strain from the examination, but also the release of tension. It was such an unusual feeling to be free of anxiety. I had every reason to skip for joy, but felt mere emptiness, albeit a happy sort of emptiness. And yet I was dreadfully passive, tired, worn out, and had to force myself to tidy away my medical papers. Just looking at them made me feel uneasy, reminding me of the uncertainty surrounding the deferral I'd been granted, on condition that I report every two months to the infirmary in Vöcklabruck for examination. In my mind I was still pleading my case before the doctors: head, nerves, nose, nerves, tablets, head, nerves. And the night was a continuation of the day.

Finally I'm sitting back in a railway carriage. I'm happy to be out of Vienna. I'm no longer used to the commotion and the tension. And I can feel the pull of Mondsee. When I think of Margot I sense that I can have a happy life too.

I put my notebook away again and looked out of the train window through a gap in the boards. Only a handful of windows on the train still had glass panes, most were boarded up, giving a dim light in the carriages. Outside the landscape flew past. Near Linz there was an air-raid alert and we had to wait in some woods for an hour while the aircraft passed overhead from the south. All in all it was a pretty journey, as the train went via Gmunden. It was hard to tell what the weather would do; there was the odd shower and the fragrance of damp earth wafted through the boards. I breathed it in deeply. It smelled of rain, of summer. I peered frequently through the boards, glimpsing freshly mown meadows, blood-red poppies standing at the edges of cornfields, and all of a sudden a narrow, bright shaft of light fell onto the countryside. The fields in the foreground shone very brightly, an unnatural yellow. A church tower flashed white, while everything around it slumbered in a purple-blue storm light. Then the sun broke through and the first lakes came into view. I felt like rejoicing.

I got out at Bad Ischl and walked to the edge of the village, where a military vehicle took me to Mondsee. It was now half past seven in the evening, and as I walked up the gravel road, dusty and tired, and saw the greenhouse bathed in evening light, it felt as if I'd never been away. The dog roses were blooming, the meadows were iridescent with flowers, and I was pleased that they hadn't been mown yet. And just behind the greenhouse, as if by way of a greeting, a deer stood by a stile. I had to take several deep breaths to calm my heart.

Margot stepped out of the greenhouse and beamed when she saw me coming, greeting me in that by now familiar salute of flicking two outstretched fingers away from her forehead.

I'm still bewildered

I'm still bewildered that you ran away, supposedly. I can't understand it and I shudder when I think about it. I've tried everything to forget for a while the thoughts that haunt me all day long, but even in the cinema I got up in the middle of the film and raced out, because I kept thinking: My God, what's wrong? My God, what's wrong? Where's Nanni? / I wandered the streets alone, talking to myself and people turned to stare at me. / And Mama and Papa are making my misery even worse by being very harsh on me at the moment. I keep having the shivers.

I'm continuing to write poste restante and I really hope you get in touch soon. And please don't be angry with me, I did want to come to Schwarzindien even though Ferdl's older brother said that the barriers at the station are manned by gendarmes and that you have to be especially careful of police on the trains. That wouldn't have stopped me. But the course in Kledering was arranged at short notice – I sent you a postcard immediately. Did you get it? I could have dealt with Papa and Mama, but not with the recruiting district headquarters. / We had instruction from morning till night, ballistics, aircraft recognition. And at night I slept in a heated sleeper carriage, imagining that I'd wake up the following morning at Schwarzindien station. But every day I woke up at the marshalling yard in Kledering. I can't tell you how unhappy I was. / Now I think I ought to have run away too. I'm really sorry, Nanni, my Schorsche. Papa's book says: People do not stumble over mountains, they trip up over stones.

It's now half past two in the morning, I've been awake since half past twelve and thoughts are churning in my head. You know what they are. I'm so worried about you, and on top of that there's the trouble with my parents. Both of them are very tense and in the evenings I have to act as lightning conductor for their bad moods. They're getting at me for everything at the moment, but all I want is a little peace and quiet. Instead I get nothing but nagging, scolding and reproach. Sometimes I stick my fingers in my ears and I often feel as if I'm living in a total daze. I could just run away, if only I knew where to go.

Today, when I was sitting in the kitchen, I had such a weird sensation, it felt as if there were no relationship between Mama and me, and as if we hadn't spoken to each other in ages. Let her go into Susi's bed when Papa is on night shift. I'm no longer going to tell her what's on my mind. I might tell her the unimportant things.

When Ferdl picked me up early on Monday morning I said a curt goodbye to Mama. We were already on the floor below when she came out of our apartment and asked whether I'd come back up. 'No,' I said. / 'It's like that, then?' she said. / When we'd packed everything onto our bicycles I called up a few times to say we were going. It took forever for Mama to come to the window and say, 'Look after yourself, Kurt.' / I know it wasn't nice of me not to give her a kiss goodbye, but what can I do seeing as she loses it so often.

Ferdl and I usually take the train to Schwechat, but when the weather's nice we cycle because we're angry we don't get Wehrmacht tickets on account of our H Youth armbands. Because an air-raid alert can happen at any moment we have to be ready at all times. Our school tuition takes place in the artillery battery. But when nothing's happening we have to do drill or field exercises. There's never enough food and all of us are completely starving from the physical exertion.

I'm not sure about being with the listening personnel. Those on the floodlights at least get to see the aircraft in the beams. Those in the artillery see the shells explode in the sky.

With the acoustic locators you sit in your dark room and you can only think: *I've got it! I can hear the aeroplane!* You have to keep quiet. It might be great to see successful hits, but we only get told about them. / I like the acoustic locator on quiet days, because it means I can be alone. When I mentioned this to Mama she said that I could do my schoolwork in there. But all I do is kill time. I listen to flocks of crows and think of you, dear Nanni. / Sometimes I'll use the acoustic locator to follow a flock flying over the fields of Mannswörth, I hear the contented squawking and the slow beating of their wings when the wind is in the right direction. I'm tired a lot of the time. I often shut my eyes and feel as if I'm in the middle of the flock on my way to you.

There's constant noise outside, which you wouldn't notice so much usually. Somewhere a nail is being knocked in, somewhere a cuckoo is calling, somewhere a child is crying, somewhere a shot is fired, somewhere a flute is being practised, and somewhere somebody is lying beneath a tree, snoring. It's one big jumble of sound. And I'm always hoping that into this jumble of sound comes your voice and I can direct the acoustic locator towards it, and then I can hear you talking at the station, where the trains are whistling, a single to Vienna please, I've seen a bit of the world, rejected a Maharaja's hand in marriage and now I'm going back home, I bet Kurt is completely listless by now and Mama is on her own in the evenings.

Your mother is very lonely, she wanders around like a ghost and her face looks like a corpse's. I brought her a kilo of cherries a while back and she gave me such a funny look. I don't know what she was thinking, nor do I want to know. Sometimes she comes over and sits with us, and just stares into the distance. She's really very pale.

You've no idea what it's like in Vienna at the moment. Somehow we muddle through, but it can't get any worse. Mama too feels great anxiety now and she jumps at the slightest thing. It's good that she can take her mind off things on Sundays when she sees her cousin. They go to the cinema in the evening. Not many people go any more. I don't know why.

There were reports on the wireless about the air raids last week. Maybe you heard them. I was really scared when the bombs fell on our positions. / Flyers were dropped, warning of attacks in advance, and the most grisly rumours went around that the city would be reduced to rubble and ashes. The authorities issued denials, claiming that the enemy was just trying to scare people. / On Friday morning it was cloudy, murky and everyone was exhausted after the tension of the previous days. On the wireless they announced from Berlin the beginning of the retaliation. At half past nine everyone went for a late breakfast and I stayed in my post for a while to listen to the crows. I didn't want to have to queue so long to get my food. Then I left the acoustic locator because it had started to rain. Outside, small drops fell onto my face. I was surprised by how soft the rain sounded outside the acoustic locator. I hurried the two hundred metres back to the barracks and for the first time in ages I suddenly had a slight feeling that the war had nothing to do with me.

Afterwards the wind broke up the clouds and a warm sun came out. I returned to my post because I wanted to write a few lines. I was nervous and had the strange sense that something was looming. In this mood I sat there alone, the headphones in front of me, and then the pre-raid warning sounded. Five minutes later we reported we were ready to fire.

Now I have to thank God that I escaped unscathed, for it could have ended very differently. On both sides of the road that leads to our position the bombs made large craters, some of them so large that you could have placed a house inside them. Endless clumps of earth, stones and shrapnel fell on us. Our lives were seriously in danger. It felt like hail on our metal helmets. I wasn't even under cover, because my device was damaged right at the beginning, so I had to help reload an artillery piece. I just had my metal helmet and one piece of shrapnel landed right by my feet.

To the left of the road the oil refinery has been destroyed and several tanks with a total of 10,000 tonnes of crude oil are in flames. The final fires have not yet been put out and there are always several fire engines at the fire ponds. In Schwechat lots of windows have been blasted out. The last little house on the right, quite a way out, has been flattened. Eight people who were in the cellar were killed. It's a very sad sight. The parish church has been closed because it's in danger of collapsing. Four bombs fell through the roof and ceiling, but not a single one exploded. We need a bit of luck from time to time, the church would have been flattened too otherwise. Out where we are they say that five oil plants have been burned to the ground. I wonder what else we will live to see, or not live to see.

It's always Americans who come, which makes me feel a little sad.

You know how I wanted to go to America when I'd finished school and spend a few years going around the country on a decent motorcycle, stealing a bit of money here, a bit of food there, and just enjoying life. Have you made up your mind whether you'll join me, Nanni? If so, tell me.

You have to dream of India to find America.

The swirling dust and the fires have darkened the sun. The wind is blowing dust and ash into my eyes. The burning oil tanks are pouring black smoke into the wind and the wind is carrying it southwards. All I can make out of the refinery is the outline.

Our lovely world is falling apart, dear Nanni, it's over, and the next attack might come tomorrow. What will be will be. So, my good angel, don't forget *your* Kurti if he doesn't write to you any more.

In the evenings I'm always in bed by nine o'clock, I hope you believe me when I say this. I'm missing you so much, Nanni, I want you to know that. When I'm lying in my room at nine in the evening and there's nobody knocking on the wall I feel anxious, I can't get used to it. At night I wake with a start because I think I've heard knocking, and I sit upright and listen to hear whether you've come home, then I knock and there's no answer and I know it's not true. I'm listening all the time, at my post during the daytime and at night in bed. I think I'm going mad. And I'm so miserable that I haven't heard anything from my Nanni. I have the entire day to dream and to wish. I'm at a loss as to what to do. My whole life has come to a standstill.

I often feel such longing for you, I can't tell you. I can't believe I haven't seen you in so long. In my dreams you would be back in India, I'd dress up as a girl and live there with you in the same room. Sadly that won't be possible because I've grown again. I'm only a couple of centimetres shy of Papa now and his brown suit fits me nicely. You'd be astonished at how well I've developed over the past six months, and if you look closely I already look quite a lot like a man. / I've swapped my coat with a comrade as his one was too large. The army socks are useless, so almost all of us wear our own.

The plague of mice in our barracks is almost unbearable. When I sit at the table I can see the mice playing amongst the traps. They squeak and leap around all night long. Thank goodness there's enough food lying around the place, otherwise they'd start nibbling at me. Whenever I open my schoolbag it's perfectly normal to see one of the creatures scurry out. We asked the platoon commander for some poison to try to control this nightmare, but he doesn't care. / When a yellow cloud drifted over from the burning refinery to our position after Friday's attack, the platoon commander declared a poison alert so we tore our masks from our belts and duly put them on. Hardi immediately wrenched his mask off again because he couldn't breathe. Fearing for his life he whacked the filter and a mouse leaped out of the tube. You can imagine the scene. The bomber squadron overhead.

It's been high summer for the past two days and ever since this morning the usual smell of the refinery has been wafting over to us. It's working normally again. During the day you can wander around barechested, the roads dry quickly and it's dusty almost everywhere. With the improvement in the weather we can possibly expect more attacks, at the moment it's still quiet. But of course, a decisive outcome would be most welcome.

When we go swimming in the fire pond in the evenings, the war sometimes vanishes from my thoughts. And sometimes I believe that one day I'll find you waiting for me beside our post. From the barracks window all I ever see are my comrades' girlfriends. And when they kiss it weighs heavily on my heart.

Yesterday evening when I knocked on the wall I heard a knocking back. Excited, I knocked again and another response came. I ran out, called your name and woke everybody up, including Susi, and it turned out that your mother had been sleeping in your bed and she knocked back because she was so lonely. Her eyes were tear-stained, she kept saying everything was Greek to her and she kept wandering around in circles. Then we all had a glass of wine together, all apart from Susi, and your mother looked at me with sad eyes, as if she still believed I know where you are. Eventually I plucked up courage and said, 'I miss Nanni just as much as you do.' / We decided that when you're back you'll get those omelettes and puddings you love so much, assuming of course that we've got white flour. At the moment there's only one kilogram per month, which means the potatoes have to do the job. Your bed is exactly as you left it in January and your mother wishes with all her heart that you'll be sleeping in it again soon. I hope you've got somewhere warm to sleep now.

I have such a lovely picture of your homecoming in my head: you ring the doorbell and immediately throw your arms around me. Then the two of us go to the Prater and ride the carousel and the roller coaster. These are the thoughts I have before going to sleep at night.

And I dream of feather beds while lying here on a straw sack, being bitten by lice. / I hope the time will come when all of us can sleep in our own beds again.

Frau Brand from block 6 has married again. You know the woman I mean, the tall blonde. She found her first husband too serious, and now she's married to a Herr Jarosz, who Mama says is even more serious. *It takes all sorts*, as you would put it. And Frau Angela from block three says she's not long for this world, but she wants to go to Anton Hikker's wedding, it'll be a joy, number 3 will go wild with excitement. You'll be back in your lovely bed, Schorsche, you'll sleep so well and never go away again and I'll knock on your wall in the mornings. I don't care about anything else so long as you come back. I'm so terrified that something might have happened to you. / Bye-bye, Schorsche, I can't write any more today, I feel so unhappy because I don't know where you are.

Yesterday came the latest serious air raid, and a bomb that fell nearby blasted half of the field into our position. From inside my acoustic locator I can't see anything, but the others say they're dropping bombs like you'd shovel coal. And in all honesty the flak is hardly hitting a thing. / You sometimes feel a tiny tear in the eardrum from a blast, and then you know that one was really close. / There was a direct hit on an incomplete, uninhabited house within sight of our position. The woman hadn't lived there for ages because she became deranged after her husband was killed, our platoon commander told us, so now she's in a sanatorium.

We spent the afternoon cleaning up the oil tankers on the Lobau, and now we're sitting in the barracks, killing time. Two comrades are playing chess, one is assembling some wireless pieces he found, two more are plucking a chicken, which they found too, of course. And the last one is lying on his bed, writing: that's me.

Apparently a dozen concentration camp inmates in Zwölfaxing used the air attack to escape, so we've been instructed to report any suspicious-looking persons. But all of us reckon that they must be in Vienna or Hungary by now. Zwölfaxing is the neighbouring village, they build aircraft there and supposedly everything's been destroyed. Many inmates and camp guards died. / But otherwise, if you discount the bombs, we're all quite well here, my darling.

Sascha was in Vienna a week ago because her father was on leave. Ferdl took me to see her and she talked about Schwarzindien. I let her speak, hoping she would say something about you. But she didn't talk about anything important, not a word about you, even though I made several attempts to encourage her. / I also met Frau Musil, your schoolfriend's mother, and asked her what news she had from Schwarzindien. But I didn't get very far. Either she didn't answer my questions or made a real song and dance about it. In the end I told her that the way people were treating me wasn't easy for me. She seemed to understand my point and didn't say another word.

Please, please don't think ill of me for not having come at Easter. Please don't be angry any more. I'm not my own master here, you know, quite apart from the fact that I don't have money for tickets and the like. It drives me mad. I get quite cross too when I think of how long it is since we last saw each other. The two of us.

It's now midsummer weather: sultry and stormy. You have to forgive my handwriting, it's not very nice any more. I'm sitting in the acoustic locator, sweating badly. The flies and mosquitoes are really bothersome, you can't sleep at night with everything imaginable crawling around and your whole body itching. / In Schwarzindien they'll be doing lots of swimming now. I'm really quite tanned too. We sweat buckets when we march off to bomb craters with our shovels.

When I sit in the acoustic locator during quiet periods and listen to the world, I sometimes feel that I'm on the verge of hearing what I need to hear so that I finally understand. But I never get close enough. This often happens. I keep feeling there's a whole heap of things other people know, they're born with this knowledge, and I hear the crows squawk.

Mama only gave me one bollocking today. She didn't have the

chance for any more because I spent the whole day hiding. Not really hiding, I was just always somewhere else, including at your mother's. / Ever since your mother knocked on the wall we've been getting on better. I visit her regularly, she calms down a bit when I'm with her. During the day it's all right because she's got her work, but when she comes home . . . I can understand how she feels. Everything is torture for her. I tell myself that you never know if helping others is a good thing or not. It's been such a hard time for her, but that's now passing too. And hopefully you'll come home soon. / In the evenings your mother and I sit in the same room, listening to the wireless, I write and she massages her hands. She's still riveting spade carriers, but it's no longer piece work, which means she's only earning twenty-two Reichsmarks a week now, for she can't manage two hundred and fifty carriers per day, and she doesn't want to completely ruin her nerves for a war profiteer, as she calls him. Mama has got hold of some Buerlecithin for your mother, which she's taking to get herself back on an even keel. Your mother says she's feeling better already. Four weeks ago she just sat there staring into the distance.

There are lots of air-raid alerts. It's definitely not ideal here. Mama and Susi sit in the cellar amongst the coal and potatoes, the explosions shudder wave-like through the ground, mortar trickles from between the bricks and the air pressure causes the ventilation flaps to clatter. After the last air raid the damaged houses on Alszeile sank even lower. When I visited them they looked as if they were only still standing out of habit. / It's such a shame for our beautiful Vienna. It's raining today. No other news.

At Schwechat station they apprehended an escaped convict, who put up serious resistance. They beat him until he was unconscious. / Yesterday we lost a football match against the flak helpers from Laxenburg. The others watched from their positions and bunkers as if they were in boxes at the theatre.

Now then, dear Nanni, dear Schorsche, please don't do anything silly, and come home soon, I beg you. I spend most of the day thinking about you, and even more so when I go to sleep. I must sign off now, I can barely see any more. The storm has died down a little. Whenever I write to you it always becomes a little calmer in here.

When I think of you I picture you in Schwarzindien, and until I know where you've got to, you'll remain in Schwarzindien. *Schwarzindien* . . . it sounds so different now from back in March, now it sounds as if it's not just around the corner. You've been away for three months, I haven't heard a peep out of you. All the things that can happen in three months! How far away can you get in three months? And why aren't you writing me a postcard from wherever you are? From the Ganges. Please send a card from the Ganges to make me feel less anxious. Your mother says she thinks you're dead. That makes me shudder and I can't help but think of what Erhard says about war: 'You won't believe what a human being is capable of.'

School is slowly fading away. They've decided to exempt us from the final school year, it's all part of Total Commitment. I've had to mobilize my dormant studiousness and I've been distracting myself with my books. Unfortunately I'm not able to concentrate as hard as I did a year ago. My thoughts forever wander astray. And the magnificent summer weather outside. Sometimes I sit with your mother in the evening, but mostly I sit amongst walls of books. It'll work out somehow. / I will have easily passed the written examinations, they weren't so difficult overall and they want everyone to pass them. The oral examinations will be a mere formality. Then it'll be our turn soon; it seems as if they're trying to win the war with Ferdl and me.

They've just been playing your favourite song on the wireless: the 'Dorfschwalben'. It was so lovely when we were all together at New Year and you sang the song for us. / Where are you, Nanni? Is where you are better than in India? Do you really not understand what you have to do? It would be best if you came back to Vienna, I mean it's now three years since we last saw each other. If you came I would give you so many kisses. No inch of you would remain unkissed.

And if the Schwarzindien wilderness still has ears, let me just say that I don't understand any of this. I don't understand what you want from Nanni and me. / Another saying goes: In the end everything is all right. If it isn't all right, it isn't the end.

Our farewell to Vienna

Our farewell to Vienna may have been brief, but it was no less haunting for the memory, a sombre affair. It set the tone for the entire journey and only started to ease off as we gradually became settled in Budapest. Vienna? For all of us the city of our birth. Because we'd delayed our departure for so long, it prevented us from feeling homesick immediately. In a funny way the homesickness had already come and gone while we were still in Vienna. We soon became detached from the city, in fact the day after we moved in with István in Stáhly utca. Today Vienna practically doesn't exist for us any more.

We arrived at István's block absolutely shattered. It felt as if we'd expended our last reserves of energy to escape to somewhere that was dark and mysterious to begin with, and only became light after several days. / My first impression of our new digs was dismal, I had never imagined it would be so small and squalid. I said nothing to István, of course, but he apologized. I said he mustn't be sorry, our expectations hadn't been high and we weren't particularly surprised. He looked mortified. / Whenever you need the loo your bladder bursts before it's finally free, it's appalling. The neighbours are nice. When we moved in Frau Földényi brought us some cake.

That first night the three of us slept on István's sofa, one above the other. Although it was cramped, we felt mightily relieved. The following night Georgili slept on the floor on a bed made of clothes. Thus we settled into the stuffy room and lived as well as the circumstances would allow. / All in all the loo is passable, when it's finally free, just a little small. Whenever I sit down I hit my head against the door. It's usually clean.

Once we'd arrived in Budapest, Wally's state of mind quickly changed. I hadn't seen her so happy in ages. She was so delighted that we were living in Budapest. Living! We were allowed to go to the parks and to the Danube. We even enjoyed the fog. 'We thought we really knew Vienna, but that can't have been right,' Wally said. 'For if we had we would have left earlier.' / I bought her a cotton scarf from a street merchant, and Wally liked it so much that she said it made her feel like a young woman again. / Our luck had not deserted us. Every day Wally thought about how she could do something nice for Georg and me. And hopefully the money issue would soon resolve itself.

We ate breakfast at nine, then we went for a two-hour walk, the fresh air did us the world of good. On the Danube promenade it was as if all our difficulties had been swept away. Georgili did cartwheels and talked a lot. How different life was here from in Vienna. We stared goggle-eyed at the bridges. Magnificent! And the shop displays were decorated so splendidly, with splendid things on display. But don't ask about the prices. / When we were hungry we bought fruit or vegetables and ate them outside, in the sun. I'd never have thought that I would prefer Budapest to Vienna. The city is laid out more beautifully with the river and the bridges. Everything's livelier here. And for the first time in a long time we started making positive plans for the future.

In the summer before our arrival the Hungarians had handed most of the non-Hungarian Jews over to the Germans. For that reason the first thing we needed was a legal status of whatever kind, for protection. We had to get rid of the passports with the large J on the front that had been forced on us in Vienna. Unfortunately we lacked the money to buy good papers. But István – God bless this wonderful man – managed to get us the papers of a Hungarian Jew who'd had the means to become Aryanized. / According to these I'm fifty years old, too old for the labour brigades. / Sometimes I feel certain that we'll be able to stay in Budapest until the war is over.

Thanks to the relatively good food here we improved physically too. In Vienna we'd reached the stage where we looked terrible. I was pleased to see some colour in Wally's and Georgili's faces; we'd got over the worst. Georgili started playing with other children too. He ran around Kerepesi Cemetery and brought back bread and sweets from the old women. I expect the children sometimes stole fruit too, but I never asked him for any details. / Things went better than anticipated initially. And because in this total era we had become total have-nots, we sent Georgili to school so as to give him something that couldn't be taken away from him at the next street corner. For a few months he went to the school in Wesselényi utca. The curriculum was tailored for emigration, with foreign languages given top priority.

The double-enveloped letters that come from Fairfield Park in Bath, Somerset, via neutral countries bring me nothing but good news of my Bernili boy. He's having a really good time there, staying with the local scout leader, a family showering the boy with love. Bernili is tall and strong, life in the scouts is good for him. He's already reached the third rank, is learning diligently how to cook, and he can tie knots and give signals perfectly. He only speaks and writes English now because neither his first host family nor the current one speak a word of German. Given that there's no future for us in Germany, it's not so much of a shame about his German. / Bernili makes me very happy.

Today is a leap day, 29 February 1944. We've now been in Budapest for two years and three months. How quickly time passes and how slowly the war progresses. Georgili has been in hospital for seven weeks, and will remain there until 3 March, but he's already better and no longer has a fever. He's really been through the mill. In the fourth week he had a second bout of scarlet fever. And every day we're waiting for the authorities to decide whether he should be sent to England. I have great hopes for this, because staying here in the long term is very difficult. Wally has really been through it with Georgili too, for you can imagine what it means to be sick in this terrible situation and in this wretched neighbourhood, and such a horrible illness at that. I wander around all day long, begging for the things Georgili urgently needs. He should eat lots of fruit and sugary foods and he greedily asks for them too. / In the beginning his rash was bad, his arm red and very hard, he cried all night long, and I'm afraid to say that Wally and I are not good at doing without sleep. / Now I'm sitting beside his bed, writing. Later I'm going to sew a button back onto my coat.

I've learned a lot of Hungarian and I speak it rather well now. I can follow the films in the cinema and also make conversation with people, which I really enjoy. Wally still has trouble with the language and doesn't like speaking it any more. Now that I'm reasonably fluent she gets me to translate everything. I've tried giving her lessons in the evenings using the book, but she wriggles out of it, claiming she's too tired. In other words, she doesn't want to, though it would be very useful for us. / Maybe it will start falling into place when Georgili speaks better Hungarian than German.

In our early days here I worked as a night watchman at the paper factory. Towards the end of 1943 I became an assistant at a grain mill on Czepel island. Then I crushed the nail on my little finger while pushing an iron wheelbarrow. Later the fingertip started to suppurate. Everything was cut away, including the nail, a large bandage was wrapped around my finger and I was no longer able to work. / They put me to sleep for the operation. That was a funny sensation: you can actually feel your heart fading away. Someone who was given the same anaesthetic before me screamed out in fear. I shouldn't want to go through this too often. / My finger is better now, the nail is slowly growing back and in the end you won't notice anything. There's no discomfort, but I have to be careful not to bump it hard because the fingertip is still sensitive.

I started work again a week ago, now at the Tungram warehouse. I've grown a Hungarian 'tache and it makes me look like someone suited to this sort of work. It's hard labour, though, heavy loads that leave one panting for breath. Up till now I've just about survived, but I've lost weight again. / Unfortunately I'm the kind of person who needs a quiet life and so in many respects I'm not a man for a hard struggle.

Georgili's sick again, we're sitting permanently beside his hospital bed. Because his body is lacking vitamins, he's developed a rash on his eyes, which is terribly painful. I hope he can be back home again soon, even though it's *very* sad here. / Jeannette, my dear, dear, kind cousin, please write me a few lines, make me happy by offering me a ray of light during this sad time. And if you possibly can, send us some money to István's address.

You must have heard about the German occupation of Hungary. It's all starting over again here now. Everyone is awash with fear, we're open-mouthed with terror. Yesterday, after Georgili had gone to sleep, we whispered to each other our worries. 'What's going to happen now?' 'Are we going to flee again?' 'But where to?' We're at our wits' end.

The city is seething and pulsating as if it were the eve of Doomsday. Everybody urgently needs to sort something out, everyone's trying to earn a few pengős or jockey themselves into a better position some other way. On a human level too, the city is having a closing-down sale. We watch the chaos in the street from our window. I've stopped going to work, it's too risky now.

In the end coming to Budapest was a mistake. One often has bad luck, and sadly I seem to have it more often than most. Sometimes when I lie on my bed, all is quiet, and my soul detaches itself from my body, I can see myself with Wally and Georg on board a ship just before it comes into port in Haifa. On the horizon is bare Mount Carmel. / István is angry, he doesn't like me railing against fate. You can't expect anyone to have an imagination that just predicts the worst, he says. A sound mind doesn't always anticipate the worst. / I turned to the window and had to put my hand over my mouth to stop myself saying anything.

I only leave the house when the sun's shining, and then I stick to the shady side of the street. It's less dangerous, you encounter fewer Germans and those you do meet are preoccupied with their own business. Nobody has ever taken exception to me on the shady side of the street, whereas on the sunny side I had to get on all fours and turn myself into a desk for a young soldier so he could write a letter several pages long. *Dear Margarete . . .*

I'm just back from the post office, where I was sending a letter to Bernili. He's doing fine, thank God. I had to hurry, for who knows whether I'll be able to send letters via Switzerland tomorrow? It's not nice here, my only happiness is to know that all of you are away and in safety. / I don't know what's going to happen to us, we're just going to have to stick it out, no matter what comes our way.

It's getting increasingly difficult to move around safely under a false name. I go out when necessary, hurrying, running from the Community to the Committee, intent on changing my identity again. You really have to help me get dear Wally and dear Georgili away from Budapest, by somehow sending either a cheque or money to my brother's address. I don't know what will happen otherwise. The law on Jews means my brother has lost his job, and even before that he had nothing to his name, so he's at rock bottom.

I went wandering through Budapest this morning in search of help, making enquiries, earning money, keeping watch and endlessly going from one place to the next. Life is consumed by daily routines like this, always with my head bowed to get from one place to another as inconspicuously as possible. I'm very careful not to attract attention, I've become a coward. I slip almost invisibly past my former countrymen. I avoid contact with Germans, but whenever I hear an Austrian accent I'm especially wary.

A few Jews were sitting in the Committee's backyard, exhausted and tormented by uncertainty, discussing the rumour that only the Hasids in the East and Transylvania were being deported. The atmosphere there was conducive to blasphemy. When I said that I envied the Hasids' faith in God, a Pole replied, 'God? Let the Germans kill him. He deserves it most of all.'

It's always the same with these Poles. They come here, never with their families, but with dark rings around their eyes, telling their stories, this was no exception, children beaten to death and some tossed into the air and shot. 'I'd rather be killed three times over right now than fall into German hands,' he said. He wiped his face with his hand and claimed that a secret of human nature had been revealed to him: human inhumanity.

Because the Poles are now trying hardest of all to get out of Hungary, we talked about other escape possibilities. The Pole said he'd arrived last winter, and that someone who'd struggled for sheer survival had an advantage in winter over those who weren't forced to be out in the cold. The best chances of getting through were on the darkest nights with the hardest frost. He advised me not to let any opportunity slip by, as you never knew what was around the corner. He'd known people who'd missed out on an opportunity merely for a child's birthday. He was an experienced victim of persecution, an expert at escapes. It was a new profession which had evolved over the past few years and you couldn't afford the slightest carelessness any longer. He was going to join the partisans in Serbia.

'A large fortune would be an advantage,' the Pole said. 'The Germans make a business of everything. They pretend to be disgusted by any dealings with money, but in reality they're the ones who've made themselves the slaves of money. The Germans are waging war hand to mouth. If they don't find any new plundering grounds in the next six months, they're finished. It's been going on like this for six years and now it's Hungary's turn. Nobody is greedier for money than the Germans, they'd fill bottles with Jews' piss if they could charge for it. And do you know what they have a particular passion for? Offsetting human life with money.'

He appealed to my intelligence and breathed directly into my face. He mentioned concentration camps and the construction of huge factories, and that anybody unable to work was sent to the gas chamber. / 'You're not being serious?' I said. / 'Yes, because killing people is such an effort otherwise. It's far less bother that way.'

I'd become used to rumours of this sort, and because the Pole could tell that I didn't believe him, he said I must be prepared for the worst, most of us would perish. Those were his parting words. / Because he'd looked so serious, I told István about it and begged him to ask his better-informed acquaintances. He came back with the information that there was no acute danger at present because we were needed as labour. But if so many refugees continued to flood in from Moldavia and the Ukraine, they soon wouldn't need us any more. He was going to join the first labour detail he could find.

As István packed up a few things, I knew that life would be difficult without him. I waited until this feeling subsided, then I thanked István for the support he'd lent us over what had been almost two and a half years, giving him a hug and kiss. 'Who knows, Oskar,' he said, 'maybe I'll see the Kremlin again.' / István went to the goods station where the labourers were assembled and transported away in brigades. God bless him!

Yesterday was warm after a succession of cold days, as hot as Vienna in July. Wally and Georgili were out for an hour and came back home exhausted. Wally ran downstairs immediately to fetch some fresh water. And while she had a wash I caught myself thinking of the Pole and what he'd said about letting opportunities slip by. When Wally finished washing she poured the dirty water into the bucket beneath the basin and said, 'And so it begins again, another long period of living in fear.' / Georg sat at the table and drew the view of St Rókus Hospital. Later he played with the skipping rope, Georg, my handsome boy.

I haven't worked in weeks. We're living off beans, peas and lentils, or nothing at all. To put on our bread we've got some lard, which in this heat we're all fed up with. / Apparently, endlessly long goods trains with Hungarian vegetable oil and preserved peaches are going to Germany. People say that the goods trains would be twice as long if they had sufficient rolling stock.

Unfortunately I've now got to take greater risks to be able to cover the rent for István's room. On the twenty-fourth, God be praised, I had some success: I bought an electric cooker off a German for seventy pengős, then sold it on again the same day for a hundred pengős more. That keeps us going for a few days. / When I showed Wally the money she said her heart wasn't beating, it was singing. I was happy to see her smile, something that happens all too rarely. And Wally said, 'This is a miserable time, but we'll struggle through again and one day we'll be through this.' / Her sudden faith in my fighting spirit made me apprehensive.

I'm horrified to see my reflection in the shop windows. I've become so thin and my hair is streaked with grey. I'm a man with an ashen face in a badly fitting, worn suit, walking on the shady side of the street. All the bones in my body stick out, I have stomach cramps almost every day, I'm no longer useful for anything and my appearance is rapidly aligning with the age given in my passport. A homeless refugee, a homeless and stateless individual, going under a false name, with false papers, with the wrong blood, at the wrong time, in the wrong life, in the wrong world.

I could tell time was passing by things such as my fingernail, which had now grown back completely. And Georgili had grown too; Wally had let down the hem of his good pair of trousers, one last time, I won't be able to do it again, she said. / We were all hoping that the war would soon come to an end.

The war! There was the hope, of course, that everything would end abruptly, talk of this was everywhere. For a year and a half the Red

Army had been pushing the Germans back, and yet the Wehrmacht continued to strut around Budapest like cockerels, looking far less hounded than myself. / BoomBoomBoom-Boom . . . BoomBoom Boom-Boom . . . This is London! . . . This is London! . . . First, the headlines! / We learned from the news that the Americans had taken Rome and had entrenched themselves on the French coast. Several German armies had been annihilated by the Red Army in Byelorussia. That sounded promising. Unfortunately, the front was moving westwards more slowly than we'd been hoping for months. The Red Army's major efforts were focused on the Baltics in the north and Roumania in the south.

Yesterday there was an air raid on Budapest. Flyers were dropped alongside the bombs, warning the Hungarian government and calling on the population to protect the Hungarian Jews. There was silent jubilation amongst the Jews of Budapest and angry remarks at the Hungarians' sudden concern that their reputation abroad might be damaged.

Despite this, orders threatening people with being shot reappeared in display cases. The handwriting was familiar: these were the very slightly modified decrees of the Reich. And so Wally and I decided to go to Roumania. We'd managed to get out of Vienna without too much difficulty, and Wally had faith that God would be kind to us. / Wally had to do the majority of outings, for the danger of her being dragged away for labour service wasn't as great. At every turn my threadbare suit marked me out for what I was. I envied those men on the street in their unblemished suits.

Near Elisabeth Bridge I met Berl Feuerzeug, whom I knew from Vienna. He had Aryan papers on him and felt safe. He said he was well, he'd got engaged. We didn't say much more as both of us were afraid that strangers might be listening. To tell him something personal I said that I often had nightmares. He comforted me and said he had them too from time to time. We then went our separate ways.

As we planned our next escape I could feel how worn out I was. I felt as if I'd spent a day carrying bricks to one place only for someone to turn up and tell me the bricks needed to be taken somewhere quite different.

The food allocations were like starvation rations, we suffered from not having enough to live on. At the Jewish self-help organization I begged for some soles to double up my shoes, as I'd already worn through to my socks. The money was nowhere near enough, I was going around in a permanent state of hunger. / On Friday I queued up for something to eat, they were serving cholent, which tasted so good that I really wanted to ask for the recipe. I imagined cooking cholent for the whole family on a Friday. Not in Vienna, but in Accra, Gold Coast, in a single-storey building with a straw roof. / All of us looked terrible again.

I wonder how our handsome Bernili is. We regard him as an islander at liberty, the proprietor of a better future. Here he would be forbidden from going to the park with his friends. Even in the inner courtyard of the star-marked building we've been forced to move into, the children risk having their ball taken away. / I'm glad that I've been able to protect at least one of the people I love.

Last night I dreamed of potatoes for the first time. In the past my dreams used to be more sophisticated.

I threw away our real papers two years ago because they were the wrong ones to have, and the false ones we now have are not real. With the real ones I'd get a letter of protection from the Vatican. But with our false papers it's hard to find someone who might help us. / You can tell how bad a time is by the fact that not even your minor mistakes are forgiven.

I haven't written for six weeks, for I've been so anxious and worried and haven't been able to gather my thoughts. The worst possible thing has happened, the thing I have been fearing all this time. It's worse than terrible, I feel as if I'm in free fall, unable to hold onto anything.

On Sunday 16 July, we got up at eight o'clock. It was a windy day, but no rain, unfortunately, for the wind had blown the clouds away. We breakfasted on the dry bread and bitter tea we've been reduced to. Wally took Georgili to Sunday school. I accompanied them as far as the front door, we kissed and I watched them until they'd turned the corner. That was our goodbye. / When they hadn't returned by the afternoon, my anxiety grew by the hour. I went to the Community, where they told me that Wally and Georg had never arrived at Sunday school. After a few more enquiries I learned that there had been a round-up on Klauzál tér, but nobody could furnish me with any more details.

When I went to bed late that night I didn't realize how bad it would get. For a long time I ruminated on how things might straighten out, begging that this dark day would soon be forgotten too. Three days later I was so miserable, anxious and tense that Dr Weisbrod shook me. I wouldn't survive for long if I went on like this, he said, I might as well hang myself now; this wasn't helping anyone.

Wally and I had agreed on a meeting point if we ever became separated and it was impossible to return to the apartment. But Wally and Georgili didn't appear at the agreed place, nor did they leave any sort of message there. And when I voiced my distress, a neighbour asked for Georg and Wally's clothes, saying, 'Others need them more urgently now.' / This unhinged me once and for all. For several days I was more listless than I'd been since we were kicked out of our apartment in Possingergasse. Everything was far away and seemed to be getting ever more distant. Nothing was of any importance. If someone had told me they were giving out New Zealand visas on Vörösmarty tér, I'd have simply said, 'Please leave me alone, do what you want with the New Zealand visa, but please spare me, I can't go on any more.'

I'd often imagined coming home and not finding Wally and Georg there. I'd resolved not to leave any stone unturned, and even risk my life if necessary, because life without Wally was worthless. But now I was completely apathetic.

In the course of my enquiries a secretary told me quite insistently that there was nothing I could do for Wally and Georgili at the moment, and that I ought to get myself to safety. / If I were to disappear now too, nobody would notice. There's nobody waiting for me here, nobody who wants anything from me. If I were not here, there would be a free mattress and one fewer sleeping on the floor. / My heart pounding, I eat the last of the plums.

The routines every person has have been stripped from me. You turn around to say something, but nobody's there. It's in such trivial moments that I realize how much I miss Wally. / Wally, with whom I went hand in hand for fifteen years, sometimes her in front and sometimes me. Then this person disappears all of a sudden, slips from your hand, you turn around, but there's nothing there, literally nothing. It's simply been extinguished, as if blown away by a gust of wind. / Dear God, take me away one night and nobody will know a thing. Peace, peace, that's what I need and I cannot find it. Who is here to tell me they love me? Nobody any more. I'm going to bed now and I beg never to wake up again. Never again.

It's raining and I'm exhausted, distraught at how life is kicking me into a corner. I live in a state of permanent tension – that's not good either. And I've been very jumpy of late, I think this is down to my loneliness. I live in unbearable, rigid loneliness, I am alone in a hopeless situation. I'm barely alive. Barely.

There are two things I clearly remember. First, our arrival in Budapest when I bought Wally the scarf and we were so happy that we danced in István's room, laughing and crying until we collapsed, out of breath, on his bed. And then our holiday on Lake Garda, when we sat on the bench eating peaches, peaches fifteen centimetres in diameter with the most wonderful juice. And Wally said, 'I can hear the wind on David's harp.' / In my dream I whisper to Georgili, 'Drink this, it'll make you better.'

And day and night it's always the same: self-reproach. Why didn't I take greater care? I go through our final days together, looking for what I missed, and imagine things, such as Wally telling me she and Georgili were moving into the Swedish embassy, which was only taking in women and children. Then this nightmare dissipates and I see Wally and Georg enter Klauzál tér, which is cordoned off behind them. / 'No, Wally! Run away! Head for Vörösmarty! Quick!' / Then I bite into the scarf I bought for Wally outside Keleti station, a connection to happier times.

Dear God, I am content with everything, I'm not asking for a soft bed, I'm not even asking for our old apartment back. Just Wally and the children. We will struggle through if we're allowed to live. Nothing is so important, one can even live off someone else's discarded potato peelings if one is otherwise left in peace.

Yesterday I threw the keys to our Possingergasse apartment into the Danube. I'd been carrying them around with me for ages, the key to the front door, the key to our apartment door, the key to the cellar. Then I sat in the courtyard of the yellow-star block and allowed myself to be warmed by the autumn sun. Not that it's cold, but I haven't eaten my fill in days. I wouldn't have imagined how cold you can get from feeling hungry.

I can't write any more, nor do I wish to. It's all too sad and I'm almost at the end of my tether. There is no more help to be had.

Dear Jeannette, I cannot tell you anything about where Wally and Georg are now. They've gone away. Georgili had completely recovered and I'd been striving to give the child as much fruit as possible to supplement his diet. What with his illness and the poverty, we had a real struggle bringing up that sweet boy, but despite the human wickedness around us we were able to steer him through all the sad times. I can say with some satisfaction that I more or less managed it by force and by taking many roundabout ways. Georgili was a brave boy, he spoke good Hungarian by the end and was an artful little lad. Although his father Oskar went missing and I, Uncle Sándor, looked after him so well, he and Wally had to go away. I don't know where the two of them are. So it makes no sense for you to write *Dear Oskar* in future, because he is either missing or dead. But Wally and Georgili are certainly very brave, even if Wally might think she can't go on any more. If you have contact with them, tell Wally to stay calm because she has Georgili with her and because Bernili is doing well in England. / Love and kisses from your Uncle Sándor.

Sándor Milch is writing this.

Debrecen has finally fallen.

As I wrote in my 'sign of life' card

As I wrote in my 'sign of life' card, I'm alive and our house is still standing. Ninety-nine per cent of Darmstadt is destroyed. Light, gas and water are supplied by the local Party organization, though sometimes we're without them altogether. Five of my siblings' houses are in ruins, as is Aunt Emma's. I hope they're still alive. Nothing's happened to Aunt Liesel. Berti and Möschen's places have been *totally* flattened. All that remains is the air-raid warning. Everyone's fled from the development. The only ones still here are Luft, the Kressers, the Stegels and Frau Dösch. Heimstättenweg, the school, Pulverhäuserweg, Forstweg: almost everything burned to the ground. I would say come home, but the barracks here are still standing and they might try to bomb those too. Rheinstrasse's just one big heap of rubble, the second post office is destroyed, the station partially destroyed. I haven't heard from you in a long while, the last letter was the one in which you wrote about the storm. A postal car should be coming now to collect the mail. Hopefully it will bring something soon. Countless people have died. Dear Margot, I hope to God you and the child stay well, and hope I do too. / Uncle Flor, Jokel, Ernst, Georg Hinz and Hinze Erlenfath have lost everything, Aunt Gusti only the glass in her windows.

The sky droned, the earth droned, the air in the cellar droned. It felt as if mountains were crashing down. I kept thinking the next bomb had our names on it. The pastor says the blast made the organ pipes ring out. / In our cellar they first tried to get over their fear by playing cards, then they got down on their knees. And outside in the streets people with blankets wrapped around them ran for their lives. Soot and smoke everywhere, it burns your throat and eyes and the sun can't shine through. Everything's destroyed, all cables disconnected . . . everything!

The atmosphere's been very different these past couple of days. It's eerily quiet and sooty, and there's not a single child on the streets. Helen and Helga are still missing, so many bodies are burned to a cinder, and often you can't even tell whether they're male or female.

Uncle Flor has seen lots already. I already said in a previous letter that Uncle Flor, Heinrich, Ernst, Jokel and Hinze Erlenfath had been bombed out. We've only got damage to the roof and windows, but I hardly dare say this. Some of your colleagues might have died. I don't see anyone because I don't have a bicycle and can't go into town. There's no light either and no sirens to signal when the bombers are on their way back. There's no water or gas, hopefully it'll be over soon.

Berti was just here and said that everyone from the Jagdschloss is still alive but they've all been bombed out apart from Fräulein Speier (Liebfrauenstrasse). Kläre's in hospital in Eberstadt with two burnt hands and a burnt foot. Her mother, grandfather and uncle are dead. Her father's on the Siegfried Line. She dragged her mother out until her hands were burning and she couldn't hold her any more. Then she lost a shoe and her sock came off too, and she kept running with her bare foot. The foot's in a terrible way, it's covered in a thick layer of ointment. There's not much to see at the moment, the bandage is being changed every day. It's all so horrific. They say 22,000 people have died so far. Aunt Emma and Uncle Georg still haven't been dug out of the rubble yet. Corpses are unrecognizable. It's still so hot in the cellar that the soldiers can't stay down there for long. Herr Weingärtner couldn't pick out Aunt Helen from all the dead bodies in the public air-raid shelter. He collapsed unconscious, unable to look at the children to see whether Helga was amongst them. He would have recognized her by the shoes if they weren't too badly burnt. I haven't been able to sleep in the eight days since. Dear Margot, you know what that means for me. I've bandaged my right hand as I've got a burnt thumb. I'm finding it hard to work and yet I'm forever having to wash potatoes for the goats. The skies have been quieter the last couple of days. Bombs with time fuses are still exploding. They don't wake yesterday's dead.

Dead ducks are floating on the ponds, loads of trees have come down in the parks, everything's destroyed, so many people dead. On Tuesday night I had a family of five sleeping with us, who used to live above Friedl on the second floor. All the beds were full. I also have to tell you that Manfred Diesle has been killed in action, which means almost all of your former admirers are now dead. Nothing but very sad news. / I'll see to it that I get my money tomorrow, because everything was locked up on Friday, bank, pharmacy, laundry . . . none of these are still standing.

Today I went to the parish hall in Kahlertstrasse to get an old letter from you. And also a card Papa sent from Baumholder. I very much doubt Papa is still there, but I sent him a telegram anyway. You must have received my two sad letters by now. Berti popped by to say that everyone from the Jagdschloss is alive. But all of their homes are bombed out save Fräulein Speier in Liebfrauenstrasse. Kläre's in hospital in Eberstadt, both hands and one foot burnt. She can barely speak due to the smoke poisoning, and couldn't see a thing for a day either. Only a few people are still living in that very narrow street, Kiesstrasse. / As he was running away Herr Hans had two rats on his coat, which were also trying to flee. They were so afraid of the fire that they leaped onto Herr Hans's coat.

Apparently there's nothing left of some houses save for a pile of ashes. The keys and a few other objects sit as clumps in the ashes.

Here in Eichbaumeck it's not as bad as it is in the city centre, but it's bad enough. Some houses have collapsed, telephone booths flattened by the blasts, lighting pylons knocked over, tangles of wires. Gerda Göller and Fräulein Meisel were buried alive for a few hours. Four rabbits died when their lungs burst, including the old Giant Papillon. I buried them behind the goat shed.

I don't know whether you've been getting post from me recently. As I wrote in a telegram and three long letters, our beautiful Darmstadt has been destroyed. We had a major air raid on 11 September, which cost many thousands of lives, sadly including Aunt Emma and Uncle Georg, Aunt Helen and Helga, Walters, Frau Beck, Uncle Heinrich's parents and siblings, and many, many people we know. There's no trace of Aunt Helen or Helga. These are very difficult times we're living through here. Ninety per cent of Darmstadt has been destroyed and all your work colleagues have been bombed out except for Fräulein Speier in Liebfrauenstrasse. I've already told you all of this, but the entire city centre, including the main post office, was burned to the ground in the attack. The following day the second post office (main train station) was hit. So they moved the post office to the parish hall in Kahlertstrasse. You had to collect the post yourself, there was a huge throng of people there, and it's where I got your letter from 7 September. But now that post office was bombed on Tuesday. I was there in the morning and as there was nothing for me I was going to return in the afternoon. Luckily I was detained, for otherwise I would have been amongst the dead. Many, many letters were burned too, including I'm sure from Bettine and Papa. I wrote telegrams to everyone but didn't get any replies.

Last night Papa arrived for five days. His lieutenant called for him, you see, and asked whether he was from Darmstadt. When Papa said he was, the lieutenant told him, 'You're going to go back home today!' An hour later Papa had packed and was taken by military vehicle to the station. / I hope you can come too. / The main thing, Papa says, is that we're alive. He got up early and mucked out the goats. After lunch he went into town and looked at the aftermath of the bombings. He said it was impossible to find your way around now because none of those buildings are there any more. / As there's still no electricity the bakers have to knead their dough by hand, which means there's very little bread in the shops.

Our work consists of sitting in the cellar every day. Yesterday there was a memorial service at the Waldfriedhof. I wasn't there and I don't imagine anyone from the family was either. In the morning Gretel took her father and mother to the Odenwald so they could get to the air-raid shelter more easily. Yesterday there were four alerts, including during the memorial service. If they'd dropped a few air-mines into the crowd I bet you would have said, if only you'd stayed at home, Mama. Aunt Emma and Uncle Georg ended up in a coffin for seventeen people, nothing but bones from people in their building. As I've already told you, Kläre's mother, grandfather and uncle are dead. They say that Kläre dragged her mother until her hands were burning. She's in hospital in Eberstadt apparently, her right foot charred and her voice still terribly hoarse. Write and let me know her surname because I'd like to visit her.

I've just been up to the field again to fetch fodder for tomorrow.

I've been feeding the rabbits beet. Although I'm exhausted after working all day, I love collapsing into bed and falling straight asleep, not having to dwell on how miserable everything is.

Just in case, this is the number of your savings book: 123 410. Papa's is 121. Aunt Liesel's: Städtische Sparkasse 1418 and Deutsche Bank 26014.

Aunt Emma and Uncle Georg were buried eight days ago, seventeen of them in the same coffin. No relatives turned up because of all the air-raid alerts. They didn't deserve that. They're at rest by the memorial, grave 181. Apparently there are still corpses beneath the rubble. Papa just kept shaking his head, he never imagined it could be so awful. When it's evening you can't help but get the willies.

Your last letter is from 7 September. I didn't show it to Papa, because he would have spent those five days arguing with me on account of the comments about Herr Hans. Papa's very anxious and uptight. Since he left it's been wonderfully peaceful here, apart from the air raids. We spent the whole day in the cellar again today. As I've already said three times in my letters, Frau Bader's living with me. / I hope you don't have lice any more. I well believe you when you say just what trouble they've been giving you, those tiny bugs can really drive you potty, especially as you're not used to that sort of filth in our family. It wouldn't have happened at home.

On Wednesday I went to the hospital in Goddelau with Liselotte. We wandered through five large rooms looking for Aunt Helen, but she wasn't even amongst those patients with really severe burns.

A few days earlier Aunt Sophie had taken all her good knitted dresses, porcelain and silver over to Aunt Helen's. All of it burnt too. Frau Birgel and Herr Berg from Rossdörferstrasse are dead. Uncle Jakob got them out of the cellar (fourteen people) and the two of them went into another house that then collapsed. I'm enclosing a newspaper cutting from yesterday. Once you've read it you'll know all about our beloved Darmstadt. Please send it back to me.

As I've already told you three times, Frau Bader's living with me. She's been bombed out twice now. Most recently she was living in the cellar beneath the castle and it was a miracle she managed to escape from there. The blast threw her against the castle wall, then someone grabbed her by the collar and threw her over the wall. She has no idea what happened after that. When she came to three days later she was in Dieburg. / The people that got away have been through so much. Still no trace of Aunt Helen and Helga. What's poor Uncle Ernst going to do when he comes? Elfriede was here with Herr Weingärtner yesterday. She's has four days' leave from her job as a navy auxiliary in Stralsund. Yesterday she found a dead child in the laundry room at 11 Saalbaustrasse. It wasn't Helga, but a one-year-old belonging to the woman who lived with Aunt Helen. Heinz was also here yesterday, with Marga. The poor boy hasn't even got a shirt any more. Everything he wears is borrowed. / On Saturday Uncle Jakob was married in Arheilgen. He's living with his parents-in-law. His wedding suit was an old work outfit burned at the sleeves. Dear Margot, you see how people can become impoverished overnight.

We're all very angry, but Herr Kresser says that's what it's like when you spit into the wind. Herr Kresser has gone again. Lulu sends her regards.

Has your neighbour been released from jail yet? Surely he must know they'll keep him locked up until he sees the error of his ways. It's really not a good example. Herr Hans says that pessimism is treason. Should we perhaps give up the war and let ourselves get shipped to Siberia where it's forty degrees below zero, you're given bread and hot water, and have to do forced labour until you collapse? I'd rather be dead. / We might not know how this will end, but I'm hoping for a good end, because if we lose then it will all be over.

Frau Lenz was in prison for a fortnight because she used her mother's identity card dishonestly to get an early-boarding ticket for Frankfurt station. She said they were given sugar beet jam every day, and almost every day someone went out of their mind. Sometimes the walls shook with the screaming, she said.

Uncle Ernst came yesterday. He's not staying with us in Eichbaumeck, but with Aunt Liesel, who's closer to the ruin in Saalbaustrasse. He went straight there today, but there's nothing he can do for the time being. They haven't found anything of Aunt Helen and Helga. They must be amongst the charred bodies. / Ellen now knows that her parents are dead, I feel very sorry for her.

Dear Margot, who would have thought that Darmstadt could ever look like this? There are no shops any more, so I've no idea where to get hold of the things you want me to send you. On Monday I will post you some darning thread and toothpaste in a hundred-gram package. You can forget about the rest. I only get one little bag of washing powder per month and I need that for myself.

Papa was back on leave again and repaired the damage here. Then he left for Speyer and was meant to go on to Metz the next day, but only got as far as Neustadt, and from there back to Baumholder. After four days in Baumholder he went on to Pirmasens and that same day back to Germersheim. With the state of the railways at the moment those journeys took two days and two nights.

I cannot send you all the things you want. You have to understand that we don't have any shops any more. I don't even have any hair clips left myself. Why are you wearing out your good knickers? Put on your old ones when you're working in the garden, what does it matter that they're grey? And if you're going to the doctor, just wear the best you've got. I'm out of shoe polish. There isn't any more to be had. I'm sorry I can't get you everything you ask for. Make sure you dress up warm in the bad weather, seeing as you've already got the sniffles.

Bettine always wants something sent to her too. I'm starting to worry that you're losing your minds. The best thing for me to do would be to put wheels on my wardrobe and hook it up to the postal van. I'd have thought that away from home you would have developed some common sense, but evidently not. To Bettine I could sing: *You're mad, my child, you have to go to Berlin!* Especially when she writes, you *have* to send me all these things. How much nicer it would sound if she wrote, dear Mama, you *could* send me them. Now she wants the Sunday coat. But who can guarantee it won't go up in flames on the way, or in Berlin? In Darmstadt even doctors and professors would be delighted to have a coat like that. Some don't have anything any more, not even a handkerchief. We're princes by comparison. How many free Sundays will Bettine have in Berlin anyway? I bet you can count them on the fingers of one hand! You wait, in the end she'll be grateful I *didn't* send the coat. Write that to her, Margot. I don't even know the new address to send it to. She might not be able to take receipt of the package tomorrow. Write and tell her that too.

Uncle Ernst has finally returned from Italy. But what a state he's in! He spends the whole day searching for Aunt Helen and Helga. It's a hopeless undertaking, but he says he has to find them nonetheless. / Today a short letter arrived from Uncle Jakob dated 2 October, which means the post arrives here quicker from Russia than it does from Mondsee. He writes *Corporal* as the sender, but there's not a word about this in the letter. Papa must be in Germersheim, he hasn't written yet. Aunt Liesel sends her regards.

Four thousand victims have been named so far, but many, many thousands more are unidentifiable. I'm sending you some of the death announcements, the paper carries a few every day. On the section with Aunt Emma's name, Walters should be underneath, but it tore off unfortunately. Twenty thousand have died, so they say. Dear Margot, you cannot imagine what it looks like. There's no more school, the buildings have been destroyed, the teachers were complaining about pupils showing no interest. We sit in the cellar day and night. You can only cook a little food and sometimes you can't even eat that.

I can't get it out of my head that you've got lice. It hadn't crossed my mind that it might happen to you. It's different with Uncle Jakob in Russia, that's to be expected, but not with you. Well, dear Margot, it's better for you to have lice and otherwise be well than to have no lice but have something happen to you. Just take care that the child doesn't catch them too. And please write to Bettine and tell her she doesn't need a Sunday coat, and that she mustn't do anything stupid in Berlin and she should stop trying to be a know-all.

I'm at Aunt Liesel's where we're waiting for Uncle Ernst to arrive for lunch. He's going away again tomorrow without having made any progress. Today Russian prisoners of war are taking away the porch. It's his last hope that he'll find them there. Poor chap. Dear Margot, please take care always, so that nothing happens to you. I can't get any peace these days. If only you were closer to Darmstadt so that I could come and visit you from time to time. Can't you come back home when Papa's here again? After everything that's happened since 11 September it might be quite good. The air-raid warning has just sounded again, you can't even have your lunch any more. Until Uncle Ernst gets here I'm going to write to Uncle Jakob, he's a corporal. Then I have to attend to the rabbits, it's always the same old story with them.

Papa missed the train today because he'd jotted down the wrong departure time. He left unwashed and without having had anything to eat. He was raging and shouting like a madman, that was his goodbye. / Two days ago he had a go at me about Herr Hans, who had come here for the first time in ages. Liselotte was here too and Papa didn't like the cosy way they talked to each other. The moment Herr Hans left Papa launched into an argument, telling me that he wouldn't put up with the way Herr Hans came and went as he pleased here. To make matters worse, when Papa discovered his mistake with the train this evening and was busy studying the timetable, there was a knock at the door and Herr Hans asked, 'Do you mind if I come in?' Perhaps you can imagine how my heart was racing. Papa was calm at first, I was sorting out his boots. I could see straightaway he was thinking what to say and it didn't take him long to blurt out that there would be no more visits of this sort when he was gone. Having already been tipped off by Liselotte, Herr Hans played the gentleman and said he was most pleased to have made Papa's acquaintance, and that Papa had told him this. He understood perfectly well, he just wanted to ask whether his wife, if she came, might not sleep here too. Papa said he had no objections to that, even though he'd told me earlier that it wouldn't happen again. I told Herr Hans he shouldn't be angry, it was just because of the way people talked, and that if his wife came here he could happily join her.

Once again you write asking for all those things you'd like me to send you. I'm afraid I can't get hold of most of them, you must have forgotten that there are no shops in Darmstadt any more. The Walters are dead. Aunt Emma and Uncle Georg are dead too, their shop no longer exists, and what you want most of all are hair accessories. What do you want silk stockings for? You've already got a pair for going out in, and winter's on its way. I could understand it if you wanted your gymnastics trousers. But would you please send me some cigarette papers? Ask someone what's a good brand. I think *Aladin* is meant to be good.

What's the news in Mondsee? Has the greenhouse owner been

released from jail? How about the soldier from Vienna? Is he back at the front? He's missed enough time. I believe I know you well enough as my daughter to wonder sometimes what Papa and I were thinking of having children. / Your old colleague Gela has made up with Zobel. She doesn't know what she wants and what she has in him. If Zobel behaved like her you can bet she wouldn't be happy. But I didn't say a word. / Yes, dear Margot, autumn has taken hold, the roses are now bare, and it becomes more noticeable by the day.

Just so I don't forget again, there's no way I can get you any bows. The Walters are dead, there aren't any shops in Darmstadt now, so where am I supposed to find them? You took half a suitcase full of them with you. So, save them and ration them! I was going to write you a long letter yesterday evening, but we were on major alert the whole time. I'm quite stiff from sitting in the cellar. It's also been raining non-stop for several days. Where have the aircraft dropped their bombs? There was a terrifying din in the air. I hope they're not heading your way too. Dress up warm if you go down into the cellar, it's cold and damp. The best thing would be to set up a makeshift bed for yourself and the child. I'm waiting impatiently to hear from you. Yesterday two letters and a card arrived: old post again. A letter from 12 September, a card from 20 September and a letter from 4 October. You can rely on the post, you see, sometimes it just takes a while. It's only now that I know you know our relatives are dead, which was more than six weeks ago.

You will have heard from Bettine how Ilse ended her life. She was wanting to throw herself off the balcony even back in the days when Oskar paid more attention to her sister than to her. She told me this herself in the orchard, when Hanne was still a little girl around four years of age. And your work colleague Monika has had a baby, the wedding will take place when the child's father is back on leave. Some people have the baptism before the wedding, that happens.

I haven't been up to the field in five days. My rear tyre keeps losing air again. Herr Hans had patched it up. But at least I mucked out the goats again. I don't think they've ever been mucked out so thoroughly as today. When I was weeding it crossed my mind that you're weeding too now. I can scarcely believe it, I can't stop shaking my head. But I don't think I'd have cause, as you say, to praise you if I could see you. I've worked so much in my life that I don't see any reason to praise someone for their work. / Are you still eating onions? If so, keep eating them, they're good for you.

I hope the two of you are well and you're not getting up to mischief in Mondsee. Who stays with the child when you go to fetch manure? I'm going to put some money in the envelope for you all the same, I don't know how much yet, I'll have to see what I've got in my purse. Please buy something for Lilo, I know I don't have to worry about you. I just hope Bettine doesn't do anything silly in Berlin. Both of you are in my thoughts all the time and I'm very sorry that Papa has to be deployed, that Bettine has to go to work so early and that you've got so much work.

In the second week of July

In the second week of July a violent storm passed over the Salzkammergut, with hail that fell particularly hard on the northern shore of the Attersee. In Mondsee too, it looked as if it might hail, it turned as dark as night, but the rapping against the windows came from small branches buffeted by the wind. Fortunately the greenhouse survived the storm without damage; I was pleased that the strong winds didn't dislodge any of the glass panes and hurl them into the garden. / The farmers frowned, hoping that the corn would stand up again soon. We just have to wait, they said, there's nothing we can do about it.

The evacuees by the lake were on holiday between 19 July and 8 August. The groups were instructed to travel via Leoben, and the girls were gone the very next day. I don't know whether they left on the eighteenth or nineteenth, but it happened before the attempt on the F's life. / Because love can make even the war seem remote, ever since my return from Vienna, the vagaries of world history had only reached me from afar. But the assassination attempt on the F shook me, as it was carried out by officers from the F's closest entourage. For the enemy the episode was most gratifying. But practically everyone back home now believed that the poor men at the front had definitely had enough of the war. / Sadly, the F was not going to give up his throne, which meant the war, which had become like a chronic illness, continued to be pursued with even greater bitterness.

From the newspaper I learned that Brazilian soldiers were fighting alongside American troops in Italy. Well, one enemy more or fewer wasn't going to make much of a difference to us, was it?

Margot's husband wrote to say that he was now not far from the East Prussian border and he kept wondering what was going to happen from hereon in. Being so close to the enemy day and night, and unable to sleep, was wearing them down over time, he said. And the suspension of leave was the final straw. He was hoping that the war would soon be over. At the end of his letter he asked whether his daughter could walk yet. But the girl was only eight months old, it was far too early to ask the question, revealing how everything was in turmoil and adrift.

And yet I was happy that the relationship between Margot and me was *working*. I was always amazed when I visualized this young woman from Hesse trembling with excitement in my arms. Even now I'm unable to think about it without feeling overwhelmed. Sometimes we were really wild in bed. Margot would say, 'It seems I'm capable of anything.' / It worked so well. The two of us opened up, we weren't trying to impress each other, or not much. We spent a lot of time in each other's company, making the best, as we saw it, of the situation. And from time to time I would hallucinate about other children we would have together. I was astonished at myself. But then again, why not? By Margot's side I cherished the hope that I might become a normal person, a person like any other.

After the 10 July storm it stayed cool, the nights were as chilly as in September and the sun seldom shone. It was such a miserable July, the kind of month people like to forget, but I didn't care, for there's something protective about the rain. The children stayed at home and the adults held up their umbrellas.

Since my recent deferment I'd tried my best to remain as inconspicuous as possible in Mondsee. Those voices saying I was shirking my responsibilities on the field of honour by holing up in the Darmstadt woman's bed were getting louder. My uncle told me this, adding that he was critical of my behaviour too, but there was probably nothing that could be done. / When Margot and I went into town at the end of June, children trotted behind our backs, gesturing horns with their fingers. We pretended not to notice anything, nor to hear their reedy laughter. But the episode served as a warning to me.

Whenever we wanted to go on a walk from then on, we left the house separately and met up again outside Mondsee on the way to Schwarzindien, where the Schleifenbach flows into the lake. / Near there we once came across a dead doe, which had clearly been run over, while a stag was going round in circles in the meadow beside the road. The doe lay there, her legs outstretched like poles, blood around her mouth, and Margot said, 'Poor thing!' We thought the stag wasn't running away because he didn't want to be separated from the doe, but in fact he'd been run over too, which we only realized when an elderly gentleman out on his bicycle stopped and said, 'It's obvious he's in terrible pain. He's dying.' / The circling became a twisting and a stagger and I was appalled at myself for not having recognized the creature's pain for what it was, too wrapped up as I was in my own situation. / We didn't wait for a hunter to come and shoot the stag, we went our separate ways back to the house. / I remember vividly the gloomy, charged atmosphere of that afternoon, and I also remember the shot I heard in the distance as I was mowing the grass in the Brazilian's garden.

For a while Margot had lice. Where she got them from was a puzzle, for I didn't have lice and nor did Lilo. Margot said she'd probably caught them at the station waiting room. She was bitten all over and was desperate to scratch herself sore. If she put on fresh underwear it was even worse, likewise washing herself, for that's what the little blighters really liked. I got her some Mitigal, a sulphur-based lotion to rub in. When she went to bed she put moth powder in her panties, but she was only rid of them when she went to Salzburg to be deloused. I was familiar with the procedure from Russia, including the burn marks on the clothes. But Margot felt as if she'd been reborn afterwards.

By the end of July Margot was so worn down by all the rain that she wrote to her mother in Darmstadt, asking her to send fifty kilograms of sun by rail, for that was what she most urgently needed at the moment. In August, however, the summer focused on producing fine weather and often it was so swelteringly hot that you might think you were in Africa. Sometimes I felt so exhausted that I couldn't gear myself up to do anything until the evening, even though it wasn't much cooler then. Margot and the child didn't seem to feel the heat; Margot could have lived in the desert and her daughter clearly took after her. Lilo spent most of the time in the water, the mornings in the tub in a shady spot outside the greenhouse, and the afternoons in the lake. I was surprised that she didn't grow webbed feet.

In such scorching heat I was glad when we had a downpour in the evenings. But the sun always came out again straight after and then roofs would steam as they dried quickly in the wind. The tomatoes thrived accordingly, and we harvested and watered at dawn, as during the daytime we would have been overcome by the heat inside the greenhouse.

The plums ripened too, and following instructions the Brazilian had given to us in a letter, we dried them on boards in the greenhouse, for more difficult times. We managed a total of ten kilos.

In the sticky summer heat, the lavatory in the animal shed became even less attractive a proposition, but as grim as it was, I liked my brief chats with the pigs. I talked to them about the weather, the war and my employer, to whom I felt no allegiance. Margot, on the other hand, complained that she felt the pigs were inspired by her to do their business too, and she didn't like this sort of familiarity.

My greatest concern was Uncle, who was ill throughout almost the whole of August. It was his old complaint: emphysema. He lay in his bed for three weeks, his temperature occasionally rising to forty degrees, which took a lot out of him. He lost eighteen kilograms and looked terrible afterwards. I was pleased when he slowly recovered, but it was a difficult process given the food shortages. I regularly brought him fruit and vegetables from the Brazilian's garden. He'd have rather I brought him tobacco. But Margot sent the tobacco I had left over to her mother in Darmstadt, and I couldn't tell Uncle that. He must have had his suspicions, however, for he said, 'That Reich German woman is causing difficulties for the both of us.'

Despite the rainy weather, in July people were already heading in droves into the mountains, before the bilberries were ripe. At the beginning of August the trains could have attached livestock wagons to the back to deal with the masses of people carrying their buckets. I'd have loved to have gone climbing in the mountains too, but such an undertaking wasn't compatible with the controversial subject of my health. I was rightly worried that any carelessness on my part could result in my being enlisted. / The landlady was making caustic remarks again, reminding me regularly of the F who got up at five o'clock every morning, sacrificing his health for idlers like myself. She was in a foul mood all summer long. First they'd taken away the Polish woman who'd looked after her house and was now working in the factory in Lenzing. And then the political news was worse than ever: the beginning of the Warsaw Uprising, Roumania changing sides and finally the surrender of Paris without a fight. On several occasions the landlady angrily kicked the metal bin across the front yard, cursing all scoundrels and shirkers. 'This entire cowardly world disgusts me!' she snarled. / Just to be on the safe side I would always round up the rent now.

Once Margot went to forage bilberries on her own. She left at five in the morning and I looked after the child, gave her the bottle, fed her, changed her nappy. While I was writing letters the little one crawled over to me on the floor, grabbed my leg, got to her feet and looked delighted by her achievement. And I imagined that there was no war.

The girl was much bigger now. When I bathed her I was startled by how quickly she had grown to fill the tub, and she was almost unable to perform her usual routine of slapping the water because her body was in the way. Everything else was the same as ever: the laughter when I wrung out the flannel over her, and the tears when I lifted her from the tub. What she liked least of all was my drying her; she howled with indignation. / I laid her down at half past six.

From the middle of the afternoon I went to the window every ten minutes, looking out for Margot. As it got later I became very tense and very worried. After the girl's bath and the inevitable tears that followed I couldn't take it any more and didn't move from the window. I felt quite strange again. To calm myself I made a tea. But as I left it to brew I was overcome with the idea that Margot might be dead. And then I was suddenly assailed by the most violent onslaught of images and I started to swear. Memories from Russia mixed with fantasies from my Mondsee life. Russia and Mondsee came together, intertwined like the root systems of two trees, it was impossible to disentangle or banish the images, and I became ever more ensnared. Sweat dripped from my nose.

Fortunately I had already put the child to bed at this point. I took a Pervitin, the child was sleeping silently, as if dead too, and I touched her several times. And while I waited for the Pervitin to take effect, I was alone with my demons.

Supper is over now. Margot came home soaked to the bone and half frozen with five litres of bilberries. The moment she opened the door I could see how pleased she was to see me. I told her that I'd gone to look out of the window at least thirty times to see whether she was coming. She said she'd had a wonderful day. / Now she's sitting wearily at the table, her eyes barely open, reading a letter from her sister who works as a conductress on the trams in Berlin and who is in love. Margot is still drinking her tea, but I can see in the corners of her eyes that her lids are closing. At once I feel crestfallen, without knowing why. It's something serious, maybe the happiness I feel with Margot, but which I'm convinced I will lose. / It's probably true what Margot's close compatriot wrote: that there's nothing harder to bear than a succession of happy days. But perhaps I'm just too exhausted after my long day as a nanny, which began for me at half past four too.

It was a peaceful night. Margot fell asleep instantly and I snuggled up without waking her. The child didn't make a peep until half past seven in the morning. Good girl. Margot, who could scarcely believe her luck, said that being able to sleep in again was a lifesaver. / Then we sat at the table together. I liked sitting in Margot's apartment in the mornings. We were almost always in pyjamas, drinking coffee and chatting, while Margot would feed the baby and I would watch the two of them. Once Margot asked if it bothered me that she was married. / 'Yes.' / And did it bother me that she had a child? / 'No.' / We fell silent and stared into each other's eyes. And when the child was lying back in the washing basket we lay down again too.

In the middle of August the evacuees returned to Mondsee and so we no longer had to send the tomatoes by rail to Salzburg. / Three of the girls who'd been in Schwarzindien in the spring remained in Vienna, but there were four new girls, one of them a refugee from Lvov. / It was good to see the girls looking refreshed, their buoyant gait, arms swinging, and their smiling eyes.

During the three weeks the girls had been away the trampled grass around the Mondsee camp had first regained its colour, then turned straw-like in the heat. To begin with they didn't have much opportunity to trample the grass down again. Because it was still the school holidays they were called up for agricultural work. The remuneration for their labour went into the camp coffers. And, so I heard, when the weather wasn't sufficiently inviting for swimming, the girls went on *reconnaissance patrols* in the woods, looking for mushrooms.

There wasn't a single new lead in the Annemarie Schaller case, apart from my uncle's insisting that she couldn't have drowned because the body would have risen to the surface long ago. / The girl had been missing for more than four months now, and Kurt Ritler hadn't sent any letters to Mondsee for several weeks, which was a shame because I'd developed an affection for the boy. The only reason why I didn't write to him myself was because I shouldn't have been reading his letters to Nanni.

The first of September marked the beginning of the sixth year of the war, more than one thousand eight hundred lousy days. Margot continued to look after the greenhouse, while the girl got her fourth tooth and was forever chewing at the edge of the shabby carpet in Margot's room. The evacuees in Schwarzindien finally brought their amphibian existence for the summer to an end because school was starting again on the Monday. And Uncle applied himself to maintaining order again. He was not as steady on his feet as he had been in the spring. Now that he'd lost a substantial amount of weight through his illness, I could see the resemblance to Papa.

I met Frau Bildstein, the teacher, once. She told me she'd spent her holidays in Schachen, where she'd been at a children's evacuee camp the previous year. She grumbled about the authorities in Linz, who were making life difficult for her because the father of one of the girls had complained about all the spelling mistakes she made. Reading her letters made him ill; he had the impression that the more his daughter learned, the more stupid she was becoming. The father had also raised a serious objection to an essay title: *He whom the gods love dies young.* The teacher said that if there was one thing they couldn't stand in Linz, it was problems with the parents. Parents who complained meant work, and the authorities held this against the teachers rather than the parents. She grinned bravely and said she hadn't written the schoolbooks.

The squadrons flying over grew bigger by the week, it was a flourishing industry. I still found it eerie, lying in the Brazilian's hammock, the girl on my stomach, and watching the aircraft glide past in sparkling formation as they flew back to Italy. At the same time the so-called weapon of retribution was constantly on its way to southern England and London, a kind of winged and unmanned bomb. Nothing was known about its actual effectiveness. Did it meet expectations? Probably not. On the Eastern Front – in the central section – the expected major offensive was underway, and because it didn't look as if my employer could gain the upper hand, not even sporadically, it was easy to see which way the war was going. But stop? That would have been totally against the firm's style.

Hamburg was flattened, Hanover was flattened, Frankfurt was flattened. Like Warsaw, Rotterdam, Coventry, Belgrade, Smolensk and Voronezh. I'd seen the last two of these and we were always told that there was a beautiful city up ahead. But what use was all that beauty? By the time we were inside all that remained of the city was its name.

Margot avoided listening to the Wehrmacht reports on the wireless by tuning to another station, as if by hearing someone sing about the South Pacific she could make the here and now disappear. But sometimes she didn't have a hand free, and then the precarious limbo we found ourselves in was disturbed by news from the outside world. One such occasion was when Margot was cooking a load of hawthorn jam and I was jiggling the girl on my knee to distract her. Because there hadn't been any rain for almost six weeks the floorboards creaked and the child was frightened because the creaking sounded so sinister. / Margot stuck her tongue out in concentration as she filled the jars with jam.

On the wireless it was reported that there had been a major air raid on Darmstadt, and the figure of twenty thousand deaths was mentioned. Margot moved the pot from the stove and looked at me. She asked what the name of the city was they had just mentioned. / 'Darmstadt,' I replied.

Now Margot went through all the other stations in search of more information. When a longer report on a foreign station announced that Darmstadt had been destroyed, Margot fell on the bed, crying, hesitantly at first, as if uncertain whether she were still capable of something she'd half forgotten how to do; then, as she got used to it again, she let the tears run their course, as they say. She howled for the next hour. Occasionally I heard the words, 'I can't go on any longer, I need a break,' part sobbed, part moaned. Then she swam her way out of her tears and I heard almost nothing for a while, a sniffle perhaps when Margot wiped her upper lip, the meeting point of everything that had run from her eyes and nose. She gasped for breath, I handed her a fresh handkerchief. And after a while she uttered the name of her home town again and continued to cry. / Once she got up, looked at her tear-stained face in the mirror, her uncombed hair and smudged make-up. Margot breathed out and I could see her steeling herself. 'I look dreadful,' she said. Then she went back to the bed and fell onto it, burying her face in the pillow. All the while the child was playing with my fingers.

Over the next few days Margot waited for news from her relatives. First came a letter from Kläre, a former work colleague at the health insurance company. Margot grabbed the letter outside our building and read it, pacing up and down and sobbing, until the landlady rebuked her, saying she shouldn't howl in the streets, that was what her bedroom was for. Margot pressed the handkerchief to her lips and a silent shudder ran down her body. / Afterwards she lay again for hours on her bed until she was completely exhausted and had a sore throat from all the crying. For a while she sat there, her legs drawn up, staring pale-faced into the distance. At one point she stared at the girl, and when she didn't return the child's smile, didn't even notice it, the girl was quite perturbed and stared back.

'Come, come, what's all this crying about . . .' was the only thing that came to mind. And in truth there really wasn't much else to say. As we gradually learned, large parts of Darmstadt had been transformed literally into piles of rubble and ashes. The dead bodies, insofar as anything remained of them, had been lined up on the cleared streets. Entire queues of them could be seen. If you didn't know better, you could have mistaken some of the bodies for children as they'd shrunk so much in the heat. And although the stench was one they'd never smelled before, they knew what it was, they always had. / Kläre's letter described all of these things in detail.

Yes, that's what it's like when you spit into the wind.

The first time I saw Margot smile again after that was on the morning when a great tit got caught on the flypaper in her room. Margot and her daughter were sleeping with the window open, it was six o'clock, and I was woken by screaming and a commotion from the next-door room. When I went over I saw the tit becoming more and more entangled in the flypaper until it could almost no longer move. The child cried anxiously. Margot set the bird free. We washed it and put it in a box. The bird looked so pitiful that I didn't hold out any hope. Around lunchtime we cleaned the tit's feathers again with turpentine, an hour later we took it into the garden and it flew off. That's when Margot smiled.

Steam was rising from the dung heap

Steam was rising from the dung heap, which was generating heat, a product of decay. I noticed that the September warmth also came from a type of fermentation: summer was decomposing and autumn was settling in with its quicker days and cool gusts of wind. / The swallows gathered by the lake and prepared for their departure.

At the same time the Brazilian returned to Mondsee. He'd been locked up for four months and now he'd been freed because he'd served two-thirds of his sentence and the local Party leader had put in a good word for him, mentioning the renovated greenhouse. It wasn't too late yet to plant the winter vegetables and the children's camps in Mondsee needed to be supplied with food, as the prison governor impressed on the Brazilian when he was released.

It had taken half a day to get home from Linz because the train had stopped for hours after an air raid somewhere. He completed the last section of his journey on foot. A few elderly gentlemen called out 'Robert, how are you?' but only from a distance. / Nobody came over to him, even though he had much to tell. People lived with their eyes closed or were reserved in their dealings with those who'd insulted the supreme commander. Our allies were dropping out one by one. Finland had withdrawn the previous week, following the example of Roumania and Bulgaria. Everywhere the mood was sombre.

The Brazilian arrived back with practically no luggage, just a few clothes and the two books Margot had been permitted to send him in prison. He set his bundle down outside the greenhouse, went inside and came out again eating a beef tomato. He wandered across the field, through the orchard and cleaned his rubber boots, which I'd worn that morning, in the fountain by the greenhouse. Then he put on a record of *Suite Popular Brasileña*, sat on the small bench outside the greenhouse and closed his eyes. That's how he was sitting when I crossed the road and went over to him. Without opening his eyes, he said, 'Bom dia, Menino.'

His greeting in Portuguese was the first sign that he wasn't yet fully back in Mondsee. Prison had been unpleasant, he said, so unpleasant that he'd looked forward to returning to Mondsee, but that wasn't saying much. On the journey here, he'd been appreciative of the beauty of the landscape for the first time in ages, but that wasn't saying much either. The window in his prison cell hadn't offered any sort of view, and the skin on his face looked as if the prison wall had stained it grey. His eyelids were swollen. When he talked his upper lip quivered, as if he were wanting to say something quite different. His hands didn't know what to do either. He was a bag of nerves.

The Brazilian breathed in the air of freedom, of which he'd been deprived for too long. Although it was still light, we could see the waxing moon between the Schafberg and the Drachenwand. It was certainly better than prison.

He fetched two more beef tomatoes from the greenhouse, passed one to me and ate the other slowly. In between bites he seemed to be in contemplation, seemed to be chewing on the future, then he nodded and said, 'I'll muddle through somehow.'

I showed him the dog's grave. He thanked me and said such proof of friendship rekindled his belief that at a time when all values had been reconsidered there were still good people who deserved to be acknowledged as such. Surely it went without saying, I said, and he replied that nothing went without saying any more. Then he slapped his palm against the earth three times, below it was the dog, and it gave a hollow sound. The Brazilian shook my hand again. His rough gardener's skin had softened during his time in prison, something I'd noticed earlier when he first arrived.

Still standing beside the elder bush he told me what it was like in prison. He hadn't been expecting preferential treatment, but neither had he thought he'd be dealt with so severely. / As I listened, I scratched my ear awkwardly. One glance at the Brazilian's distraught face was enough to put you off probing any further. 'And yet I had it far easier than most of them there,' he said. 'Torture is routine, death an everyday occurrence.' / He followed up with some details of things he'd heard in conversation. At night they'd used rags to empty the waste pipes of the toilets, and then used these pipes to talk to each other across all the floors. The really important things were said by those detained in the cellar, those who would soon be corpses. 'Any halfway rational person must look at a political system through the eyes of the dead.' / I heard him say this three or four times over the weeks that followed. In some respects the Brazilian had changed during his time in prison, but in the fact that he never tired of repeating himself he was still the same man I'd known.

Overall, the shadow he cast on this earth hadn't just got smaller, but weaker too. Besides his newly acquired anxiety it was noticeable that he isolated himself more often than before. And I was also concerned by his sudden staring into space. From time to time he would for no apparent reason pause mid-sentence and appear totally absent. At other times he might stop moving for several minutes while working and his sleeves would flutter in the wind like a scarecrow's. When he started moving again he would look around sheepishly before continuing with his work, very slowly, as if his strength might desert him at any moment. For the first time I witnessed him display something akin to clumsiness and he looked overstretched, unable to cope on his own with the work that needed to be done. And yet, when you saw him like this, his imprisonment seemed to be something he'd needed to get over and done with, and that in spite of the exhaustion he could see a positive side to the experience.

A few days after his return Margot settled the accounts with him. We'd sold nine hundred kilograms of tomatoes, almost a tonne. But a substantial proportion of the profit that Margot handed over to the Brazilian went on covering what was owed to the glazier. An unsuccessful year. / The Brazilian said he felt incarcerated in this time of war and bandits. Nobody in the entire country was free any more, the entire country was a slave ship run aground. The first thing he had to do was rid himself of his chains, and not just him. For the time being, sadly, he could only dream of his journey to freedom in the southeastern part of the Americas.

And he dreamed often. He listened to records of South American songs, sung by a tenor, and dreamed of the longest trams in the world and the largest bus stations in the world and butterflies as large as one's palm and the intoxicating fragrance of the heliotrope. And of the sky-scrapers that surround Sugar Loaf Mountain like bodyguards. And mandarins that lie on the paths strewn with white sand that nobody stops you picking up. 'Of course you can buy them at the Syrian shop too, they're cheaper than onions back home.

'All the same it won't be easy, I'm not going to fool myself. Nowhere's ever welcomed me with open arms. The good life doesn't wave at you. Life doesn't wave anyway. But just one last time, in the jungle, I'd like to enjoy the four freedoms we were promised so firmly. The freedom not to freeze, because in South America energy falls from the skies. Not to go hungry, because in South America fruit, fish, worms and crocodile eggs aren't rationed. Not to live in fear, because the so-called savages are better people than the European robots. And not to: everything else. You can enjoy all these freedoms in the jungle without ration coupons, and that's where I want to be. Here, on the other hand, in the Great Reich of Justice, where the individual and his freedoms count for nothing, here I'm just going mad. In fact I'm half mad already, or three-quarters.

'Jungle *hell*, Menino? Only a robot can come up with an idea like that. Hell is here. Killing with the help of machines. Electric chair, machine gun and all those other things.

'You know, Menino, there's nothing coarse, boastful or arrogant about the people in Brazil. They're calm, dreamy, sensuous people. All those qualities which are missing here. Only during Carnival do they have a stab at being loud and boastful. The black people take their shoes to the pawnbroker so they can celebrate fittingly, but never their hats. And if a poor person doesn't get any leave from his employer for Carnival, he'll give up his job so he can summon the dead and dance with them when they return. But after four days he'll go back to his little, worldly life and be content with it.

'H is a homeless individual too, but he's now into his sixth year of dancing with the dead. And just as he appeared from the void, so will he disappear back into the void with his horde.

'Once I was lodging with Frau Lúcia dos Santos Mota, a washer-woman. During Carnival she always made a den out of wood wool in her room, and people could leave their children there for a small fee. It was in and out all night long, around three dozen small children were left there, lying tightly packed together. They were allocated numbers and their mothers were given the same numbers, like when you leave your coat in the cloakroom at the opera. The children lay in the wood wool, children of every colour, all jumbled up, a mixture of all the world. Sometimes a child would cry, but then it went straight back to sleep. The little ones kept each other warm and their sleep was conta-gious. The noise from the streets lulled them too, the wild hooting, the crashing of pot lids, the firecrackers. Frau Lúcia dos Santos Mota sang her songs and I gave the children watered-down milk to drink. From time to time one of them was fetched on presentation of a number that would have been kept safe in a brassiere during the hours of dancing samba. And the child was lifted from the warm wood wool. And all the mothers that came, sun priestesses and moon princesses, still had the frenzy in their eyes, and the children went on sleeping in the arms of the moon princesses or woke up, for now it was daytime, and as they left the shack the harsh light pierced their eyes.

'Although all the effort will be out of proportion to my life expect-ancy, the point is, I belong in Brazil. And if I hadn't been on my own I wouldn't have come back to Germany a second time, only to be deposed from my responsibilities as the eldest by a crook imported into the family by my crazed sister, and by the treachery and mistrust of others. Trude and the varnisher ruled our parents' house and every-thing went to the dogs, just as this entire community of German criminals will go to the dogs.

'And even if I have to spend the rest of my life in a remote village eating black beans, cassava and bananas, which grow pretty much by themselves there, or you can get them cheap from the Syrian, I just hope that I'll soon find my way to the land I long for. Because I don't wish to live in a society where every other person is a murderer. Murder cannot and will not be pardoned, not by God, nor by my philosophical convictions. This is why humanity won't find peace and freedom again until it stops killing, animals included, and until it finally stops eating the flesh of animals, like a hyena, the only difference being that human beings kill animals with instruments, cook the flesh, lard it and serve it up on Meissen porcelain. I may still be leading an errant life myself, but it's far less errant than it used to be.

'So keep your fingers crossed for my journey to freedom. Surely it'll be possible in a year or two. I'd rather flee Germany at the age of fifty-six than stay here. And when finally I'm able to feast my eyes again on a mestiza, those women I've worshipped ever since I first set foot in South America, then, my dears, I will feel as if I'm in paradise, the search for which is perhaps my quest, overcoming all the obstacles in my way.'

His eyes half-closed, he smiled to himself in anticipation. 'Viva Brazil!' he said. Then he got up and, because it was midday and there was not a single cloud in the sky, he used the burning glass to scorch some lettering into the picket fence by the road. Margot and I watched the old wood smoke as it blackened, while the Brazilian extolled the power of the sun and said, 'If you fail to find any happiness for yourself, then you are lost. Other people only inflict suffering.'

Margot sat on the fence right next to where he was burning, dexterously maintaining her balance with the child on her lap. The top buttons of her blouse were open, revealing a triangle of her décolleté. When she leaned forward one could see the shadowy hollow between her breasts and some light skin, light-blue craquelure in the milky white. Noticing my gaze she winked at me. I knew her well enough to know what that meant; we were worse than cats. / Margot sat there calmly for a while longer, listening to the Brazilian, then said, 'Only the Austrians, it seems, are able to recognize the truth.' She burst out laughing and the Brazilian looked at her fiercely, because he wanted his efforts to be taken seriously. But all in all I could see that Margot's cheerfulness did him good. / Blinking in the harsh sunlight, Margot said she didn't mean any offence, but she didn't agree with him on many things. She liked the fact, however, that he was so thoughtful. Then she climbed down from the fence and poked her finger into my belly, which electrified me. She put the child down on the grass beside the Brazilian and asked him if he could look after her. It took him a couple of seconds to realize what was going on. Then we went up to Margot's room and made love.

Afterwards we lay for a while side by side in the narrow bed. Dreamily, I ran the fingers of my hand through the bushy dampness between her legs. Margot muttered something into my ear which I didn't understand, gave a contented grunt and was probably close to nodding off.

Later I had one hand on Margot's hip and, as I began dozing too, I regretted having suffered so much anxiety since childhood. I sensed it would have been in my power to be happier more often, to delight more often in the beauty of the world. For it was beyond doubt that the beauty of the world did exist, had always existed and would continue to exist in future. So why had my life always seemed so grey? Why? What for? I couldn't understand. And at the same time I suspected that I'd soon be plagued by a feeling of bleakness again, whether I had my hand on Margot's hip or not. What a pity, I thought idly.

When we went back outside the lettering on the picket fence was done and we could read the words: *Little Brazil*. The Brazilian had taken the child with him to the rear of the greenhouse where the workbench was. The girl was taking her afternoon nap on the dog blanket that was still there. She slept with the carefree contentment of a child, and it was still warm enough inside the greenhouse that you didn't need a coat. / I don't know exactly what happened between the Brazilian and Lilo while Margot and I made love, but the Brazilian said she'd been a good girl. Nonetheless, in our absence he'd started to build a playpen for the girl. And because he refused any help, Margot and I harvested tomatoes, which after all we had practice in.

That night, before going to sleep, I heard music coming from the greenhouse again for the first time in many months, as well as the occasional hammering. And the following morning when I got up the Brazilian was already at work again.

I had a brief chat with him and suggested it would be better if he adhered to the night-time blackout regulations. He risked making life difficult for himself otherwise, which would be a particularly bad idea at the moment. I wasn't sure whether he heard much of what I was saying; he was staring at a piece of wood, sanding down its edges. When a twitch in his face revealed at least a slight recognition I went back outside, lay in the hammock in the garden and made sure that nobody went to pick the apples. A lovely task.

Since the Brazilian's return I'd often been unnerved by the lack of jobs urgently needing doing and by the fact that I could just lie there peacefully, idling my time away, as if there were nothing to do. But by doing nothing I was missing out, because I wasn't spending all my time with Margot. I realized that my appointment at the infirmary in Vöcklabruck to have my frail body checked had elapsed six weeks earlier. I felt slightly uneasy about this, but for the time being I kept calm, with the intention of allowing the war to enjoy some more time without me.

Uncle was outside

Uncle was outside when I bumped into him, brushing his uniform on the front steps of the gendarmerie. He finished by cleaning his peaked cap with a soft clothes brush. Uncle responded to the greetings of passers-by with a barely perceptible nod of the head. This nod was his pièce de résistance: too slight for a greeting, but substantial enough for everyone to feel that they'd been noticed. *I can see you! Never forget that I can see you!*

A man with a prosthetic right leg teetered over from the cemetery, intent on complaining about the grazing steppe cattle belonging to the refugees. The refugees were housed in the barracks built for the construction of the Reichsautobahn, which had been shelved some years earlier. Uncle explained in detail the complaints procedure, presenting it as rather convoluted, which succeeded in its aim of deterring the man. He hobbled off, disgruntled. / Uncle told me that he had a lot of work, but he was approaching everything very calmly and coolly. One ought to remember, he said, that everything came around again, and sorted itself out in the end too. / We went inside, where my uncle cleaned the buttons of his jacket with scouring powder and an old handkerchief.

The institution betrayed no sign of zealousness. As I was about to put my feet up on the desk, Uncle asked if I'd be so kind as to give him two cigarettes. He lit the first immediately and smoked it while I leafed through Polzer's *Guide to Recording Criminal Evidence*. It contained the advice that one should always bear in mind a dog may have licked up blood from a crime scene. 'Interesting, interesting,' I sneered. I read out another passage to my uncle: 'Someone who is truly hard of hearing makes an effort to understand the interrogator by pulling a face and moving his head close. The charlatan just sits there without moving.' / 'I can confirm this is true,' Uncle said.

As he clearly had nothing else to do, my uncle bathed his feet in a tub of hot water. In the water, to which he'd added a yellow essence, the feet looked like they belonged to a corpse. / When a little later I saw my uncle sitting apathetically at his desk, he reminded me of Papa and I felt my throat constricting.

'I went to see the doctor a couple of days ago,' he said. 'He's imploring me to give up smoking, as he says my lungs can't cope any more. Maybe I should follow his advice, I mean, I don't actually want to die without seeing the end of the war. But I like smoking and there's nothing else in my life.' / Then he lit his second cigarette, very sedately, in his torpid way. He tried to catch my attention and suddenly I saw his eyes twitch, as if he were not going to allow himself to burst into tears. A spasm ran down his face and into his spine, as if he had caught another fever.

He told me that a former colleague had sent his Iron Cross Second Class by post to the gendarmerie. It had arrived, but without the two packets of tobacco and one hundred cigarettes for Uncle which the accompanying letter had mentioned. From the wrapping paper it was clear that the package had been opened and then resealed once the tobacco had been removed. / Uncle looked at his Iron Cross, which hung from the framed photograph of his colleague between the two windows, and said, 'If that represents true Volk Community, then nobody's going to put a stop to this disaster. It means the war is lost.' / Those words from his mouth – he was really upset.

Once Uncle had finished describing the incident, he was unrestrained in venting his frustration. He was the most stupid idiot in the entire Reich, all his pleasure was being taken away. The three cigarettes per day that he obtained on his tobacco ration card were too little for the long working days. In all weathers he had to set up roadblocks in the hunt for spies, he had to carry out lice checks on refugee transports and ensure the blackout regulations were being observed. At night he shuffled through the streets with the dog, and when in the deep darkness there was not a glimmer of light save for the twinkling of a few stars, he felt like a cigarette. Especially if somebody had failed to observe the blackout.

'I know I'm smoking myself to death. But so long as I have to continue in my job I can't cope without tobacco. I'd very much like to retire, but in the current circumstances I'm obliged to keep going until I'm no longer physically able. Then it'll stop of its own accord.' / He fanned himself with the cap then took a bar of Hershey chocolate from the drawer – heaven only knows where he got that from – and said, 'I have a great favour to ask you. Would it be possible for you to get hold of some tobacco, even if it were to cost you dearly? I'll reimburse you in full. Nowadays I have no needs apart from my cigarettes, and if I can't have those then nothing gives me any pleasure.'

I would have happily done him this favour if I hadn't felt that I was merely being exploited. I told him, therefore, that I would do what I possibly could, but unfortunately my own needs were greater on account of my anxieties. / Uncle took a deep drag and began his next sentence as he breathed out the smoke. 'But there's no reason for you to suffer from nerves, my boy. You've got a room with a lakeside view. You spend too much time looking backwards and you look too far forwards, that's your problem. You ought to go home and have it off with that Reich German woman, that'll set your mind on other things.'

Afterwards Uncle admitted that for a long time he too had suffered from memories that suddenly came flooding back, but they stopped at some point, so I shouldn't be unduly worried. In 1916 and 1917 he'd been in the Friulian Alps, for a time close to Malborghetto, which was where he'd taken up smoking. The Italians had occupied an embrasure on Monte Piper and on the Due Pizzi. At night he often had outpost duty, which was a thankless task, for at any time an avalanche could sweep you into the valley, and that often happened. After the war he would sometimes hear a sound and in a sudden panic the feeling would shoot through his body that the avalanche was coming and it was all over. / He looked up and I saw the sadness in his eyes. I held his gaze for a few seconds, then Uncle lowered his head and said, 'It's all stored up inside me.'

I gave him another six cigarettes in exchange for the chocolate. He thanked me, then said, 'Your friend Perttes should always remember that he's being watched.' / Shocked by this harsh shift in tone, I asked in horror, 'Has something else happened?' / 'I'm saying this for the sake of good order,' Uncle reassured me. 'He ought to know that a sharp eye is being kept on him and that the best thing would be if he didn't get anyone's hackles up, for in addition to another possible punishment he would have to serve the remaining third of his prison sentence which he was spared. Given the current circumstances he would no doubt wish to avoid this. And tell him that if he's looking for a taker for the cigars he used to be sent from Brazil at Christmas, he should come to me.' / I recalled hearing my uncle mention the cigars before, without my having given the matter much thought. Now I said, 'I cannot imagine these cigars are still around, Perttes has strength of character.' / Uncle fanned himself once more with his cap. 'Apparently he's keeping them as emergency currency. Perhaps his need is urgent enough.' / I didn't like the way my uncle said that. I took a sip of the coffee he'd given me and stared at the wall. / 'If we help one another it'll be easier for all of us,' Uncle said. And he reinforced this by saying, 'You need someone to keep an eye on you too.'

In the morning it poured down relentlessly. Margot and I sat in her room, talking, and Lilo was rattling her playpen. Sometimes she shook it so hard that Margot had serious worries about its longevity. I said that if necessary it could be strengthened with string. / Later Margot received a letter from her mother in Darmstadt, who still seemed to be without any news of her daughter. She asked for the fourth or fifth time whether Margot knew that several of their close relatives had died. And to confuse the situation even further, another of Margot's letters that was months old had arrived in Darmstadt, in which she begged her mother to send more underwear as what she had was so grey and torn that she felt ashamed when visiting the doctor. In between her laments for the dead relatives, Margot's mother informed her that she wouldn't send anything; the old underwear would suffice until the war was over.

Margot was grumpy. Wearing an expression I'd never seen before she went over to the playpen, took the child out and gave her the breast. I lay on the bed and listened to what Margot had to say about her mother's stubbornness, that it was always noisy at home and she hoped her life might take a different direction. She talked and wandered around the room with stiff, hesitant steps, feeding the baby all the while. I watched her and outside the rain hammered against the window.

There was a knock at the door; I opened it a crack. The landlady pushed it right open and said to me, 'I thought I might find you here.' With these words she handed me a flyer which the schoolchildren in Mondsee had distributed that morning. It contained the most important provisions concerning the people's militia, the Volkssturm. / The children had gone from house to house in soaking uniforms and had even tried to give the Brazilian a flyer. But as the Brazilian had been declared *unworthy to bear arms* by the court, he'd sent the children away gruffly. Now the landlady said that this call-up was more aimed at shirkers like myself. / As I felt no need to point out that I was already a soldier, I took the piece of paper and promised to look at it. But the landlady stood there, her arms crossed, and gave me a malicious smile. This made me so angry that I said, 'What about you? Why haven't you been working in an armaments factory all these years? Given your convictions you ought to have volunteered ages ago.' / Doubtless this was not the cleverest way of telling the landlady to leave me in peace. But once I'd got going, I kept piling it on: 'They should send you women to the front one day to change your minds. Anyone still alive after three weeks there would have an idea of what it's really like and would be talking very differently.'

The landlady was still standing there, arms crossed, smiling to herself. Then she reached for a fat candle on the chest of drawers beside the door and hurled it at me. I parried it with my hand. / 'Now get out of here,' Margot ordered. 'You're not quite right in the head.' / 'I'm not going to have anyone tell me what to do in my own house,' the landlady said, but didn't resist when she was pushed out the door. She stood for what must have been another five minutes in the dark hallway before we heard her go back down the stairs. / 'Don't let her upset you, surely you can see she's not right in the head,' Margot said, and put the child back in the playpen.

The following day saw the first air raid on Salzburg. Even when the bombers were in formation over the city, the streets were still a hive of activity. Until then people had believed that Churchill would spare

Salzburg because he'd been treated at Wehrle sanatorium. But they soon realized that this was no longer just an air display. / Even in Mondsee we could hear the shelling and powerful explosions. The second early train to Salzburg waited for two hours on the line at Eugendorf. Margot sat with a damp head in a hairdresser's air-raid shelter.

Because the inhabitants of Salzburg hadn't anticipated that their city might be bombed too, there were many dead. And lots of buildings were now open to the sky, including Mozart's house on Makartplatz. The flak shot down a number of aircraft, but this only served to emphasize just how many had arrived to wrench the Salzburgers from their dreams. One bomber plummeted in flames onto Maxglan, its crew saving themselves with parachutes. Another soldier fell into the Salzach by the Protestant church, was fished out and taken prisoner. / That same evening a Party man gave a talk in Mondsee school hall on the topic: *When is the war going to end?* He struck a popular tone and briefly addressed the question right at the end, admitting that he had no idea.

Now the landlady only ever turned her nose up at me and called me 'the shirker from Vienna in clover with his Reich German whore'. She seemed to harbour so many wicked plans that I decided to get my papers in order before my employer took notice of me again. A few days after the bombing of Salzburg, therefore, I went to Vöcklabruck for an examination. I knew only too well, of course, that my failure to turn up there in August had put me in a precarious situation which, if it came to the worst, might mean my facing a court martial.

I felt horribly queasy as I entered the barracks and I started to sweat at the thought that there would be nothing on file if I claimed that my report from August had gone missing. I wondered whether I wasn't hoping for too much by imagining I could worm my way out of it again, and all of a sudden my confidence vanished. Which is why I didn't waste any time when I found the orderly room empty. I hastily stamped two sheets of paper that were in a pile beside the typewriters, and before I could tell myself that I was completely mad I was already out of the room again, my heart thumping so wildly that it felt as if it were about to leap out of my throat. I bumped into an officer in the hallway who made a remark about my ashen face. When I told him I felt sick he pointed to a door at the end of the corridor. I ran straight there and locked myself in. / In retrospect, I could have taken the long leather coat that had been thrown over the back of a chair in the orderly room. Barracks life in the sixth year of the war.

Back out on the street I didn't know whether to praise myself for my coolness or chide myself for my recklessness. But it galvanized my feeling that I didn't want anything more to do with all this crap; I wanted to lead my own little private life, which in a better world would be taken for granted. I shuddered when I realized who I was dealing with here. But a good mocha in a cafe cleared my mind again and I told myself that the sheets of paper I'd stolen meant I was in a better position today than yesterday. Which gave me a vestige of security again.

It was a sunny, windy October day, and as I was already in town and had some time to kill, I bought Margot a set of underwear, which I got for ten points on my clothes ration card and eleven Reichsmarks. It really didn't matter what I spent, I had to buy things while there *were* still things to buy and, more importantly, while I was still alive.

What struck me about Vöcklabruck was just how many perambulators were out and about. The town was making an effort to revive its population numbers. I was ambivalent about what I saw, for although I liked children, I felt perturbed when I recalled how many of these children had been fathered by men seeking to be promoted up the list of soldiers eligible for leave. They'd got married because they'd been promised leave, and they'd fathered children because they'd been promised leave. People would do whatever they could. And me? Most of all I regretted that I couldn't get pregnant myself and thereby withdraw elegantly into private life. Instead I had to steal paper from the writing room of Vöcklabruck infirmary and falsify reports and signatures, knowing full well that if my deception came to light I would lose my head.

I would have laughed at the idea of a world where men could fall pregnant if I'd been slightly more relaxed about laughing in general. If such a possibility were open to men, the front line would be emptied in a trice, I thought. In my despair I said this to Margot.

'I'd even go to bed with the landlady if that could get me pregnant.'

/ Margot looked at me in surprise and pulled a face, then she laughed a couple of times before pulling the face again. / 'Oh no you wouldn't!' / 'I bloody well would! As I said, the front would be emptied in a trice, not because everyone's against the war, but because nobody who's even got half their wits about them wants to take part personally.'

Margot was thrilled when I gave her the new underwear and it allowed us to move on from that miserable subject. / I'd never experienced such pleasure in giving gifts as with Margot. Most people have no sense of this. Either they're greedy, or they're swept up in an obnoxiously false or genuine modesty. With Margot everything was joyful, heartfelt and natural. She even showed her child the underwear, and turned around in front of the child and did a little dance in front of the child, and she closed her eyes.

Thus the days continued to pass, one after the next. The potato haulms were burned in the fields, groups of children stood around the fires thick with smoke and waited until the potatoes put into the embers were cooked. Trails of smoke streaked the sky, and the squadrons, which were now bombing Salzburg almost weekly, flew over on their way to destroying the roofs of Mozart's city. The leaf canopies of the trees came down too, but under the burden of the season. Frau Bildstein, the teacher, continued to educate the children who had been entrusted to her. And Uncle tried fruitlessly to rustle up some tobacco, while the Brazilian jealously guarded the cigars that Frau Beatriz de Miranda Texeira had once sent him from Rio de Janeiro. The Brazilian said that an industrious collector of butts could cobble together two kilograms of tobacco per day in Rio, but no Brazilian, no matter how poor, would ever bend down to pick up a dropped cigarette, even if they themselves dropped half a packet, which frequently happened, intentionally on occasion, to show that you were somebody. By contrast my uncle was mentally in the gutter, the Brazilian said, and I should tell him that. / I was smart enough to keep this to myself when I next visited my uncle. I was planning to use his typewriter.

The weather had been wonderful since the previous day. After a week of rainfall and fog, during which Margot and I had started to heat the stove, the sun had returned. When the first rays slanted through the fog, everyone breathed a sigh of relief. Although I'd quite liked the fog too, when it knotted together, then pushed out its tentacles like an octopus and climbed up the Drachenwand, the sunshine was more pleasant.

With my hands thrust deep into my trouser pockets, I walked through the town and brought Uncle the tobacco he'd been requesting with such urgency. He was delighted and asked what he owed me. I said that in return he should try to find me some sole leather as I had to reinforce my boots. I raised the prospect of my being re-enlisted soon and said that perhaps one fine day at the front the two of us would be able to shake hands as soldier and Volkssturm man. / 'Dear boy,' he said, 'we don't have to joke about it. We just have to take everything as it comes, there's nothing we can do to stop it.'

He swallowed a tablet of nitroglycerin, shook his head and said he was going to take a stroll. It was good for the heart, he continued, good for the stomach, good for the lungs and good for work, because people thought he was out on patrol, whereas he was just going for a walk. / He put on his jacket and peaked cap.

Sitting at his desk, with my legs across the scattered papers, I asked whether I might stay. The type elements were filthy, I said. I wanted to clean them and then write a letter to the army headquarters to which I was affiliated. The endless shirking and killing time was getting to me and I wanted to put an end to this unbearable state of affairs. / 'I see,' Uncle said, coughing with irritation, but he didn't appear interested in my plan. / Before he left the office he handed me a cloth, half a bottle of turpentine and a box of toothpicks. Then I had a good hour to myself, disturbed only once by his assistant, whom I also helped out of difficulty with a cigarette. I got the typewriter back in running order and then I drafted the documents for August and October, deferring me from duty. The most important words were *demonstrably* and *signs of paralysis*. / The wicked man with the little moustache stared at me from the wall.

With the intention of keeping myself as safe as possible for another couple of months from the downtrodden existence I'd suffered long enough, I went out onto the steps that were steaming in the heat. It smelled of mushrooms, autumnal fruit and rotting potato haulms. Lost in thought, I watched a car drive past which used to belong to the beheaded butchers Lanner and Lanner and was now the property of a sawmill owner in Bad Ischl. The gas bottles on the roof looked like the illustrations of the weapons of retribution in the newspapers. There was something inexplicable in everything. / I was just about to get on my way when Uncle came back, panting and shouting that the body of Nanni Schaller had been found on the Drachenwand.

'I certainly earn my money, I must say,' Uncle said. He fetched his motorcycle from the shed and rattled off towards St Lorenz.

Annemarie Schaller's body

Annemarie Schaller's body was found by two soldiers, Ludwig Holzer and Franz Weng, who were on leave and making the most of the good weather to go mountain climbing. They found her in the so-called 'Hochstelle' of the Drachenwand, around three hundred metres from the bottom. As all of the evacuee children have name tags on their clothes, Holzer and Weng were able to identify the corpse themselves. The recovery of the body was carried out by the head of the local gendarmerie, Johann Kolbe, with the assistance of mountain rescue officer Max Schmarl from Mondsee, and gendarmes Kasper and Kollman from Unterach station. The body, which was already heavily decomposed and down to the skeleton in places, was taken to the mortuary of Mondsee Cemetery. From what could be established at the scene of the accident the girl must have fallen about two hundred and fifty metres from the ridge and come to a rest in one of the ditches in the 'Hochstelle'. In all probability death occurred in the course of the fall itself, for on her way down Annemarie Schaller may have hit several rocks protruding from the mountainside. The authorities established that feet, spine and ribs were broken. The fall must have occurred from a great height, for at the scene of the accident, or where the body was found, shoes, stockings, a torch and a satchel, all of which had been torn from the girl's body as she fell, lay scattered around. / The official search for the girl has been called off. / [Signed:] Johann Kolbe, head of the gendarmerie.

For several days everyone was distressed and numb with shock. I was filled with horror at the thought that the corpse, its eyes hacked out and no longer recognizable as Nanni Schaller, lay in the mortuary, without sleep or thoughts. A forearm was missing too, taken by a large bird, perhaps, up to its eyrie. Uncle said that a child's body missing its eyes and right forearm was a dismal sight.

When the other girls in Schwarzindien were told that the body had been found, most of them started whispering and one passed out. An elderly lecturer came from Salzburg and comforted the girls sitting in the garden and beside the lake by stroking their knees. The innkeeper didn't trust the lecturer's good heart and insinuated that the girls' crying was arousing something quite different from his pity. Fisticuffs followed and the term *child molester* was uttered. My uncle intervened and personally accompanied the lecturer back to the station. He said he wondered where all these madmen had suddenly come from.

There was no wake for Nanni Schaller as she'd been dead for far too long. Owls had held the vigil.

I went over to Schwarzindien too, but didn't stop at the camp. The flag was flying at half-mast. It was so quiet by the shore of the lake that the grazing of the few cows in the meadows seemed to echo around the countryside. A chill drifted up from the water. Everything was so neat and tidy; even the surface of the water and the sky gave the impression that they'd been tended, cleaned and given a fresh coat of paint where necessary. The blue-grey mountains faded into the distance.

I recalled Nanni standing calmly yet inquisitively in the garden of the Schwarzindien camp, one of the few girls who had radiated a sense of contentment. I recalled a girl who had held my hand while sweat had dripped from my nose. Something about the puzzling impression I'd gained from this encounter had stayed with me. / Then I felt deeply ashamed when I remembered that Nanni had asked me to write to her mother and tell her that being in love was a beautiful thing. *As a soldier*, I heard Nanni say again. And then her disappointed, angry scrunching up of the letter when I turned down her request. / I fancied I could see her before me, sometimes knee-deep in snow, defiantly climbing up to the ridge of the Drachenwand, eating the occasional biscuit and in the sunny spots looking at the hellebores that were already blooming in large quantities. I was able to put myself in her shoes and understand why she hadn't turned back. What she had done was ill-advised, but it bore the stamp of independence. / Eventually, or so I imagined, Nanni had reached the ridge of the Drachenwand and once there, freed from the burden of the previous weeks, she'd recovered her breath and gazed out proudly at the landscape. Mondsee lay below her, the mountains to the east and south stood in the sunlight, and in the distance the Attersee glittered. Nanni had scribbled a few lines on a postcard for Kurt, slipped the card into her satchel and then attempted the descent. She had slipped on the stone of the ridge, which was difficult to negotiate and hard to judge because of the snow that still lay on the ground.

Her inquisitive, challenging, slightly mocking eyes were still fixed on me. She seemed to be made from a different substance to her fellow schoolgirls; she'd been subject to different laws. And again I thought of Kurt and how it might be a good idea if I wrote to him. But I didn't dare, so put the idea on hold.

In Mondsee and the surrounding area the discovery of Nanni's body caused much disquiet. And yet one more misfortune didn't knock life in the village off track. The last few apples fell from the trees, there was beetroot in the garden, as big as a child's head. And for a few days the sky was bright blue. Its cheerfulness astounded me.

As there was no suspicion of any third-party involvement and because, as my uncle said, there was no need to suspect a murder behind every accident, only a routine medical examination took place. Uncle said the corpse was no longer in a fit state for a proper post-mortem; they hadn't even been able to establish whether the girl was still a virgin. He pulled a face. / The only thing they'd established with certainty was that the girl had died. Any appropriate experts? 'They're all digging trenches,' Uncle said. 'Or working as guards in Mauthausen, Ebensee, Zipf,' the Brazilian said. In any case he thought that any experts had long forgotten how to look for causes of death, something that was bound to happen when one was in the pay of killers.

The case was closed as far as my uncle was concerned, and he intended to feel pleased about this with no caveats. 'The Drachenwand in April isn't a very clever idea,' he said, shaking his head. 'I get dizzy standing on a chair.'

He drafted one final protocol relating to Annemarie Schaller. With his two index fingers he crudely hit the keys of the now cleaned typewriter. He described the scene of the accident, which, as he said, in itself gave an explanation of the tragic course of events. All you had to do was interpret the clues correctly and put them in the right order. Done and dusted. He attributed the accident, as he did everything in connection with young people, to the state of mind brought about by the onset of puberty, mixed with juvenile recklessness. Putting his signature to his composition, he said, 'These things just happen from time to time.' And he shook his head once more at the tragic case.

It didn't look like suicide either, Uncle said. 'And why should it?' Why would she need reasons? I thought. All right, it didn't matter. / I remembered a roommate wanting to kill himself during our basic training. He'd got such a roasting because the buttons on his coat were poorly sewn on. I then got a fellow recruit who was a tailor to sew them on properly and paid him with a bottle of beer. That sorted that out.

Once in Russia some comrades and I found the head of a corpse in a meadow, an unsettling sight. We played football with the head, God knows why. I think we did it out of disrespect for death rather than disrespect for the dead man. He could have been any of us. We kicked the head in high arcs over the meadow and for a few minutes the war released us from its clutches.

The mayor provided a grave from communal funds; like almost everyone in the town he was deeply shocked. Nanni's mother agreed that the girl should be buried in Mondsee, and as the police file was now closed the funeral took place four days after the body was found. / As we all felt the need to be at the Mass, Margot made the snap decision to take Lilo with her. She rejected my suggestion of leaving the child with the landlady, for that woman was now on the verge of insanity. One day she'd head off to the post office with a cup of coffee in her hand, the next she'd turn up at the neighbours in a frayed dressing gown. 'She's not even capable of lying straight in bed,' Margot said. 'There's no doctor who can help her any more.'

A good crowd had already gathered in the square in front of the church. Some old women in mourning clothes and with matching harsh expressions stood between the representatives of the evacuee schoolchildren from the western suburbs of Vienna, who had already marched to the church. In uniform and spruced up, the girls stood in compact blocks. Last to arrive were the girls from Plomberg. In formation, with drums and flags, they showed the progress made in children's drill, moving in nightmarish geometrical sequences, a sort of surreal Leni Riefenstahl choreography. The worst part of it was that, on this day of the funeral, the girls seemed to really enjoy the drill and the robot-like behaviour, as if marching in time could protect them from death.

The marching in time, two abreast, cast its evil spell over me too. As I watched these girls, mesmerized, I felt the tension in my body. Only the Brazilian remained calm. 'I feel sorry for them,' he said. 'It's like at a military cemetery: everything in rank and file. At a military cemetery the graves also try to convince us that the soldiers died because orderliness demanded it.'

Of Nanni's relatives, her mother came, whom I'd met in the spring, accompanied by a woman and a girl of around ten, who ventured curious glances from the shadows of the two women. I happened to overhear that these were Kurt's mother and sister.

The priest read from the service book, his arms open wide. The book was probably as large as it was to avoid the priest having to turn the pages so often. Turning pages must be annoying if you're standing there, arms open. The text was about divine Jerusalem and the precious metals refined there on a large scale. It reminded me of a film they'd shown us at the front: *The Golden City*. Essentially, everyone always said and promised the same things, the fact that redemption came through demise. / The priest scratched his beard. And I kept thinking of where Nanni had been found on the Drachenwand when he said the Lord make his face shine upon thee, and the light shineth in darkness and the darkness comprehended it not. / But the idea of death being redemption? I'm not sure, I can think of better things than lying buried in a wooden box a few metres beneath the ground while worms and beetles delight in my dead flesh. / I do, however, believe that all people go on living somewhere, I just don't know where.

I liked hearing the priest say, 'The ox-cart of our life has become stuck in the mud. The devil is hanging onto the back of it. If God doesn't pull us forwards because we don't harness him, how are we ever going to get out of there?' / Although this was pure Catholicism, I fancied I could hear an undertone of restraint.

An unfamiliar genuflection – left or right leg? Or didn't it matter? Couldn't be that rigorous. Interesting all the same. Now the entire congregation made its way down to the cemetery.

When the coffin was lowered into the grave we were standing some way at the back, and because the ground was dry Lilo ended up crawling around amongst the graves on a strip of grass. We let her crawl and she was delighted to be left to her own devices; she was looking after herself. She nibbled at the edge of a gravestone and squealed a couple of times without being loud. The uniformed girls stood all around, not daring to move. Lilo pulled herself up on one of the gravestones, looked over at us and slapped the stone with her free hand. At that very moment a gentle breeze rose and wafted into the bushes beside us, gently rustling the leaves. A swarm of birds flew up from a large oak tree.

The evacuees sang 'The Good Comrade', the song of a soldier who can't hold the hand of his friend who's been struck by a bullet because he has to reload his rifle.

I'd witnessed many funerals during my four years at the front. I preferred the ones that took place on the spot, without pomp or embellishment. In most cases the short speeches were kept very general to avoid the possibility of sounding insincere or hypocritical. All over. You've got stones in your mouth now. My university. My lectures. Salute!

Digging the graves felt good too; one had the sense of doing something that wasn't entirely pointless. It was something serious, at any rate. Usually the earth wasn't especially stony. We'd shovel earth for half an hour and then place the body in the pit. It was so simple and so natural that you soon stopped thinking about the horrible aspect of it, or only sometimes, such as when the body was so badly mutilated that the sense of it seemed to be lost too.

I once visited a large military cemetery in Roslavl. I counted more than seven hundred and fifty crosses standing side by side in long rows.

On three of the graves were wreaths with ribbons and harrowing messages from the relatives. One grave, for Max Wild, reminded me of a fellow pupil by the same name, the year was right. Was it him? No idea, I didn't pursue the matter any further. But in that cemetery I was reminded of one of the F's comments, the full significance of which many people possibly only realized much later: 'The last battalion on the battlefield will be a German one.' Or perhaps only half a battalion . . .

While the evacuee girls sang, Nanni's mother suffered a sobbing fit and had to be supported by her sister. Susi, Kurt's sister, cried too, but was thoughtful enough to hug her aunt. And Margot cried as well. But none of the evacuee girls shed tears, they merely swallowed hard, fixed their gazes on their shoes and fell silent so that the singing gradually became quieter.

I thought about the beauty of life and the senselessness of war. For what was war except for an empty space into which beautiful life vanished? And one day, as final confirmation of the senselessness, the space into which beautiful life had vanished would dissipate too. What then? Whatever it had been, it no longer existed.

'The Lord is my shepherd; I shall not want,' the priest said, his hat slipping over his eyes. He said something about the life hereafter being better and the heavenly bridegroom. I found this last bit rather bold considering all the insinuations that had been made about the girl. Then some earth was thrown onto the coffin. Rest in peace.

When we left the cemetery, clouds towered overhead and their shadows appeared abruptly, as if someone with broad shoulders had approached unnoticed and planted themselves over Mondsee. At the same time a cold wind blew over from the lake. At once the depressed-looking people became animated and a few seconds later the first fat drops of rain fell with a clunk onto the base of a metal watering can upturned on a stick. / A man called out to the girls who were marching away, 'Just as the Lord God makes things wet, so he makes them dry again.'

Now Nanni's mother left the cemetery too, walking unsteadily. As she passed the gate she lifted her red face and looked around in that strangely distanced, sober manner that I'd seen in Nanni too. Her face was notched with a few severe lines. She sucked in her lower lip and looked at the teacher who was coming to say goodbye. The two spoke a few words, their lips moving weakly. / When the teacher had left, the mother stood there, unmoving, torpid, beneath the few heavy raindrops.

Eventually my uncle came over from the other side of the road. Now Frau Schaller smoothed down her skirt self-consciously. / My uncle handed her a golden necklace which had been found beside the body, a filigree chain with the image of a guardian angel, also golden. He placed the piece of jewellery in her hand, she looked at it briefly, then closed her fist and didn't open it again for the whole time we stood on the square.

When the rain became heavier the street by the church emptied. The Brazilian wanted to go straight back home, but Margot and I said we wanted something to drink and went to the pub. The Brazilian wouldn't come in with us at first, he just took shelter, but the downpour was torrential. Soon afterwards there was another loud deluge and so it went on. The Brazilian became increasingly anxious, for Margot and I had sat down. Pea soup. Eventually the Brazilian came in too. At times he forgot his manners, leaped up from the table and ran outside to check on the weather, but only because he felt smothered by the air and the conversation. People were discussing the war in its different facets and their faces soon relaxed again; one had to think of tomorrow too, after all. And seeing how apprehensive he was, the Brazilian ought maybe to laugh if people were cracking jokes. He was certainly not what you would call composed; I could see that only the utmost effort of willpower was preventing him from becoming verbally abusive. His anxiety spread to me and I believe that if we'd sat there for five minutes longer, I couldn't have guaranteed anything. The Brazilian growled impatiently. / 'Time to go,' I said.

On the way home the wind was still buffeting the odd raindrop. And late that afternoon a grey rain set in, falling lethargically. I immediately sensed that the next few days would be murky too. And indeed the rain didn't stop for three whole days. The wet and cold part of the autumn had begun.

It's still light enough to write

It's still light enough to write. It's just getting chilly. The moon is shining yellow in the light bluish-grey sky. I can still make out the yellow and red of the trees. Margot is playing with the child outside. The little one walked on her own for the first time today and she's been laughing. A great day. When Lilo took her first steps there was jubilation in the whole house: shrieks of joy from Margot, shrieks of joy from me, and even the landlady applauded and later brought sweets. The smell of leaves rises from the garden. I'm amazed. No moment passes without wonder.

Margot came up with the child, took off her coat, hung it over my chair and finally sat down. I love it when she sits beside me, but it means I can't write any more; all the strokes of my pen go askew. She sat next to me and I kept talking to her, either asking questions or saying I had to note something down. She said I should be quiet and continue writing, and she told me not to forget that Lilo's walking now. / 'I've already mentioned it,' I said. / 'That's good.'

Margot fed her daughter, holding her handkerchief under the child's chin. Afterwards she started writing too, letters, because the whole world had to know that Lilo had taken her first steps in a rented room above a pigsty in Mondsee. And what a joy it was to watch the girl try out this new skill, still shaky, but refusing to be discouraged when she fell. / From one chair to another. From the knee of one person writing to another knee of another person writing. And again. / It's a shame you never remember later on how much pleasure you got from repetition when you were small.

Margot wrote first to her mother, then to the child's father. He was now in Memel. In his last letter he'd said that nothing much had changed, but the water was terribly cold already and it was occasionally sleeting now. His hands were stiff, so he was writing with gloves on. Thank God some winter clothes had finally been delivered; now they wouldn't freeze so badly as they stood day and night in the trenches in worn-out hiking shoes rather than boots and so on. / He said he'd dreamed of Lilo and that Lilo really seemed to have grown up. And that he was very pleased Margot had her hands full with the child, for at least it prevented her from getting other ideas. Comrades of his here were telling him that a wife couldn't remain faithful with such a long separation. And when he was unfazed by their teasing, rejecting it, they said, well, pigs might fly.

A lovely expression isn't it? But so what. / I'm sending you some more money today. Do what you want with it, dear Margot, who knows whether I'll ever have any of it. Use it, go on an excursion, travel, buy whatever can still be bought, and make life better for you and the child at least.

I felt bad when she read out these lines. But Margot was my first successful attempt in years to rectify my luck and I didn't intend to be shy about it. Well, what can one change?

Whereas Margot's husband had been without leave for almost a year, the landlady's husband turned up again at All Saints. Supposedly there were official reasons for his being back home, the firm had full confidence in his reliability, there were things that needed to be done. / But there wasn't much evidence of anything being done; all we noticed was, as the Brazilian put it, his emphatically spreading the fug of his ideology. Fortunately he would often disappear into the cellar for hours, where he carried out a detailed inventory of the supplies stored there.

Outwardly the varnisher continued to signal his conviction that not only had his hour come, but that it would last. That, after Paris, Belgrade would be reconquered too. He didn't appear to be perturbed by the fact that the Red Army was outside both Prague and Budapest, while the Americans and the British were getting ready to cross the

Rhine. And anyone who wanted to could now get from the Eastern Front to the Western Front in a day. A day passes quickly. And how quickly an hour passes. The varnisher's hour was over. And there was something enervating about the adamant, rigid, obstinate honour with which he defended his position. Going up to Margot as she was washing the nappies, he said that so many people in the world envied the F, but what could the F do about the fact he was such a good man and had chalked up so many successes? Margot told me her face went numb.

After Dohm had finished his cigarette he went back down into the cellar. Being a smart aleck and cautious old fox, he'd stored crates of Marseille soap down there years ago, occasionally adding other items to his collection, such as raisins from Sarajevo and washing powder from Sofia. This time he'd got hold of several canisters of sunflower oil, which implied that rather than anticipating better times he was making provisions to ensure that a military collapse wasn't followed by an economic one.

I felt uncomfortable in his presence. Whenever he looked at me he sneered and indicated my insignificance with a fleeting glance. We spoke once, albeit very briefly, a rather one-sided conversation, for I had very little to say to him after the episode with the dog back in spring. He seemed surprised that I was still here and he questioned my laxity. In the hope that he'd be off again soon, I told him that it gave me no pleasure, but I already had my recall papers in my pocket. He was pleased to hear this and he reminded me of my sacred duties. It struck me that I had more in common with an Eskimo than this fool.

As one might imagine, the Brazilian made less of an effort to hide his aversion to his brother-in-law. The sheer hatred they felt for each other was palpable. Already on the second day they almost came to blows; the subject of their slanging match wasn't politics, but the shooting of the dog. At some point they ran out of swear words and were just snorting. For a few seconds they stood facing one another like mortal enemies, until they both turned around as if to order and stomped off in different directions. / When the Brazilian had calmed back down he said, visibly satisfied, that just like the biggest fool of them all, H, his brother-in-law couldn't come to terms with being a pipsqueak, and that was where his wickedness came from. He rubbed his hands with glee.

I often sat with him in the greenhouse again, knees up to my chin, cigarette in mouth, and listened to him talk. Sometimes I helped him out with work, also with the odd cigarette in my mouth, which he reluctantly tolerated because he didn't want to send me away. He was dependent on my assistance, for it didn't seem as if he could muster sufficient energy or will to work his way out of poverty. Although he had plenty of seedlings – lettuce leaves, chard, cauliflower and a few orchid beds – if nobody kept him company he would fall asleep mid-morning on the dog blanket, or in the hammock if the weather was fine, wilful and withdrawn from the world, despite the squadrons of bombers flying over the lake. And the snails that at night invaded the greenhouse in their dozens from the neighbouring fields stripped the young salad plants bare.

Maybe it was will that the Brazilian lacked more than energy. The way he wore his Panama hat with the elegance of a loafer was remarkable. And when he finally got down to work his movements were so routine they could only be those of someone who knows his work inside out and is thinking of something completely different while doing it. He seemed utterly indifferent to the world around him and sometimes would stop and not move for several minutes.

His *back to nature* got on my nerves, but he swore by it, insisting that every other approach was the road to madness. I listened patiently. But when he started talking politics, which didn't happen very often any more, I put on the record with the South American songs, sung by a tenor to guitar accompaniment, and demanded he translate them: *I see you in everything that is hot and has the colour of the sun.* / We looked at each other and laughed.

In the dampness rising from the earth he leaned on his hoe. 'Sometimes I could do with a little affection,' he said. 'I don't want to sound pathetic. I enjoy my isolation for the most part and feel complete in my solitude. But sometimes when I'm tired it would be nice to be embraced. I miss affection more than I miss the south. Maybe it's because I've never had very much of it.' / He smiled apologetically. / Another rain shower then pelted the roof of the greenhouse and we continued with our work while the tenor launched into another melody: *Ai, yoyo . . . ai, yoyo . . .*

On Tuesday there was a record-breaking Föhn wind that made one's knees turn to jelly and stirred feelings in the heart that ranged from melancholy to bloodlust. The bluest sky. The Drachenwand had moved much closer, the lake was an improbable shade of green. The aftertaste of the discovery of Nanni's body was an extra ingredient in this dangerous cocktail. The only solution was more work therapy.

The Brazilian and I shook the last apples from the tree. Then Margot and I baked an apple cake, using baking powder tablets instead of yeast. They did their job. As I tucked into the first slice Margot was ironing the washing and the room was filled with the smell of hot fabric and steaming dye. / We talked about her husband; Margot apologized for not having mentioned me in her letters, saying she wanted to wait until the war was over. I told her she wasn't accountable to me. / 'I see it differently,' she replied. / I gazed at the slim figure of this long-haired woman. As she ironed, her breasts swung gently beneath her blouse. Her slim, bony hands and her arms that were too long appeared to grow even longer in her anxiousness. She was folding one of Lilo's dresses. As she pulled herself up the girl made the blanket dirty with her fingers, sticky from the cake. From the bed the child looked at me with curiosity; she could see that I was thinking.

And the Föhn shook the branches of the cherry tree, now denuded of almost all its leaves. And suddenly the branches froze as if the tree had been given the order to stand to attention. And I was haunted by the blackest visions: that my falsified reports would be found out and I'd never come back here. And I was overwhelmed so suddenly by images that I got the shivers and no longer knew whether it was day or night or something in-between that would never be whole again.

I don't know much about what happened after that, except for the fact that I took a Pervitin and toddled off to bed with tiny steps, feeling the whole time that my legs would fail me. Margot told me later that I lay down and fell asleep almost instantaneously. Something else new.

Now I can see the coffee pot on the table and beside it the small metal tin with the Pervitin. Margot puts the child's bottle to her cheek to test the temperature and I wonder how all of this fits together.

Margot gave Lilo the bottle and when it was almost finished the child brought it all up again. Margot was so frustrated and exhausted that she burst into tears. 'All of us are clearly at the end of our tether,' she said.

Soon afterwards there was another slanging match outside. There's no point going into all the details, but the Brazilian and his brother-in-law swapped insults. To begin with I got the impression they were arguing about healthy food and how harmful smoking was. The Brazilian swore by his love of the sun and said he'd rather throw the cigars he still had on the fire than leave them to a bunch of criminals, compared to whom Nero, Tiberius and Caligula were moral giants. He railed against all meat eaters. The worst thing about his stay in prison in Linz, he said, was the industry there, which gave off a permanent foul smell. How appropriate that they'd named the large factory in Linz after the fat Reichsmarschall. Whenever they'd processed a big batch of rotten eggs, the stench had been so horrific it was as if the carnivorous Reichsmarschall had farted. 'Only the farts of meat eaters smell like that,' he yelled.

Dohm shouted back that he was sure there must be a bug-infested pallet bed free in Mozartstrasse; the back-to-nature evangelist was clearly desperate to revisit Linz. The Brazilian yelled he was desperate to get to Rio de Janeiro because he didn't want to live amongst people who thought they were inherently superior. Gobineau, who'd virtually invented racism as a philosophy, had been the emissary to the imperial court in Rio de Janeiro, and Gobineau had hated the country. That was the most wonderful thing about Brazil, he said. 'Members of the master race aren't happy there.'

'Damn you!' / 'Child molester!' / 'Negro king!' / 'Megalomaniac!' / 'Dead loss!' / 'Professional crook!' / 'Arsehole!'

'And let me tell you one thing: the only reason you robots want to make life difficult for people like me who've retained their sense of independence is that I remind you of the time years ago when you lot were free too. Go off to your F, who's given ghastly European civilization its last incitement to violence and irrationality, crawl up his arse until just your boots are sticking out. Then you can click your heels one last time before the F shoots his dribble. And I hope the devil breaks your neck.'

It was silent for a moment. Margot and I were huddled by the open window. The landlady stood to one side, her fists braced against her hips, waiting for what was to follow. The varnisher looked around in consternation, in case anyone had heard the last crude insults that had been hurled. He glanced at Margot and me, and he saw the sneer that was a permanent feature on his wife's face. Then he took out his pistol and poked the barrel into the Brazilian's left eye. The two of them stood like this, both with scarlet faces. / 'One weakling fewer,' Dohm said coldly. Then he relaxed, put his pistol away and said, 'I'm not going to bother even spitting at someone like you.' / With a stiff smile he went over to the barn. A few seconds later we heard the motorcycle revving and the varnisher drove off without shutting the barn door behind him.

When I asked the Brazilian what had got into him he said nothing. I waited for an answer. Slowly, embarrassment took hold and I sensed he wanted to be left alone. Then he said, 'The Indians wear shrunken heads on their belts and the lips of these shrunken heads are sewn together with human hair so they cannot talk. But I'm not like that, I just can't resist.' / He put his hand in his trouser pocket and gave me his keys for a second time. / 'I know I'm an idiot, Menino. But not as big an idiot as others, which is why I'm now going to vanish into thin air. I'd rather be in my hole than in theirs. Even if I have to share my hole with rats, it's better because I've chosen it myself.' / He looked at me with his pale grey eyes. Rather than any hint of reproach in his eyes, they exuded an affection with which he seemed to acknowledge that I had changed too. / I put the keys in my pocket. / 'You've got complete authority here, Menino. The cigars are under the floor in the dining room. Take them if needed.' / Then he plodded off to the house, spitting as he went, and disappeared behind the door.

Margot and I stayed beside the broken handcart and waited. It was the beginning of November and the warm Föhn was blowing. The sun was already setting and a yellow moon was briefly visible between the gathering clouds. It would be dark soon. The Brazilian came out again with a large sack over his shoulder and he hastily stuffed a few folded pieces of paper into his back pocket. He probably wanted to say something else, quite a lot perhaps. His eyes gazed at us sadly. Then he nodded. To his sister, who was still standing at the fountain outside, he said, 'You prefer looking at me from behind than from the front, Trude, so please leave me in peace now.' / She went into the house. / Then the Brazilian was standing, shivering, in the rear garden by the boundary to the open field. He braced himself. He knew that his life was no longer worth anything, but this didn't seem to bother him as much as might be expected. Free to die as an individual was better than to lead the live of a slave, he said, before trudging off with the sack over his shoulder and his trouser legs flapping. One more refugee.

I took a look at the rooms

I took a look at the rooms where the Brazilian had been living. Dangling from the ceiling of the pantry were lengths of cord cut through with a knife, from which the sacks of dried fruit and vegetables had hung. I took the bunch of feathers that stood watch over the pride of the person sleeping beneath to avoid it falling into the wrong hands, as well as the cigars: five boxes of twenty-five. / It was hard work taking up the boards carefully so as not to leave any traces, while having to get the job done very quickly. I was on edge and again haunted by the feeling of being in danger. / I carried the cigars over to my house in a crate covered with work clothes. It was handy that it was raining. But, most importantly, I'd waited until the landlady and her husband had left the house to go to the local Party evening.

When I entered Margot's room she was sitting at the table, sewing the moleskins into a small blanket. Lilo was sliding across the room on her pot, her eyes wide with expectation that I was about to praise her, but I didn't feel like it. I asked Margot where I should hide the cigars. She said I ought to have left them where they were. / But housing in the village was getting more and more critical. The Plomberg camp had been wound up seemingly overnight and was now home to Slovak German refugees. I said it was unlikely that the Brazilian's house would be left to stand empty, and the moment fifteen people were housed there I would lose my access. / Margot agreed with me; I could rely on Margot. She thought for a while, then raised a number of points, needles between her lips all the while, which I begged her not to swallow. / 'One needs to learn how to do these things,' she said. / I begged her to take them out all the same as I was feeling nervous enough as it was. She obliged me without further comment or even shaking her head.

We stowed the cigars away in one of Margot's lockable suitcases. From the same case Margot fished out a German-manufactured pistol bought on the Polish black market and which her husband had made her keep for emergencies. I took the pistol because the sight of it reassured me at once.

I now realize too that I write best when the pistol is on the table beside me.

I didn't fall asleep until long past midnight, then woke again with a coughing fit soon afterwards. Going back to sleep was out of the question. I was also disturbing Margot; I could hear her tossing and turning next door. In the morning I was exhausted and my muscles were aching from the exertions of the previous day. This made me realize I was back in the war, for they were the same aches I'd often had for weeks at a time at the front. The poison was seeping into me again. / For several months I'd tried to sustain the illusion that I could sit tight with Margot until the end of the war, but now reality was knocking at my door and I sensed that life wouldn't return to calm waters any time soon.

From somewhere the landlady's husband brought a few cases of French wine, which presumably had been hastily evacuated across the Rhine without consulting the owners. A lack of everything, a lack of everything . . . And that lackey Dohm leaped onto his motorcycle, heading for the catastrophe, oiled and greased. And never washed. He wouldn't even give water to anyone unless it was for money. Such was my opinion of the man.

But before he left he took me aside again and apologized for his irritability. He was often depressed too, he said. His work in the General Government was so bloody stupid; all he ever did was write lists, queues, queues, it annoyed him so much that he often felt like kicking up a rumpus. And when he came home for a few days he wanted to relax, but instead he had his hands full with his wife and her family. / Now he came to the point. He somehow had the impression that I'd be here for a while longer and so he asked me whether I'd keep an eye on his wife. He knew she could often be difficult, but he felt attached to her and he liked her. She had a trapped nerve in her neck from all the work she did, which gave her terrible pain and circulatory disorders. That was why she was so vicious; she would even rant and rave at him, using foul language. If he answered back she would say: *Don't annoy me or I'll knock you to the floor.* She was never able to find peace anywhere, although she felt most at ease by the lake or when she was in the animal shed. She was restless all the time and it was best not to aggravate her. / 'So, no hard feelings,' he said. 'And please keep an eye on Trude and be lenient on her.'

I had to take a morning Pervitin or I wouldn't have been able to deal with what I'd heard. It's impossible to listen to such talk if you're unwell yourself. As I've already said, no moment passes without wonder.

Dohm the varnisher rushed down the stairs one last time and checked that the cellar door was locked properly, then he departed for the war, which he trusted more than peace on account of his *bloody stupid work.* / And that very same day another train of refugees arrived, Danube Swabians who'd driven large herds of steppe cattle westwards, the last of their possessions. Most of the refugees were billeted in hastily vacated camps and schools. The barracks along the line of the motorway were already full and a large herd of longhorns were grazing between Mondsee and Hof. They put two families with many children in the Brazilian's house, and so now longhorns were grazing outside my window that faced the street too. Margot and I had managed to salvage the gramophone and the records from the greenhouse. Margot had taken another look around and wanted to take some tomatoes, but I'd felt uneasy and so we hurried home. Less than an hour later the local Party leader told us that the refugees would take over the market garden business.

In the presence of the landlady – as the Brazilian's sister – the local Party leader and my uncle, the Brazilian's most personal effects were locked in a room. The key to this room was given a tag and a nail on the key rack in the gendarmerie. Everything else was handed over to the refugees. / In Mondsee the Brazilian was as good as dead.

Uncle remained puzzled by the whereabouts of the cigars. He asked whether I knew anything about them; I said I didn't. Despite this he asked me to visit him at the gendarmerie the following day. He didn't know how much longer he would be here, for the latest regulations might mean he would have to leave at once. Fear and despondency were reflected in his tired, bloated face.

Total war was a total sham. In particular it was the call-up of boys with fluff still on their cheeks that now revealed in horrific clarity to those back at home just how lunatic and inhumane the firm was as it pressed on in the service of blood and soil, ever ready to demand utterly pointless sacrifices that served nobody. It just effaced the happiness of those affected and, in the worst case, their lives too. All they were doing was shovelling more coal onto the fire, irrespective of the cost. / I felt an icy chill rise inside me at the thought that the children, supposedly the F's most precious asset, were now to pay the price for what their insane parents had cooked up. By contrast I didn't feel sorry for the old men. They'd supported the whole enterprise from the start with their loud cheers when reports of victories came through, and with these same cheers they'd led the parade to the Prophet's arse, only now to be hit by the realization that wars are won at the end rather than the beginning.

The following day I paid a visit to my uncle, as requested. It was raining and the wet weather had brought to the fore the sloth that was always latent at the gendarmerie. When I entered the office, Uncle was sitting at his desk. 'Do you know what the front face of a coin is called? Seven letters, apparently.' / I shrugged. / 'I urgently need it,' he said. / As ever, he was friendly, more friendly than me, because he was getting on my nerves. / So when he handed me the sole leather for my boots I felt bad. One of Uncle's good traits was his reliability in such matters, one had to give him that. / I placed ten cigarettes on the desk and he thanked me with a swear word that was meant appreciatively. Then he pinched the back of my neck, his usual manner. / 'I'm short on cigarettes again, I'll be having to suck my thumb soon,' he moaned. But his office was so full of smoke one could barely breathe; the air was blue with cigarette fumes.

My uncle moistened his fingers with his yellow tongue and leafed through a couple of pages of the newspaper. 'Just read that, top left.' / The article was about remuneration for Volkssturm soldiers. It said they received a wage of one Reichsmark per day, were entitled to food and lodging, but no financial assistance or recompense for clothing was possible. / 'If there's a shortage of uniforms,' Uncle said, 'then you can be sure there's a shortage of more important things too. They'd better leave me in peace. None of this has got anything to do with me!'

It might not be particularly flattering to say something like this about your own uncle, but I feel it's accurate: being a total opportunist, Uncle was the biggest arsehole of them all.

His main concern was to avoid all trouble and eke out as many advantages for himself as he could. Everything else was of minor significance. This explained his profound dislike for the Brazilian, who caused him work. I regret to have to say it, but Uncle hated everyone who failed to live by the motto: a citizen's first duty is peace. / Not for nothing was it in this region that the Christmas carol was composed with the line 'sleep in heavenly peace'.

'Admit it,' I said, 'here at the gendarmerie you'd easily last another ten years of war.' / This made my uncle cross. Contesting all arguments with his cigarette, he claimed that he'd lived through his war years ago and had nothing to reproach himself for. And the fact that young, insolent whippersnappers like me now had to live through their own war gave great satisfaction to an old man like him. / 'It's not my war,' I said. / 'So who drove a plundered Citroën all the way to the Caucasian steppes and hung around in the Soviet Union for years? Did you have a doppelgänger there?'

I lowered my eyes and said nothing. In all honesty my uncle was right, it was my war too, I'd played my part in this criminal war, and whatever I might do or say later, my role in this war would exist for evermore, something of me would always be part of it, and something of the war would always be part of me. I couldn't change that.

'I think it would be best if we stopped talking politics,' Uncle said. 'I mean, we can't change things, and anyway there's never going to be an outcome that satisfies everybody.' / It was meant to be conciliatory. / Then he thought of something else and said, 'You're just like your father, he's such a miserable know-all too.' / It was fair enough that my face registered disapproval, and my uncle insisted that there were definitely some things about me that I'd inherited from my father. / I had no desire for a conversation that was like an arm-wrestle, but a few things sprung to my mind too, such as the fact that, like Papa, Uncle

Johann was unable to express any emotions except for self-pity and contempt for others.

Someone ought to take the time to consider whether self-pity and contempt might actually be the most disastrous combination of emotions in our lives. It's a question that needs thorough analysis. I don't trust myself to get to the bottom of it. Not me. Perhaps this honour will fall to someone else.

Uncle had to go and check a refugee transport, which he found an onerous task. He said that the fleas would now become established in Germany again. And, as if trying to find something I would entirely concur with, he added, 'Life shouldn't be easier for us here than for the soldiers at the front. The flea will have more pleasure from a washed German woman's body than from the filthy skin of a private.'

When he had fastened the buttons on his jacket and was doing up his dark-blue oilskin, for it was still raining, I turned the subject of conversation to the Brazilian. I thought that he was the real reason my uncle had asked to see me. To my surprise my uncle appeared quite dismissive. He wasn't interested in the Brazilian unless he turned up again; personally, he couldn't care less about the man. If the Brazilian felt the need to risk his neck with careless talk, that was his lookout, nobody was forcing him to talk like that, but oh well, in the end everybody was a mystery even to themselves. / Uncle uttered this last comment with the expression of a philosopher, and at the same time reached onto one of the shelves and took from it a package containing a few things that had belonged to Nanni Schaller. Would I do him a favour and take the package to the camp at Schwarzindien when I was on one of my strolls? He couldn't go himself, for the world was a place of work and pleasures were thinly sown.

I didn't probe any further, but I suspected my uncle wished to avoid a conversation with the teacher. He seemed to have plenty of time for his crosswords. / Outside in the street we brought our quarrel to an end with a handshake. Uncle said we shouldn't discuss politics, it couldn't end well and we ought to draw a distinct line under today. Thus we parted company, him breathing in deeply the fresh air that dampened his almost non-existent bronchioles; me hunched because of the oppressiveness I felt at every turn.

The next flag day for schools and authorities was 9 November, commemorating those members of the movement who had fallen. Without being asked I put up the flagpole the previous evening, allowing me to avoid a discussion *and* spare the nerve in the landlady's neck. All the while I was marvelled at by the refugee children, who were very trusting, immediately getting in my way. The following morning, when the weather had improved, I went down to Schwarzindien with the box that Uncle Johann had entrusted to me. Margot stayed behind; she wanted to listen to a Wagner opera on the wireless: *Lohengrin*. That was fine by me as it gave me some time for an aimless wander by myself in the ever-changing blue.

After the rain of the previous day the paths were in a sorry state, especially the farm tracks. At one point the stench of dead animal wafted up from a bush, stirring a vague memory of the mattress I'd burned in the garden in the winter. I peered into the bush and saw a dead cat lying there. Swathes of mist hovered in the spruce woods that extended up the mountain slopes to my right.

As I approached Schwarzindien I could see the camp leader doing gymnastics with the girls by the shore. Two girls with the suburban accent that was familiar to me, one with blonde braids and the other with nickel-rimmed spectacles, sauntered down to the lake from the house, looking self-assured and pretty in their gymnastics outfits. I watched them until they had joined the rows of girls and were doing the exercises in rhythm. The girl with the braids gave me a smile, then immediately bent down to her toes again.

I looked around hesitantly. The innkeeper sat on the wall, his sleeves rolled up, blinking in the sun. The flagpole was bare; I'd heard from Uncle that the girls were pleased not to have to hoist the flag at morning roll call any more. Now the camp only had the flag on the roof because the other one had been stolen. / The girls were doing loosening-up exercises, some scratched their tummies and others straightened their spectacles. The girl with the braids pointed at the house; I followed the line of her arm that led to a window in the bar. / It was astonishing to me just how attentive the girls remained beneath all their discipline. While everyone was drifting in different directions, seemingly unsure as to what was going on, and the girl next to her was absent-mindedly picking her nose, the girl with the braids had let me know where I could find the teacher.

Plucking up my courage I entered the house. If the teacher had noticed me come in, she didn't let on; frowning, she kept her eyes fixed on the blue exercise book she was marking. As she reached into a blue ceramic bowl and was about to put a dried apple ring in her mouth, I said hello. She flinched, put the apple ring back and blushed.

This was the second time in almost a year that there had been something approaching intimacy between us. The first time was after Nanni's disappearance, when the teacher ticked me off for my poor appearance and threatened me with a *spanking*. And now this blush; I'd never have expected that from her. For a brief moment it mitigated my discomfort. But the teacher looked at me spikily and, as if she were trying to snuff out for good what had just happened between us, or what might have been, she said gruffly, 'What are you doing creeping around the place? You gave me a fright.' / She edged the bowl away from her slightly; it contained pieces of dried tomato too. Our eyes met again.

To make the moment pass more quickly the teacher started talking rubbish. She said that not a moment went by without one of the girls wanting something from her, and that by the evening her head was smoking because of the continual blathering from all sides and at high speed. And when the weather was bad the house turned into one big fleapit. She hoped it would stay fine for a few days now. / She tried to act relaxed, but our nervous glances saw through each other. And I had to keep checking whether what I'd seen in the blue bowl – dried tomatoes and apple rings – were really there. / Eventually the teacher asked what I wanted. I gave her the box with Nanni's things. She took it without a word of thanks; she wasn't unfriendly, but not particularly nice either. After a moment of silence she remarked what a shame it was about that clever girl. Nanni had wanted to become a teacher. This was followed by another of those don't-touch-me glances.

'I probably won't be coming back to Schwarzindien for a while,' I said. 'But if there's anything I can do for you away from here, just let me know.' / The teacher stroked her hair behind her right ear and replied peevishly, 'Thank you, that won't be necessary.' / 'It was just an offer.' / Without looking at me, she muttered, 'The camp is being wound up.' And then, meeting my gaze, 'Supposedly it's in the girls' best interests. They're going to be divided up and sent to Stern and Stabau, if they don't return to Vienna. As for myself, I am to be subordinate to a more capable camp leadership.' / We sized each other up once more. 'It's a shame about Schwarzindien,' I said. / 'In Linz they claim the camp is too isolated. And in the eyes of the school inspector I proved to be inadequate in German and History. Then there's the dead girl and ten thousand refugees moving in from the south-east.' She made a gesture as if tossing dust into the air; what has been squandered can never be won back. / 'It's my view that people ought to be patient, I've thought that from the age of twelve, and ever since I've developed a patience that would do credit to ten psychiatrists.' Surprise filled her face, as if at that very moment it had struck her that she'd never intended to grant anyone an insight into her thoughts and feelings, and so she said, 'But let's leave this now.'

Confused, I found myself outside the house again. The girls were doing handstands. The white of the vests was now at the bottom and the black of their trousers at the top. And their toes were pointing towards the sky and their feet were moving like the tail assembly of aircraft in turbulent air. Some ponytails were lying in the damp grass. From time to time one of the girls tumbled over and then got to their feet with a red face before having another attempt at a handstand. And beyond them the lake babbled as if as a reminder that everything is in flux and that nothing is permanent. Wild ducks floated on the water.

I looked up at the house that towered behind me. There was probably a room up in the attic that couldn't be heated; the teacher had mentioned it when talking about the request for another person to help out at the camp. I also recalled the teacher having said that someone had used the coal cellar as a lavatory. / 'The rain's on its way again,' the innkeeper said, still sitting by the wall and reacting to my upward glances. / 'Not until tomorrow,' I replied. / As he nodded, a heron squawked, and at that moment life felt uncanny again. / I quickly turned away and left, the mighty rock skull of the Drachenwand at my back.

I made my way home like a sleepwalker, slipping several times on the paths dotted with puddles, leaves and dung, and arriving back splattered in filth from head to toe. / Margot looked flabbergasted and said, 'Darling, what on earth do you look like?' / I was pleased by her use of 'darling'. / Lilo tottered over and squeezed herself into the boot I'd taken off, which came up to her shoulder. She squealed, probably liking the damp warmth inside the boot. / I carefully stuffed my boots with newspaper, hung my jacket over the chair, told Margot about what had happened during my day and revealed my suspicions as to where the Brazilian might have gone. / 'Don't get involved,' Margot warned. / 'I don't need telling on that score,' I said.

Margot made tea to warm me up, and while it was brewing she said that her period had come. She looked over at me; I had just tapped my knee to give Lilo something to aim for as she practised her walking. / Margot then said she assumed I wasn't particularly disappointed. I told her I wasn't. The idea that my employer would, one way or another, soon be looking for me again ruined any idea I might cherish of a future in civilian life. / 'Not now, when everything's so up in the air,' I said. / Margot didn't appear disappointed either; the last time she'd been two weeks late was when she was eighteen. She hoped it would work out again.

She poured her tea away, fetched some schnapps and we toasted the children we intended to have together in the future. / On a whim I proceeded to get drunk, I don't know why. And the following morning, after we'd been awoken by the mooing of the longhorns, Margot asked me if I remembered what I'd said to her in the night. No. I must have been blind drunk. I'd said really lovely things, she told me; I could be very affectionate when I let myself go. 'Why don't you do it more often?' / I put my arm around Margot, though in truth I was supporting myself on her, and said, 'I won't stop loving you till we're separated by the man reputed to be the greatest of all lovers. And I will hold it against him.'

Lilo staggered through the room and fell over, taking the wastepaper basket with her.

It would soon be a year

It would soon be a year that I'd been idling in Mondsee, a year during which the war had failed to come to an end. The anniversary of my being wounded had passed and I was surprised that I'd managed to avoid the war for so long. When I received a summons from Vienna at the end of November I couldn't complain, or not much anyway, for in truth I'd managed to steer a middle course until now, which – let's say – veered between the extraordinarily good fortune of some and the harshest lot of many. / The order said I was to report to the barracks at Breitensee within a week. I spent hours poring over my medical reports to see whether anything stuck out. The *signs of paralysis* may have been slightly exaggerated. On the other hand, if you weren't missing a leg you were considered to be fit. / Hopefully nobody would notice anything.

Even Margot didn't know that the most recent reports were faked; I carried the knowledge around like a secret illness.

There were moments when I felt relief at the thought that I had to go back to Vienna, for the uncertainty of my situation was straining my nerves and it was a real effort to keep a clear head. I was almost consumed by self-pity. And I'd also become slightly dependent on the tablets; I no longer waited until I felt really bad, but swallowed a Pervitin at the slightest sign of any malaise. And as soon as the tin was empty I went to the community doctor to fetch another one. Too weak to break out of the vicious circle, I just took each day as it came and hoped that everything would sort itself out by the curtain falling on the war. I was reluctant, however, to admit the gulf between my desire and reality, for the general opinion was that wars don't end in winter. / And yet something had to happen, I had to change something. I couldn't carry on like this with Margot suffering the consequences. When, once again, I snapped at her for some minor thing, she asked, disconcerted, 'Why that tone?'

Sometimes I sat beside the gramophone player, the Mauser pistol aimed at the ceiling, listening to the tenor's love songs, accompanied by the guitar: *Ai, yoyo . . . ai, yoyo . . .*

The first snow had fallen in mid-November, ten centimetres of white. Margot and I had built a snowman for Lilo in front of the house. There was a dog around the place again now, brought by the refugees from the Banat. It was a handsome young sheepdog and Lilo loved him. He peed around the snowman. When the sun shone the carrot fell from the snowman's face, and now he was just a pile of sludge.

I often stood by the window, doing nothing but watching the long-horns graze and relieve themselves in the Brazilian's garden. When the sun came out after a shower, the animals' grey backs would steam. Their long horns with dark tips were twisted in an intimidating way and reminded me of ancient pagan figures. But they couldn't stop the winter. / Then I gazed at the greenhouse, in which the men and women who'd fled the lower reaches of the Danube were doing the Brazilian's work. The presence of these strangers unsettled me. They were both an opportunity to expand my horizons and also to confirm my belief that nothing was absolute, nothing was *total*, background, race, social status, conviction. I just had to go over there.

Instead I went to see my uncle to ask him to issue me with a travel permit for Vienna. Outside the gendarmerie hung a sign saying that it was unstaffed. / A message girl, recognizable by the lightning bolt on her cap and the armbands on the jacket of her uniform, hurried past, a package under her arm, something wrapped in newspaper. She called out to me that the police were carrying out a check at the bridge over the Zeller Ache, where the road led to St Lorenz. / I went in the direction she was pointing. The leaders from the Stern and Schwarzindien camps were coming up the road. As it was raining they were both carrying umbrellas and neither of them looked at me.

At the crossroads the message girl had mentioned, Uncle and his assistant were standing in their dark-blue oilskins. Uncle had a face like an unmade bed, he looked exhausted, but he was in a good mood.

Because of his respiratory difficulties he had been rejected by the Volkssturm, whereas almost everybody else had been enlisted apart from those with visible debilities. He coughed, gasped for air and tapped fondly on the tin of tobacco in his coat pocket, as if it had saved his life.

'I've had a summons from Vienna,' I said. 'I have to go there in the next few days and need a travel permit.' / 'Are you joining up again,' he said, pensively. / 'Only because there are regulations that force me to.' / I oughtn't to have said that, I thought immediately after opening my mouth. But Uncle seemed to think my answer was a good enough reason; the jarring connotation was at a pitch he could barely register. 'Sometimes this is just how things are, it's not worth digging any deeper.' He shrugged his shoulders in a gesture equivalent to the words: *One just has to come to terms with it.* / Then his face assumed a friendly expression and he said, 'We're waiting for the girls from Schwarzindien to pass through, they're moving to Mondsee. As soon as they're out of the way we're going to perform an arrest.' / 'What sort of arrest?' I asked nervously. / 'There are people listening to foreign broadcasters, who've been shopped by their relatives. You know how people are, full to the brim with envy, resentment and tittle-tattle,' he said, giving me a wink. I tried to find out exactly where he was going, but Uncle wouldn't be drawn on the matter and I soon gave up.

Now the small group of evacuees appeared between the trees. As with their arrival in January, the girls were accompanied by a detail of young H Youth boys, the same handcarts, the same suitcases and rucksacks, and similar wet winter paths. But whereas the girls had arrived in Schwarzindien as a disorderly rabble, they left it marching two abreast, giving the impression that they were complete, the ranks closed. The girls' outfits were not quite as impeccable as almost a year ago. I saw that some shoes had different coloured laces, and the odd coat was now too short. / I was surprised to hear the girls sing 'All My Little Ducklings' several times over, always starting from the beginning again. Only when they got to the bridge over the Zeller Ache did they stop marching and singing; one whistle had sufficed.

'You're late,' my uncle said. / 'We got caught in a downpour, but we were able to shelter under some trees, thank goodness, and escape the worst, otherwise all our luggage would be soaked,' the teacher said. We smiled at each other apprehensively. / 'Are you all present?' Uncle asked. As a formality the teacher briefly scanned the rows of girls then nodded. Then she discussed the final details of the liquidation of the camp with my uncle, and neither the old man with his cigarette nor the young woman with her bobble hat paid me any further attention. / But some girls were peering over at me, as ever, making no attempt to hide their irritation at having to move camps. Only the young photographer, who'd been documenting camp life from the beginning, seemed to take pleasure in the sullen faces. She took photographs of Uncle and his assistant, the evacuees and the dark clouds providing the background. / As I moved aside for the girl, I said, 'After you, young lady,' at which some of the other girls hooted and whistled with their fingers. Order had totally collapsed in a flash and the teacher had to restore it with some sharp instructions. Within seconds the girls emanated a sense of discipline once more.

The marching column set off again soon afterwards: a H Youth boy with a flag at the very front, then the other boys pulling the handcarts with the luggage, and finally the girls, passing by in step.

My uncle was now ready for action. Where did this come from? What did he hope to get from arresting an individual who listened to foreign broadcasts? That the stripes and stars on his collar, which had never harboured any particular ambition to multiply, should now enjoy some belated parental joy? That he would be put in retirement if he managed to pull off five more arrests as brilliant as this one? I don't know. / Uncle's assistant pushed the motorcycle forwards, put his foot on the starter and the engine hummed as he revved it. With a disquieting glint in his eye, Uncle jumped onto the pillion and the two gendarmes puttered away along the lakeshore.

It was getting dark. The first fox strayed into the village and started sniffing at the doors to the animal sheds. The dogs barked and tore at their chains. / I went home, where Margot had made soup. I wanted to get changed quickly first. When I took off my boots, now repaired, I realized that Uncle had deceived me. It was the Brazilian they were arresting. Why else would they have had to wait for the girls to move out of Schwarzindien camp?

It can't end like this, I thought. But this is exactly how it will end, I said. What if I'd misread the signs? Unlikely. So what should I do? Without answering this, I put on the Brazilian's work clothes and his boots, and everything that happened from then on seemed to follow the logic of dreams. I reached for the pistol from the beams, and took a precautionary Pervitin, which would soon take effect given how my heart was thumping. And without a word to Margot, I leaped down the stairs, went out through the rear barn door, pulled my woollen hat down low and hurried over the saturated fields into the rapidly descending darkness.

We all know how quickly night moves in at the end of November, it falls from the sky and comes creeping out of the ground too. And when the two types of darkness meet one another, they clump together in a mass of unusual density as if one were facing a sea of tar. That's how it appeared to me. Everything seemed to lead to a dead end – the day, the war, my life. At the same time I was astonished by every step the darkness allowed me to take. It was only through experience that I knew all of this existed: path, footbridge, and most of all the nightmarish Drachenwand.

Whenever I got to open ground, such as the bathing spot behind the Höribach, I was able to see a little more. The trees in the meadows appeared to be twice, three times as numerous, and then all of a sudden a tree would hide behind another and the darkness would again become so black that everything seemed to have been swallowed apart from the noise of my footsteps.

It was still pitch black when I reached the inn at Schwarzindien, but now I could see better, for it is true that the eyes get used to darkness. The building vacated by the evacuees would have given the impression of complete abandonment if the gendarmes' motorcycle hadn't been by the front door. Everything was quiet. Only when I went up close to one of the windows did I see the thinnest crack of light between the window frame and the edge of the blackout panel.

As I didn't really know what I was doing here I squatted behind an elder bush on the far side of the road beside the outbuilding that belonged to the inn. I tried my best to take shallow breaths, but only managed three in succession, after which I panted all the more acutely, for I was out of breath from running. As soon as my pulse had calmed somewhat, I could hear my watch. The long hand divided the seconds with a regular tick-tock, tick-tock; it sounded as if the seconds were being stamped out, as if they were clattering, momentarily tangible, into a container that was collecting them: small nails, nails for my coffin.

Now the door to the inn opened and the assistant gendarme came out cursing, followed by my uncle, who stopped in the open doorway. All I saw was his long shadow that fell onto the forecourt. As far as I could make out in the light, someone had inflicted a serious injury on the assistant's right ear. Blood was pouring through the cloth that he'd wrapped around his head. Uncle said he should call the community doctor to have the wound stitched as soon as possible. Their colleague from Unterach would leave immediately and be here in fifteen minutes. / The assistant kickstarted the motorcycle and the noise of its engine echoed across the lake. Most of the headlight at the front had been covered up, with only a narrow strip of transparent paper allowing blue light to trickle onto the road so the driver could get his bearings. But it wasn't enough to allow him to drive fast, and I heard the motorcycle rattling away for a long time.

Uncle stood motionless in the open doorway for several seconds. The long shadow he cast over the forecourt and road reminded me how thin he'd become since the summer.

Eventually the door closed, immediately plunging everything into darkness again. / For a while I remained hidden behind the elder bush, waiting for the sound of the motorcycle to die away.

On the other side of the lake the moon emerged fleetingly between the clouds, throwing a glittering trail across the water. Everyone has to take the plunge sometime in their life. / Emerging from my hiding place I knew, of course, that the path I was about to go down was an unfamiliar one. Did I really want to do this? No idea, I no longer had time to give it much consideration. / The Mauser pistol in hand, I walked over to the building and slipped in through the door unnoticed. In the bar somebody had turned on the wireless, from which a military station was sending greetings to a world that for German soldiers was getting smaller by the day. Almost all the chairs were on the tables, their legs pointing upwards. Only two chairs remained on the floor. On one sat Uncle Johann, on the other the Brazilian. The two of them appeared to be surrounded by the chair legs beside and behind them.

In one corner of the bar was a heap of things left behind that afternoon because of the rain. On the blackboard someone had marked the departure with a tongue-twister in a child's handwriting: *If a dog chews shoes, whose shoes does he choose?*

The Brazilian looked wretched: bluish-grey skin, unkempt, filthy clothes, dirt and straw in his hair, exhaustion and frustration on his face. What surprised me most was that he didn't give the impression that he'd been sleeping in the building, more like in a hole in the ground. / Uncle looked worn out too, ancient, his face bloated. He struggled to his feet. And while the Brazilian stared at his hands, my uncle looked through the cupboards until he'd found a bottle of schnapps. / 'I have to smother my coughing,' he said, taking a swig straight from the bottle. He offered the Brazilian some too, but the latter shook his head.

I must have been standing in the hallway for two minutes now, and I knew I couldn't just leave things as they were. I had to take decisive action, and decisive action is something from which there is no way back. So I entered the bar. Without giving me a sign of acknowledgement, the Brazilian leaped up and moved away from my uncle. Uncle looked at me with bloodshot eyes, then he got up too. I told him to sit back down, but he ignored me. In a conciliatory tone, almost begging me, he said, 'Please don't play the knight in shining armour, just go back home. I haven't seen you here, all right?' / I couldn't make up my mind, so I let my uncle talk until he became totally unsure of himself and no longer knew what to do. 'Enough harm has been done already,' he said, words that rekindled all of Uncle's meanness, and I harboured no sympathy for him, just as he'd never harboured sympathy for anybody else. I'm certain the Pervitin wasn't entirely blameless in my decision to pull the trigger. It didn't require that much courage, but I felt uncomfortable, and the very next moment I couldn't believe that what I'd just done was the good deed everyone should do in their life. No, it was far from good.

My uncle's eyes flickered crazily, everything in the bar became blurred, which was also partly on account of Evelyn Künneke's singing the beguiling song 'Das Karussell' on the wireless. Again I told my uncle to sit back down. / 'Spare the advice,' he stammered barely audibly, gasping for air. And he stared at his hands across his chest. He was spitting blood, the sight of which made me ill. With a painfully grim face he said, 'Shit.' Then something inside him collapsed, fell apart, and as if with that last word he'd expended his final reserves of energy, he sank onto the chair I'd pushed over for him, but then fell straight onto the floor. And there he died, his eyes open, but with the most dreamy expression on his face. / Hopefully, dying is easier on a November night, when you're tired and dark clouds hang in the sky outside.

The two of us carried Uncle out together and hid him behind the outbuilding on the other side of the road to buy ourselves as much time as possible. Now my uncle was merely one more of those corpses tossed into the dark, over and done with. The Brazilian went to the loo, and while I was turning off the light I thought, he's mad, they'll arrest both of us. But he was back a few seconds later, having just gone to get some soap, which they still had here, a bar of all-purpose soap. He asked me why I hadn't switched off the wireless, and because I didn't want to tell him I'd left it on for the dead, I just shrugged.

Finally it was time to go. An icy east wind blew sleet into my face. The Brazilian thanked me again and said I shouldn't worry about him, for he had a second hiding place and enough dried fruit and vegetables for half a year. He would rely on his knowledge of biology and the terrain. / He went down to the boat shed, climbed to the upper floor and threw down his sack. 'We'll talk again, Menino, some day,' he said. / 'That would be lovely,' I replied, 'but hard to imagine.' / He cleared his throat. The sound of it faded in the snowy rain. I listened and the Brazilian listened too. Silence unfolded and the Brazilian said, 'The heart will not be calm until we have become what we are meant to be.'

With the sack over his shoulder he hurried away. The darkness immediately closed behind him, and the same happened to me too. When I shot a brief glance back at the Schwarzindien inn, there was nothing there any more, not even an outline to give a hint of where the building stood. Everything had dissipated in the jet-black darkness. / And so I turned my back on all of that, the Schwarzindien camp, the

Schwarzindien teacher, dead Nanni and my dead uncle. Something tightened in my heart, and I was seized by that deep sadness to which I was disposed. It's all over now, I thought. It's true that what's been squandered cannot be won back.

On the way back to Mondsee I stopped several times and cried. Once I hid for half an hour. The dogs barked. I crept past a farmhouse. From the animal shed I heard the rattling of a pail and wooden shoes on the concrete floor. I passed one of the camps. When you wandered past the evacuee camps at night, you didn't hear a sound, not even in summer when the windows were open. How quietly the children slept.

I washed my hands and face at the fountain by the house. On the other side of the road the longhorns were snorting and stamping their hoofs. I groped my way cautiously to the unlit steps and climbed them. Back in my room I had solid ground beneath my feet again, even though I couldn't turn on the light because the blackout panels weren't up. / Crouching on my bed, I listened out for the sound of Margot's door opening. At one point I realized I was crying again. Afterwards I put the pistol back on one of the beams and tried to collect my thoughts. It didn't work. Perhaps it does a disservice to your thoughts to try to collect them; I gave up.

Later I took the pistol back down from the beam and kept it with me in bed, warming it beneath my pillow. And for the first time in almost three-quarters of a year I covered myself with my military coat. I listened. I could hear the longhorns mooing. I resumed my sleeping position and the noise of the cattle accompanied my brooding. In an attempt to get to sleep I recited sayings in my head, such as: *When the ox falls there are many that will help to kill him.* I fell asleep.

Two comrades appeared in my dream: Josef Gmoser and my co-driver for the first two years, Helmut, who died in our escape attempt from Tarnopol. The two of them arrived at a hotel where I was staying. They stood by the door and looked in, lost and confused. Interestingly it was Josef who did the talking, while Helmut leaned back and smiled.

Helmut's hair was wet and Josef had a scar on his face. I can't remember what we talked about. But I know that they hadn't come to complain; the impression I got was that they were doing well in the circumstances.

Dazed and freezing, I was woken immediately afterwards by the sound of the sleet whipping against the window. I got up briefly and had a glass of water. The next time I opened my eyes it took me a while to get my bearings, then I saw to my great relief that the earth had already turned substantially to meet the new day. The darkness in the windows was no longer so harsh. Now I was sleeping two hours at a stretch.

At half past nine in the morning I went and sat in Margot's room. She had been out shopping already and knew about Uncle's death. She gave me a cup of coffee and asked whether everything was all right. 'Yes, so far,' I replied. / 'I'm glad,' she said. / I fancied she suspected something, but she didn't probe any further, I offered no more information and we spoke no more about it.

Soon they'll all be gone from Eichbaumeck

Soon they'll all be gone from Eichbaumeck. In the factories and offices they're replacing men with women, and the men are complaining how lots of people had thought it would be easier. / Herr Kresser says we're now reliably getting what was written in three bold letters on the tin right at the beginning: Wilhelm, Adelheid, Richard. There's always someone trying to walk all over everyone else, he says, and it keeps going like this until everyone's flat on their backs, then there's a bit of peace and quiet again for a while.

Before Herr Kresser joined up he helped me shake the pear tree. Now all the fruit is on the ground and though it's small, it tastes delicious. Twenty-five kilos. I cooked the pears up on Tuesday. I didn't want to throw anything away – you know your mother – so I ate the cores and ended up spending the whole of Wednesday in bed. I'm still a bit weak-kneed today. I ought to have thrown the cores away, my delicate tummy can't take them any more.

Then we had two days where it was so cold and stormy that I had to light the stove. Thank God the harvest was already under cover, the potatoes in the house, but sadly not the children. The beautiful flowers in the back garden that were supposed to be for All Saints have frozen. / Many of the things that still hung in the trees after the huge air raid of 11 September came down in the storm: curtains, window frames, clothes, satchels. All flung out by the blast. I can't imagine that there was much of use there apart from firewood. / It devastated our garden, I had to pick up four baskets of winter apples and now my legs are aching.

On All Saints' Day I wandered from one cemetery to the next, envious of those who could visit graves with their families. On days like that you feel twice as lonely. / At Bessungen Cemetery I met Frau Albus, who asked me to send her regards. She'd just been on the telephone to Anni, who's found a source of coffee beans. I'm going to get a pound myself, which will cost thirty-five marks, but so what? I'll be happy to have some to combat the tiredness. It does nothing for your nerves, of course.

The Brinkmann tobacco you sent me was excellent. Give my warmest thanks to the soldier, even though we've never met. You don't mention him as much as you used to, that's something I ought to be familiar with. You were like that as a child too, always with your torch under the covers. / At any rate, I'm pleased you finally got a letter from me letting you know about Aunt Helen, Helga, Aunt Emma and Uncle Georg's deaths. Your letters are now arriving all in a jumble, I sometimes get three or four a day and have had eighteen or nineteen since the air raid, all within a few days.

So your neighbour is back in his hammock during an air raid? You're no longer responsible for the market garden, then?

Nelli came to visit yesterday evening. She was in Darmstadt for the day. How she's changed, she looks dreadful, it made me wonder if she's got lung disease again. Our family has such terribly bad luck. Now Käta's had a relapse and of course she can't stop crying, which can't be good for her sick heart. I wonder, no, I don't wonder, I know it's not right that some people have no luck at all whereas others seem to get everything they want.

We haven't had a dense fog like this in ages. When I was feeding the rabbits after Nelli's visit, the fog followed me back into the house. It smells of mouldy leaves in the kitchen too and the bedclothes are damp, which means I can't get warm at night. / I'm so anxious about the winter, dark at five already, and more time to be alone. I can bear to be without you all for a few days or a week, none of that rushing around and yelling. I'm not saying, dear Margot, that I'm always delighted by the shenanigans, there are times when I get fed up to the back teeth with the ruddy *lot* of you. But it's not right that there's nobody at home these days.

I've just remembered that you still want me to send some clothes, but the post won't make an exception to its ban on packages just for you. Besides you never know if something's going to arrive because those bombers make a mess of everything. / Couldn't you come to Darmstadt and show me your daughter? After all that's happened since the massive air raid it would be lovely to have a little one around the house for a few days.

I haven't told Papa about my bad legs, he wouldn't understand and he'd say it's my own fault. I'm afraid I've got to go and lie down again. I've had the most unspeakable Sunday. Lulu's got to feed and milk the animals for me. Frau Kresser's worried too. / I'm happy to say that Lulu's being nice to her mother again, after I gave her what for. Write things in your letters so that I can give them to Frau Kresser to read and put some stuff in for Lulu so she realizes that life wouldn't be any better for her than at home. She still hasn't gone back to work yet as they don't have any electricity. She thinks Darmstadt's boring now, no cinema and nothing since the air raid. But Belida's supposed to be opening again soon, and she's really looking forward to it. I mean, all she ever sees these days is rubble. You get a really strange feeling nowadays if you go somewhere where there aren't any ruins. Lulu went with Gertrud to Wolfskehlen recently and she felt like she was in Australia.

I want to go to bed now, dear Margot. Usually we've not been lying there ten minutes before the sirens start. They're real experts at this and you can imagine how furious I get. Then we've got to sit in the cellar, where there's plenty of time to write letters, but the war doesn't make it easy for your thoughts, which just go around in circles. / Maybe tomorrow we'll be nothing but rubble and ashes, and all our hope will have been in vain. Two days ago a soldier who was just back from Russia, where his battalion had been encircled, shot himself. He was delighted to finally be *home* again when he arrived at the station, but it hadn't occurred to him that bomb damage doesn't just affect buildings. So it hit him hard when he learned that his wife and three children had been buried eight weeks earlier.

Papa too is wearing himself out with all the thoughts swimming round his head. I tell him to stop, he's going to need all his wits about him when he's back home. I also tell him he's not the only one, others have to be far away from their wives and homes too, it's hard for everyone. But he seems to find it particularly difficult. / I'm missing Papa as well. During the day I'm overwhelmed with work and errands, and I'm fed up to the back teeth with all the domestic chores. If Bettine's here for the weekend she's got her own life and own friends to be doing with, and I don't begrudge her this because I know how busy life is in Berlin, it's exhausting.

Now they've lifted the ban on packages, dear Margot, I've sent you some underwear by express post. You'll have to pick it up from Mondsee station. / Send me the bow and paper back, because we've got nothing here. / I didn't send you any nighties as you've only got sleeveless ones and winter's on its way. And I need the ones I've got with sleeves for myself. I've sent you a few warm mittens instead.

Dear Margot, it's very different if you've got your nearest and dearest around you rather than strangers. Last Saturday Frau Bader got an apartment in Kaiserschlag. She only comes here to sleep now as they haven't got any beds yet. Today they fetched mattresses and hopefully they'll get the rest soon. / I'm sleeping in Bettine's bed. Mine is where the sofa used to be and the sofa's beneath the clock, and that's where Frau Bader is sleeping. I like her being here. I'm starting to get anxious about being on my own and my head's spinning. When things get really bad I ask Lulu to spend the night here.

Lulu's back in Hügelstrasse, which she likes a hundred times better than Bessungen even though they haven't got a toilet in Hügelstrasse. The girls go upstairs and sit on a pot in what used to be their offices, and of course the gents make jokes about this. The girls never go on their own, they always have to take someone with them to make sure nobody disturbs them. In a few days' time they'll be making a start on the yearly accounts. Lulu's already moaning because there'll be a huge muddle following the bombing raid and she'll have to work some Sundays for sure.

Käta died, sadly, of natural causes, which is rare around here. I went to Arheilgen to pay my respects and found her on a bier in a cellar, covered with a cloth. She was completely changed, very pale, and barely recognizable. As a final goodbye I stroked her face, then left. I couldn't cry. It's over now. The old fortune teller, who once predicted she'd live to the age of eighty-nine, wasn't right. / I didn't meet Uncle Gerhard, he was in hospital in Dieburg.

At the moment Papa's working as a locksmith in the workshop. He hasn't got any materials or tools and yet he's still working. His letters are really whiny, I think these few months have been enough to turn your father into a different man. Some of his opinions seem to have changed completely. In the past I've really suffered from his views, which are fanciful sometimes, but now I think he sees the world through different eyes. Maybe he's finally realizing what a lovely thing a comfortable home is, where you can relax for a bit once your work's done. / Maybe it'll be *our* good luck that he was called up again.

You know that Klärchen is the worst off of all of you, don't you? She's got nothing except for her skiing trousers and a coat. And you know that her mother's dead and her own hands are badly burnt. Frau Emmerich's dead too. Who would have thought that back when the two of you were in the same office? / Apparently Kläre's going to stay with her cousin in the Westerwald when her hands have healed.

They're now catching up on the memorial services. This morning I was at the Martinsgemeinde for a commemoration for Aunt Emma and Uncle Georg. Pastor Widmann spoke very poignantly and there were plenty of tears. The pastor had some harsh words too, saying that after this brief earthly intoxication many people were in danger of waking up to a cruel sobriety.

Yesterday I got official police notification that Aunt Helen and Helga gave their lives for Germany on 11 September, serial numbers 4261 and 4262. / Today Aunt Liesel too was notified that a pile of bones from two corpses was found under the rubble of the porch that Uncle Ernst had arranged for prisoners to carry away. Only two people are still missing, but it's hard to tell whether the bones are actually Aunt Helen's and Helga's, though we have to assume they are. / I went to the cemetery yesterday and laid down a bouquet of flowers. They're going to be buried in plots 2294 and 2295. It's all very sad, and Uncle Ernst's letters are heart-breaking. He's asking if anyone's got any photographs of the christening or photos of Helen, the rose of central Darmstadt. I can still see her beaming smile as she stood opposite the pastor. The photographers ought to be very busy making copies right now, but they don't have any materials.

It's all very sad. I'm going to have to chip in for Käta's funeral, because her husband, the cad, has foisted all the costs onto her relatives, saying he's got no money himself and that he's been divorced from her for a year.

I've got some more news: I think your Peterle is going to become a mother soon. I hope she doesn't give birth to her babies in my bed, she loves crawling in there. / And the Kressers' Fritz is going to be put down soon because he attacks all and sundry and he won't even let Herr Kresser into the kennel. Like all males he has to show off, always wrapped up in his own importance, which I bet isn't far from the truth. Even when I see him from a distance I'm worried he's going to go for my legs.

Bettine was here at the weekend. She had a decent lie-in and met her friends. I believe her when she says that it's not easy working on the Berlin trams, now in the freezing winter. There must be a way they can let her come back to Darmstadt, seeing as the trams are starting to operate again here too. Eberstadt to Arheilgen is working, as is the Griesheim tram. I mean, me being alone with my bad legs is good enough reason.

Bettine had only been gone six hours when Papa arrived. What a shame they didn't see each other. Papa went sniffing around the house for her for a while.

He's got lots of work to do, he cleared the area where the cucumbers were, tipped everything into a big heap and then immediately sowed corn for green fodder in the spring. He dug and sowed everything he could in the garden. He didn't even visit his parents. He says everything goes to rack and ruin when he's not at home. I helped him out a lot and we snapped at each other because all this frantic working isn't healthy for either of us, me because of my legs and Papa because of his back. / But Monday was wonderful. We went out in the evening for a beer, played cards and missed you children. / Hopefully we can all be together again soon. For good. Maybe you'd even like to be back home.

At lunch Papa asked me if I knew what it would mean if we lost the war. Out of interest I said no, but he didn't give me any information. / 'We'll get by in the future too,' I said. / For a long while Papa just stared at his plate, a frown on his face and the veins throbbing at his temples. Then he showed his irritation by gobbling down his food, shovelling in his pudding and shooting out the door without saying another word. / When I told Papa today that Rudi had died, all he said was, 'That's our twenty marks down the pan.' He won't have written that to you. / Believe me, it hurts me so much that someone could lose all affection for a person like Rudi. Such things have become commonplace in wartime. But all this talk is pointless. Life goes on somehow.

Your child's almost a year old now and I haven't seen her since she was three weeks. The year's gone quickly, bringing many terrible things. I hope next year brings us only good things. / Thanks for the photograph. How the little mite has changed! I've got the drawings of the hands and feet, so I'll knit some mittens and stockings for Christmas. I've already unravelled Bettine's old bathing suit. / It wasn't very clever of your neighbour to insult his brother-in-law, he'd have been better off keeping out of his way. / Have you got your clothes and the money yet?

When I went out earlier to fetch water for the goats, my cape billowed in the wind, the cold rain lashed my face and all of a sudden I could have jumped for joy. Please don't think I'm crazy, dear Margot, but it makes me so happy when it's stormy like that and I find myself brimming with energy. I stood beside the fountain until the jug was full, watching the clouds race past. I never want to have to leave Darmstadt, I want to rebuild this city, have you children back at home and a few grandchildren playing in the garden. / Life just goes on here, we get up and go to sleep, sit in the cellar, feed the rabbits and queue up at the shops only to be told they've got nothing left. And the next day we start all over again, but it doesn't hurt, or at least it doesn't hurt as much as one might imagine. And amongst all the rubble and misery you see the occasional chink of light.

I'm happy that our correspondence is almost back to normal and I'm getting replies from you. That story of the girl who climbed the mountain on her own at Easter is very sad too. And it gives me the creeps whenever I think about how she was pretty much just bones when they found her. I have to shake myself.

You say you don't love your husband. But you married him. So what now? If you don't know yourself, then how could I know?

Where is he, the spiv? Did he get out of Memel with the evacuation they talked about on the wireless? In any event all I can do is give you some good advice, which I don't for the life of me imagine you'll heed, knowing you as I do: don't get yourself mixed up with anybody. I feel so sad when marriages end like roads that haven't been finished.

But you've never felt strongly that you need someone to tell you what to do, have you? Even at your wedding you ignored my advice, otherwise I'd have told you that a marriage is just the wretched luck of the draw and that you mustn't push your luck. / Papa and I have been married for twenty-four years, you know, which is quite a long time from this perspective. I know you don't look to us as an example, but we've never found it necessary to go our own way. And of course I'm not so foolish as to imagine that Papa is without his flaws. But I'm not an egotistical person by any means, and that's my biggest mistake. I've paid for it often enough over the years but I've never learned my lesson. Perhaps you're luckier, Margot, you're better at breaking away. I can never really be finished with someone. Once I've accepted some-one, then I stick with them even if they disappoint me. / So do as you wish. Behaving in the way you do requires character. Now that you're finally free of the garden work and winter's on its way, you've got time enough to think.

I'm forever getting letters from Bettine, who sometimes asks for a dress, then for her Sunday coat and now she wants me to make her some pyjamas. Where does she expect me to get the material from? Next time she's here she ought to take back her old gymnastics trousers and sleep in those, or Papa's old pyjamas, which will hopefully be good enough for someone living in a communal shack. I expect she thinks that because her address is Rubensstrasse, exercise trousers aren't good enough.

To hell with all the shenanigans, I'm sick to the back teeth of the trouble and worry you *all* cause me with your stupidity! It's ruining my life! Bring my grandchild back so that I have some pleasure at least. I'm assuming she's already saying her first words, so she should be saying Nana too.

There'll be no sign of Christmas in our house. I'm going to be heading to the gloomy cemetery on the holy days. Everywhere there's just emergency lighting instead of Christmas.

I'm very tired, Margot, I'm going to lie down for an hour. I miss you.

Papa just wrote to say he's going to Greudenz or Graudenz, I can't make it out, but it's in Pomerania. He's really hungry and hasn't changed his clothes since his leave in November. His socks are wet and ripped. He's still very whiny and he thinks I'm not going to take him back when he comes home after the war. He can't know me very well. I wrote to say that he can come and stay anytime if he doesn't swear.

He had to hand in his boots and was given lace-up shoes instead, at the beginning of winter. His good boots. If he'd known that earlier he wouldn't have gone to such trouble looking after them. He's livid with rage and says that those in the barracks and the SA are going around in the best-quality boots. He's also surprised that the Russian women who work with them are allowed to keep their boots, why can't they take theirs instead? And in every ministry in Berlin there are boots for an entire division. A good pair of boots can make all the difference on the front line, he says. You know what Papa's like when he gets worked up.

I hear from Bettine that she's standing firm in the hustle and bustle of the trams and she's going to be very busy with work over Christmas. She mustn't forget that Aunt Resel got ill as a conductress on the ruddy trams because she went to work over Christmas even though she had a fever. / Uncle Flor also says that Bettine should never go out in the evenings on her own and she should be careful not to get mixed up with anybody. He heard that in Vienna four girls working on the trams were killed. Did you hear anything about that in Mondsee? If not, keep it to yourself and don't create a fuss.

Yesterday we got our fifty-gram allocation of coffee beans as compensation for the 11 September attack. Fifty grams of coffee beans to prevent all of those still alive from losing their zeal. I'd rather have the glockenspiel back as well as Helen and Helga and Aunt Emma and Uncle Georg.

I believe you when you say you sometimes feel a real longing for home. The fact is, it's only when you're far away that you learn to appreciate your home. Hopefully you'll be able to pay us a visit soon, I'm keeping my fingers crossed. But don't expect a nice train ride, as I shouldn't be surprised if it's anything but pleasant on the railways now. Maybe when you come you can stay for good, which is what I would really like. But I know you've got your misgivings. If you don't come or if you arrive late, on Christmas Eve I'll be going to church at 4 pm, that's the one in Liebfrauenstrasse, and then on to Aunt Liesel's. I won't be coming back home until Boxing Day evening as I don't want to spend those silent nights on my own. I'll leave the rabbit I was going to kill until you come home, so you can get your fill for once.

I went to their's on Wednesday and had Liselotte Schaffnit give me finger waves. Four and a half hours I sat there, because each time she started on my hair there was an air-raid alert. Sometimes that's a real disaster. Liselotte said they've had a boy in Griesheim.

It all happened very quickly

It all happened very quickly. General Schubert appointed us to a Volks-grenadier division, then there was schnapps, cigarettes, biscuits and boiled sweets, that was our send-off from home. Our class was scattered in all directions, as was to be expected. Those still doing their leavers' exams got good grades, quite a few even got distinctions. As you know, dear Ferdl, I've never thought much of the rest.

Those crooks put us in a cattle wagon for the journey. The windows were broken and so it was terribly cold. The train took four hours to get from Vienna to Hainburg. We stopped outside every station and by every signal. I slept on the draughty floorboards and when we arrived I was frozen. They had to help me off because my legs were so stiff.

I hadn't felt comfortable at home any more. Here, there, here, there, and why don't you understand, Kurt, that we've got enough worries without you too. I felt like a spinning top, turning and turning until I fell over. / From the Sunday till my departure Papa only said the bare minimum to me. What should I do? I can get on with anybody if I try, and I certainly want to get on with my parents.

Now I'm in this desolate, gloomy box of a room. Even back in Vienna I'd get the creeps whenever I passed a hovel. Where I'm sitting now it's bleak, there's virtually no light in the corridors and we're sleeping fifteen to a room. It's dark in the room, everything grey and drab, my mood is roughly the same as that of my comrades and the surroundings, but I'm already feeling so listless that I don't care about anything.

On the second day we filled our cupboards. We had to cover the surfaces with paper and attach paper doilies to the front edges of the boards. They're mad in the army. / Sometimes Nanni would stand there and pretend to faint. She's brilliant at it, I don't have her talent, but anyway you have to be careful here as my superiors are sensitive souls.

I'm now in possession of a spade and thus a spade carrier too, like the ones Aunt Hilli has been riveting for the past two years. I tell myself that Aunt Hilli personally riveted my one and so I especially cherish it.

I wonder where Nanni is, my Schorsche? Whereabouts unknown. I wish she'd come back. Or at least I'd find it much easier if I knew where she was.

When Nanni and I were sheltering from the rain in the concrete pipe they'd laid for the sewerage and the war was still far away, I suddenly got the feeling, which I haven't had in ages, that none of it had anything to do with me. This is just between the two of us, Ferdl, don't breathe a word of it to anyone. There I kissed Nanni for the first time and she had a laughing fit. But later she enjoyed it. / Then she almost burst with pleasure and I was delighted that she liked it so much. / The next day she said it would be nice to do it all over again. She didn't find it awkward to say this, unlike other girls she didn't have that fear of coming across as embarrassing. And so of course some people thought she wasn't quite right in the head.

I can't remember what we talked about, but I do know how I felt, so buoyant and happy, as if I'd actually arrived in life, not the usual feeling that this was merely a dress rehearsal for the real thing.

The town isn't particularly big, but there are women here, by the way, rather a lot of them, and they look forward to us going out. There are few girls amongst them and they're not really from here, but *bombed-out* women about whom our superiors have given us the strictest warnings.

Civvies on and down into town, mingling amongst people for the first time since we left Vienna. You get a quite peculiar feeling, one you've never felt before. To be back out, away from the barracks, without having orders barked at you by a superior.

The Danube is six hundred metres from the barracks and here the wind always comes from up ahead. On the slopes of the Braunsberg the forests are turning yellow and the plains outside the town are now a rusty colour. It's properly autumn now, the wind is blowing thistle seeds across the fields and the Danube carries its green water towards the front line. Sometimes the sky looks transparent, the autumn light drained, the air so thin, Ferdl, that you think the birds might fall to the ground. / Thoughts pass by too and I look up, my mouth open, and think: how can I keep on living normally when I don't know where Nanni is? / You go quite mad if every day you're waiting for something that never comes.

And what they're making us do! Drill! Snouts in the mud! We move our noses across the ground like minesweepers. Those not of good heart can't get up again. Then exercises with gas masks, singing, running. I wonder what effect it's all going to have on me. And they're almost training us to be housewives, not just cooking, but all the rest too, mending, washing, cleaning, darning socks. One man's screaming because he's pricked himself, another's cursing because his hand won't do what his head is telling him to, and another's scrubbing so hard that sparks are flying. It's a hard school in every respect, they allocate your duties in such a way that every minute of your day is filled and you hardly have time to breathe.

Yesterday in our one hour of lunch break we had to copy out the roster ten times because we didn't know it well enough. You can imagine how those soldiers feel who've just returned from the front and are now resting. They say that only three days ago they watched people die and now they're being compelled to do this desk work. It's a bit weird if you ask me. But is anyone asking me?

At least I've finally washed my trousers now, that's one worry out of the way. But I don't know what to do with my coat, which is covered in boot polish stains, ink stains and burns. I think it must have been in continual service since the 1920s. / I'd be happy to get away from here, it's much stricter than in Schwechat. It's true, of course, that I'd be more willing to help out at home now, without all this drill. And it's also true that they've smoothed some of my rough edges, as Papa said they would. I'd be interested to see if he'd be satisfied with me yet. Because I've had enough now.

You can tell that the Eastern Front is moving closer too, because we've already seen the first Russian aircraft coming from Hungary: two MiGs. They look strange, squat, with short wings, a bit like a cuckoo. I fear we're going to have to get used to the sight of them.

Dear Ferdl, I'm again looking for someone I can pour my heart out to, and apart from you I've got nobody. You already know from Sascha that Nanni is dead. I can't believe it. I keep breathing, keep moving, do what has to be done, and yet it feels as if everything has frozen in time.

Aunt Hilli often said she thought Nanni was no longer alive. I tried to persuade her that wasn't true. I didn't believe it or I told myself that if I did then that would increase the likelihood of it being true. But I also had a bad feeling, like in the fairy tale where the wanderer anticipates that at any moment he'll come face to face with his worst fears. That's why I wasn't particularly surprised. What did come as a surprise was the intensity of my emotions. But my feelings aren't of interest to anyone here and so I force myself to bottle it all up. I accept it, just as I accept that there are things I don't understand.

It's also pouring with rain from a dark sky. And I'm not especially thrilled that we've got to go back into the woods tomorrow, the sopping woods where everything that doesn't run into the top of your boots drips away. Because our training's about to begin I've got to stick this letter in an envelope. Sorry it's so short. I have to surrender at every turn, it's so sad. / Time is passing so quickly, Ferdl, I'd love to know why this is happening, because I can't see any compelling reason.

When I wake up, normally around half past five or even earlier, in total darkness, my first thoughts are: Can it be true? Nanni dead? I'm seized by anxiety and I can't think straight, I'm so upset, I'm shaking and I'm all at sea. / You know, dear Ferdl, the clover is blossoming and I'm . . . I'm withering.

Somehow I manage to contain myself. Being an adult means above all being able to contain yourself.

Yesterday it snowed for five minutes and I froze like an ice cube. In the night I wrapped myself up so tightly that I felt warm. But in the morning my teeth were chattering and to cap it all we had to work without gloves. The water in our flasks froze. / On the hill down the river we're building a camp for forced labourers who'll be coming from

Hungary to dig trenches. From the hill you can see the Danube, the shimmering ribbon of the river, you know, always the same river and always different water. / It's bloody cold up there, and the wind up on the construction site is no joke either. Talking of the construction site, you hack at the ground with your pick, then stones and earth rain down on you. The subsoil's bloody awful. / By mid-afternoon my joints are creaking and only my daydreams get me through to the evening.

Then, for a brief second, I get the feeling that I've just got to dash to Burggasse and hop on a tram. But the very next moment it dawns on me that I can't do that because I've joined up. Such are the dreams of recruit Kurt Ritler, an imaginary happiness that cannot become reality. All the same, I spend my days wishing for things. How sad it is that people have wishes all the time even though they can't make them come true. Everyone more or less knows this.

What's going on here is indescribable. Thousands of refugees with their carts pass through this small town all day long, heading for the Vienna region. It's a proper war zone now. This is worrying. They're already coming from Budapest.

Our toilet on the construction site is out in the open, a wooden hut on top of the hill above a ditch, and when you toss away the toilet paper it flies back up and dances on the ceiling. That tells you how draughty it is in here.

Last night another soldier and I had to stand guard at the construction site. It was so dark that you couldn't see the nearest trees. A cold wind was blowing, creating an uncomfortable draught in my steel helmet. And whenever a branch snapped I jumped with fright. / Last winter when Nanni and I went out walking late, there was something particular about the night, it was so dark. We got lost on the Wilhelminenberg and had to feel our way with our hands. I used to like the night with Nanni, huddling up together makes the darkness more pleasant. But here the night just makes you afraid. On watch I atoned for all my sins, I was so afraid, and there was nobody for miles who could have helped had anyone crept up on us. I trembled with fear, I'm not a brave person. / Then I think I fell asleep leaning against a tree. When I awoke I was slightly more composed. / But whenever I remember that Nanni's dead I break into a shiver that shakes me right to the bone. If I didn't have you, Ferdl, life would be unbearable.

Today someone returned from home and told us about the air raids. It's such a shame about our Vienna, our beautiful city. Just so long as nothing happens to the family, that's what everyone thinks. Sometimes we're so irritable towards each other that it's best if everyone keeps out of the way of everyone else. In the barrack room I've seen someone suddenly pick up an object and hurl it against the wall. / For my part I suppress everything as best I can, and if the others start drinking I pick up a book. But sometimes nothing helps.

I can't tell you much about the funeral, which took place in Mondsee. In her letter Susi said that the clouds hung very low over the lake and lots of people cried. Mama writes that there was something spooky about the church and the priest, but the grave was in a nice location. And Aunt Hilli writes that she couldn't sleep for three whole nights beforehand and it was like when a ghost passes through another ghost, she couldn't remember anything. / That's about all I can tell you.

Susi writes that Aunt Hilli sometimes drinks and then gets tipsy. Papa writes that whenever they find some brandy nobody can put the bottle down until the flames are leaping out of his throat. But I'm sure it's not as bad as all that.

Of course I've known for ages what they think of me at home, and it doesn't bother me any longer. So long as this war goes on I'm living from one day to the next and for the time being I'm not going to worry about anything else. Papa reckons I might think it the end of the world if my home no longer existed. But no, I want to feel at home everywhere and nowhere. I've never felt so indifferent about everything.

Recently we've been getting all types of schnapps too, and you can imagine the result: everyone becomes melancholic. The soldier on duty has to remain sober and keep an eye on the others to stop them from taking the place apart, because when anyone talks about leave and home there's no stopping them.

The camp for the foreign labourers is ready and they've already moved in. And so the days have passed when I could barely stretch out my sluggish fingers from which the pickaxe dangled. The shed for the guards has a concrete floor. I left my footprints in the wet concrete and so those are my marks. / Ever more processions of refugees pass through, farmers with sheepskin hats driving their herds in front of them. And then there's the December grey over the landscape and the calls of the hooded crows that only vaguely stand out from the slate sky.

We're going to be moving away from here soon, but we don't yet know the official date. Another column just went out the gate, sent northwards. / There is much talk of the newly established divisions bringing about the turnaround. Not for nothing did we sing at the top of our voices a few years ago: 'F, give the orders, we will obey!' / That's the next stage now.

As I'm being paid I now have money, quite a bit in fact, and I have to keep it in my fat wallet. If I'd had this in Vienna, my God, what a life I could have enjoyed. On the other hand, I'm no longer the sort of person who feels the need to spend money the moment they get it. There's so much you can leave and do without, it's something I'm going to get used to, it's good, dear Ferdl. No beer, no dancing, no women.

I sent the surplus money home. Let them put it away for the *victory celebrations*, see if I care. I was almost back at the barracks when a soldier approached me. He'd come from Mondsee to return the letters I'd written to Nanni. He was very sombre. When I told him Papa had advised me to always keep my civilian clothes on me and chuck away my uniform if the worst came to the worst, he took Papa's side. But they can stuff their advice. / The soldier said that Nanni helped him once when he had a nervous fit. Then he smiled at me slightly anxiously, now he was nervous too and looked terrible. Oh well, it takes all sorts, as Nanni would have said.

Once I told Nanni that she was a rather brazen girl. I believe I was thinking of the time when she took my arm in Mariahilferstrasse. In her boisterous way, she replied, very excitedly, 'Yes, you're right, I always have to keep a check on myself!'

As we're leaving here tomorrow, our captain has ordered us to write as much as we can today, which is what I'm doing. Apparently we're going to Silesia. Maybe all those inexplicable things in my life will find an explanation in Silesia, then I'll fall asleep and wake up a normal human being. / Don't laugh, Ferdl, but a spectacular change will come over me. / And you know I'll write to you as soon as I get the opportunity. If you don't receive any more letters from your Kurti you'll know what's happened.

To the left of the window in the attic of our cottage in Penzing, under some rags, are my sheath knife, my dynamo torch and my fishing tackle. There's all sorts of clutter in front of it. Such objects aren't safe anywhere, but they're well hidden. / Tear up this note, you'll remember what I've written. / And please understand that this is the greatest trust I've ever placed in another human being. I hope you appreciate it.

Otherwise we keep on going through the biting cold, across meadows and woods, it's never-ending and boring, by which I mean empty, deserted. You see the odd abandoned pig or horse here and there. We grab them at once, we can make use of everything. Picture it, a pig, we're going hunting like fine gentlemen. We shoot squirrels too if necessary. When you're hungry you grab whatever you come across.

Yesterday I had some things washed (shirt, pants and a few socks). When I gave the innkeeper's wife the soap she was pleased, because she needs plenty of it for her dirty children. They've got five of them, still very young, but they're making a lot of noise today, a rainy day, and they stare at me wide-eyed. They're between three and nine. / As I said, perhaps I'll find some solid ground again in Silesia, although I suspect I never will because it doesn't exist for me.

Every time I hear knocking at night it sets my teeth on edge. Here it's the children thumping the wall with their heads as they dream.

It's a strange feeling to think that back home, particularly in Vienna, the streets are full of activity and everyone's trying to buy Christmas presents for their loved ones, while we're lying in boxes of straw and every day is the same as the next. Time moves on with an engine that sometimes stutters, runs smoothly as we do nothing, build bunkers, eat and sleep, then ta-ta-ta-ta-ta, the entire vehicle lurches forward violently, a few men fall down, and then it putters on again peacefully as we do nothing, change our lodgings and organize food. / But in the current circumstances Christmas in Vienna is difficult too, of course.

After a two-hour journey we've arrived nearer the front. It is still some distance away, but we can hear the rumbling. Tomorrow we'll be in action again. We're already dreading it, but our captain says, 'This war is a battle of true honesty against the greatest wickedness.' / It really puts you off when it's whistling around your ears and thundering so hard that the ground shakes. But yesterday we had a swim when we stormed the outside pool of a spa hotel. I bet you can picture it, I dived in like a hippopotamus. It was wonderful, ten boys and Lobau-style naturism. In the distance we heard the thunder of the war, we didn't care, we had full cover in the water. You can get used to anything.

I'm still in this barn, so you can imagine the position I'm writing in, lying on the floor, some hay beneath my arm, that sort of thing. / When I step outside I can see in the distance the reflection of battery fire, this ghostly spectacle. / Otherwise there's not much in this godforsaken place worth mentioning. There's not even any point in photographing the area. It breaks my heart whenever I think of home.

I'm so shocked to hear that Franz Stranzberger has died. The Hübsch boy was unlucky too, he was badly injured when leaping onto a lorry and apparently he won't recover. / Scheichenstein is at home with jaundice.

What can I say about you joining the paratroopers? In the end it doesn't matter where you are, you can buy it anywhere. Have your parents calmed down now? My mother too takes a dim view of having to give away *children*. She got very upset when it rained on my head one time when I was sleeping in the hut. She's got a very unrealistic view of all this. In one way that's good because she wouldn't get a wink of sleep if she knew the whole truth, but nor is there any point in pretending. / I wrote to her that she should stop being so anxious, it's not worth it, nobody's going to give her anything for it. / Papa, meanwhile, is very cross because the municipal authorities won't give him any leave. He says that's real gratitude for all he's done, even back when the Party was illegal, and so it's no wonder that he's losing his idealism. As far as he's concerned, all his political activity is now done and dusted, and anyway he gets the impression that the Austrians are treated like idiots, there's no mistaking that.

My first soldier's Christmas has now begun, as my first Christmas package has arrived, from Aunt Hilli. My corporal has forbidden me from opening it before 24 December, but when I was on night duty yesterday and everyone was asleep I cut it open carefully with a knife. I'm now emptying it piece by piece and I always tie it up again afterwards. They'll be in for a surprise on Christmas Eve when they see the package is completely empty. This is just by the by.

I was last in Vienna three years ago. I often think back to that normal time when we went to school, got up at a quarter to seven and by lunchtime we were free again. But now we're soldiers, for the time being. / Once I dreamed that Nanni and I were getting married, the Schrammel music was playing and we were sitting together happily. That's never going to become reality. / So, dear Ferdl, keep your fingers crossed for me and hope nothing happens. All the best from me and good luck! / Goodnight!

Just one more thing: I realize I don't know much about life yet, but I'm gradually resigning myself to it and I don't find it quite so painful any more. And please excuse my poor handwriting, I'm freezing already. I haven't heard anything from you in ages. The post doesn't arrive with all this snow. Or it could be because of the high demand for ordnance – the field post draws the short straw and munitions take priority.

A terrible battle has been raging in our area for days. At night the sky was stained blood-red. The artillery has been pounding for three days non-stop. Those poor people in the trench up front. We're in the village where the main dressing station is. The wounded arrive on foot, on carts and in cars. It keeps going day and night. A picture of pure horror. I will *never* forget these images. / On Thursday morning I was with a few others in a village near the front, and by the evening the Russians were already there.

I'm often reminded of one of the Indian sayings in Papa's book: If one goes out hunting tigers, one must expect to encounter a tiger.

Retreating German units

Retreating German units piled into Budapest and the city became one big military camp. The Danube was teeming with hooting barges and freighters carrying heavy equipment. Whenever a cloud drifted in front of the sun the Danube turned grey. The ships were painted in camouflage colours, which rendered them barely visible. Autumn had secured its dominance over the city; it was a colourless time.

Then the rumour went around that Hungary was going to drop out of the war in a few days' time and strive for neutrality. We Jews were full of hope one day and full of despair the next. It was announced on the wireless that Admiral Horthy had been arrested and Szálasi had become prime minister. Now the unanimous opinion was that the threat was more severe than ever. / And in fact a racial fanaticism was stirred up in the Budapest population too, and the little man came forward and spat at whomsoever he wished to, something he wouldn't have done a few weeks ago, nor had he seemed to need to, but this need appeared overnight.

In September I often loitered around the Danube, the city just waiting in a state akin to catalepsy, strangely unreal, as the Red Army advanced. By the banks of the river I ate plums and chatted to Wally and Georgili, I called out to them, called them by their names, wished them luck and apologized. Now bands of Arrow Cross members were murdering Jews there, taking them to the riverbank and shooting them into the water. / Life isn't pretty here. As soon as one leaves the house one has to anticipate being shot dead like a game animal.

When this morning I looked despondently in my empty bread bag, I realized that I had to leave the house if I wasn't going to starve. I've no money any more, and the easiest way to get some is by changing up

Reichsmarks for pengős with a German soldier. It's a lucrative business, but very few people have the courage to do it, for it has its pitfalls. One mustn't ever get involved with the wrong man. / I've already developed a certain skill in begging for support from aid organizations, committees and neutral foreigners. This allows me to just about keep my head above water.

Guard posts keep appearing at new points in the city. Occasionally a street is sealed off by security forces and they carry out a raid, with pursuits through rear courtyards and across roofs. It's all down to luck whether the men who break into an apartment are looking for people or items of value. Either there are no clear instructions or the instructions are interpreted freely. / This morning Dr Schlosser tiptoed over to the window and peered out. He said I should be careful. / Leaving the house is becoming increasingly risky. Even those who are experts at navigating the streets are getting caught by checks, death lurks everywhere, nobody knows whether he'll be killed by an Arrow Cross bullet, a German tank or a Russian strafer.

I paid a visit to Brandt and begged for money. His wife gave me a small offering. I asked whether she could find out any more about the whereabouts of Wally and Georgili. Frau Brandt said they were still trying to make enquiries, but it was a chaotic situation. / Goodness gracious, where is Wally? Where is Georgili? Where?

My feelings of guilt often bring me to my knees. There is a time by which the pupil has to learn his lesson by heart. After that no more learning is possible. This hour struck for me in 1940 when we could have gone to the Gold Coast, to Accra. / Great opportunities pass and never return.

On the way home I bought something to eat, half a kilo of green peppers and a loaf of bread, a hunk of which I ate there and then in the street. It had a musty-cellar taste, which soon sated my hunger. For us Jews they're now baking bread from potato peelings, flour and chaff. I've almost become used to it. I can barely remember being able to go into any old bakery in Vienna and buying large white loaves and pastries filled with plum jam. / In the house I live in, which is marked by a large yellow star, most men can count their ribs in the mirror.

Whereas a few months ago I would pass people in the street as if invisible and they would treat me as if I wasn't there, latterly I've been attracting looks again and I live in terrible fear. With the musty bread and peppers under my arm I hurried back home, and when I saw one of us *zsidó* people being manhandled outside a cobbler's shop in Lendvay utca, I thought, good, they're busy for the time being. / It's only ever when I get back home that I'm ashamed of my thoughts.

The house in Bajza utca, which I was assigned to at the end of the summer, is right beside Nyugati station. They cooked this up because there's a greater likelihood of being bombed here. If there are to be bombs, then let them fall on people like me. / The house was already hit by a bomb a year ago and because of the damage it hadn't been inhabited until quite recently. Ever since the roof was repaired they've been sticking Jews in here, even though the house is lacking things such as the steps from the third floor up to the attic, water, electric lighting etc. All the locks on the doors have been stolen and even the hinges on the windows. Because of this it rained into the rooms, causing mushrooms to grow. / This is where I'm spending my unhappy days.

I don't have a bed, but a piece of coconut matting and a straw sack. I have my own blanket.

Imre Mendl from Pécs, who subsidized me to begin with until I couldn't pay him back a debt on the agreed date, has lost a lot of weight and is lying on his back, covering his face with his crossed arms. I'm sitting on my berth, writing, sometimes staring at the wall, and time and again my gaze alights on a patch swollen by the dampness and stained yellow at the edges.

Then Hersch Leichtweis comes and says that Wintersperg was apprehended and taken away outside St Stephen's Basilica. On Thursday Frau Horvath's body was washed up on the banks of the Danube near the airstrip at Tököl. / We discuss the news from the nearby front and offer up our current assessments. Then we put ourselves in a foul mood by talking about politics. All of a sudden there's silence in the packed room, and soon everyone is preoccupied with their own concerns again. One can truly sense how common worries can turn into individual worries, not just today but in general. Penned up in such a confined space, one is eventually repelled by the thousand routines and bad habits of others. I often fly into a rage in the room and it's only down in the courtyard or on the street that for a few moments I think warmly of poor Wintersperg or dead Frau Horvath. / But I've become hardened overall, I often think what's the point, I could be next in line at any point.

In the courtyard I have a dark little corner where there's half a metre of space between a garden shed and the massive wall of the neighbouring house. There I lie on the old leaves and relax. Now I realize that the greatest blessing that can be granted me here is peace. To be left alone, to forget that I am a social being. / I take out my cigarettes that I removed from the coat pocket of Gyula Karpati who died a few days ago and light one. As I take the first drag into my lungs, time seems to stand still. / And then I think of Wally again, blearily and sleepily.

This is now my world. I look at it as I might a button in the palm of my hand. And then I think again: Adieu!

Maybe Wally and Georgili fled to the country, unable to contact me, and are living in hiding in Németkér or Jászkarajenő or Balinka. Perhaps Georg is hidden in a Catholic nunnery and Wally is working in an underground munitions factory. Maybe they were taken back to Vienna; it's possible they're waiting for me in Possingergasse.

Lajos Teller, who lives in the same room, escaped Miskolc for Budapest in spring. When once our conversation turned to Wally and Georgili, he said the two of them were in the gas chambers, in the ovens, at any rate anywhere but alive. / I said he should spare me his sick mind. He shrugged and said, 'Nobody believes me. That's bad luck. But strictly speaking it's normal.'

In the meantime I too have been entertaining the possibility that Wally and Georgili are dead. Well, what if they are? Then I'll have to go looking for their graves, I'll have to be brave and keep my chin up, however much I shan't want to. I'd much rather lie down and be dead too, in any case I don't know what I'm still living for. / Fortunately there's Bernili in England. And yet . . . my life is painfully incomplete. Something inside me has been destroyed, and this is causing the part of me which is still intact to suffer from this. I can't say what an effort it is to keep going. / If Bernili didn't exist . . . I've been able to protect at least one person I love.

We listen to the artillery fire, mesmerized by its rhythm. 'Sounds like it's getting closer, doesn't it?' Dr Schlosser says. 'It can't be long before the city will be liberated.' / We try to persuade ourselves that the advancing front line will bring the much-anticipated salvation rather than the peremptory arrival of the next catastrophe. But I'm not one hundred per cent convinced, nor are the others.

I'm also disturbed by the relentless presence of several men who've always got something to say, and on top of that, night after night my sleep is restricted by the industry of families of mice underground. Unfortunately we can't get to grips with them. There's no obvious hole in the floor and the woodwork in the walls is covered with mortar. / I often lie awake in my bed of rags, unsettled and tormented. It feels as if I were lying on a flight of steps to the cellar. And whenever I hear an unfamiliar sound I think, oh really? What a shame! Now it's time, they've come to get me.

The worst night was the one before All Saints' Day, when I had such bad toothache from the wind blowing through the windows that it drove me mad, I couldn't sleep all night. When the curfew was over I wasted no time and went straight to the hospital in Maros utca to have the tooth extracted. The closer I got to Margaret Bridge, the more nervous I felt, but it all turned out fine, even in the hospital. Beforehand I'd worried that they'd mistreat me. On the contrary, the doctor injected my tooth and removed it without the slightest pain. Now the broken tooth was out. And a second one was filled. / The facility was very simple: the drill was operated by foot and I sat on a normal chair. There wasn't any water. It took quite an effort on the dentist's part and he started panting, but he didn't lose his sense of humour and we parted company as friends. / I recalled how after some treatment back in Vienna, Georgili had told Dr Neumann he was no longer his friend, and all the adults laughed.

At the gate on the Pest side of Margaret Bridge a young Jewish man was beaten up. All day long the inhabitants of the city would behave as if they were focused solely on their own concerns. But the moment someone was being beaten up in the street, such a large crowd of people would form that you could barely squeeze past. Already back in Vienna I'd repeatedly ascertained that there was less danger of being harassed if no audience was present. And the abuse didn't last as long. Everyone who stands there and stares adds to the crowd, lends it status, thereby prolonging the suffering of those being tormented. For this reason nobody should imagine they're ever just an onlooker. / Two Arrow Cross men were beating up the boy with full authority to do so. He was already lying on the ground, begging for mercy silently, with his eyes only. Up till the very last moment he couldn't believe that this was actually happening to him. What would his life mean to others if it no longer existed? He couldn't understand and his face was writ large with terror. / Seconds later he was still moving, but as I walked past, these looked like the final movements of a dying man. I closed my eyes, I didn't want to look, but it was in my head already.

I'd also looked one of the Arrow Cross men straight in the face. I wondered where he got such self-assurance from, it was striking how confidently he acted and he still had the energy left to make a joke, asking the dying boy if he'd numbered his bones. I shuddered.

The present era, I believe, belongs to killers more than to anyone else and for this reason killers will always exist.

I was so dazed by what I'd seen that I noticed too late the German soldiers standing in front of me. I couldn't go back any more, so I steeled myself internally and pushed my way to the middle of the throng, some of whom eyed me suspiciously. When I think back to it now I'm horrified by how reckless I was. But at the time I felt I was doing the right thing.

Back in my berth at home I thought of my cousin Jeannette, who from South Africa had advised me against going to Budapest. From a distance one has a better view of things. I ought to have gone to Hlatikulu too, but the name had frightened me and so we stayed in Vienna and then plumped for Budapest, those long-familiar, civilized cities. / I ought to have been frightened of Vienna and frightened of Budapest and I ought to have gone to Hlatikulu. / Looking back I realize that already in Vienna they were talking about us as if we were inanimate: *elements*, alien and unwelcome.

Hersch Leichtweis now has a Spanish letter of protection. I envy him. As I now have illegal status in the city and don't have decent papers, I'm gloomy about my prospects of getting one of these myself.

I'm first going to try to obtain better ID papers. In Spain I could start building a new life for myself until Wally and the children join me. Dental technicians are needed all over the world, even in Accra, Gold Coast, 30 to 35 degrees every day, why not? / Today I had to urge myself not to think too much about the future, it's over and there's nothing I can do about it. It's pointless to keep thinking about it, brooding and brooding and brooding. Now it's all about today and tomorrow.

Again I approached Va'adah, the help and rescue committee, and finally got some new papers, but never mind. It would be fine if I were to change my name another thousand times. It feels as if I haven't been real for many years anyway. My name is Stefan Horvath. Kálmán Grosz. Andor Bakos. Ignáz Braun. I don't know. I barely recall my name any more.

Living conditions in the house are getting ever more cramped. Old Földényi has gone mad; he stood by my bed and peed on it. And to cap it all he shouted abuse at me too. But I'm not going to argue with that lunatic.

Being cooped up like this, day after day, is wicked, thuggish, irksome, demoralizing. For weeks there's been no progress in these dismal living conditions. It's gruelling. Rigid adversity is the worst adversity – stiff, pinned-down adversity. How it assaults one's character! There have even been fisticuffs. All ties we had are being torn apart.

In the city major preparations are being made for war. Budapest is like an army camp; everyone who's not required has to leave as the military needs the space. There's so much other worrying news too. The wounded returning from the East are saying that as the front is pushed back the Germans are not allowing any Jews to stay in the cities and are making short work of clearing them out. The way things are going and the worsening chaos do not bode well. / I don't want to stay in Budapest when the battle commences. The new gap in my teeth is holding up well; today I was able to bite normally on the right-hand side and hopefully by Friday it will be all right.

On Friday morning a transport of volunteers is being put together. They are to meet at the assembly point behind Nyugati station, as was announced over loudspeakers in the street. / Hersch Leichtweis is of course shaking his head: 'No way! I can just imagine what that work is like!' / He can talk, with his Spanish letter of protection. By contrast I've got nothing, no papers, no money, no luck. Officially I've got no special status of any sort, I'm a poor devil and poor devils end up in hell.

As far as we can get information on this, they're planning to send the volunteers to the West as trench-digging Jews. So I'd have to shovel, hack, saw, build, plane and concrete.

Opinion about this voluntary labour is unanimously negative. Lajos Teller says those going will be treated as people treat those who cost nothing and have nothing to say – appallingly, they'll be worked to the bone. Although he told me just how much human beings could endure, he also said, 'God protect us from all that humans can endure.' He said I should think of my brother István, from whom I've heard nothing for weeks.

But the possibility of an escape from this forced idleness is encouraging, and I'm no more horrified by the idea of hard labour than I am by the consequences of staying here. Besides, I can't survive much longer in this shabby room between life and death.

If I ever get back to civilian life again, I intend to be satisfied with everything, even hard physical labour. To me it would seem to be the greatest happiness. Is it possible, perhaps? / Oh Wally, don't be angry with me. I'm not myself at the moment, I feel utterly miserable. I'm sending you a heartfelt kiss. I would happily give up everything else if I could only see you and the children again.

When I woke up in the middle of the night and listened to the sounds outside, I couldn't help thinking of how we passed Halbturn Palace on our flight from Vienna and imagined living there. I sometimes see these images in my head . . . lying with Wally on a divan in a south-facing room in Halbturn Palace. Or lying in a boat covered with planks and sailing down the Danube to Roumania.

At the registration I bumped into Berl Feuerzeug, who's got thinner since our last meeting, and this scrawniness lent his face a hawk-like appearance which turned him into someone quite different. / 'You ought to know,' he said, 'that names are written down in a list with the intention that they can be crossed out again one day.' / He must have recently been on the wrong end of a beating, as I could see by what in Vienna is known as a German Master because of the colour of that regiment's lapels: a black eye. / A German Master had given him the black eye.

As is so typical of Prussians, the SS, gendarmes and auxiliaries began sorting us, one group over here, the other over there. The men were totally in their element; the sorting seemed to give them inner strength. There was no call for expertise in machinery or frostbite surgery; all that counted were bodily mechanics, muscle power, resilience. / When my turn came I looked the man assessing me straight in the eye and gave the slightest of nods, which seemed to convince him. I was waved on to the place where lots of other Jews were standing. For two hours nobody bothered about us, then we were registered: name, age, place of birth, current residence, married. 'Yes.' / 'Wife's name?' / I wanted to say 'Valerie' rather that 'Eszti', to allow Wally to remain real, to keep her real name, to have her real name appear on this list as proof. But then I said, 'Eszti. No children.' / None of us existed any more.

I took Wally's scarf, which I'd kept and carried around in my coat pocket. Once after we'd got married, Wally said quite unexpectedly how wonderful it was to be able to write her new name on the envelope. It was fantastic to have this new name: Wally Meyer.

We were lined up in rows, and the Hungarian guards told us to kindly hand over our valuables, which would stay in Hungary . . . It's your last chance, they said, to do this for Hungary, otherwise they'll fall into German hands. / I didn't have anything anyway, apart from a small penknife for cutting bread, the small notebooks with my shorthand writings, and Wally's scarf. / The other volunteers seemed to be without possessions too, nobody handed anything over and the Hungarian guards gave us angry looks.

Because there was dangerous shooting nearby, the organizers of our journey were worried that things could get awkward if we hung around any longer. So they started shooing us aboard the carriages that were waiting there. We obeyed the orders without hesitation. / Most of the gendarmes had powerful diaphragms, as if this were a selection criterion for the job. Whenever they noticed any attempts at being leisurely, their rifle butts were brought into play and one of the gendarmes complained that the butt of his rifle had splintered and clearly wasn't going to last. / The gendarme had an Austrian accent and, as I had on that occasion back in Rotenturmstrasse in Vienna, I decided to make a note of the face.

'Where are we going?' This was the big question. 'To the West,' some said. 'To our deaths,' others said. 'To the depths,' the Hasid said. / 'Come on, for God's sake! Hurry up!' the gendarme bellowed.

We were transported in closed cattle wagons, the doors of which were locked with wire on the outside. But before we left, our wagons were shunted back and forth for two days on sidings. In Győr too our wagons were shunted around for two days. We didn't know what was going on. Finally, when we got to Heygeshalom, the instruction came to get out and we were ordered to march. They said we were heading for the Bratislava area.

Please God, let me survive the exertions. I am bound to collapse, but others will probably collapse before me, and then we'll see.

Things went better than expected. There was something comforting about being ordered to march, as if I were now in a phase where there was a rhythm carrying me to the end. The ground soon became characterless, flowing beneath our feet, and gradually the landscape disappeared, getting ever more distant, while everything became quieter, the footsteps, the calls, the whistles of the railway trains.

We were back on Austrian soil. My odyssey was like the River Niger, the third-longest river in the world, which after four thousand kilometres flows into the sea not far from its source.

Because the main roads were reserved for the military and processions of refugees, we were directed across farm tracks which snaked between fields and past villages, through little woods and along the Leitha. Occasionally we were followed by children, as if they were following a circus troupe. They imitated our walking and pulled faces at the dogs on leashes so that the dogs bared their teeth. / I was astonished to see life going on as normal outside of my own situation. I watched the birds fly from one tree to the next, and sensed myself growing ever smaller. / The wind was cold and biting, but it was at our backs, which seemed to me a positive thing. / The Hasid marching right in front of me said, 'Wind is wind, regardless of whether it blows from the east or the west.'

Sometimes movement slowed and the procession came to a halt. Everyone waited, staring lethargically at the back of the man in front, until we got moving again, unevenly to begin with, then uniformly again. A strange shuffle moved along the path. / By the afternoon I barely noticed these brief pauses any longer.

Beside me marched a boy, a former student or graduate of the business school, not much older than twenty. We didn't talk, we just exchanged the odd glance. He was thin and pale. All of a sudden he started shouting, 'Why!? . . . Why!? . . . Why!?' I took care not to lose step or falter despite the shouting. It was the task I'd set myself at that moment. And I could hear the gendarmes further back shouting too: 'Close ranks! Come on, close ranks!' And soon afterwards, 'Stop! Halt!' Then a few gunshots. I didn't turn around. But I could hear the shuffling of footsteps around me far more clearly now. And I thought again about what Januk, the Pole, had said to me in Budapest: Never give yourself up to them, and if you fall into their hands, run away at the first opportunity.

These slaves come from Hungary, they look like ghosts but there's nothing inherently unreal about them, they've just been turned into something unreal. First they were transported by train in wagons, given food worthy of the name, from Budapest to Győr, where the Raab flows into the Little Danube, and from Győr to Heygeshalom, right by the border with the German Reich. Then westwards on foot. And now they're shuffling, exhausted, through the winter haze and they look like they look.

I feel as if I'm sweating out my cold through exertion. At any rate I can't feel anything any more. Either I'm going to get better again or I'm already half dead.

Then one man gets given a tin of sardines by a Waffen SS motorcycle rider who drives past us. In the end the Waffen SS man will have something to be proud about. The Hasid says, 'Every soldier has to do that once, so he can talk about it. He does it once and talks about it a hundred times. It keeps things ticking over. The sardine is soon eaten and it's of more help to the soldier than the Jew. The soldier gives it away once and back home he can talk about it one hundred times.'

Whenever anyone collapsed with exhaustion, couldn't go on any more and was shot, there was usually a profound silence for a while. Even the guards had to take in what had happened. But usually, a flock of birds taking to the wing or a goods train passing with fifty tank wagons was enough for everything to click back into its routine.

The lists that had been so carefully compiled were in fact fairly insignificant. Whenever our numbers were decimated, the only issue was how to deal with the body, never updating a list, of whatever sort. Nobody particularly noticed when someone disappeared. I saw at least four bodies which in a better world would not have been lying where they lay.

When it started to get dark we arrived in German Haslau. We were taken to a large barn where we were to spend the night. First we sat outside and I searched for lice which I'd picked up from the cattle wagon. I squashed them between my fingernails as if I'd grown up with companions like this. / Two hours after our arrival we were given soup. Then I was so exhausted my head started to spin and I could barely react when we were ordered to go to sleep. / The barn had a concrete floor. We were forbidden from making use of the planks piled up at the rear of the barn to mitigate at least the worst of the cold coming up through the floor.

We staggered inside. It was hard to find a space as the barn was too small for all of us, and now it was night-time. I was knocked, shoved and hit. The room was quickly filled with curses and cries of pain. One man was crying because someone had broken his spectacles. / 'Shut up, you nutcase!' another said.

As soon as I'd got myself a halfway acceptable sleeping position, using Wally's scarf as a pillow, I felt better. And because we'd been told that it was less than fifteen kilometres to Hainburg as well as Berg, where there was a camp, I wasn't so worried about the next day. I just had to fall asleep soon. And in my sleep I leaped onto a horse!

Then I saw Wally standing beside the pile of planks, by the wall to the right. I put a hand out to her so she would come over. She looked at me, and because I was unsure whether she recognized me I called out her name. Then her expression changed, as if she'd only just become aware of my presence. Grief descended on her face, and it seemed as if with a nod of her head she was signalling she couldn't come any closer. For the first time without my heart thumping I entertained the possibility that she and Georgili were dead. / 'Wally,' I said, 'forgive me for not having been at your side when they took you and Georg. You know how much I love you. Please forgive me for not having given you adequate protection. And you too, Georg, Georgili, my handsome boy, don't think badly of your father because at a bad time he made bad decisions. I'm an unhappy man.' / I told Wally how I'd fared and what I thought of my current situation. She continued to look at me, her face a picture of grief, and waited until I'd finished talking. At that moment a smile darted across her face, accompanied by a nod, and it felt as if she'd given me permission to no longer feel guilty. I kissed the scarf again and when I looked up once more she had gone.

The following morning I found walking easier. I focused completely on my walking, taking care not to fall out of step. And once I heard Wally's voice: 'Courage, Andor, courage! Keep it up, Andor! And run away if you get a decent opportunity.'

I was surprised that she knew my new name. Andor, that's who I was now. / I thanked Wally for her support and for everything she'd given me in the years we'd spent together. 'Thanks for everything, Wally,' I said, then I took my leave of her, sending my love to Georgili.

[Written in the margins:] // I'd love to have some decent gloves, mine aren't up to scratch and it's painfully cold. / I hope the hands of my late parents are over me and that the Lord will shatter all the teeth of our tormentors. / All the best, my dearest ones! I'm near Hainburg now. I'm wearing your scarf, Wally, even though the others tease me for it. Mist is drifting across the Danube. Best of luck, Bernili, Georgili! Thanks for everything! God bless you! Kisses! Kisses to you, my loved ones!

I'm plunging into winter again

I'm plunging into winter again and I realize that in some respects we're coming full circle. It was almost exactly a year ago that I wrote my first diary entries, on a winter's day, in the military hospital in the Saarland. But that was a damp, rather foggy day, not cold and sunny like today. Back then I was daunted by the passing of time, as I still am. The difference is that now I don't feel like my days are being ground to dust; on the contrary, they're becoming more solid, and even if their substance is sometimes serious, I nonetheless feel that my life is my own.

How lovely that Lilo has celebrated her first birthday. She's not an infant any more, but a little girl who's getting smarter by the day, and who's learning what her surroundings look like and what you can and must do in them. The annoying bars of the playpen often prevent her from going where she would like, but they do have the advantage that she can use them to pull herself up and to hold on tight if necessary. Knowledge like this is already bordering on wisdom: everything has two sides. Lilo watches to see what she can make out of it.

One of her chief interests is other children. When she sees a child she scrutinizes it, starts speaking in her own language and appears happy. Her other great passion is the pig shed. The moment she sees the door she launches herself at it and tries to open it. She's keen on her mother when she's unhappy, but otherwise she's fairly indifferent towards her. She has a particular fondness for men in uniform and older gentlemen. And then there's the watch on Uncle Veit's wrist, which is especially interesting with its tick-tock, because there must be a reason for it. If only she knew what. The little one will figure this out at some point. If not now, then later, after the war, she'll delve into it sometime.

For her birthday Margot gave Lilo a coat, her own plate and her own spoon. From me she got a blanket with blue flowers on it. Lilo adores the knitted yellow hat from her grandmother in Darmstadt, she wears it day and night, and the girl almost looks like the late professor's wife from the second floor who refused to be separated from her violet bonnet. / Margot and I toasted Lilo, that was two days after I'd shot my uncle.

I had shot my uncle dead; this thought went around my guts the whole time like worm powder. Only when I slept with Margot were there moments when I felt free from this terrible episode. In a way I was happy to have the order to go to Vienna, as I no longer felt comfortable in Mondsee; I fancied I could smell Uncle's blood whenever I turned around.

The authorities weren't really able to figure out the murder. It was established that he'd been shot with a pistol. Nobody could explain where the Brazilian was suddenly supposed to have got a pistol from, but he was presumed to be the killer. / They couldn't pin anything on the innkeeper from Schwarzindien; everything pointed to the fact that he had nothing to do with it. Nor did it occur to anyone that the shrew might be involved. *The shrew* was what Uncle's colleagues called the former camp teacher at Schwarzindien on account of the severe expression she always wore in the presence of men.

It was even more dismal than usual in the gendarmerie office. The assistant sat at Uncle's desk as if sprawled out on a throne. His right ear was thickly wrapped in white bandages, making the hair at his parting stick up like a comb. / Instead of consoling me, the assistant said, 'Well, well, who do we have here?' / 'I've come to say goodbye,' I said, showing him the order to go to Vienna, where I expected to be certified as fit for service. The assistant showed his pity for me with a shrug. I shrugged my shoulders too. 'It's about time I got out again.'

As the assistant was filling out my permit to travel to Vienna, he asked me what I thought of the Brazilian. I tried to contain my nervousness by being sincere and said that before going to ground he'd been embittered about his ship that had sailed around the world and ended up stranded in this one-horse town. And he'd suffered from the fact that the F had met with such approval while nobody took him seriously. / The assistant asked whether the Brazilian had again spoken derogatorily about the F to me. I thought about it and said that he'd called the F a cursed man, cursed by the god of beauty and cursed by the god of love. / 'He's got problems . . .' the assistant commented, then inserted a report form into the typewriter and poked at the keys for a while, with two fingers like a stork's beak. His brow furrowed, he gave the consummate performance of the reluctant bureaucrat, annoyed at a world that generated work, all of it stupid and avoidable, and which ultimately harmed the entire German Volk Community. / The familiar ring of the margin bell and the purring of the typewriter carriage as it was pushed back made me sink into my thoughts. First the world around me faded, then I saw my uncle in the bar in Schwarzindien, looking at me in disbelief before falling to his knees in pain and fear.

When the assistant pulled the report from the typewriter, the sound of the badly oiled roller made it seem as if the machine were shrieking in horror, and the jarring note hung in the room for several moments. / 'Where is that bastard?' the assistant muttered, grimacing again with vexation.

I acted as if the matter had nothing to do with me and claimed that, a few days before his death, my uncle had asked me to take Kurt Ritler's letters to Annemarie Schaller back to Vienna, letters that weren't important for the file. / The assistant tugged thoughtfully at the bottom of his head bandage, then he went over to the shelf, took from the relevant file the letters, some in light-blue envelopes, others in dark-red ones, and handed them to me. / 'Such a sad story,' he said. / I could see that he'd been Uncle's apprentice.

We talked a while longer about my late uncle, how he'd enjoyed smoking as well as apple pie. Then I took my leave. And with the gloomy feeling that hasn't left me since I first enlisted, I wandered away from the gendarmerie, thinking that the image I had of myself hadn't been made any more attractive by having shot my uncle. I was sure, however, that overall the good outweighed the bad. And this feeling gradually grew stronger as I walked home in the lightly falling snow.

Who killed / whom / when / where / why / with / what?

Margot raised her eyebrows when I entered her room, but I didn't have any news for her. 'I wouldn't like to be in the Brazilian's shoes,' I said. 'I hope he's able to help himself.' / Margot gave me a critical look and advised me to calm down. It wasn't good to be so steamed up, she said.

We talked about my forthcoming examination. I knew full well that my hope for a further deferment was incompatible with the war situation. There were no compelling reasons. The mere fact that I was alive underlined my deployability. And so I told Margot that I'd probably be enlisted again. She took her large suitcase from under the bed, opened it, threw the grey, torn underwear and nappies onto the bed, stacked cigarette boxes to one side, and took out a tin that contained the tomato money. Stuffing the wad of notes into my hand, she said, 'Veit, I beg you to do whatever you can to ensure you come back. I'm not expecting any other heroic deeds from you.' / We exchanged glances and I swallowed hard.

She had recently received a letter from her husband, who'd finally got out of the bridgehead in Memel. He'd been taken by ship to Cranz on the Baltic, where they'd stayed for three days in a beachside hotel, three really lovely days. In the evenings they strolled around the town or went to the cinema, and from there he sent a postcard and a registered letter with the certificate for his Close Combat Clasp. / From Cranz they'd been taken by train to a desolate backwater near the Polish border, where they were also able to rest. Almost all the inhabitants were gone and there was no light. Such were the resting quarters for soldiers in Germany; it hadn't been any different in Russia. How long their resting period would last depended on the overall situation, and it was widely known that the overall situation was not particularly rosy. / He didn't think he'd be granted leave until the war was over.

'When the war's over,' Margot said, 'it'll be fine by Ludwig, too, if we get divorced.'

Everything lay in a profound silence when we woke the following morning. The village and the lake were a milky grey, and the longhorns, although they came from far away, were well suited to this misty milieu, silently chewing the little they'd been given to eat. They pawed at the snow with their hoofs. Margot and Lilo accompanied me to the station. Margot held my hand the whole way, regardless of any looks we might get. / Back in spring, our being together had at least in part been motivated by the desire not to be alone. But now, as we stood on the platform of Mondsee station in the winter dawn, waiting for the train to arrive, I knew with absolute certainty that we'd started something which would last, if circumstances allowed.

'These last few months will be fine too,' Margot said. We kissed. I lifted Lilo and made her laugh. But when I boarded the train I felt a pang of anxiety and was desperate to get off again at once.

There was no chance of everybody getting a seat from Salzburg to Linz, so I stood in the aisle, and later too, as the train was chugging along the Danube, I spent some time in the vestibule. By now the exhaustion of the passengers was palpable. The air was damp and stale. I heard moans, groans and discussions about politics. One woman said, 'Christmas is the festival of peace.' / 'You know where you can stick your peace,' a voice growled from somewhere. / As the railways were pretty much at a standstill anyway it really didn't matter that we lost half an hour after Linz because we had to let two fast trains pass. Overall we made relatively good progress, and I thought I'd be very happy if the journey back was just as quick.

As the train approached St Pölten, I recalled my military service, which I'd done there in the last year of peace, about a hundred or a hundred and twenty years ago. Back then I would often cycle to Vienna on Saturdays, because recruits were only allowed to use public transport with a leave pass. Sixty kilometres there, sixty kilometres back, a total of seven hours in the saddle. / How happy I'd felt at the kitchen table at my parents'. And now I was going back home, thinking gloomily: I'm already anxious about those stupid lectures.

Everything passes, everything comes to an end, everything, even one's youth and life itself. As the sergeant had sneered during our basic training: 'Now then, gentlemen, we're not here to enjoy ourselves, just you bear that in mind.' / At the time I didn't have any idea just how dearly the military would cost me.

Outside the bleak fields drifted past, where forgotten beets and rotting cabbages lay like skulls and blackened bones.

The Westbahnhof was thick with smoke

The Westbahnhof was thick with smoke from the steam locomotives. I immediately slipped into the mass of soldiers arriving, changing, leaving, all types, all armies, all ranks, auxiliary personnel, forced labourers, ripped uniforms, filthy rucksacks, dirty faces. And amongst them hundreds of refugees, some of the women in unfamiliar-looking traditional costumes, old men with unfamiliar-looking beards, sitting on suitcases, surrounded by sacks, bags and large bundles of clothes blocking the soldiers' way.

And of course the sky over Vienna was lower than elsewhere. The ash and dust from poor-quality coal blew into my face and throat. / On a wall I saw the following words daubed in paint: *H, the knave, belongs in a grave*.

At home I had a wash, and when I saw the scars on my right leg they looked unfamiliar; I couldn't recall sustaining these injuries. And most of all I couldn't believe it. Was that me? Me, who . . . ?

What was new in my parents' apartment was that it went tick, tick, tick all the time, incessantly. It took me a while to get used to this. When the ticking stopped momentarily, a cuckoo sounded on the wireless and a woman's voice read out the status in the sky: 'Aircraft incursion from the south . . .' / Papa had built the ticker himself and linked the telephone up to the wireless. As soon as enemy aircraft were approaching, the normal wireless transmission stopped and the Party broadcast came on via the telephone. I didn't understand how it worked exactly and I gave my father great credit for it. / 'You could do that too,' he said. / 'Perhaps,' I said. / But I was sure it would take me months, if not years, to refresh the knowledge I'd acquired by the time I'd finished school.

The conversation very quickly turned to Uncle Johann. How much should I tell them? Internally I tried again to bring myself to show a level of sympathy, but it went no further than rebuking myself. The underlying feeling remained: Uncle is dead, but the Brazilian and I are still alive, and that's the main thing. / And so everything I said was unreal and not what I wanted to say. I'd be better off keeping my mouth shut. I claimed not to know very much about it, only what I'd picked up from the newspaper. The authorities were cagey and fully preoccupied with finding the suspected killer. / 'Uncle Johann will have wanted to live out his final years in passable happiness,' Mama said. 'But fate put a stop to that.' She faltered and then added, 'I don't know where it's all going either.' / 'He's dead and that's that,' I let slip. / Papa and Mama looked at me aghast. Mama's eyes went red and she shed a few tears. Papa also assumed an expression that was conceivably one of shock. Then Mama began tinkling away at the piano, playing some Christmas songs in an attempt to salvage the evening, but it didn't work.

I was horrified too. My God, it hit me, I'm just like my uncle. Once when I'd asked him what had happened with the two Lanners from St Lorenz, Anton and Anton, who'd been executed for illicit slaughtering, he'd replied tersely, 'They got carried away.'

There was a second critical moment when Papa said that 1944 had been one big disappointment for him, the entire year so far. I asked pointedly whether the previous years had been any better. He didn't answer me. / 'If only we hadn't been so stupid,' I said. / He asked whether he'd misunderstood what I'd just said. He'd understood me correctly, I muttered, bracing myself for endless discussion. But he said, 'All right, all right.' / I got the impression that Mama had begged him not to start any arguments with me. / When I asked what was new in Vienna, Papa was even in a mood to joke. 'Some are complaining about the inflation in addition to the misery of the air raids, others about the weather, which just goes to show that Vienna will always be Vienna, no matter what happens.' / I kept out of the conversation after that and filed my nails instead. Of course there were comments that I could have reacted to, but I exercised self-restraint and not another cross word passed my lips.

But I noted again that Papa never made fun of himself, a

characteristic he shared with the men he'd sworn allegiance to twenty years ago, men who never laughed at themselves, only at others.

I quietly lay down and covered myself. My thoughts as I was going to sleep were of Margot. But whenever I woke up at night my head was filled with everything else; thoughts of the war became too much, pressing down on me like a heavy burden. And then there were the dreadful dreams. / A dream I had about the Brazilian was the most agreeable. I was talking to him when a lorry came racing down Possingergasse towards us and for safety's sake the Brazilian pushed me to one side, away from the road.

It was a wet night. I heard the rain. Now a car was beeping in the ash-grey light of the morning, a bicycle rang its bell and these familiar sounds banished my fear. / Margot would be getting up soon too, the child must be awake already.

Over breakfast it occurred to me that the overwhelming impression I had of my parents' apartment wasn't the familiarity of the surroundings, but the unfamiliarity of what had once been familiar. I was uneasy at no longer having my own home and I realized that the war hadn't just robbed me of six years of my life, it had wrenched me from all that I had been used to. During my absence the furniture and the pictures on the walls had become little more than junk.

Mama asked whether I'd be going to see Aunt Rosa that morning. I gave a lacklustre wave of my hand and said I wanted to visit the cemetery. Mama reminded me of what she'd already told me in a letter: that Meidling Cemetery would remain closed for the duration of the war due to bomb damage in an air raid, and they'd be holding no more funerals there until then. I insisted on trying my luck. / As I slipped on my boots, Mama said she hoped she stayed in good health, otherwise they'd have to bury her provisionally in Vienna Central Cemetery and then exhume her after the war so that on the instructions of those who outlived her she could be definitively laid to rest beside Hilde.

Quite a few mourners were standing outside the locked main gate, chiefly elderly people, some crying, others begging to be let in to visit their relatives' graves. The municipal cemetery officials were notoriously unsympathetic; they would have liked nothing better than to be able to instruct people when to die. At any rate, they didn't care whether you got the opportunity to visit your relatives or not. This also reflected the harsh reality inside the city. / An old woman said I was still young and the fence had been blasted backwards by a bomb. Although you had to negotiate a crater, that wouldn't be an obstacle for me, many people took this route. And I did. There was water at the very bottom of the crater and I had to be careful not to fall.

There were more craters in the cemetery, but these were easily bypassed. Many gravestones had been destroyed, but our family grave was undamaged, albeit scruffy-looking on account of the cemetery closure. Everything was overgrown with weeds. Amongst the weeds I spotted the decomposed remains of a swastika pennant. With my handkerchief I wiped the dirt from the indentations of the inscription: *Hilde Kolbe 11.III.1913 – 20.X.1936.*

Graves and craters and rubble and evil spirits. Is everything just a nightmare? I stood there in disbelief, the grave a pile of weeds, my family reptile-like predators ready to eat me alive. The usual cold, grey life.

In the end Hilde's coughing had disturbed Papa so much that he set up his bed in the kitchen. A week before she died Hilde was very anxious the whole time. At night she kept switching the light on every hour and when anyone asked, 'What's wrong, Hilde?' she'd reply, 'I can't say, I feel so strange.' / On 19 October at seven o'clock in the evening the doctor was here and she gave Hilde an injection, saying, 'You'll sleep well tonight.' / When I briefly went up to Hilde to give her a glass of water, she said, 'How fresh the water is!' Then she said, 'Go to bed, Veit, I want to sleep too.'

She had beautiful skin with faint freckles on a large face, and usually two plaits dangled down her back. Towards the end she wore her hair in a coil like the girls from Galicia. She was twenty-three years old. Her death still unsettles me today.

I remember being still awake, we were all awake. Despite the injection she'd been given by the doctor, Hilde couldn't sleep and she was talking about suicide. My parents paced up and down the apartment nervously; I was terrified. At one point the windows creaked, then a door slammed shut. The linoleum in the hallway was springy, it was like walking on a moor. The entire apartment gave me the creeps.

Above my bedroom was the attic, where I heard objects falling to the floor. I don't believe in ghosts, but the threats Hilde had issued in her distress had made me jumpy. I told Papa that the two of us should go up to check on what was going on up there. We opened the door to the attic and inside everything was neatly in its place. We went back down and tried to finally get some sleep.

Around four in the morning there was more noise, so I checked on Hilde in her room. She was sitting in her bed, bathed in sweat and gasping for air. No more retching, no wheezing, the sweat dripped from her body as if she were sitting under a shower. My first thought was: God, get out of here, she's dying. / Mama sat beside Hilde, wiping the sweat from her brow, while Papa had dashed to the telephone to call the doctor. Mama implored Hilde to be patient, the doctor was on her way. Then she rushed out of the room, had a chat with Papa, and I followed her because I didn't want to be alone in the room with Hilde and have to assume responsibility. No sooner was I out the door than I heard a bang against the bedside table. Mama ran back in and a moment later she came out again, wiped the snot from her nose and told us that Hilde had fallen backwards and was dead. We ran into the room and looked at her, eyes skewed and one arm hanging from the bed. Mama sent us out, we sat in the kitchen and the doctor arrived, spoke to Papa for a while, then we all went back into Hilde's room. The doctor was just about to listen to Hilde's heart, and Papa to close her eyes, when Hilde sat up then immediately fell against the bedside table again. All of us blanched in horror. But after we'd exchanged glances, the doctor confirmed the death, she said that now Hilde was actually dead.

The lights were on in our apartment until the morning and I kept asking myself the whole time: Why, why, why? Why did it have to be this way? It was the question the living person asked into the void, and the dead person didn't reply, nor anyone else. All of life is like a dream.

At the end of the week another girl's bed was carried up into the attic. Hilde was now on her wanderings and wasn't coming back; I waited a long time for her to come back.

Years later I comforted a few dying people . . . not that you can ever make up for anything . . .

My thoughts returned to such things as I stood at Hilde's grave, and I felt as if here, amongst the dead, everything was collapsing too, another world of rubble, without a centre, everything crumbling, rolling bit by bit in different directions. The same applied to language too; words like *promise* and *faithfulness* had become hollow, and they shattered when I tried to form them with my mouth.

In the afternoon I strolled here and there, in a city where everyone was in a hurry, even those maimed through war who were reliant on crutches. Half the world seemed to have been maimed through war. From the Wehrmacht office in Hirschengasse I went to see Uncle Rudolf in Siebenbrunnenfeldgasse. On the way back I tried to buy a 1945 diary, but it was as if all the shops had been swept clean of everything. The longer I spent amongst people, the more anxious I became.

Late that afternoon I returned to the 15th district and went to the Grassingerhof to give back to Kurt Ritler the letters he'd written to Nanni Schaller. I looked for the right door and, before knocking, I waited a moment for my tension to ease a little. After knocking I noticed a shadow at the kitchen window, but I couldn't see who it was. Then Susi opened the door, Kurt's sister, whom I remembered from Nanni's funeral. She informed me that her brother was a soldier now and was at the South-east Wall. 'They're digging like crazy there,' she said. / As I was in uniform she readily gave me information. Although she couldn't quite make me out, she shied away from asking questions. She might have been eleven, with bright, alert eyes, and looked slightly mistrustful, as if she were already aware how serious life was. At once I was convinced she would read her brother's letters if I gave them to her. I mean, I had read them myself, which you can interpret as you like, but I'm not his little sister. Rapidly changing my plan, I asked for Kurt's address. The girl knew it off by heart: 'Jägerkaserne in Hainburg, Marschweg, Barrack 1, Room 3.' / I gave the girl one Reichsmark, which she took unabashed with a beaming smile. And so I left without having achieved anything.

I was wrenched out of bed during the night by the siren, which started howling just after five o'clock. Alarm! I quickly got up and, half-asleep, threw on some clothes and dashed down into the cellar with my belongings. / We sat on crates and stared between our legs.

The ceiling in the cellar was supported by beams, on the principle of too much being better than too little, and there was an opening to the cellar of the neighbouring house, which was covered with a shutter. / When the ground began to shake, an elderly woman who'd recently moved into the house said, 'They're demanding a bit too much of everybody.' Her words hung there in the others' silence.

At seven o'clock we were back up in the apartment. None of us went back to bed, we muddled along, no gas, telephone not working. Apparently the Elisabeth Hospital had been hit twice. Papa said that even in hospital one was no longer safe, that was a real outrage.

At breakfast Mama asked me why I was so silent. I said I was nervous. Papa thought about this for a while, then said, 'Do you know what, Veit? With all these bombings and air-raid alerts my nerves are shot too. I don't think I can put up with much more anxiety. But that's the enemy's intention, isn't it?' / Then he started talking again about the future, for which our many sacrifices were being made, and I said, 'Just see how the city looks nowadays. There's no sign of life any more. People go about their business apathetically and joylessly, and written on every face is the fear of the future you are glorifying. What are your grandiose words against all those tired faces?'

The tone in which I talked to Papa was fairly harsh and this was what ultimately cut me off from the family. He said that if I spoke to him like that again, et cetera, et cetera. Well, of course I'd be only too happy speak to him like that again, and I told him this. His threat of never wanting to set eyes on me again if I continued in this vein now became definite, without it having to be spelled out. / I just murmured 'Fuck you.' / He turned as red as a tomato.

Now the past twenty-four years made themselves felt, that permanent lashing of a child with criticism, only hearing negative comments, never praise, never a little white lie: 'Well done!' Instead: 'I hope you won't be satisfied with that, Veit.'

Childhood is like a piece of wood into which nails are hammered. The good nails are those that are just deep enough to hold; these protect you like thorns. Or later you can hang things from them. The bad ones are those that are thrashed so hard into the wood that their heads lie below the surface. You can't see there's something hard there, a foreign object rusting away. / Papa always drove the nails deep into the wood by continually hammering away at the same spots. And for that he now expected to be heaped with gratitude. / I have a certain attachment to my childhood, which is why I respect my father. And yet, over the years I've realized that *steadfastness* and *consistency*, to name two of his favourite words, have their dark side. Papa ruined my childhood with words such as *steadfastness* and *consistency*. Others had ruined my adolescence and early adulthood, but with the same words.

What the family had begun in the destruction of my personality, the war continued. At the front I watched personalities being wrecked. Sometimes goodness emerged from the wreckage, but more often than not it was wickedness.

Then I went to the Breitensee barracks for my examination. As soon as I entered I bumped into someone from my former army unit, who told me that Frenck was here too, our wireless operator. / When Frenck learned that I was here he came running, took my bag from me and we went to the mess and had a beer. He was very warm and emphasized how glad he was to see one of his old comrades. There weren't many of us left now, the familiar faces were getting fewer and fewer, and he missed them. Tomorrow he was leaving to rejoin our unit in Insterburg, and he urged me to follow soon. / He still had my bag on his lap and I said it contained all my belongings. 'Where are they going to send you?' he asked. / 'To the gallows, the front or to be gobbled up by the devil.' / He laughed, wondering perhaps why I was not laughing too. Then he said he was being given three days' worth of travelling rations. 'In the good old days we got eight days' worth,' he added. 'In the bad old days,' I corrected him.

Then I was instructed to go to the orderly room; they wanted to carry out my examination at once. The corridor that served as a waiting room, with chairs arranged along the wall, was narrow, dark and packed. My mood immediately sank lower. Most men were waiting as if crippled. But one, who appeared half-mad, was soliloquizing, convinced that the whole world must know what he thought of military doctors. He said that somewhere else an army doctor had patched up a lieutenant so badly that the officer was now a hopeless case in a lung sanatorium. The only way they'd certify you unfit for military duty, he continued, was if you were literally on the verge of dying; nowadays anyone not carrying his head under his arm was passed as fit. This was no longer the seriousness of life his grandfather spoke about, this went beyond seriousness. They were toying with you and seeing if you came out of it well. If not, they chucked you onto the dung heap. Two years ago he'd had three toes sawn off his right foot, and the doctor responsible for that deserved a right thrashing. It was unbelievable that they let someone like him loose on soldiers.

I was unsettled by the man's words. I was desperate for a Pervitin to help me get through this, but was worried that it would work to my disadvantage if I was in a good mood during the examination. I gradually broke into a sweat and was gripped once again by the unreal feeling, but at least by now this was familiar. / And I kept thinking: Am I really destined for war? Wasn't I actually destined for something else?

A medical assistant called me into an examination room, and told me to get undressed and stand on the scales. With my underpants I weighed sixty-six kilograms. A doctor with a stethoscope hanging from his coat pocket came and asked me why I was here, I ought to be at the front. I said it was all there in the documents. Ignoring these, he held out the prospect of a suitable place soon being found for me in the army. Every man was needed at the front, he said, and hopefully I realized that somebody like me, who knew the workings of the army inside out, was worth more than ten boys. I'd been astute at keeping myself away from the fighting for long enough now.

Although it was hard to predict the outcome of my examination I made every effort to explain everything. I told him, amongst other things, that I was depressive. / The doctor almost burst out laughing. He said he acknowledged this, but in his experience men at the front didn't have the time to give in to their depressive tendencies; this would be delayed until they got back home. That was why many depressives were capable of work, but not capable of living. / Incensed, I said that someone not up to living had no place at the front. / But this made no impression on the doctor either. He said that it might even be possible to overcome the condition by confronting the causes; that's what he'd learned at university. / 'Who from?' I asked, in anticipation of hearing a few names that had now become unpopular. No reply. / 'The only way to be rid of your fears is to confront them,' he said stubbornly. 'One must come to terms with one's weaknesses and find a way to prevail.'

We sat angrily opposite one another, and again it occurred to me that I was going to be twenty-five soon. Thousands of other feelings washed through me, mainly fuelled by the things I feared at night. / The money that Margot had given me rustled in the left breast pocket of my uniform jacket. And because anything was more desirable than what I'd experienced for years in the war, I decided to do what I'd never have done otherwise: I took out the money and placed it on the table. It was a thick bundle of notes. / 'My bonus for four campaigns,' I said. / For a few seconds the money stayed where it was, without a master in the land of the master race. And the man who was keener to be the master than the other one reached for it. I mitigated the embarrassment by saying, 'The headaches give me problems with my vision.' / I closed my eyes, my ears roared with the tension, and when I opened my eyes again the money was gone.

As I waited for my papers I braced myself for being certified fit for certain types of work, such as clerical duties or as a driving instructor at a garrison. I didn't think I could be deferred altogether, and this suspicion proved correct. / When I set eyes on his decision I had to look twice to ensure there wasn't a mistake: *Fit for active service in the field.* It struck me with such force that I had to sit down. I felt the provocation in every cell of my body and it burned as if acid had worked its way into the wounds. / This lousy bastard had taken Margot's money and certified me fit for active service. My marching orders were for Wednesday.

When I'd composed myself, I looked for the orderly room. I realized that, after all that had happened, it was better not to protest. The mere fact that I hadn't had any objections to the sparse evidence from Vöcklabruck took some of the sting from all of this. But I demanded a concession, which took the form of two doses of Pervitin that the medical officer willingly gave me. As I accepted the medication I was overcome by a real hatred of these tablets. But I needed them now, unfortunately. / I showed my registration form, which said Mondsee, and said I had a child out of wedlock there. And without asking for one

I was granted a two-day extension. My marching orders were now for Friday rather than Wednesday, Vienna North station, destination Insterburg, East Prussia, where my unit was located, as I already knew from Frenck. The bone mill in the East.

Because I didn't feel like going home, I got a haircut from the barracks barber. And as I was still wearing the old uniform I'd been in when I was discharged from the military hospital in the Saarland, I paid a visit to the stores. There my request for a new uniform was approved. / Sitting on a bench in the stores, as I was taking off my boots, I had a moment of semi-stupor, wondering to my surprise why Lilo wasn't crawling towards me, laughing as she reached into the boots. Oh yes, because I was in Vienna, from where I was being sent back into the field. War drags you along like scree in a river.

Ever since Margot

Ever since Margot turned out to be somebody I could talk to and who encouraged me to stand by my opinions, I'd no longer felt inferior to Papa. When I told them back at home that I had to return to the front, he said he loved his children more than anything and he wished me the best of luck. I lacked the courage to say straight out that he only loved himself, but I prepared myself mentally to do so. Unfortunately I didn't get another opportunity. / And how sad I felt at the sight of the old sewing machine which Mama had used to mend our clothes. In my mind I could still see her fingers fiddling with it. And so, in great sorrow, I left our apartment early in the morning to go and see Kurt Ritler in Hainburg. His letters to Nanni refused to give me any peace.

It was snowing so heavily that no trams were working. With my luggage I had to make my way on foot to Schönbrunn, from where I took the city train to Hauptzollamt. There I changed onto the Bratislava train. / It was snowing and gusting until the Central Cemetery, after which the snowfall subsided. / My carriage emptied when we got to Schwechat. The only other passenger left was a gentleman doing a puzzle in the corner to my right. When he got out at Kroatisch-Haslau he left the puzzle behind. Read from bottom to top, the solution was: *Into the new year confident of victory.*

Because I'd had too little sleep over the past few days my senses were foggy, my body felt jaded, everything was dimmed. It wouldn't have been an unpleasant feeling had I been able to abandon myself to it. But fear of falling asleep prevented that.

The train passed through Carnutum, and because I have the gift of always being able to see through the skin of things to the bare bones, I could make out the remains of the former city beneath the fields. I don't know if this distracts from what's important or points to what's important, but it's strange that here, where fields now sprawl, Roman emperors once resided and were proclaimed, and that nobody knows any longer whether Carnutum had twenty or thirty thousand inhabitants. Everything is covered, only a few stones lie around, and it's barely imaginable that here Emperor Marcus Aurelius wrote self-justificatory meditations in the midst of the madness of the wars he waged. / *For the stone that is thrown in the air, it is no misfortune to fall back down, just as it was no misfortune to be thrown up in the first place.* (IX, 17.)

In Hainburg I continued my journey through the centuries that stood cheek by jowl. From the station beside the Danube, which seemed to have come to a standstill, I went up Blutgasse into town, passing at the Fischertor the plaque set into the wall that commemorated the bloodbath of 1683. Almost the entire population of the town had been butchered by the Turks. And life went on. Towns came crashing down, were built up again, people were slaughtered, sometimes here, sometimes there, on one side and then the other, *caramba*.

Supposedly the Niebelungen made their last stop in Hainburg before riding into the kingdom of the Hunnish king Etzel, where every last one of them perished as a consequence of blindness, arrogance and pride.

Single snowflakes were falling and I put my hat on. The clouds, no longer hanging so low, shimmered brightly, light occasionally appearing in the cracks. I heard a lorry change gear behind me and allowed it to pass. Then I moved back into the middle of the road.

When I arrived at the Jäger barracks I was tired, dishevelled and grumpy. The guard listened to my request, made a telephone call, and after a while informed me that Private Kurt Ritler had gone into town and ought to be back soon. So I waited. And while I waited I braced myself emotionally for our meeting. In the snow that continued to fall gently I paced up and down alongside the depressing barracks, kicking with my boots the iced-over puddles, for the plinking, crunching sound of the ice as it shattered made the waiting easier. Far to my left a tall metal fence, separating the site from the town, allowed me to see through to some of the living quarters.

Several soldiers came to the barracks gate. I scrutinized each one because I knew Kurt's face from the photographs he'd put in with his letters. That's why I recognized him when he arrived. The way he moved made him look older than I'd anticipated. He didn't saunter; he walked at normal speed and purposefully, his hands in his coat pockets that sat too high because the coat was too small. Shortages wherever you looked. / Like Nanni, he seemed to be a small powerhouse. But unlike her he looked obdurate, rather than full of curiosity. / I asked him if he was Kurt Ritler, to which he said yes. From the photographs I'd expected him to be smaller, but now I had a strong young man before me, and terribly handsome. 'What is it?' he asked confidently. / I told him where I came from and what my relationship was to the authorities in Mondsee; it ended up being a rather complicated explanation. And when I handed the letters over to Kurt, he recoiled slightly, unsettled. He blushed, deeply embarrassed at receiving his love letters from the hands of a stranger. He stuffed them at once in the right-hand pocket of his uniform jacket.

At that moment I felt all the disappointments of the past few days: things coming to a head with my parents, Vienna as a moribund city, the disappearance of a world familiar to me, and the war in which I was supposed to let myself get shot for nothing, nothing at all. On the train to Hainburg I'd imagined that my meeting with Kurt Ritler would bring something positive into my life, but now the two of us faced each other uneasily, and everything felt as if it were weighed down with stone.

'To my knowledge, only the local police commander read these,' I lied. 'And he's dead, he was shot a week ago.' / This was of interest to the boy, he gasped for air in relief and his face brightened. / 'In the course of an unsuccessful arrest,' I said. / 'It's extraordinary what . . .' he muttered, leaving the sentence unfinished with a shake of his head. The two of us were probably thinking about Nanni. His thoughts may have been of walking arm in arm down Mariahilferstrasse, mine of the ferocity with which she'd scrunched up the letter from her mother by the shore of the lake.

I told him that I'd met Nanni several times in Schwarzindien and that I'd been impressed by her. / It was as if Kurt's face had frozen again, and I felt I wasn't getting through to him. / 'I'm really sorry about what happened to Nanni,' I said. 'She was a nice girl. She helped me once when I had a nervous fit.' I lowered my eyes and stared at the trampled snow beneath my feet. Then, after a brief pause, I added, 'You knew her better than I did, but I believe that when she got something into her head she was unstoppable.' / He didn't look at me, he just chewed his lip. Behind his head I saw the sky, from which snowflakes were falling. Further on, down in the town, the smoking chimneys of a factory towered from the bone-white scene. / 'One of my three sisters died when she was about your age,' I said. 'I would always imagine her wandering, especially in winter.' / Kurt continued staring out into the landscape, his right thumb tucked into the open pocket the letters were in. His unease was palpable and intensified by my own unease. / Then he said, but not directly to me, 'I imagine Nanni to be sleeping.' / We fell silent. I could see Kurt's breath in the winter air. Finally he raised his head, and now it seemed that he was aware of me and was talking to me. / 'Nanni always slept a lot,' he said. 'When we went swimming we would look at each other for five minutes, then she'd fall asleep. And if I wanted to wake her up I had to call her name several times, she really slept like a log.' He closed his eyes briefly. 'Once, when I said *Nanni!* really loudly, she opened her eyes and looked at me, and I asked her: Did you just doze off then? And she said, astonished: No, I certainly didn't. And she shook her head in surprise.' / Kurt was now more relaxed than at first, and I thought I could see a hidden smile in his face just as a tear rolled down his cheek, which he wiped away with the back of his hand. / 'It's because of the cold,' he said. 'The snow.' He shook his head as if he were baffled by it himself, then he assumed an expression of indifference again. And the two of us said nothing for a while. I felt that both of us were waiting for the other to speak; I sensed our meeting was coming to an end.

'What's going to happen to you now?' I asked. / 'We're being deployed tomorrow. We don't know where we're going, but I imagine we're heading towards the front.' / He seemed to view their transfer with indifference, but this was probably just feigned courage. I was quite shocked and I think my voice was quivering when I said, 'The only thing that can be of any importance to you is that you survive.' / He listened to what I was saying and told me that his father had advised him always to keep some civilian clothes on him and to throw away his uniform if necessary. But he wasn't going to do anything like that, he said. He wasn't going to let anyone else down. / Now he was as obdurate as he'd been at the beginning of our encounter, but I could also see the vulnerability behind it. / 'It's likely we're going to lose the war,' I said. / He shrugged. 'I don't want to live under a foreign regime anyway,' he said, then shrugged again, and his eyes said the same.

We parted company without saying any more. Kurt walked unsteadily down the snowy street to the large gate, through a complicated life. The packet of letters bulged in the side pocket of his coat. Then he deftly vaulted the barrier by the guardhouse.

I was crestfallen and wanted to go back to Mondsee as quickly as possible. At the Ungartor stop, which was closer than the station, I was told by an official that all trains were delayed for at least two hours because of damage to the tracks in the vicinity of the Vienna city boundary. I therefore left Hainburg on foot. By walking I intended to overcome the feeling of bitterness growing inside me. The bell in the church tower struck midday. I headed eastwards, following the road alongside the railway towards Wolfsthal, the next station.

Refugees were pulling their belongings through the streets on carts, battered pots and pans dangling from string tied to the crossbeams. There was congestion at Ungartor, where the horses' breath steamed snowy-white from their mouths. One horse was nibbling away at a picket fence by the side of the road. / In France and when the nastiness in the East got going they'd still had battalions for regulating the traffic. Now this felt like a dream to me. And yet, if I'd encountered a soldier from one of these battalions standing here I would have been no less surprised than if Dante had personally shown me the way into the underworld.

For a while I followed a straight road that led across a flat expanse, between fields encrusted with ice. The wind was biting. Sometimes the grey spat out a farmhouse or a crow, which came close to me in the drifting, floating snow. And because this stroll was affording me a temporary release from the tension of the past few days, I crossed Wolfsthal and then entered a dark wood at the edge of town. Where the road emerged from the wood again I came across a building site, where a dozen filthy men were erecting a collapsible obstacle: if the supports were knocked away, it would block the road to Bratislava. I moved to the side to give me a better view. 'Can anyone tell me who thought this up?' I said to an old man in the Volkssturm, who was wearing civilian clothes just about fit for purpose, with the obligatory black-and-red armband. 'It's totally crazy!' / As I was saying this, two Messerschmidt 109s flew overhead, and the man I'd spoken to said, 'I didn't hear what you said!'

As I wandered on, the landscape opened up again, everything opened up. I walked between, and stumbled across, fields, I wanted to get to the mountains, but it was much further than I'd imagined, as it always seemed to be these days. In the icy silence of the winter, disturbed occasionally by the blow of an axe or a hammer, I saw more construction work for the defensive position, more visible symptoms of madness. Anybody who'd fought in Russia knew full well that such a defensive position wouldn't be able to hold up an army that had made it across the Dnieper and the Carpathians for more than a few minutes. But thousands here were hacking and shovelling away, monotonously, in the rain, in the snow, the trenches filling with water and caving in, while the thousands continued shovelling until they collapsed. These fucking trenches were assets from the estate of the morally bankrupt. And whenever the wind threw up another finely spun curtain of snow, I felt as if this entire hallucination would dissipate at any moment.

The closer I came to the village of Berg, the more clearly I saw the ruptured and churned-up earth, while ever more concrete humps and barbed-wire obstacles came into view. From a distance I could see a forced labourer on the edge of an anti-tank trench in construction being beaten by a guard with a stick. The labourer fell to the ground and was now out of sight, but the guard and the stick that kept being raised and brought down with violence were still visible. No sounds drifted over to me, no screaming, no groaning; everything was weighed down by an eerie, icy silence. It was a cold, dull day, everything was hazy. / But the arm went up and down with the stick as if being pulled by a string. Who was pulling the string? Me? Possibly. / At some point the guard stood back up and stretched his back as if he'd just performed a heroic deed. For a while he stood in this pose on the mound of earth, then he raised his chin in a peculiarly thrusting movement, turned away and left. Two other forced labourers came and lifted the man who'd been beaten under his arms, but despite several efforts the victim couldn't stand on his feet. So they lay him back down and left too. / I observed the scene in horror, but did nothing. I just stood there, watching. Then I moved closer; there were no barriers. And the closer I got to the construction site, the softer the ground became. Now I realized why the forced labourers were walking off like drunkards; I too almost got stuck in the mud with my boots.

Next to me a man was working in ripped clothes, a nameless soul, covered in mud. His trousers looked as if they might stand up of their own accord if the man took them off. The reason why he'd caught my attention was a colourful scarf: orange and light-blue with a touch of green, glowing colours in all the dirt and grey. When the man noticed me staring at him, he looked back for a few seconds with penetrating, reproachful eyes, but he held his head high in defiance, as if his neck, wrapped by the scarf, had turned to stone. / A whistle pierced the air and the man went on with his work, shovelling to one side the cold, heavy earth that had been thrown up from the trench. With concealed hatred, he shot me another sideways glance. Then one of the guards turned and gestured for me to leave. Which I did, as if I had no desire to disturb what was going on here. As I walked away I was briefly overcome by a profound inner silence which amplified further the harsh noise of the shovelling and the muffled blows of the hacking.

In front of me there was nobody, nothing but the snowflakes that continued to flutter their way down. As the ground moved beneath me I knew that I would irrevocably remain in this war; no matter when it finished or what happened to me, I would remain in this war forever, as a part of it. It was hard to admit this to myself.

Yes, what a shame it is that nothing which lies behind me can be changed. What I have learned from the past six years is that wisdom goes behind me, seldom out in front. In the evening it comes and sits at the table with me as a pointless diner.

As we were advancing into Ukraine, it didn't escape me that

shootings were taking place in the rear area command. But I was so preoccupied with my own fate that I thought: The Jews aren't any concern of mine. / Once I had a visit from Fritz Zimmerman, who told me in some detail how things were in Vyazma – Zhytomyr – Vinnytsia. We were sitting in my lorry, and outside a tempestuous summer shower was pelting down, which lent Fritz Zimmerman's account a certain unreal quality. Now I'm able to separate the summer shower and his stories; they don't belong together.

Fritz Zimmerman's superior shot on the spot a Jewish barber who'd cut him while shaving.

Time and again I heard of shootings. The family of the baker, from whom we'd bought bread during a few days of rest, was taken out of town, four people in total, and shot in the back of the neck. I heard of incidents like this every few weeks, and whenever I was repairing my lorry such thoughts went through my head. I tried to imagine being assigned to a shooting myself. What would I do? And what would it be like? And although these scenarios were never particularly concrete, I got used to the idea of them. / I would never have thought I'd have to contemplate these things. For thinking about them means becoming familiar with them, which means changing one's understanding of normality.

Such were my thoughts as the Danube flowed and the clouds drifted overhead and people died and the train from Engerau let out a whistle.

When I arrived back in Vienna it was already dark and I could see large fires in Simmering. The Simmering-Graz-Pauker plant had been hit and the factory's coal store on Simmeringer Hauptstrasse was ablaze. Many dead in Simmering. I questioned passengers who were boarding. A gust of sooty air flew into the carriage; ash and dust lay heavily on our lungs. I heard that even Vienna Central Cemetery had been ploughed over in a carpet bombing. Everything was being bombed now, nobody was safe any more, not even the dead.

At Hauptzollamt station I deposited my rucksack. Outside the station stood a woman about my mother's age, asking whether I was looking for a room. I said yes. She said I could stay with her. When I asked her how much it cost and how far away it was, she said one and a half Reichsmarks, and very close. So I followed the woman beneath the charred sky. As we were turning into Marxergasse I told her I had to get up at half past five. She promised to wake me.

I went to have something to eat and to take a look around this part of the city. At an inn I had horse goulash, which was mainly just sauce, more sour than spicy; I suspected the goulash had been coloured with brick dust from the last air raid rather than with paprika. / Then I wandered through the impoverished and shabby streets, meeting all their impoverished and shabby inhabitants, and I felt at danger from falling masonry from the unstable walls, and my one wish was to get back to Mondsee as quickly as possible, to Margot.

Soon after ten o'clock I wrapped myself in the blanket in the room that had been provided for me. It was the woman's son's bedroom. On the small bookshelves was a deflated leather football. Over the bed hung a Simmering AC pennant beside the Reich war flag. / I had a fairly restless night, waking a few times from dreams and other disturbances, such as the door clicking in the wind.

Despite her promise the woman didn't wake me the next morning, but I woke up of my own accord and got dressed. When I was ready to go I discovered that the front door to the apartment was locked. So I knocked on the door of the woman's bedroom and asked whether I might be able to leave. / At which she said, 'It's high time you got up!' / I couldn't help grinning, for this was a welcome distraction from the war. / I told the woman I was already up and dressed and asked her whether she'd be kind enough to let me out of the apartment. / She came out in a floor-length red dressing gown and unlocked the door for me.

On the way to the station the wrecked streets were dark and empty. The only person I saw was a woman with a nurse's hood who, visibly anxious and in despair, hurried past me, crying, wearing a yellow armband with a star. The lapels on her coat flapped helplessly, like a wounded bird.

I sat on the windowsill

I sat on the windowsill and listened to all the news Margot had to tell. The baker didn't have enough yeast and was worried that he might run out of coal in a fortnight. The community doctor had bought two horses from the Banat refugees because he couldn't get hold of enough petrol any more. But they weren't beautiful horses, the doctor told her when he came to examine Lilo's cough. He'd spotted better ones at the last horse inspection, but the Wehrmacht had nabbed those. That's why he was content with the bad horses, at least the Wehrmacht wouldn't want to requisition them.

Things hadn't been good during my absence, Margot said. Lilo had been ill. Every night she'd sat up in her bed with a dreadful cough, and in the end she'd thrown everything up. Then there was the never-ending bad news: huge flyovers, the occasional dogfight and an American fighter crashing a few kilometres away in Zell am Moos. No light at home for hours on end. And a damp room that never got warm, no honey for her tea, nothing of all those things one took for granted. And the landlady as angry and unfriendly as ever. 'Arguing with the old bag is such an effort, she's becoming madder by the day.'

Margot pushed herself away from the table with her bottom and came over to me. She was happy to have me back in Mondsee, if only for a couple of days. I tried to make a mental note of everything: the orange speckles in her brown eyes, the curve of her hip leaning against me and the rustling of her hair in my ear.

It had stopped snowing and, in the garden opposite, an other-worldly winter light glistened due to the unbroken covering of snow, intensified by the glass panels of the greenhouse, which were at varying angles to the sun. Most of the longhorns had been sold; only two pregnant cows remained, rummaging in the rustic food trough beneath the walnut tree, clouds of condensation around their mouths. There was not a breath of wind and everything was filled with crystal light.

Seeing the greenhouse reminded me of my concern for the Brazilian. Somewhere around here he was leading a ghostly existence. Hopefully someone had given him a bed in an attic room. And even if he was barely able to move from there, at least it wouldn't be snowing on him. I don't know why, but I recalled all the marvellous-sounding names of the women from Rocinha that the Brazilian had mentioned: Lúcia dos Santos Mota, Beatriz de Miranda Texeira, Leticia Carvalho da Silva Maciel.

I asked Margot if there'd been any developments in my uncle's murder case. She said that the assumption he'd been shot by the Brazilian was now being treated as a certainty. / I hung my head in shame. Not that it particularly mattered, but I felt sad; for the first time I felt sorry for what I'd done. Sometimes feelings need a while to take effect. / And in this moment of sorrow I also felt a sense of peace because I made the decision to leave Uncle where he was and move on.

Margot then asked me for news of Vienna. / 'Lovely snow,' I said, 'lovely children and otherwise rubble and grotty people.' / I was in fact pleased to be away from the city again; I wondered how people managed to live in such a cold place. Then I told her about Kurt and the woman who'd let me her son's room.

Because it was so nice outside we left the house. I had to do some shopping for my departure: loo paper, razor blades, sugar cubes, notebooks to write in and Nivea. The last of these isn't one of the clichés of soldierly life, but almost every experienced soldier has a jar of skin cream for the cold, the dirt, the petrol, the rifle oil. / My exercise outfit was already washed and Margot had given me some thick stockings.

Lilo ran over to the longhorns. She was good at running now, only ever stumbling when she had to lift her legs to negotiate small bumps. She wanted to scramble under the fence that the refugees had hastily built, but I grabbed her by the collar, which led to tears. Lilo soon calmed down, wandered in a different direction, then came back and held on tight to my trouser legs when the longhorns started kicking at the fence. Full of curiosity, the cows craned their heads towards us with those pagan-figure horns. I stroked the black nose of one of them and she licked my hand. I imagined the cow with her long tongue being able to free me from the curse of history. / Snowflakes were falling again. Lilo tried to catch some in her hands. When she made another attempt to slip under the fence, I lifted her and put her on my shoulders. With squeals of delight she threw the cap off my head several times, so I put it in my pocket.

A man and a woman were busy in the greenhouse, where Margot had come to help me work all those months ago. The Brazilian's dog that was beaten by the police had lain under the cart, and Lilo beside the gramophone player in the greenhouse, kicking her legs in the air.

We went into town. We didn't talk much to begin with, but then I said we ought to discuss everything that needed discussing, for a letter might take two weeks to arrive and the reply another two weeks, and if unresolved issues needed dealing with in circumstances like that, it could quickly get you down.

So we worked out all the important matters. If everything goes to pieces, where will we see each other? How will we find each other? Where will our meeting point be? What's our contact address? I said Margot should write to Inge, my sister in Graz, and I would write to her mother in Darmstadt. / 'But you must come back straightaway, at the very first opportunity. I'm not happy if you're not with me,' Margot said, blinking into the harsh light reflected by the snow.

'I will always try to write,' I went on. 'But there might be interruptions in the postal service, so please don't worry unduly. All in all, don't panic. I won't write when I'm tired, I'll sleep. That's more important.

'And always go to the cellar, Margot. Promise me you'll be careful.' / 'You too.' / 'I've managed to survive these past five years, so I hope I'll get through the rest. Unfortunately, at the front it doesn't make any difference whether you're stupid or intelligent. The only thing you mustn't be is unlucky.' / 'But I hope you realize you'll be lucky.' / We stopped, turned to one another and exchanged squinted glances. I didn't know what else to say, so just nodded. Then Margot added defiantly, 'As compensation for this we're going to live to a hundred.

'Veit?' / 'Yes?' / 'Please don't take so many pills.' / 'Yes.' / 'You need to find other ways of dealing with it.' / 'Yes.' / 'You can't lock away forever things that aren't meant to be locked away.' / 'I'm aware of the symptoms.' / 'Imagine that the attacks are disaster drills.' / 'Yes.' / 'You need to get out of it without pills.' / She was right, of course, I had to relax, let everything go. It wasn't good to be so permanently fired up that everything sounded like a child's trumpet or an emergency brake.

Lilo tugged at my hair; she wanted to get down and walk on her own, so I let her. Even though she fell in the snow a number of times, walking was good for her, her cough was better. My hands were cold so I put them in my coat pockets. Margot's face was freezing and she said, 'I ought to wear more make-up in this bloody cold weather.'

By the time we'd done all the shopping it was late afternoon, the sun was already low in the sky, reminding us that the clock was ticking. We set off for home, and as we walked I was surprised by how small Mondsee looked, smaller and brighter than before. This couldn't be anything to do with the town itself, it must be me. The town looked harmless with its acquiescent houses and the lake, its shore venturing a step out into the water with a thin layer of ice. And the tarred pylons with their white insulators stood there like close friends. Strange, I thought, after all that had happened. I looked around. I wasn't frightened by the gigantic trees that looked blue against the background of the snow; everything was perfectly normal. The mountains too, with their bone-white contours that stood out against the grey sky, painted a normal winter picture, only now everything appeared smaller and friendlier than before. / And I fancied I knew the reason for this. It was because I knew it was coming to an end. The imminent end of the war was making everything small again, now that many things were foreseeable. And we'd see whether I too would be shot dead. But it felt good to know that after more than five years the war was coming to an end. The war's going to be over soon, I told myself again.

You have these moments when all that matters is that something's over and done with. And of course I hoped that it would turn out all right for me. But even if it didn't, I'd rather the end came soon than to have to endure this hazy nightmare which went on and on, getting worse by the day, leading us into ever darker years, hollowing out all that is civil in life and bringing people's wickedness more clearly to the fore, even my own. It almost felt inevitable that the more people were sick of a war, the more brutal and merciless it must become. That was the impression I had. And so all that mattered was that the war would be over soon, putting a stop to all the misery. This thought bolstered me: yes, I know it won't be long, the end is in sight and then we'll see.

Another strange thing was that, since Uncle's death and since I had my marching orders, my head had been clearer again. I didn't dare think too closely about the whys and wherefores of this, nor did I wish to. But the fact was, before I'd felt sorry for myself, whereas now I was focused and felt hope again. Margot, however, was grumpy because she was stuck in Mondsee with no greenhouse, no tomatoes, a small child, yes, but otherwise it was just a case of waiting. She said, 'I've got two husbands, a wrong one and a right one, and soon both of them will be at the front. And even if all of us survive the war there's no guarantee we'll see each other again soon. And if we did, where? Rebuilding a Russian city, maybe. Just the idea that I won't get a letter for weeks and that I've got nothing to do here apart from sitting around – good God, I can think of better ways of passing my time.' / She raised her eyebrows.

I lifted Lilo back onto my shoulders. She wanted to talk, which put an end to our conversation for the time being. The crunching of the snow as we walked and Lilo's babbling were soothing. Maybe these will be the last few happy moments in my life, I thought, the last moments free of fear.

Later, in bed, Margot reiterated how much she liked being with me. She seemed to find it enriching. The unsustainable aspect of our relationship had acquired something sustainable; I was in a state of permanent incredulity. In my disbelief, I wanted to reassure myself and asked Margot what chance she thought our relationship had in the future. / 'One hundred per cent,' she said calmly. / An unequivocal answer. / For a while we said nothing. Margot seemed to be deep in thought, then she gave me instructions for when I was at the front. I should do what was asked of me, no more and, if possible, less. / 'I'll try.' / And I asked her to let me know what was happening with Ludwig. / 'Of course. I mean, it concerns you too.' She fell silent again, breathing regularly beside me, and after a while she said, 'I think Ludwig has the necessary level of detachment.' / 'I doubt it.' / 'Sure he does.' / 'We'll see.' / 'Night, night. Sleep well.' / 'Sleep well, Margot.' /

She snuggled up close, pressing her back and her bottom into the curve my body makes when I'm asleep. And I fell asleep with my right hand cupping Margot's left breast. / Lilo woke us twice with her coughing. Margot comforted her with some juice, and when it was quiet again I could hear a low humming in the chimney.

The following morning something unusual happened: we built another snowman, helped by some of the refugee children. Even the landlady was there for most of the time, standing just outside and gazing over at the longhorns, whose presence she seemed to find calming. Eventually she went over to the fence and fed the animals some small, shrivelled apples. One of the refugee children hurled a snowball at the landlady, which hit her on the head. It couldn't have been hard, for the snowball burst into powder, but that didn't make it all right. The landlady ran after the child, who may have been around six years old, and I was amazed at how fast she could move. She gave the boy a kick up the backside to let him know that the Volk Community wore boots. With a serene, yet severe look of satisfaction, she watched the boy dash into the house.

'Leave the child alone,' I called out. / At once the landlady stomped over, looking as if she were about to breathe fire and brimstone. 'I'm not having that riff-raff behave as if they're at home here.' / And, as if the wind had gusted into a heap of new snow, the other refugee children hurried away, clearly wary now. I watched them in astonishment, and all of a sudden I found myself in the mood for a fight. 'Where else should the children behave as if they were at home?' I said. 'Were the children at the table in Berlin when the plans for wholesale slaughter throughout Europe were forged? You ought to be happy if they feel at home here, but I very much doubt they do.' / The landlady scoffed at me, a small, wicked laugh that came from the depths of her bitter, corrosive self. Her face turned into a grimace and, as if she'd known me for a long time, she said, 'Which can't be said of you, can it? You feel particularly at home here. It's high time you went back to join the masses at the front. I mean, you've been knocking around here long enough. I expect the front's too dangerous for you, isn't it, the smell of powder? I do hope they send you back to Russia and I wish you the very best. No doubt what you're missing will be sent to you by post.'

/ As she uttered these last words she looked at Margot and there was an unrestrained brutality in the slant of her mouth. Then she gave the half-finished snowman a kick.

I had no desire to try to teach the unteachable, so I spared myself the bother of explaining to the landlady that my employer no longer had a foothold in Russia, and that at least where I was going I wouldn't have to talk with my hands. / I took Margot by the arm to let her know we should leave. But Margot wanted to get something off her chest too and asked the landlady what the hell she thought she was doing, harassing peaceful people, what was wrong, couldn't she be a bit more reasonable in the sixth year of the war, it was sickening, some people just had nothing else to do. / At that the landlady began shouting and screaming, so we left her there, but she followed us and burst into Margot's room without knocking. She made such a scene that after a while I'd had enough and ordered her out of the room. She said she had every right to come into this room, she called us scoundrels and snake-charmers, said we were having a relationship and living a seedy existence, whereas she had nothing but work and trouble, and if anyone was going to throw anyone else out here then she would be doing it to us rather than the other way around. To our surprise, with these words she left the room.

I slumped onto the bed and lay there motionless for a while. Then I said, 'You ought to move, Margot.' / 'Move?' she said, squatting on the floor beside her coughing child. / 'You'll go potty here otherwise.' / Then I spoke more quietly, as if I were worried the landlady might be listening in, even though I'd heard her crash her way down the stairs. 'The old bat isn't right in the head and she'll taint every hour of your day. When I leave tomorrow you shouldn't stay here any longer.'

We went into town together and enquired about somewhere to stay for Margot. We were quickly referred to a butcher, whose assistant, a French woman, had been assigned to the factory. I hadn't been into a butcher's shop for more than a year, because I couldn't stand the smell any more. When the bell rang as we opened the door it was an alarm. And when the stale smell of meat pricked my nostrils I had to force myself not to rush straight outside again.

We waited our turn. The shop had grey floor tiles and white ones on the walls. On the counter some innards – veal hearts and calves' liver – lay beside large chunks of meat. The rail on the wall at the back was full of grim S-hooks, but only one paltry salami hung from several metres of metal. A shiny cleaver lay on a massive butcher's block. / My ears immediately detected a hollow, echoey gurgling coming from the room to the rear of the shop. It seemed to keep saying, 'Wait! Wait! Wait!' / And again the bell rang; someone had left the shop. And while the butcher chatted to Margot I allowed the images into my head; I was ready to accept them now, for they showed me things I needed to know. And it made it easier for me not to be alone in my anxiety. Only for the butcher, a man of robust appearance, did it seem to be rather strange. When I glanced up at him, I saw in his face a quizzical expression, surprise.

When we were back outside Margot said I'd been humming the whole time, without having to take breath, like a ghost, like a light bulb. She was so happy that she embraced me as best she could with Lilo on her arm. Not only had the butcher offered her a room, a room above the garage with outside steps, she was also his shop assistant now. / 'So who's going to look after Lilo?' I asked, panting. 'The butcher's half-blind mother,' she replied, beaming as if she'd been called to King Arthur's Round Table.

On the way to the old quarter I had to stop every few paces, as I kept thinking my legs would fail me. And when I walked I teetered uncertainly, as if I were an old man. As we climbed the stairs to our rooms I panicked that I was going to trip and fall all the way back down. Even Lilo made her way up more nimbly and quickly than me. / Turning back round, Margot said, 'Come now. Come on up!' / It was helpful that she treated me normally, as always.

I lay on Margot's bed, watching her pack, until I felt better again. She'd told the butcher that she would move that same afternoon. She'd explained what furniture she needed and what she didn't need, and he'd promised to arrange it all while the butcher's was closed for lunch.

As we loaded our suitcases, bags and the gramophone player onto the pram, the landlady gave us an evil stare, her mouth pinched to a short line. We were already overladen, and I was amazed when Margot arrived with a nappy case too. The one-year-old girl had to walk because we were using her pram to transport all our things.

We said practically nothing to each other, walking side by side in silence. I was busy manoeuvring the crammed pram down the roads made bumpy by snow. All Margot said was the occasional 'All right?' / 'It has to be,' I replied.

Two evacuee girls coming our way helped us by carrying the child and the nappy case. With coats that were now too small for them and worn shoes, they were little war veterans too.

We arrived at the new place safe and sound. The room provided for us had been heated by the butcher's mother in advance. The moment I stepped through the door I sensed that I'd broken free from something and I finally had my own life. / We put everything down and I constructed the playpen. Margot stuffed all her gear into the cupboard; she would have enough time over the coming days to put everything in its rightful place, so that order prevailed and any item could be found when it was needed. Just for the moment she couldn't find anything. / For now, we felt secure. The shortcomings of the place were insignificant, we thought. The room was small and the bed too soft; it was unlikely the French woman missed her former lodging. But here in the centre of town Margot wasn't so abandoned, not with all the evacuees in the streets. And I thought: When it's all over I'm going to come back here.

Margot insisted that I fetch the seagrass mattress I'd had made in spring. I put it beneath the porch of the old house and gave the landlady back the large key that had weighed down my trouser pocket for almost a year. When she took the key, her face maintained its sombre expression, but then she stumped me again by talking perfectly normally, only griping slightly that we were walking out on her, that's how she put it. She was going to have her tonsils taken out now, as she thought this would prevent the weather from giving her such gyp. / I looked at her in disbelief; she appeared to be made out of paper, like a Japanese house in which insanity and reason lived together. When I was confronted by her reasonable side, I saw in the neighbouring room, behind a paper wall, the arm movements of insanity.

In the end she was even trying to give me encouragement, insisting that there would be another reversal of fortunes. But what she offered as proof for her convictions was nothing but fantasy, mixed with the familiar phrases about supposed miracle weapons that droned from the wireless day after day. / 'It can't end like this,' she kept saying. 'And it won't end like this.'

I left the landlady with her faith in the future, wishing her all the best. And yet I thought, I must get away from this house; it's crumbling internally. And yes, I know I repeat myself sometimes, but I have to keep telling myself: you grow into one thing as you turn away from another.

I visited the loo one last time too, because I was desperate. It was filthy and squalid, never cleaned, shit spattered everywhere. Poor old loo! / I told the pigs, whom I could see and who watched me go about my business, that I'd come to say adieu and that there had been times when I'd felt happy here. But not any more. Margot had found somewhere else to stay, whereas I had to confront the victorious Soviet army, which wasn't exactly one of life's great pleasures and a big mistake besides, for the Red Army had every reason to be incensed. The landlady would no doubt find other tenants to bully, and one day she'd perish, no longer able to halt the downward slide. / I wished the pigs all the best too, but it was clear they were facing a briefer future. Looking around once more, I said, 'You lot deserved better.'

Margot and I arrived at the new lodgings at almost the same time. She'd been shopping and was unwrapping the child from her winter clothing. Once the girl had been bathed, Margot fed her mashed cereal. We sat for a while at the window, gazing at several back gardens of town houses, where smoke rose vertically from the chimneys. A few isolated snowflakes fell like spiders lowering themselves on threads, shining whenever they caught the light. / Margot told me what her mother had written from Darmstadt: she'd received an allocation of fifty grams of coffee beans from Berlin in compensation for the air raid in September. / 'Fifty grams, how wonderful!' I said. 'What would we do without the war?' / Margot was washing. I took out the dirty water and fetched some clean water. Then I sat back on the windowsill. It was now dark, my final evening.

We'd known each other long enough to be able to discuss past times. Margot said that for weeks she'd wondered: What's he doing all the time? What sort of a person just thinks about paper and the smell of ink the whole time? And had I really thought she was cooking for me just for fun, thirty or forty times? / I defended myself, saying that whenever I'd asked she'd always assured me she was cooking anyway. / Margot laughed and shook her head at such naivety. / Then we talked about life after the war, the jobs we would do and the children we would have. Margot said she wanted another girl.

I looked at Lilo, who was shaking the bars of her playpen. The child looked back at me, quieter than usual. The new room was unfamiliar to her and she didn't feel quite at home here yet. But the resinous wood crackled away in the stove as ever, and the pots bubbled and simmered away. Above Margot's bed hung the Brazilian's feather crown, and again I heard him say, 'You only find peace once you've become who you ought to be.'

I put on my favourite record and the tenor sang of the great love he had carelessly squandered, and how it's the simplest things you learn last; that's how the Brazilian had translated the lyrics for me. Lilo got ready for a little sleep, Margot placed a hand on my cheek, I a hand on her hip, and I felt the physicality of her body. I was very pleased that I no longer heard the song as one long blubber; the chords resonated through my body and joy purred in my chest.

'Hopefully all this crap will be over soon and you'll be back with me,' Margot said.

When all the necessary preparations for my departure had been made we sat on the covered area at the top of the external steps and smoked a final cigarette together. From time to time gaps appeared in the clouds and I peered into them and wondered what the future held for me. Suddenly I heard an inner voice say, 'You'll be fine.' I will survive. And later, when everything's back to normal, I'll somehow salvage all those years I've lost.

Mondsee experienced the quietest night in its history, everyone slept deeply. / A cloud approached the moon, the war approached Mondsee, Mondsee approached the end of the year, one land approached the other. / I never wanted to leave here!

We waited for the milk van

We waited for the milk van. It had turned very cold; you had to dress like an Arctic explorer. Margot shivered in a blue quilted jacket, which was already very shabby. Lilo slept within her arm. Margot put the other arm around my neck and looked at me. She was affectionate, a wonderful, warm person. I thanked her for every minute we'd had together. And she straightened my collar. I'd never felt such an attachment to life as at that moment.

The milk van came and after a passionate kiss and a supplicatory 'Good luck!' and 'See you soon!' I got in to resume my war journey that had been interrupted a year earlier. / Margot saluted me with two fingers that she thrust away from her forehead. I put my rucksack on the broad bench beside me – both the rucksack and the bench had burns in them; the rucksack from the war, the bench from cigarettes. You recognize life by these small details. / Margot and I waved to one another for as long as the tiniest possibility remained that the other might see it.

The milk van drove through Schwarzindien. The former camp also now housed refugees, people thrown out of their home, the betrayed, criminals who'd absconded, the oppressed, poor devils. / At one house in St Lorenz someone had forgotten to black out the windows as per the regulations; one on the ground floor was brightly lit and I could see a child's face behind the glass. For a moment I sensed I could go into that house and live there until the end of the war, safe in the knowledge that nobody would find me. This simple possibility made me shudder and then the milk van had passed the house and I was heading on towards the front, even though I loathed the war and knew I was serving an unjust cause. / The driver enquired as to my destination and

I said, 'The front at Insterburg.' / 'You mean East Prussia, where it's total carnage?' / 'Yes, it's strange, you allow yourself to take part in something that's intent on killing you. A war like this is one of the most bewildering things in the world.'

It would take about four days to get to the front, maybe more. At least that gave me time to write, time to complete something.

Now the milk van driver and I engaged in small talk, about the weather and how the trees shook their branches angrily, throwing snow to the ground when we sped past. The driver pointed out how the snow wasn't melting on the farmhouse roofs, no animals left in the stalls. He said he was happy he didn't have so many churns to lift at the moment as he'd tweaked his back. The Drachenwand stood out clearly, a skull craning above the jangling woods, staring down at the landscape with empty eyes. Dawn was breaking and the first rays of light seemed to flitter across the thin ice at the edges of the lake. If it remained so cold the lake would freeze over this winter too, for the third time in a few years, all part of a cold era. / The road to St Gilgen lay before us, there was no moon, but the sky was brightening. As we drove through Plomberg I looked up one last time at the Drachenwand, where Nanni Schaller's body had lain for months on patient stone. In a few minutes the sun would be up; the shoulder of the Drachenwand shone a hue of red. I greeted Nanni with a discreet movement of my finger and wished her all the best for her time with the spirits. / Then the face of the mountain disappeared from view and I closed my eyes in the knowledge that, as with the war, something from Mondsee will remain with me, something I'll never get over.

Postscript

Veit Kolbe returned to his unit in mid-December 1944, from which he absconded near Schwerin in April 1945. He spent the end of the war in Mondsee. Margot and he were married in 1946 after Margot's divorce. Besides Lilo, the couple had two children together, Robert and Klärchen. In 1953 Veit finished an electrical engineering degree, and straight afterwards he worked two years for Siemens in Afghanistan, building a power station in Sarobi. Margot and the children were also in Afghanistan for at least one year. Later the Kolbe family lived in Vienna. Veit worked for an energy firm, and Margot for an insurance company. Veit Kolbe died on 3 June 2004; at the time of writing Margot Kolbe is still alive, ninety-five years old.

Justus Neff, Margot's father, died in Silesia in March 1945. Lore Neff, Margot's mother, died in 1961 from diabetes that had been inadequately treated. From the death announcement it appears that she had five grandchildren when she died: Lilo, Robert, Klärchen, Adam and Hanne.

Robert Raimund Perttes, the Brazilian, was living in Zell am See at the end of the war. His first postal address after the war was Gasthof Auerwirt. He wasn't charged with the murder of the gendarmerie commandant; all further investigations petered out. In March 1948, Robert Raimund Perttes emigrated to Brazil again. Via the Red Cross he sent from Genoa a crate of lemons, oranges and figs to Margot and Veit. In the Cartões de Imigração da República dos Estados Unidos do Brasil there is a record card detailing information about the Brazilian's arrival into the country. The photograph clipped to the card shows a man who looks ten years older than he must have been when it was taken. The Austrian consulate in São Paolo was unable to provide any information about what happened to the Brazilian or where he lived. The last address I have for him is poste restante at the consulate from summer 1952: Consul Austria, São Paolo – Brasil, rua Lib Badaro 156.

Trude Dohm, the landlady, and her husband moved to Freising after the war. An associate of his offered Max Dohm the opportunity to take over an abandoned electrical and radio shop. Trude Dohm died on 28 January 1953 in the convalescence and care home in Haar, Munich, from quaternary syphilis, which wasn't diagnosed until the last weeks of her life. Her husband continued to live in Freising until his death in 1981.

The Stern and Stabau camps with the evacuees from the former Schwarzindien camp left Mondsee on Easter Sunday 1945, as the front was getting closer, and went to Kaprun, where the girls from the Weisses Rössl camp were taken in. In the summer after the war the girls looked after themselves, working as sales assistants in the bakery or as farm girls. Post only arrived from Vienna with visitors; some girls had been without any news from home for six months. In September 1945, after the new school year had already begun, the last few girls who'd originally been at Schwarzindien returned to Vienna. They hadn't been home for over a year. The girls were now fourteen years old, some had turned fifteen.

In January 1945, Margarete Bildstein, the teacher at Schwarzindien, took over the Hotel Post camp in Weissenbach on the Attersee. After the war she worked as a teacher in Vienna. She never married and had no children. She died in 2008 at the age of eighty-nine in Kirchberg am Wagram.

On 21 April 1945, Kurt Ritler was wounded in the right upper arm during an air attack as his company was retreating westwards from Hamburg. He lost a lot of blood and fell unconscious. On 2 May he was admitted to the collecting station in Horsens, Denmark, where his trail went cold. For years his family tried unsuccessfully to obtain more information relating to the boy's whereabouts. Later research by the Danish Red Cross revealed that Kurt Ritler, born 23 April 1927, died on 2 May 1945 in the Horsens collecting station under the name of Kurt Ritter. Nobody had noticed the spelling mistake before. Kurt Ritler is buried in Horsens church cemetery – B514.

Oskar Meyer, alias Sándor Milch, alias Andor Bakos was killed in March 1945 as he was being transported to Mauthausen concentration camp. The men who didn't give him enough food and then dumped his body in the Danube were never brought to justice. Wally and Georg Meyer had already been murdered at Auschwitz in 1944. I know nothing about what happened after the war to their son Bernhard, who had been taken to safety in Britain. The last address I have for him is in Bath, Somerset.